MINDING HENRY LEWIS

Other books by
SARAH COLLINS HONENBERGER

CATCHER, CAUGHT

WHITE LIES: A Tale of Babies, Vaccines and
Deception

WALTZING COWBOYS

The Point Books   February 2014
Copyright@2014 by Sarah Collins Honenberger

Published in the United States of America by The Point Books
Minding Henry Lewis/Sarah Collins Honenberger—1st ed.

1.Drowning—Fiction. 2. Teenagers—Fiction. 3. Older women—Fiction. 4.
Small towns—Fiction. 5. Race—Fiction. 5. Virginia—Fiction.

ISBN 978:0615980362

PRINTED IN THE UNITED STATES OF AMERICA
First Edition
Set in Times New Roman Text

Dedicated to OBIE,
my friend and
a dog of extraordinary perception

MINDING HENRY LEWIS

By Sarah Collins Honenberger

MINDING HENRY LEWIS

His eye is on the sparrow.
And I know he watches me.
-Gospel song, 1905

Prologue

Every time there's a rainbow some body always say *make a wish, Meeka, rainbows are magic.* Just like that, flick of the wand, your wish suppose to come true. It's crazy really. Not one single thing in life is that simple. I'm no genius like my brother Henry Lewis who studies every little thing about a thing, reads every book in the library about it, and then forever after he can tell you more stuff than the teachers. But even I can see it would take buckets and buckets of rainbow wishes to cure all the evil and sadness in this world.

One time, a long time before Henry Lewis explained to me how rainbows are really millions of tiny blips of water in the air splitting the sunlight, that without raindrops people can't see the colors, I asked Mama about rainbow wishes. If any person anywhere in the whole world with any color skin can wish on rainbows, why's there no black in a rainbow? Every color in the world except black? I said to her. Seems like rainbows are for other people. Know what she said?

"Honey," she said, "you're forgetting the pot of gold at the end. That pot is black. Shiny and solid and black, all the way through to the gold center. That pot is the most important part of the rainbow, and God made it black."

"Then why so many black people unhappy?"

"They just haven't found their gold center yet, nothing magic about that. There's no need of you fretting over rainbow wishes and magic. You've got that gold inside you. You're smart and kind and beautiful, inside and out. All you gotta do is find your gold center and you can do whatever you want, however you want."

She made it sound so easy, like she does with almost everything. She and Henry Lewis, they're the smart people in our family. Back then Mama was taking night classes at Virginia Commonwealth in Richmond, studying psychology and learning how to help people who lose their houses or get beat by their husbands. I was only seven, not old enough to help anyone, not even old enough to mind Henry Lewis and Baby Girl. In the mornings before school Mama would drop us at Aunt Ruthie's and we wouldn't see her until bedtime when she picked us up in our pajamas. Her eyes so red from all that reading she could barely get us back to the apartment above the Laundromat before she fell asleep in her clothes. But that didn't stop her from singing and joking with us, hugging and kissing on Baby Girl.

When we got home, it was my job to read Henry Lewis a story, calm down his brain. That brain of his so busy all the time he had trouble falling asleep. After the second or third page he'd be in dreamland, Baby Girl curled up in between me and him, and Mama stretched out on the bed beside us.

Four years she carted us around like that. She set the alarm clock for five, did her assignments before she went to work. When I asked her why didn't she use that big black pot of rainbow gold to go where she wanted to go, she laughed.

"Go where? I'm exactly where I want to be. Good job, roof, food, and three smart kids."

All her talk about rainbows and the pot of gold, what she really meant was something else altogether, something I was too little back then to understand. The thing is, it's not as easy as she made it sound. Life's scary and everyone makes wrong turns. While you're trying to get where you want to go, you can make yourself sick worrying over whether you're one of the people who won't ever figure it out.

MINDING HENRY LEWIS

Chapter One

Across the swayback bend in the creek a shout interrupted the peaceful afternoon. A girl's voice, young, a little unsure of itself, but loud enough for Celie to hear a hundred yards downstream where she stood in the unseasonably warm April sunshine, her arms crossed on the shovel handle. Just moments before she'd rested her chin there to catch her breath, though she told herself it was to admire the afternoon light on the creek, the glittering path it carved through the marsh and out to the broader river. She would be fifty-three in another month. Birthdays were milestones she'd never paid much attention to until the cancer last year. While she blinked against the brightness something else was niggling in the back of her brain, something undefined and ethereal. She couldn't quite reach it. But as the sun penetrated and smoothed out the mental furrows, her mind let whatever it was float up and out of sight.

When the girl's voice erupted again, louder still, a distant blur of arm circled to match the girl's instructions. "In. Swim in."

Along the opposite marsh a random stick caught Celie's eye as it slid past the ribbon of mud. The tide, holding steady, was about to turn for its run out. Above the treetops the soft spring sunset was still an hour or two away. She put one hand over her eyes and squinted in the direction of the girl's voice.

A flash of white blazed at the end of the abandoned marina pier. The lanky shape in a man's undershirt was too far away to discern features. In Celie's mind the voice replayed itself, command more present than panic. But then the girl, whoever she was, jumped into the water, April water that three weeks ago had been iced over. The splash shocked Celie and she blinked as if the spray had hit her skin. When the girl's head reappeared, she was paddling madly toward the dock, the yelling garbled, but sharper, more concern than before.

Celie scanned the water. Five, ten, twenty feet. Well beyond the girl's reach a small dark circle was drifting into the channel. A dog, she thought.

The girl scrambled back up onto the dock, her head twisted at an awkward angle, her face toward the brown spot. "No, here, toward me. Swim in," she ordered. This time her fear carried across the water.

Through the glaze Celie peered harder. It was a still life, like the stark brightness of a camera flash, backlit, tantalizingly detailed inside the vague shadowy outlines where the hill lapped the sun and framed the scene. When a younger boy shot out of those shadows and up the hillside away from the creek, his sneakers were oddly silent on the old dock boards. Why would he leave?

Celie's brain jerked forward. There was no adult with them. Almost as suddenly her brain registered *trouble, those kids are in trouble.* She stared harder at the dark spot in the water. In the next blink she realized it might not be a dog, it might be a child. Even if it were a dog, she told herself as she dropped the shovel and started to run, they needed help.

By the bottom of the driveway she was gasping for air, barely one month beyond the last radiation treatment. When she swung her leg over the neighbor's fence, the other ankle caught. She lurched forward. Her hand clutched for the rail behind her. Trying to save her balance, the other arm flailed wildly. Once righted, she trained her eyes to the ground in front of her sneakers and kept moving. Along the wooden seawall half-logs and debris were jumbled together in the weeds. Weathered boards connected the jagged sections that edged the tall grass. Although she was concentrating to avoid another fall, she heard the girl's voice spiral out of control.

"No. Wait. Don't." A wail, swallowed before it could explode.

When Celie reached the place where the teenager stood, arm extended, finger pointing, there were actually more children, two little girls, and the running boy returned from wherever. Celie pushed the heel of her hand against her chest. Her lungs burned. Her legs tingled. The oldest girl's breath was hot on Celie's bare arm where she'd rolled up her sleeve earlier to garden.

"My brother's right there." The girl shook her whole arm for emphasis. "Hurry."

As Celie stared at the slick surface, the six or seven bubbles disappeared, swallowed inside a tiny shrinking brown sworl. Bent in half, still wheezing, she tore at the laces of her sneakers. In the water the weight would drag her down. Behind her branches crackled. In a rush of air a hand grabbed her arm and yanked her back onto the grass. Richard Widener, a neighbor, must have sprinted down the hill from the opposite direction while she'd been fighting the fence and the overgrowth.

He panted in her ear. "It's too deep. You can't see anything. And he may not be there at all."

The girl's finger wavered as she pointed down thirty inches from the seawall. "Please. Those are his bubbles."

Celie lowered her head, closer to the creek. Blank water stared back. *Was he sinking even now, deeper and deeper while they debated?* She leaned further while she argued with herself about whether she could swim with the bad arm, if she had enough breath left to muscle a boy in that single-arm stroke she remembered from YMCA life-saving class all those years ago. That had been a pool, clear water, bright lights, people at the edges ready to help.

Richard continued to argue. "The water's still half frozen. And they just dredged the channel. It's probably 16 feet here now. You can't go in."

Stiff and silent, the children stood in a clump. No one moved for several long seconds. Without another word passing them, she knew exactly what Richard was thinking. If they could find him, if he could be revived.

She shook off Richard's hand. "Well, get a boat then." Why didn't he do something helpful?

And then he did. He raced across the grass to the neighbor's old dinghy, flipped it over, and dragged it down the cracked concrete ramp. With one foot in and one out, he shoved the little boat into open water. The boat rocked dangerously as it pitched forward. Richard sank onto the bench, an arm on each gunwale to deter the lurch from side to side, his face hidden. Ten, twenty seconds, then a single oar sliced the surface and the bow swung around. His shoulders hunched forward, the shirt taut across his back. The muscles at his temple knotted in concentration. Without looking up, he dug through the water, paddling Indian-style, along the crooked seawall to the place where the teenager was still pointing.

Behind Celie hollow reeds from a recent storm tide snapped under the girl's footsteps—once, twice—as if warning the other children to stay back from the edge. When Celie turned at the noise, their eyes did not shift in their dark faces, the shock so much a part of their demeanor it might have been paint on masks.

She couldn't help herself. "What is his name?" The need to know overwhelmed her.

"Henry Lewis," the teenager spoke without inflection, a monotone of dread.

"Why was he in the water? It's too early to swim."

"He fell," the girl said more loudly than before, the way you might to convince yourself.

Just outside their hearing, the wooden rowboat spun in circles while Richard thrust the oar down into the lapping water in random spots.

"911," Celie muttered, as if the mere idea might raise the boy, though it had come unbidden from nowhere, a non-sequitur. She spun back toward the cottage, but stopped short when she remembered the cell phone in her pocket. Clawing at her jeans, she found the phone under the clippers and dialed. The three smaller children were staring at her now. Two steps apart, she spoke with her back to them. They shouldn't hear this.

Once the dispatcher finally let her hang up, she turned around to find the children still frozen in place as if the words had electrocuted them into permanent statues. She reached out to put her arm around the shivering teenager, but the girl backed away.

"I have towels at the house," Celie said.

But she hadn't gone to get them after all. Before she finished the sentence, while her arm was still hanging useless in the air, the rescue people materialized. Two women in police uniforms skidded down the hill. They motioned to each other and yelled indistinguishable orders. Radios beeped over the crescendo of sirens. Men in fire gear tromped through the long grass. Their heads lowered to the frightened children, they made notes on their pads as Celie watched Richard push the oar down against the weight of the water and pull it out clean. Over and over.

Twenty minutes passed, thirty. The details percolated through her and away like morning-after overflow from a storm gutter. One of the policemen led the children to the squad truck up on the road. While Richard circled in the dinghy, the police boat trolled the creek. In ominous muffled clinks its chains and hooks dragged back and forth, down and up and down again. She hadn't known that was the way they looked for a missing swimmer.

From forty feet off the seawall she watched the rescue workers and related the events on the cell phone to her oldest son an hour away. Thomas had called to be sure she'd arrived at the cottage safely. To his periodic murmurs she repeated the horror, the helplessness, the girl's howl at the boy's disappearance under the murky surface, her own hollow sinking feeling when she'd poised barefoot on the seawall with shoes, socks, and children scattered behind her.

"It couldn't have been sixty seconds, Thomas. I know I can't run very fast lately, but his head was above water when I started and by the time I got there, he was gone. In the time it took for me to run down the driveway, climb the fence and along the seawall. Eighty yards. Maybe."

When she took a breath, the newsreel ran again across the screen of her memory, random flickers, no noise, black and white. She told herself she'd been slower because of the fallen branches, the storm debris, the high grass. More likely it was the six weeks of daily radiation after three surgeries and five months of chemotherapy.

Miles away she heard Thomas's quiet drawing in of his own breath to pace himself, to give her a chance to tell the whole story.

She choked on the words. "I didn't start soon enough."

"You can't blame yourself, Mom."

"But I—"

"Would you like me to drive down there?"

"No, no. I'm fine."

"I don't think it's a good idea for you to be alone."

"I won't be. Your father's coming home tonight from Chicago."

A footstep away, a uniformed man she recognized from earlier was waiting for her to finish the phone call. He didn't look much older than the drowned boy's sister. Rocking from foot to foot he glanced at his watch, raised his eyes to her face again, but in almost the same instant he looked away. She could see that he had already adopted the guilt as his own. His arms hung loosely at his sides, useless, the uniform shirt too large for his juvenile frame, his belt cinched tight to hold up the baggy pants. Distracted, she scrambled to think of a positive way to end the conversation with Thomas, to convince him he could stop worrying.

"One of the rescue men is here with a question. I have to go. You were wonderful to call, but I'm alright, really. We'll talk again later." After she said good-bye she held the warm phone in her hand, curled fingers against her chest, not quite ready to release the connection.

Thomas was the one they all depended on because he stayed calm and clear-headed. When he had come from Fredericksburg after her treatments, he never mentioned his insurance business. He turned off his phone and spent quiet hours in the wing chair next to her without any hint that he had clients and employees and adjusters lined up to speak to him back at the office. Somehow without instruction, he knew the right thing to do and say. While she napped in the recliner, he read his bulletins and magazines. He brought her macaroni and cheese, filled her water bottle, wrapped the blanket around her feet. She guessed he'd been the one to update his younger brother on her condition and to prompt Rory to call her after the lymph node procedure, after the emergency gall bladder removal, after the tumor surgery. A flash of yearning for those insulated days ambushed her.

The policeman coughed. Still distracted, Celie faced the young man in the uniform. He was tapping the radio at his belt like a drummer warming up.

"I'm sorry," she said. "My son."

"We hate to bother you again." He rattled out the words, the politeness in the way. "But the children need to go home. The girl needs dry clothes." As if Celie were their maiden auntie.

"No parents yet?" she asked.

"The mother's been called. Driving from work in Fredericksburg. She's supposed to meet them at the Linden Street apartments."

"Linden Street apartments?" The fact that Celie didn't know the place seemed a mystery to her.

"Behind Captain Long's Crab House."

She nodded. "Oh, right." An image of the newly-sided cinder block duplex came to her. "You want me to walk them home?"

"That would be great. They know you."

She started to correct him, but their faces at the seawall flashed before her, that incredulous disbelief in four sets of eyes at her failure to reach in and pull their brother out of the water. Strange, really, that the simple intersection of their lives in the boy's final seconds gave her the responsibility to see them safely home.

After the abbreviated conversation with the policeman, she climbed the hill to where the children huddled. The little girls were backed up to the older one, the teenage boy glued to her elbow. They all faced the creek, speechless and wide-eyed, still except for the oldest one's shivers. They stared past Celie at the circling boats and the crisscross movement of uniforms at creek level, though she wasn't at all sure they registered any of it. Hope coated their faces like sweat.

Her own instant anger that someone hadn't thought to distract them made her knees threaten to give way. Deeper even than the anger, in her gut, the place where she'd learned over the last year to bury what she didn't want to deal with, everything screamed, *turn, walk away, leave them to their vigil*. They were nothing to her, strangers, the events of the afternoon a mere coincidence of timing. Their mother, when she arrived, would need them to be close, warm, alive. Celie's mind churned at that imagined reunion.

Before she took them anywhere she would ask for confirmation that home was the best thing. She glanced around for someone in charge. The rescue squad vehicle, its doors flung wide, its radio spitting and hissing, screened the bustle on the street behind them. Police tape and fluorescent traffic cones and gaping cruisers spread out along Creekside Drive and down the single side street that led west. She didn't realize the county had so many officers.

No one approached her. Everyone seemed to have a job. She was the odd man out.

"Damn," she muttered to herself.

The policeman who had delivered the order was nowhere to be seen. But then, he was trained in triage. He would be busy, following objective procedures learned in a classroom. He was too young to know anything about children. Still, if his supervisor, someone official, with training and experience, thought it appropriate to send the children home, it was probably the right thing to do. When her boys had been young, would she have wanted them to see all this? Definitely not.

She spoke finally to the older girl over the heads of the other three. "They asked me to take you home." Her voice, stilted and businesslike, came back to her as too harsh. "Is that okay?" She tried to soften it. "I'm Mrs. Lowell, from over there." She pointed to the cottage, a gray smudge in the late shadows. "We're neighbors. Kind of."

There was no change in their expression or the direction of their eyes. Everything was irrelevant except the boy who had disappeared. She couldn't fault them for that. She hoped her own face and voice did not convey the feeling of futility that had paralyzed her since the seawall.   Because the children remained focused on the rescue activity and her words seemed to make no impression, she wondered if subconsciously they connected her with that last awful moment. Perhaps that explained why they didn't seem to want to go with her, but were simply not able to voice the objection.

"Okay then, we'll go ahead now and head home," she announced. When they still didn't look at her, she prompted them with her hands. She tapped the boy's arm and patted the backs of the two little girls before she laid her hand on the teenager's shoulder. At the girl's flinch, it was all Celie could do not to withdraw her hand. Through the Rescue Squad towel and the wet shirt, she could feel bones, and muscles sliding over those bones, as they walked. The girl was so young, a long lifetime ahead of her, longer now.

As they trudged along Celie spoke airily, trying not to let any emotion show so that none could be misread, no unintended slight given, no impression of blame. She avoided the eyes of the people they passed and issued a silent prayer that no one would shout out a question or stop their halting progress toward Linden Street.

"What's your name?" she asked the teenager.

At first the girl just glared. When Celie waited without looking away, the girl shrugged concession. Her tone, though, brimmed with outrage.

"Tomeeka. But everyone calls me Meeka."

"Meeka Breeden? I heard you say your mother is Mary Breeden? She works in Fredericksburg?"

Meeka nodded, her shoulder length hair still dripping in clumps.

"And your sisters and brother?"

The girl looked blank.

Celie waved at the other children. "What are their names?"

The teenager blinked, shook her head as if clearing water from her ears. She pointed as she spoke. "Jasmine and Liné. For Grandma Carline. And Reynaud."

"Rey," the boy corrected.

The littlest one's sandals were several sizes too big and slapped the pavement as Celie nudged the bundle of arms and legs toward the apartment building two blocks away. She lowered her head and shoulders to Jasmine's height.

"Whose shoes are those?" Celie asked.

"Liné's."

It was just like a little girl to borrow her big sister's shoes for fun. Once upon a time Rory had appeared in Thomas's hiking boots, his pick-up stick legs bare to his Superman underpants, and his arms swinging in time to 'Over There,' a song he'd learned from Jake's father. Thomas, ever the big brother even back then, had yanked him out of the boots and held him inches off the ground, miniature toes wiggling madly, while they all laughed, especially Rory. The empty boots stood abandoned. Although the memory appeared out of the blue, Celie felt the tickle of a laugh, but it died instantly when Jasmine slid her tiny shape behind the big girl. The children were frightened. Were they afraid of her?

She forced herself to smile at Jasmine. "You do have shoes that are the right size?"

"I have two pairs." Jasmine looked at Meeka for confirmation.

Meeka, Celie repeated to herself, and took a step forward, motioning for the children to move along.

Liné whispered. "I have two pairs of shoes too."

"And apparently so does Rey?" Celie stabbed the air in the direction of the boy, who walked a little apart from the girls, not lagging exactly, but perhaps fighting off his own terror in boyish pretense of independence; one black high top in each hand.

The three girls stopped and looked at Rey. They all stared at the basketball sneakers in his hands. The laces dangled. Just as Celie realized he wouldn't be carrying a second pair of shoes for himself, Meeka started to shiver again. Celie wished she hadn't asked.

Chapter Two

I was spitting mad. The crazy white lady, who asked our names and prodded us along like sheep, tried to hug me once we got to the apartment. Like a hug could change the whole afternoon and bring back Henry Lewis. And then the lady turned to leave before the little girls had even scrambled up the steps. Like she was afraid. Of kids? She didn't apologize. She didn't say good-bye. She didn't say anything.

When the front door opened, Liné and Jasmine fell into Aunt Ruthie's arms and began to sob. Like people on TV do when they hold up a sign, *clap now*. I don't remember giving Ruthie's number to any of the rescue people. But someone had telephoned her to come. As she reached out to gather me in too, I waved her away. She let the door close between us, a wall against their sobs. I didn't feel like crying. I felt like yelling every curse word I knew.

It was better out here, alone. I shut my eyes against what I kept seeing, the girls and Rey staring at me. Their lips parted, their eyes wide, they had waited and waited for me to say something, anything, about it being a joke, the game's over, stop fooling around and get out of the water, time to go home. I wanted to scream.

When the images still wouldn't go away, I opened my eyes. The white lady was barely past the front yard. She'd hardly moved ten feet. Her sneakers dragged along the ground, making a wavery trail in the loose dirt. Gravel slid under her rubber soles in a gritty whine, a crooked line back the way they'd come. Like a sleep-walker. Or a drunk.

Maybe she was. Maybe the rowboat man who'd held her back from jumping had smelled it on her breath. Maybe he knew she had a drinking problem. Maybe that's why he rattled off all that stuff about how deep the water was and how cold. I grew up here and I didn't know that stuff. If she didn't know, how did he? But how could she not know when her house was stuck right there next to the creek on that hill?

As hard as I tried to come up with her name, I couldn't. Aunt Ruthie was gonna ask. Mama too. The name had gone completely out of my head. I did remember how her lips moved slow as if she weren't quite sure about the name herself, the same way she was trailing away from the apartment like she might of forgotten where she lived.

She was way older than Mama or Aunt Ruthie. Her chest sagged—flat enough to start with—and tufts of hair stuck out all over her head like a moth-eaten wig from someone's attic. That's what people meant by a bad hair day. A very bad hair day. Halfway down the block she zigzagged across the pavement, smack across the middle line, without paying the least bit of attention to the traffic. Lucky for her there weren't any cars driving around. They were all jammed up at the creek end of the street, parked every which way on the grass, clogged together in driveways all the way to the police blockade. And all those people from those cars and houses clumped together this side of the orange cones, googly-eyed at the rescue workers. They leaned forward like buzzards on a fence, so intent on what wasn't any of their business. Vultures.

When the white lady walked us past those cones, there was a sudden hush like when the candles came on during the church nativity pageant. Everyone watched, but no one spoke as we passed. I remember the wash of relief I felt, that she was talking low, enough low that the strangers couldn't hear. Our little group had moved past people and cars the way ghosts slipped through walls. I was dazed. We all were. Maybe the creek lady did that talking soft on purpose, so we could get through without being bothered. Smart of her, if that's why. Or maybe she guessed I couldn't answer any more questions after the police and the rescue people made me repeat it all a hundred and twelve times and still no Henry Lewis to show for it.

But while we walked, there was that pounding pulse inside my head in spite of my being so relieved not to have the blank water staring back at me anymore. Something was pushing and shoving against my ribs to get out, ready to explode. That a woman we didn't even know was put in charge of us, that all those grownups assumed we couldn't find our own way home.

Grownups always take control of things just because they've lived longer, the number of years you existed supposively being some formula that makes you smarter. Grownups love to tell everyone what to do, as if there's only one right way. Like the grandmas at church order the kids around, *Hush now,* or *go on and get your mama more lemonade* or *time for ducklings to go off to Sunday school.* The older they are, the more they can't help telling other people how to do, what to do, when to do, especially kids.

Or it might be the creek lady was a crazy person, not just one more grown-up who thought she ran the world. At the seawall she was so busy spouting off what everyone else suppose to be doing she didn't do the one thing that might could have saved Henry Lewis. Jump in and grab him before he sank too low to reach, too low for his bubbles to rise up and show where he was, too low for him to catch enough air to make bubbles at all.

All of a sudden standing on the front porch my face was burning up, just thinking about how it was when my own head went under the water. The feeling of instant panic came back in a huge wave, how I thought my own fool self was done for. I'd forgotten all about Henry Lewis. My legs shivered and wobbled like they might would give out any second. I gripped the porch railing. To distract myself I concentrated on the white lady wandering down the street. At the sixth or seventh house she stopped smack in the middle of the road. I had the weird sensation that the same feeling of panic gripped her too.

One hand clutched the jeans slipping off her hips, she's so thin. The other dug through that raggedy buzz cut. Was she trying to look punk? If she thought she looked younger with that hair, she was crazy for real. Someone should tell her it made her look a little off, those invisible eyebrows and the dead-on stare. She could be one of those movie aliens who disguised themselves as humans and gobbled brains to absorb their thoughts. Why was she looking back so many times? She never seen a black girl before?

In one way she acted kind of like the teachers, the way they shook your hand, asked your name, pretended everything was fine, and then the next minute acted like they'd never seen you before, blaming you if you were anywhere near the trouble. In another way she was altogether different. She wasn't angry. She hadn't raised her voice. Although she said she wanted to help, she hadn't done anything. Least not anything helpful, except call 9-1-1.

I tried to recall the exact way it happened at the seawall when Henry Lewis disappeared. I remember that same sickening feeling from the fights in the girls' bathroom, that if you had left thirty seconds before, you would have avoided the whole mess. The two or three times I'd been stuck in the middle school bathroom when the teachers steamed in to break up a fight, they used a ticked-off voice, stepped up a notch or two in volume from their everyday hallway bossing, but they never seemed surprised. They acted like fights were exactly what they expected. They made it crystal clear they were irritated they had to waste their time with it, even though they were being paid to do exactly that. What they really meant with that tone of voice was that's what kids did, they screwed up, and adults simply had to soldier through and clean up the mess, things never changed.

But whenever Jasmine or Henry Lewis or I acted up, Mama's voice was different, filled with surprise and hurt. She was shocked her children could misbehave after all she'd taught them. And the white lady was shocked and hurt too, not in the least little bit irritated or angry.

Everything was so mixed up. I let my back slide down the railing until I was sitting on the top step. My shorts made a slurpy hiccup as the water squished out. My legs ached. It had to be all the standing and waiting because it couldn't be that little bit of swimming. I hadn't been in the water more than a minute. Half a minute, maybe.

Through the apartment door footsteps pounded up the stairs over the blur of radio static. When the static cleared, I recognized the jingle of the local station WRVR and the voice of Mr. Harmony, the father of one of the other eighth grade girls, as he read the menu for tomorrow's school lunches.

"Batter-dipped fish and home fries, peaches, and lime jello." Mr. Harmony's cheerful voice went on to list the middle school and high school menus, a Santa Claus show in April. It didn't seem possible, after what had happened, that school would go on tomorrow like they did every other day.

One time in fourth grade Birdie Harmony brought her father as her Show and Tell. Even though you were supposed to bring things you could explain to the class, Mrs. Brighton let him stay. Birdie wasn't dumb. She knew the whole point of Show and Tell was to practice speaking before an audience, but with her lisp she probably figured her father could do the talking better. Because of Birdie's lisp the teachers were more careful with her and she milked the special treatment for all it was worth. Where a normal kid, to get attention, might brag about a new video game or going to Kings Dominion, Birdie took it to the next level with much smaller issues. A whole lot of overcompensating taking place, Mama said.

When Mr. Harmony did his radio voice for the class, we all laughed. Except Birdie. She grabbed his hand and stomped out. She probably thought we were making fun of him like we made fun of her. I felt terrible. Not because we laughed—Birdie's dad was funny—but because she didn't understand that we liked her Show and Tell. She was so busy being touchy.

The apartment steps were cool, shaded by the line of trees that edged the gravel parking lot. The rough concrete pressed the wet shorts into my thighs. My hair clung to the back of my neck. All of a sudden I saw myself from earlier as I'd looped across the grassy hill to the dock. When I leapt into the air, the muddy water came up fast and I was under before I knew it. It was how I imagined the swirly torture Rey described from the boys' locker room, but worse because it wasn't just my head in a toilet, it was my whole body falling down and down, round and round, deeper and deeper. I plowed through the water with my arms and legs to get my head out where I could breathe. Without even thinking, I kicked and kicked to get free of the water. And it worked.

Back at the surface my throat was scratchy from swallowing too much water. When I twisted around, only Henry Lewis's head was above the surface. His mouth was a little round O of surprise, but he didn't say anything. I kept on kicking because I was afraid of sinking back down. I told him to kick too, only his head bobbed under right then. He might not have heard me. Even though I yelled my head off, when he came back up, he just floated out into the channel like he couldn't figure where he was.

Please, God, I was thinking, *don't let a boat come through now and hit him.* For the quickest second I took my eyes off him and looked toward the dock. It was four or five feet away, the distance widening. I was drifting out too. I lunged for the post and grabbed fistfuls of water. When my body moved in, I realized this must be how you swim. I pulled faster, like a dog digging a hole, until my knuckles hit the dock. I was so happy to be holding on to something solid, I started crying. Henry Lewis's head was still up, but he was much farther away and I couldn't see his eyes anymore.

Sitting here now, hours too late, it hit me that I prayed for the wrong thing. I should've prayed for a boat to come because they could have scooped him up out of that water and saved him.

For a long time after the girls went inside with Aunt Ruthie I sat on the apartment steps. While I rubbed my arms and legs, I tried to figure why Henry Lewis hadn't tried. My arms and legs had done it all by themselves. Surprising how magically it worked, a person acting like a dog could swim like a fish, an amazing thing. But Henry Lewis hadn't pulled the first time. That was the real mystery.

While my teeth chattered, a tiny rattle echoed in my head. My jaw ached and my shoulder muscles throbbed. A regular one man band, one of Grandpa TomTom's sayings. I knew I should go in and change out of my wet clothes. But I was scared. I didn't want to see my brother's things scattered all over, looking like he was just late from Cub Scouts or whatever. With my arms wrapped around my knees, I tried to think about something else, anything else.

The funny thing about Birdie Harmony, her voice was so 'zactly like Mr. Harmony's. The stretched-out words and the way the sentence ends fell off into slurs you couldn't make out. She even moved her hands the way he did. I wondered if my voice was like my father's. Was it genes that made that happen? Or something more? Because it couldn't be genes when we three kids were so different, our voices, and the things we were interested in. It made more sense with the Harmony's. Birdie and her dad lived together. She heard him talk all day long.

I didn't like to think about Latrelle. He hadn't come by for years. And the last time, before Jasmine was born, he'd been all sorry and sloppy, with his hands all over Mama. He'd been stinking with that jumbled sour sweet smell I learned later was whiskey. I hadn't known drunk then. Most of the men throwing dice behind the Laundromat with their paper bags all scrunched at the top smelled and acted like my father had that day. They lean sideways and help themselves along the cinderblock wall with their palms open. The slurred nonsense of their boasting and the whiskey sourness drifts across the street.

Before that day at the trailer with my father, I'd never been that close to a drunk man. And never since. The next week Mama moved us out of the trailer park to the apartment above the dry cleaners. She thought it would be safer, and it was. My father never came there. But it turned out to be almost as bad as living in the trailer. Late night arguments and street jive that Mama didn't like us to hear or see. All that was before they built the Linden Street apartments, where we moved a year ago, where nothing ever happened.

That day my father was drunk, he came through the back door and was inside before Mama realized. I was sitting on the floor, playing a game with Henry Lewis and his plastic trucks. Latrelle didn't even say hello to us. He went straight for Mama, repeating her name like it was a song. My mother talked to him like she talks to Henry Lewis about not throwing his toys.

"Don't do this, Latrelle. Let me be." She twirled loose from him and edged toward the back door. "Just go now," she said in her fiercest I-AM-SERIOUS voice.

But he kept on, grabbing at her from behind and backing her up against the counter. When he slid her blouse off her shoulder, she screamed.

"You couldn't just stay away like you been? Why come 'round now, when we learned to do without you?"

He slapped her face and she started to cry. I ran to her, but she pushed me away.

"No, Mee, stay away. Take your brother outside. Go."

So I drug Henry Lewis away from the little trucks and he started crying. We sat on the tree swing together, singing like alley cats as loud as we could to drown out the sound of Mama crying and our father cursing and things crashing and banging. I prayed for one of my aunts to come, Ruthie or Antoinette either, or the postman, or even one of the white boys from the other end of the trailer park who wore their work shirts unbuttoned to the waist and wrestled in the dirt for dollar bets on Sunday afternoons. When it grew quiet in the trailer, I wanted so badly to go in and see if Mama was still alive, but I was too afraid. I was eight.

Then my father lurched out the way he'd come and climbed into his pick-up truck, huge raggedy rusted-out holes along the side like the water stains on the trailer carpet. He drove away, never even saw us sitting there. By the time Jasmine was born the next summer, I had discovered a book in the library about the reproductive cycle and I knew what he'd done.

By now he could be dead—all this time passing—and Mama still so furious she wouldn't think it was important enough to tell us. I used to think at least Henry Lewis was safe from turning out like Latrelle. But after today if by some odd chance Latrelle saved hisself through one of God's mysterious ways they talk about at church when a good thing comes out of something bad, my brother will never know his own father. We'd never know if he had the same voice or the same way of swinging his shoulders when he walked. No matter which way you looked at it, it was my fault.

I slapped my leg hard. There I was back to Henry Lewis, but this was different. I wasn't thinking of him the same way. In these few minutes I'd stopped believing. I slapped my leg until my palm stung.

My brain spun in crazy circles, question after question after question. I should've asked the white lady if it was possible to hold your breath long enough to push off the bottom and come up a different place from where you went down. It would be just like Henry Lewis to convince himself he could think up a better solution and then go and try it like it was one of his never-ending science experiments. Maybe that's what he'd been doing when he hadn't answered me. He was figuring how to save energy, sink down, and bounce at an angle that would get him closer to the shore. So he wouldn't have to fight the current so hard. That sounded just like him.

He'd drifted way out so quickly he must have seen he was headed the wrong way. Still, he might have come up downstream and be out there shivering right now. Right this minute he could be waiting for them to find him and carry him home. I considered running back and asking the firemen or the rescue squad workers to look farther along the shore. They might not have thought of it. Those rescue people hadn't even marked the seawall where his bubbles were. They could be looking in the wrong place. I shouldn't never of left.

But I kept on sitting on those steps like I was glued down. I didn't get up. I didn't yell inside to Aunt Ruthie that I was going back. I stayed right there like a lump while my brain worried it round and round like those Cracker Barrel restaurant puzzles. *Please let them find him. Please let them bring him home. Don't let him be a lost boy.*

It grew darker and darker while I worked through all the possibilities. People write in books and poems about the night falling, and I could see, sitting here, how true it was. It was like God had flung out a giant black velvet cape and it was slowly sinking through the air until it covered the earth. Shapes of buildings and trees melted into the velvet and disappeared until I was alone on the steps, the smooth cool blur of the velvet on my face and arms, the world and all its troubles gone.

It was strange. I'm never alone. All day at school the other kids shove and elbow me. Knee to knee, the bus ride crowded us in on top of each other. Talking, teasing, joking, the noise filled what little space was left in the bus between bodies. After school Jasmine and Liné danced around me with their fairy tale games and Rey sulked with all his hot air. Except whenever Rachel or my other girlfriends came over, he strutted around like he the big man. Funny how he forgot all about basketball practice.

And every afternoon Mama's boyfriend Ashante called to be sure we were following her instructions. I didn't mind that so much. Ashante was nice enough, and he treated Mama good. Even though I was supposed to be minding all the kids, he only checked up on us when she had afternoon meetings. He never made rules just because he could and he wasn't like Aunt Ruthie who never stopped talking. Between Ruthie gossiping with Mama when she came to collect Liné or while they made dinner, I was hardly ever by myself.

Alone like this in the falling night with no jabbering and only my brain whirring, this is what it must be like to be the lady with the house on the hill. Before this afternoon I'd seen her a bunch of times, but never up close. She was always alone. On Saturday mornings she'd walked by the apartments with a bright blue canvas bag over her shoulder, a hat stuck on that stumpy hair. The only thing up Linden Street was the post office, so I figured she went to get her mail. Usually she passed one block over from the apartments, too far away to see much more than the hat and the blue bag. Sometimes if it was afternoon she looped from one side of the street to the other they way kids did when they were looking for fireflies. Lots of times

MINDING HENRY LEWIS

Henry Lewis dragged us along when he went to exercise the Jessup's dog and she'd be standing on her hill like one of those Hollywood Indians, her eyes shaded by one hand as she stared across the water, no telling what she was really looking at.

Imagine having that great big house to yourself with water wrapped all around you. It would be like living on a mountaintop with the whole world at your feet. Maybe she'd gone bonkers from living alone like Ms. Havisham in *Great Expectations,* all over candles and cobwebs. Except for today at the creek when her hair was loose and wild, every other time she walked by she'd been wearing a different hat. Straw hats and colored hats and baseball hats. If she owned a hat store in the city, that could explain it. It would also explain why her car was gone for days at a time. It might be the reason she spent so much time outdoors when she was here. Working inside a store all day long would drive me crazy.

In a blur of red and silver a fire truck rocked past the apartment without a siren. When the second one chugged by in no real hurry, I guessed they'd quit searching. It reminded me of the crab races at the street festival after school let out. A couple three crabs would speed down the wooden ramp like there was a forest fire behind them or a huge gooey chocolate cake waiting for them, when really there was just a wooden dead-end at the bottom. There was always one crab that dawdled, not in any rush, as if it knew nothing good waited at the finish line.

The slow crab was the second fire engine. The rescue workers had given up like the crab. If they'd found Henry Lewis, I would've felt something, I would've known. Instead all I felt was this crackling panic that buzzed around my head like a mayfly.

I hated mayflies. The sound and that bite out of the blue, just when you thought they'd finally left you alone. Mayflies were the worst. Bees, at least, could be chased away and only stung once. Not mayflies. No matter how hard you tried, they stuck with you, stung you every time they landed. On top of adding nothing to the world. Nothing good came from mayflies. God created a whole race of flies for no good reason. They could eat mosquitoes or fire ants, but no, their whole short lives—three days, I read in my seventh grade science book—all they did was lay eggs and bite. Someone ought to tell God that particular experiment had flopped. He could quit making mayflies.

Although I didn't hear the door open, Aunt Ruthie's thick-soled nurse shoes made telltale squeaks on the concrete behind me. I steeled herself for a bombardment of pint size arms and legs, but no one else came.

"Meeka, hon, what you doing out here all by yourself?" She put a hand on my head for balance and let herself down onto the porch steps. Her body was warm next to my cold one. "Your mama ought to be here any time now."

She patted the top of my damp leg, stopped, and then started again, the way she did when she was cooking and forgot what she was saying in the middle of a sentence because she was re-reading the recipe. Her voice, not quite a whisper, was low, clogged enough that I knew she'd been crying.

"The girls are watching cartoons," she said. "Leastways for the time being. No telling what they'll do once Mary comes."

I tried to imagine what Mama would do. At first she'd go straight to the creek, to the people in charge. The captain, the man with the bullhorn, would give her an official report. It wouldn't be enough for Mama. She'd pepper them with questions. After that she might call home on the cell phone to be sure her other babies were safe. Ashante and Aunt Ruthie must have worked it out on the phone already, because Ruthie was here with us. He must be waiting at the creek. The afternoon was getting more and more jumbled in my mind, the crazy lady, the rowboat, Henry Lewis disappearing under the water, Rey running away and coming back but not talking. I didn't know what I'd say when Mama came home.

Ruthie rubbed my back in energetic circles. "You freezing in those clothes, girl. Go on inside and put on something dry before your mama gets here."

But when I tried to stand, my legs wouldn't bend. Ruthie pushed low on my back, like she knew exactly what the trouble was.

"Go on, save yourself from a cold. That won't be no help to your mama."

"I'm no help, no matter which way."

"I don't wanna hear that kind of talk. Your mama's going to need you more than ever. You can't be thinking stuff like that. You gotta be strong."

When Ruthie's palm pushed harder, I pitched forward, but saved myself at the last minute by grabbing the rail.

"That a girl," my aunt crowed. "One thing at a time. Dry clothes. Don't let yourself think about anything else."

At the open door I paused. The house lights inside blinded me. It was like looking into the sun, which you weren't ever supposed to do. My eyes burned. The stuffy air in the townhouse smelled like yesterday's tuna fish casserole. My stomach twisted. I tried to think what day of the week it was. Maybe today was trash day and I'd forgotten to take the kitchen bag to the outside can. I couldn't remember. I couldn't remember much before the sound of splashing water and Henry Lewis's glee at the first cool splash on the boat ramp, before he slid, before the fear took away his voice.

As I felt for the banister, I fought to lift my feet, each one heavier than the one before. *My brother needed me this afternoon. And what d'I do? Nothing. I did nothing.* Aunt Ruthie had no earthly idea how hard it was to think about things like dry clothes when Henry Lewis was missing, sunk in that muddy river water, and never coming home. It was impossible to think about anything else.

Chapter Three

After awkward good-byes to the children outside the townhouse, Celie walked back the way they'd come, her arms across her chest to ward off the early evening chill. Hugging Meeka had been spontaneous, though the girl had been stiff and unresponsive. Too late Celie remembered that stage with her own children. No teenager wanted to be hugged, much less by a stranger. And for Meeka, worse still by a white woman who had done nothing to help save her brother.

Shame and disappointment flooded Celie, and she had to fight off an overwhelming sense of being alone, separate from everyone else, of being invisible and useless. It wasn't that she was old and Meeka was young. It wasn't about being white or black. It was more about her own failures. She'd been indecisive. She couldn't control her emotions. She'd lost her temper with Richard Widener, and she hadn't been brave enough even to try to save the boy. No wonder his sister didn't want anything to do with her. Trudging home, Celie was bleary, her eyes watery, her face flushed.

In spite of spending the better part of the cancer year forcing herself to be honest about how weak and frightened she felt and letting people help her, she kept reacting the same way. She refused to talk about it and avoided people, then worried over every little thing on her own. For a whole year she'd been upset with herself for not being able to change, and yet she hadn't changed.

Like a sports coach Jake had harped on perspective. "You have to look at it the other way, not how miserable it is to be sick, but how lucky you are to have had 53 years of not being sick," he said.

He was right. She knew it and she'd told him so later. When he apologized, she'd felt guilty all over again. He was so patient with her, though his world had changed too. He didn't complain or whine. He was being a rock, what he did best. Still the gap between them was huge. She hardly knew how she felt and it changed from minute to minute. After a full night's sleep she woke up encouraged and by the end of breakfast she was hiding in the bathroom, terrified that a new ache in her knee was the cancer metastasized in her bones. In the thick of treatments and feeling lousy and not knowing how it was going to turn out, it wasn't easy to have perspective.

He'd foreseen that argument too. "It's easy for me to say, I'm not the one who's sick, but you're strong, sweetie. You can do this."

"Me? I'm the one who let the disease take over in the first place."

"It's just a statistical probability. It's not anything you did."

"My body let me down."

"No." He was General Patton and there would be no dissension in the ranks. "You have to think of it like a war. The invading army attacked, surprise attack. How could you know? You just have to be smarter."

She shut up then. She didn't feel smarter. She didn't feel anything close to smart. She felt fuzzy and exhausted. All she wanted was to lie down and close her eyes and let the Green Berets burn the hell out of the invading army with their chemical warfare and radiation artillery. Someone else had to fight. She was overcome with disgust that her body had let the cancer in. That betrayal seemed monumental.

Even after the renegade cells had been declared dead and the doctors announced their success, she didn't feel safe and she knew she never would. But she gave up trying to explain that to Jake. The rift remained, even now months after the cancer was allegedly vanquished. The sense of being a team was gone. In the end it was her fight. She was the one standing at the other end of the rifle barrel.

With the afternoon's events he would say she'd lost perspective. His voice reverberated in her head, the instructions loud and clear. She needed to get a grip. She was the adult here. And even as she slipped away from that stridency into a hazy awareness of the rescue activity around her, she struggled not to dwell on the past, but to focus on what she could do to help.

The streets teemed with parked cars and people, heads together, their voices a steady painful drill. *What were they waiting for?* The instant she thought it, she knew the answer. She swallowed hard to keep from throwing up right here on the street.

At the corner of Stonegate and Creekside Drive the scene spread out below her like a movie set. Boats and people along the water were following an invisible but palpable official rescue protocol, oblivious to most of the onlookers. A man with a bull horn commandeered the hilltop. At his heels the radio in the rescue squad vehicle crackled instructions and questions. She was so busy looking at the yellow emergency tape that she walked by an entire block of parked cars without paying any attention to the faces, though some of those people waved at her.

Just as she crossed the street at the corner, an older blue van pulled into the last sliver of open lawn. The driver's door swung open, but before the woman could get out, a compact black man rushed over from the huddle by the ambulance. His muscled arms wide, he pinned the woman in and blocked her view of the creek.

Celie saw immediately that the woman was the boy's mother. She had Meeka's same cheekbones, the same high narrow shoulders. When the woman fell back onto the seat and beat her fists against the steering wheel, Celie tensed for the expected scream. Instead a wail spilled out, a keening so charged with sorrow that she had to look away. Even so the sound etched into the lingering portrait, the woman's hair slick against her head with perspiration, that brown forehead buried in bare arms, the man's polished shoulders circling hers to still the shaking.

"Excuse me." The same young policeman who'd sent Celie home with the children touched her shoulder.

She jerked away from him, as if he had interrupted an actual conversation between her and the boy's mother.

"Is it all right if we walk out to the marsh?" he asked. And when she didn't answer, he pointed east. "Isn't that your land?"

She nodded. Without asking she knew they were not looking for a boy swimming, but for a body. For a body suspended in the muddy water, adrift in the current. She formed the words like a line of type on the computer and made her lips move to answer.

"Yes, of course," she said. "Whatever you need to do."

Like a film negative the vision of Henry Lewis's mother pounding the steering wheel joined the other recurring images in Celie's mind. She shook that off too and traipsed after the uniformed man. Four paces behind, she threaded her way past odd clusters of deputies and firemen and bystanders. People nodded. Maybe at the policeman, maybe at her, people whose faces she recognized from her evening walks without being able to name them. As the young policeman strode across the grass purposefully, she had trouble keeping up. The distance between them grew. She was huffing again.

When she reached the seawall, she stepped onto the wide board on top. She paused a second to balance. The water looked impenetrable, as if it had swallowed the boy whole and closed over forever. He was eleven, his sister had said. Celie tried to recall the height and thickness of her sons at that age. Thomas had been so thin, his knees little knots of bone and his hands too big for the rest of him. When they'd taken him to the doctors for the leg pain that made him moan in bed at night, the orthopedist had said it was typical for growing boys. Muscles couldn't keep up with bones. Only time would cure the pain. The medical term had been four syllables long and she'd forgotten it before they left the doctor's office. After that whenever Thomas cried in bed, she let Jake stay with him. She would go out and sit in the car with the windows rolled up tight. She couldn't bear to lie there helpless and listen.

While the rescue team worked methodically, she stood on the seawall stuck in time. Her mind took her back to that morning. She'd run down to the river house in the old station wagon Rory had used in grad school, the sun roof agog and the back jammed with plants. For weeks she'd been thinking about transplanting some daylilies on the hillside that plunged from the river house to the creek. Even with the open car windows the loamy smell of dug earth was like company, familiar and almost conversational. She had sung to the radio and tried to remember afternoons in the yard when the boys were little so she could tell the stories to Thomas's wife Caroline who was expecting their first child at Thanksgiving. The first grandchild. It would be a fresh start.

The morning itself had enticed her. A perfect spring day with its unseasonable eighty degrees and cloudless sunshine had sprung Virginia from the prison of an overly long winter with record snows. Celie felt like that prisoner, finally freed. With no obligations at home and no pending doctor's appointments, she made instant plans to stay at the cottage for two weeks, maybe more. After unpacking the car at the cottage, she snacked on cheese and crackers before she put clean sheets on the bed in their room. She had slipped the brownies in the oven, set the timer, and gone out to work in the garden for twenty minutes. She should have known better.

It was late afternoon by the time she gathered the shovel and the first bag of plants. Shadows spread across the hillside like slouched soldiers weary after a long vigil. Their little dog, Maxy, fourteen and creaky with arthritis, shuffled into the ivy near her, careful to stay in the shade. After he sniffed in one direction, then the other, he plopped down with one last half-hearted wiggle. The damp earth must have been cool on his belly. With her feet apart, armed with the shovel, Celie was primed to start the process of digging holes when that voice shot across the warm afternoon air.

Last spring she hadn't been able to dig at all, her right arm a liability after the removal of twelve lymph nodes, one infected. *Had to be one bad one in the bunch,* she'd joked, but the surgeon hadn't laughed. She knew it wasn't funny—really—but courtesy dictated you would laugh if your patient did. Especially a patient headed for chemotherapy, a mastectomy, and radiation. And it must have been obvious how hard she'd been trying to be confident in the face of overwhelming fear.

Even before the cancer her garden was a hodge-podge. It never had come halfway close to her mother's meticulous garden back in Middleton, and it was worse at the river because they were only there part of the time. Her mother had a white garden circling one redbud and on the western side of her house a blue garden with her Prince Phillip vine trained to a green-wire trellis, a publicity shot straight out of the seed catalogs. Her mother's herbs formed a perfect half-moon and were graduated by height. Every spring she had lettuce before anyone else. Lovely, sweet celery-colored petals for their salads. Along her fence in August a late rainbow of zinnias crowded towards the sun like rock'n roll fans waiting for the expected limousine.

Celie's river garden was the opposite. Odd plants heeled in wherever there was empty space, watered and fertilized like sailors visiting dockside bars, without forethought, without memory. Volunteer nandina and mimosas sprouted wherever they could find a toehold. Everything was temporary, waiting for some permanent plan that had yet to materialize, waiting for her to decide.

She wasn't really a gardener at all. What she liked about gardening was the sense of accomplishment in a full bucket of weeds and the magic of flowers that reappeared every year, however haphazardly. It was only recently she could admit that working the garden was a substitute for being with her mother. She missed the afternoon conversations in her mother's rickety wooden lawn chairs when they caught each other up on the week's activities, the latest political controversy in Middleton, their tiny adopted farming community, books that just had to be read, articles from the Sunday Post.

Her mother had died in her sleep two years before Celie's cancer. Just as well, she told herself. Her mother would not have done well with a sick daughter. They had that in common, that shared Puritan blood that did not tolerate malingering, that would not admit weakness or failure. Her father had been gone for years, a surprise heart attack right after she and Jake's wedding. He'd been mostly absent during her childhood, a fanatical salesman who'd left her mother enough of a bank account to allow her to live comfortably without working.

"Maybe you inherited your father's ability to read people," her mother quipped when Celie chose psychology as her major. Clearly she had not inherited his business sense. Her mediation training had been her rebellion against the pursuit of profit he espoused as the universal human motivation.

She blamed the unusual April sun for the delay in her transplanting project. She moved slowly, absorbing each sparkle, each lift of the breeze. The sunshine was not ready to let go of the perfect afternoon either. It clung to the trees along Creekside Drive in throbbing shards of tangerine and salmon. As she carried the shovel down to the garden she remembered thinking that Jake was probably in the air between Chicago and Richmond, still hours away. With his late flight, she was free to work late in the yard and snack instead of preparing a full meal. She wouldn't look up and catch him watching her with hooded eyes, wary and uncertain of her mood or her emotional barometer, a habit he'd adopted after last February's biopsy and the long months of drugs and surgeries.

In light of the irreversible change in how she viewed life, it shouldn't be a surprise that she was uncomfortable with his constant assessment of how she felt. Never before had anyone paid so much attention to what she was doing, when she closed her eyes, or whether there was significance in the way she positioned herself on the lawn chair. With the unspoken questions she grew more miserly still. Although she suffered frequent pangs of guilt, she feigned sleep more often than not to deflect attention. The person she became was so different from the independent self she'd cultivated her whole life. It felt like dragging around a wooden leg.

The river house had become an escape from her new faltering self, snagged on the invasion of doctors and hospital visits and medicines. If he were honest, Jake hid out here too. As weekend people they hadn't cultivated neighbors or friends. Their schedule was irregular, last-minute. No one knew them well enough to know she was sick. No one brought casseroles or offered to drive her to her appointments. Here she and Jake could pretend life was normal.

Eight years back, hooked by the old clapboard cottage's spectacular view, they'd bought it after one visit. It was meant to be an oasis from the frenzied schedule of their jobs and the children's obligations. Although now the boys were graduated and on their own, she and Jake hadn't yet grown accustomed to being here without them and their constant activities. She savored the slowing of time like an unexpected gift, even as Jake worked hard to fill the weekends with projects and visits from old friends and the kids, a manic backwards grab at 'life before cancer.'

South of their property the creek fed into the river, subject to the rise and fall of the tides from the Chesapeake Bay fifty miles downstream. The beaches along the river edge were a mixture of sand and mud, the water barely waist-high for fifty or sixty yards until the channel markers. Along the shipping passage the grain barges still chuffed and chugged through the brackish water on the same route as the last remaining grand old tourist boat. On weekends it carted groups up river to see the bald eagles and the new wineries. April, though, was too early for tourists.

Spring at the river, before the burden of summer humidity, gave up these random sunny days like a birthday present from a new friend, filled with promise, yet a shade unnerving because you weren't quite sure what was coming next. Frost and thunderstorms might arrive back to back. Three weeks ago when she and Jake had come to open the cottage for the season, the last of the ice was floating past in shrunken opaque patches. In the wintertime, with only the gas logs and no insulation, the cottage was too expensive to heat. They usually drained the pipes at Thanksgiving and took a day trip once or twice after the Christmas holidays to check on things.

From the first summer they'd talked about renovating. They drew out their ideas on graph paper, pored through window catalogs, clipped magazine photos of spaces they liked. Private school tuition and college for the boys delayed the project. It was almost seven years before they finally interviewed contractors and started the renovation. Four weeks after they tore out the first wall she found the lump in her breast.

The cancer changed all their plans. They limped through March and April, most of their time spent on the road to and from the hospital. Consultations with three different doctors, internet research, conference calls with the health insurance patient advocate took over her free time. After two rushed MRIs, her 'team' of doctors insisted on immediate surgery to remove the lymph nodes. Chemotherapy started four days later. Her head spun with the schedule of blood tests, infusions, vitamin regimens, and prescriptions against side effects. Stark details emerged like Ouija words from vast chunks of hastily recited technical information. Daily decisions crystallized, only to melt into the blur of the chemicals. Her life became the weekly drive to the hospital, the dreaded return to a silent Middleton house with the boys' empty bedrooms, and the nightmare aftermath of perpetual naps, singles bites of bland food, and solo nights of gut-wrenching nausea. The dream of the river cottage faded.

Without her, the contractor soldiered on with the renovations, minimal decisions gleaned from sketchy emails or late night phone messages with Jake. Every few weeks he drove down by himself from Middleton and took photos with his cell phone to share with her. At home the women she'd played tennis with and her bridge group divided the weeks and brought gourmet meals in throw-away containers. They hugged her and left funny movies and piles of magazines, which she devoured because she could pick them up and put them down whenever she needed a distraction. She didn't need to remember what she'd read. Dutifully Jake heated portions of their concoctions in smaller pans, carried them on trays upstairs to where she slept in his recliner, and just as dutifully he took them away, the utensils barely used, the leftovers congealed and cold.

By autumn she'd had three surgeries and was ignoring the sunken place in her chest. With radiation in full swing five days a week in Fredericksburg she didn't check on the cottage all winter. She felt a little like an addict after rehab, trying to avoid relapse by blocking out remembered highs; their family gatherings, the splendor of wide water and open sky, the melting ripples off the kayak's bow. With this April visit, after they'd reopened in mid-March, she was officially in remission. She'd succumbed to the lure, eager to put the sick room behind her, not that she was convinced the cancer was really gone.

Jake had encouraged her to focus on simpler things, the river garden being one. She actually agreed with him for the first time in a long time. At first her mind seemed eager to manage the regimen of small chores, short lists, instead of reliving the endless haze of hospital visits and reactions to medicine that didn't change the bottom line. But look where her first attempt had landed her. The yard was overrun with strangers and there was this lost boy.

Chapter Four

"Celie."

The woman's voice was familiar, but there were too many faces. When Celie stepped off the seawall to walk on the grass, the voice followed her.

"I came when I heard the sirens. Where's Jake?"

Celie forced herself to stop walking and look up. The hand on her arm belonged to Tracy Anne Sheffield, a woman from church who lived in the neighborhood, perhaps on Stonegate Road itself. Celie hadn't worked very hard at remembering who went with which house. Because she and Jake weren't here full-time, they didn't always go to Sunday morning services. Some weekends, even when they were in town, she couldn't manage the low kneelers, the too-efficient air-conditioning, the flurried handshakes of so many smiling strangers. On those skipped Sundays she was undone later by the horror of not making time for God while the cancer lurked. And although Jake would go with her if she asked, he didn't seem to need that kind of ceremony to bolster his own beliefs.

Back when they were dating she had liked that about him, that confidence in God's order without the crutch of repetitive public ceremonies. Yet it was the familiar cadence of those prayers and childhood hymns that brought her back on the Sundays she did go. Comfort, not inspiration.

Tracy Anne was insistent, the manicured fingers on Celie's arm ever so competent. "Are you here alone?"

"Alone?" Celie surveyed the hillside of people. Even at the mouth of the creek a blue uniform crossed in front of their boat dock and marched along the reedy edge of the marsh. What could he see in the descending gloom? Through that wall of dark water?

"Celie," Tracy Anne repeated. "Is Jake up at the house? Or one of your kids?"

"Jake's on a business trip. In Chicago. Well, he's coming back from there. Tonight. He'll be here tonight." The words reassured her, a surprise in light of how resentful she'd been feeling over his continuous scrutiny. In spite of the tense months of being observed and babied, it struck her in that moment that being alone was worse. When he was with her, his routine returned some normalcy to her life. And although it seemed more like a performance by her, things did get done when he was home, the everyday kind of things she had done before the cancer.

36

"This must be horrible for you, here by yourself," Tracy Ann said.

Celie refused to let herself be drawn into a discussion with this woman she hardly knew. They'd met outside the church three or four times. Tracy Ann, without a wedding ring or a husband in tow, had paid more attention to Jake than to her. There was no telling whether she was referring to the afternoon, the cancer, or a traveling husband.

"It's getting chilly," Tracy Anne said in response to Celie's silence.

There was the cancer again, imposing a barrier that even nosy Tracy Anne couldn't cross. Celie gave her points for trying. "Yes. It's April." She was impatient to join the policeman at the marsh.

"Would you like to borrow my jacket?" Tracy Anne asked.

"Our cottage is right here." At Tracy Anne's flutter of shock, Celie backpedaled, the echo of her own abruptness catching her out. "A jacket is a good idea. I'll just slip up and get one of mine." It avoided the next question and a recitation of what had transpired earlier. Surely by now more than one story was circulating up and down the street.

When Jake called half an hour later during his airport layover and heard Celie's jumbled report, she was still on the seawall. She hadn't gone up for her coat, but had walked out to the marsh where the young policeman and another officer paced back and forth, scanning the creek and the wider river. Intermittent radio conversation with the rescue boat skittered over the waves like November leaves, though she had to strain in the dusk to make out any of what they were saying. She couldn't shake the feeling that she ought to be present as long as there were people on the property, a skewed version of acting a proper host. That wasn't it exactly, but if they needed something, she wanted to be helpful.

Jake barked orders into the phone. "I want you to go straight up to the house." He raised his voice over the airport loudspeakers in the background. "And stay inside. Let the rescue people do their job. You don't know those kids."

She could hear the sharp tightness as her voice skidded across the open lawn. "He was only eleven. His brother and sisters saw it all. I was right there."

"They weren't on our dock?"

"Goodness, no." She choked out, her irritation instantaneous at his single-minded leap to the question of liability. "Three houses down Creekside at the old marina. But if I'd started sooner—"

"Oh, no, you don't. Those kids shouldn't have been in the water in the first place. Or on that property for that matter."

There was no point in arguing. He hadn't been there.

Halfway up the drive, puffing from exertion and irritation, after a second terse good-bye to him because he'd called back two minutes later to be sure she'd gone inside, she remembered the brownies. The niggling in the back of her brain flashed fully illuminated like a tree line below fireworks, a shot of charred brownies superimposed on a smoke-filled cottage. She raced up the hill, past the empty flower pots on the steps, and fumbled with the screen door handle. Amazed that the kitchen was not a cave of smoke, she grabbed potholders and charged outside with the brownie pan. Once she set it on the brick steps, she realized she could have burned down the entire cottage. She was lucky.

In the last twelve months she hadn't felt lucky once. Early on when Susan Leder, one of her tennis friends back home, came with a dinner offering, Susan assured her she was in God's hands. Celie had been speechless. Stolid in her faith, Susan simply assumed that everyone felt as she did. For days after Susan's visit the simple declaration had echoed in Celie's head. Confident yet mindless like a high school football cheer. She knew Susan's unswerving faith ought to inspire her.

But she wanted more than faith. She wanted the cancer never to have come. She wanted the world to spin backwards, to defy time and gravity and take her back to the day of the clear mammogram, the grousing afterwards about cold metal imprinted on pale flesh, even before that to the breezy good-bye kiss she'd given Jake as she headed to her annual gynecologist's exam, and the month before that when she made the appointment and hoped to have time for a little Christmas shopping while she was in the city.

It had taken her weeks to even consider that God might help her with the cancer. Because it would have been so much easier if He hadn't let her get it in the first place. Months later, with the surgery scars fading and her mind a little bit clearer every day, she needed Him now to find Henry Lewis so his mother could hold him one more time, so his sister could say good-bye. There were worse things than cancer.

Sloughed onto the folding chair out of the wind, she stared past the charred brownies as the whirligig maple seeds skimmed across the pool's surface like speed skaters. Lime green, they piled up on the opposite tiles and stuck in odd waterlogged bunches. They would never be baby trees. They would never stretch skyward, greedy for sun and rain, eager to be grown and making shade. Their usefulness had ended before it had a chance.

Her shoulders shook. She trembled from the inside out. But if Jake saw a blotchy face, he'd assume she was falling apart. She forced herself to focus on the wrought iron dragonflies in the new hosta garden, the graceful pattern of black curves against vertical fence bars. The tears subsided. After she rooted in her pocket for a tissue, she planted her feet apart on the porch and swung her arms in circles. She tried a jumping jack but the jounce tingled sharply in what was left of her right breast. She pressed her hand to the spot and held it for a moment. Better. A flash of worry that the pang was significant buried itself as quickly as it had come. She'd gotten good at that. Just last week the doctors had done new scans of the other side. Yet here she was planning a week at the cottage as if the cancer had never been there in the first place and she wasn't waiting for test results.

"Do you feel something? Is that why you scheduled the scans?" She'd asked Dr. Rogers.

"It's routine follow-up," he said.

"It could be a recurrence?"

"I'd be surprised." He had made notations on her chart, too busy writing to look up at her. And when he realized she was waiting for more information, he added. "It's unlikely."

"Unlikely, but possible?"

"We'll call you as soon as the results come back."

The seeming inconsistency didn't seem to bother him. And she could hardly repeat anything so indefinite to Jake. He'd think it was more obsessing. When they hadn't offered a time frame for that call, she told herself if the doctors weren't worried, she shouldn't be. It didn't work. Every time the phone rang it reminded her the report was imminent, and that she could be dumped back into that endless night where she was falling and falling with no bottom in sight. Another reason she'd fled to the river house.

Back inside the warm cottage she flicked the light switch for the new outside lights, part of the renovation. Golden orbs appeared magically in five or six spots along the driveway like breadcrumbs that led to safety. She wondered if the rescue people noticed or were too engrossed in their protocol, intent on their checklist and the repetitive slow swing of the chains behind the steady circling boats. When she tipped the cooled brownie pan over the trashcan, the charred square fell in one solid block of chocolate. Almost black, it gleamed back at her, slick with grease from the bottom of the pan.

"What a waste," she said out loud. The packet of unused icing rattled in the box. She chucked the packet into the trash too. Otherwise she'd be tempted to eat it. "What a waste," she repeated to the silence as she folded the box flat for the recycling tub. The cancer or the infected gall bladder or both had caused her to lose forty pounds, the only good thing about being sick. In the morning she would get another box of brownie mix and start again. Their dinner guests weren't expected until Saturday. She had three days to get organized, to pull herself together.

In a way—she thought back to her phone conversation with Jake—he was right again. If she'd stuck to her original plan and read in the cottage while the brownies baked, she would have missed the entire thing. At the sound of the sirens she could have drifted outside like the other neighbors, innocent and unaware. She could have conferred at the fence line, sympathetic, but uninvolved.

After she washed out the pan, she padded through the unlit cottage in her socks to retrieve a sweatshirt and the book from her bedside table. This was part of the new daily routine as a cancer patient, to lose herself in a book, to force herself to rest. Although the pile had grown with friends' donations, each one completed was a small accomplishment. To make room for them in the living room bookcase, she'd thrown out the heavy tomes of Jake's Republican biographies, flash-in-the-pan bestsellers that overloaded used bookstore shelves in boring repetition. She hadn't shared the glee with him. Pared down like that, the shelves called out a challenge. To slip each finished book into a waiting space yielded a moment of sweet satisfaction. She'd done something that didn't have anything to do with the cancer. With each book she felt a little better. Her life was less narrow. She was more aware, like a toddler with each new word.

The latest paperback in hand, she returned to the living room. From here the river stretched a mile across, the view into forever that had sold them on the cottage. Every window oversaw a different slice of water and sky. On the far side of the white caps a thin sheer of clouds draped rose and lilac pleats across the faded blue like fabric samples flung across a table for review. The wind had picked up. More drift.

She saw again, superimposed on the evening dusk, the bubbles melt into muddy water, a snapshot of the boy suspended below, his features invisible as he floated out to sea. She was having trouble separating what she had really seen and what she imagined. She squeezed her eyes shut. When she reopened them, the clouds in all their cotton candy colors were back. After settling herself in the ancient leather chair, she turned on the lamp and opened the book. Much as she hated to admit it, Jake was right again. She'd tried to do too much. She'd worn herself out.

The vibration of the cell phone in her pocket nudged her awake. Seven-thirty, she'd slept almost an hour. She checked the caller ID, but it wasn't Jake. It was the man who'd renovated the cottage for them.

"Lots of activity at your house this afternoon," Barry Morgan said after asking about her health.

"You heard already?"

"Fire Department."

She did remember that the construction business was a sideline for Barry, one that a 24-hour fireman's shift accommodated.

"You okay?" His voice carried that professional calm that had made him an easy person to work with on the cottage project and must make him an ideal rescue worker.

"Just angry I didn't go over there right away to see what they were yelling about." *They?* She knew their names. Why didn't she use them? "I've taken life-saving classes."

"The Coast Guard will find him."

"The Coast Guard?"

"That's the helicopter down there. I can hear it through the phone."

"Oh." She went to the window. "That's what that noise is. It must have just arrived. I'm inside."

"They say the water's clear. That's a good thing."

"It doesn't seem clear. I walked along the seawall with the rescue people and you can't see a thing in the creek."

"Their divers are trained for that kind of water."

"There aren't any divers. At least there weren't when I was down there. Jake made me come up to the house." She almost blurted out that the 911 people had asked her for rope and binoculars and life jackets. But what good would it do? Barry wasn't part of this rescue team. And it was too late at this point.

"They know what they're doing," he said.

There was nothing to say to that either. What they were doing wasn't going to save the boy. Or his mother.

About the time the sun disappeared altogether Celie put on her down vest over the sweatshirt, stuck her feet in the fake Crocs from the dollar store, and stood for almost ten minutes at the kitchen door and tried to talk herself out of going down. But she needed to know.

Trying to sort out what was happening, she crossed the driveway to the grass in slow motion. She stopped where she was still above most of the activity. George, the dentist who lived in the little yellow house on Stonegate Street, ambled over and put his arm around her shoulders. "I know this probably isn't the right time to say this, Celie, but you look fabulous. And you have hair again. It's nice."

She put her hand to her head, unnerved that she'd forgotten her hat. She felt the new baby fine strands. She kept forgetting it was there. She couldn't even run her fingers through it, it was too short still. At least with the hats, no one commented on her hair. Or lack of it. She took a quick survey of the thinning clusters of people on the street and the hillside above the old marina dock. Someone might overhear him and think they were ridiculous people, concerned with her hair-do when a boy was lost in the water. A boy was dead.

She had to force her brain to move away from the thought that he was never coming back. She shrugged her shoulders and waited for George to take his arm away. He must have felt her withdrawal because he stepped apart. Embarrassed himself perhaps, he rose on his toes, up and down, up and down like a jogger warming up, as if that had been his intent all along.

They hadn't had a chance to become friends yet. When she bicycled by on her way to get the newspaper, he waved. She was curious in a sporadic neighborly way. Where was that trophy wife of his, twenty years younger, clearly dressed to the nines and not pleased to have the full time responsibility of two children while George was at work? When he took his little girls out in the boat, Celie waved back. Although the girls were boisterous, they seemed to follow his directions patiently while he untied lines and started the engine. He was gentle with them, deliberate about putting them into the boat one at a time. They couldn't be more than four or five. Other days he went out by himself. When he was alone, he moved more quickly to free the Whaler from the dock and he slipped out of the creek without looking back.

Jake said people born on the water were drawn to their boats, that they craved the solace of the waves and the way a boat rode high and proud. Although she hadn't grown up with boats she understood the need for space. At the time she'd been sheepish about spying on George. The fact that Jake had thought about it enough to articulate all that intrigued her. Not at all his usual efficient business-speak. It wasn't often, after thirty years of marriage, that he managed to surprise her. She wondered if Jake sensed her curiosity about their neighbor.

George, two steps away, was staring at her, not paying any attention to the blur of people all around them. Where his wrists poked out from the cuffs of the starched shirt the skin was tan. His neck too. Curious because, at least on the days she and Jake were here, he didn't spend much time in the yard. She imagined with the only dental practice in town, his work kept him indoors beyond normal office hours. But then she remembered the boat. The open river must be a relief, an escape for him, like the cottage was for her.

"Your hubby around?" he asked. "On his way home from a business trip."

Although George didn't say *good*, she could see from the way he nodded quickly it was what he was thinking. So . . . she didn't look that healthy. And like everyone else, he assumed the cancer had diminished her.

At the top of the hill two young men in sunflower slickers whipped around the corner. Bright flashes of color in the dusk, they jogged down to the idling fire truck. A third man, out of uniform, hurried to catch up. She recognized him as the one who had first jumped into the water, though he hadn't dived under the surface or reached down for the boy. She wanted to ask the man why he had bothered getting wet. She had wanted to yell at him to dive, go under, deeper, just as she had yelled at Richard Widener to get his dinghy and row out to the bubbles.

In hindsight she realized she hadn't been upset with them. She'd been angry at herself for hesitating, for not making a decision and for failing to follow through. In hindsight though, it had nothing to do with Richard or the temperature of the water. It was far simpler than that. She didn't trust herself after the long year of medical invasions. She might fail, and so she had failed.

"They're leaving?" she asked George.

"It's too dark. Almost low tide and no sign of him. I overheard them talk about starting again tomorrow at first light."

"I hope not where his mother could hear." In that single second Celie was hot with outrage for Mary Breeden. She unsnapped her vest and began to pull her arm loose.

He took her hand and held it until she was still. "She's gone home. To be with the other children. There's nothing else they can do tonight."

Celie let the vest hang open. Her anger leaked out into the falling night. In slow motion he rubbed the back of her hand. She watched his thumb move across her skin. She was so pale. They hardly knew each other. But it was pleasant to stand in the dark and feel the warmth that connected the two of them, a kind of effortless communication, like breathing between a parent and child.

"Dream about somewhere you've always wanted to go," he said.

"What?"

"Dreaming is the great equalizer. In a dream you can do anything. Dreams conquer all enemies, mend all wounds, lay all ghosts. Proverbial ghosts, I mean. God, I've gone and botched that, haven't I?"

"No, no, I get it. It's the nightmare thing that's been hard to control. With the doctors and all those machines."

"Equipment nightmares, I know about those."

"Occupational hazard for you, I guess."

"More for my patients. I love the chrome and grind. But not you. You always seemed like someone in charge of your life. I expect you can direct those dreams."

The image of herself in a canvas chair waving cameramen this way and that made her want to giggle, but she didn't want to break the spell. She murmured assent without words and tried to make her hand float so he wouldn't notice they were still connected there. But when the flashers on the fire truck sparked and the warning beep for backing up shrilled around them, he dropped her hand and stepped back onto the grassy shoulder. Cool evening air silted in between them and his face melted into the shadows as if he were the ghost. When he half-turned to start home, she felt the disappointment rise up in her until she had to cover her mouth to keep from begging him to stay. He was halfway across the lawn when he finally turned and waved.

She raised her hand to wave back. "Tomorrow, then," she said.

"Get some rest."

"Thanks, George."

"Good night."

When he didn't say her name, she was oddly crushed. She watched him trot up his driveway in a loose jog that signaled he was late for something. Perhaps he had bedtime duty since his wife was home with the children during the day. Although Celie had never had that luxury with Jake's constant business trips, she remembered how sweet it was to snuggle with her own toddlers after baths when she'd worked a full day mediating between angry husbands and wives.

She imagined George as he locked his back door and switched off the driveway lights. He might stand behind his wife at the kitchen sink and kiss her neck before he took the steps two at a time to tuck in his girls and hear their prayers. It felt like spying through an open window.

What was wrong with her? She had her own life. Thomas and Caroline's baby would be here in six months, the first grandchild. She had the river garden project. That stack of books. And Jake's energetic suggestions of how to fill her days. It ought to be enough. She needed to let it be enough.

And that was when she realized George hadn't been wearing a wedding ring. Not even a band of pale skin where a ring might have been. Perhaps the girls were his granddaughters, their mother his daughter, and Celie had leapt to the wrong conclusion again.

She jumped when the fire truck warning bell rang for reverse. Its dispatch radio blatted nonsense as it steamed backwards up the hill, made its three-point turn, and panted down Stonegate in the direction of St. Bernadette's School. Flashlights flickered and disappeared. Engines revved. Trucks coughed into gear and sputtered off. A low mechanical thrum filled the night. Everyone was gone. Suddenly chilled, with her hands in the pocket of the vest, she trudged up the driveway.

Mary Breeden lived close enough to hear the trucks leave. She would know they'd given up. She would feel the growing chill as night enveloped the neighborhood just as Celie did walking back to the cottage. None of the rescue squad's assurances about tomorrow would matter to Mary Breeden, if they even registered. She would be worrying about her son out in the silent night, in the frigid water, alone, drifting. She would be wondering if she would ever see him again. There would be fear and shock and rage. It was too early yet for recriminations.

The imagined horror of being Mary Breeden, the helplessness, the sudden imposition of death on a busy life, the stark night that would become a constant emptiness, the unfairness of not at least having her child to hold while she grieved, all that undid Celie. Breathing hard from the hill, she grabbed at the wooden rail and sat down on the back steps. Why couldn't one thing have worked out all right? Just one thing in this awful day.

Chapter Five

"Go away." I kicked low and caught Rey's leg right below the
kneecap. I hadn't meant to connect at all.

He crumpled onto Henry Lewis's cot with only the slightest
moan. "I thought you didn't want to be alone."

"That doesn't mean you can sleep in here."

"How'm I supposed to figure that out? All those people
downstairs, where else can I go?"

With the side of my leg I nudged the metal cot closer to the door
and lay down on my own bed without taking off my shoes. I kept my
eyes shut to avoid Rey's.

"Your mama's going to split a gut," he said.

"What you know about my mama?"

"I know she don't let shoes be on furniture."

I could feel him staring at me through the dark. "Just leave."

"I said I was sorry."

Everyone was always sorry. It was a stupid word, meaningless.
Too late, I thought, though I was too tired to say it. I just wanted him
to leave me alone. They all needed to leave me be so I could
concentrate on Henry Lewis.

Rey whispered from where he'd landed on the cot. "I didn't
expect him to walk right into the water like that."

"Shut up."

"He did it to hisself."

"You dared him."

"He coulda said no."

"He do anything you tell him to. You're his big bad cousin. You
can't expect a little kid like Henry Lewis to know what's safe and
what's not."

"I didn't know. You didn't either." Rey sat up, but inched toward
the end of the cot out of range of my feet. "Anyway, he's been in the
river before."

"On a beach. Where the water don't come up over your knees."

"It didn't look any different on that dumb old boat ramp."

I flipped herself over to my side, my back to Rey, and stared out
the window into the blackness. It couldn't really be nighttime
already. Only minutes ago we were sweating in the sun and arguing
about whether to go to the 7-11 or down to the end of the street to
see about walking the Jessup's dog. Henry Lewis kicking stones to
Rey and Rey kicking them back. Perpetual motion, those two. It was

Aunt Ruthie's phrase and it rolled over and over in my mouth, just the way it sounded.

I tried to remember back to the time when it was just Henry Lewis and Jasmine and me, when Rey lived with his own mother instead of us. Aunt Antoinette, with her bare stomach, her navel ring, and her tippy heels, had been in the middle of beauty classes at the community college last spring when she dumped Rey, her only kid, and disappeared, supposedly for a job interview. Whatever kind of job that was, it wasn't local and they must not believe in time off. It had been more than a year since Rey started sleeping on our couch.

In the silence while I was thinking, Rey wriggled the cot blanket into a cocoon. The wavery image of his reflection in the window reminded me of the page with the Indian medicine man in the school encyclopedia, the faraway look in his eyes, the way he seemed to shrink back from what only he could see, all the evil in the world. I read about Native Americans for a project last year on Virginia history. They had supernatural powers and could see the past and the future. Like the medicine man, Rey's eyes were full of pain, his mind clearly somewhere else. Reflections were like mirrors into another world. They showed things about people you never noticed in full light. The window Rey looked shrunken and scared, not at all how he was when he boasted about his free throw percentages and his new basketball shoes. Anyone's mother could afford to send LeBron James basketball shoes when they didn't have to feed their kid or pay rent. But Rey's reflection made me feel sorry for him and I didn't want to feel sorry for Rey. It was like I was abandoning Henry Lewis all over again.

When I stared at the ceiling instead, a gray wisp of cobweb floated in the corner, big as life. I'd missed that spot with the broom last Saturday. Well, Mama wouldn't notice it now.

The cot creaked. "You want me to go and look some more in the marsh?" Rey asked.

"I wish you'd go and move to Baltimore or wherever Antoinette took herself off to, and we'd never have to see you again." I kept my eyes drilled on the blank wall so I wouldn't have to look at his face.

There was a rustle, then the door opened and shut. *Good riddance*, but I didn't feel any better. I felt worse.

Hard to figure how long I lay there, trying to think about nothing, circling round and round the picture of Henry Lewis drifting away. He hadn't called out. He hadn't said a thing, just let the water take him. I wished I could know what he'd been thinking. If he'd been too scared to move or maybe just waiting, thinking the current would carry him across to the other shore and he could climb out. And like magic, we'd all be together again.

While I lay there the window filled with light. Headlights of police cars? Or rescue people? When I sat up though, the street was empty. It was the moon sliding over the top of the roof. It filled the entire window and then some, as if a lamp had been set down right outside on the roof, a spotlight pointed at my particular window. That same moon must be shining on the creek and the river. At least there would be light above his head and he wouldn't have to be afraid in the dark, not that I could ever remember Henry Lewis being afraid of anything.

With it so bright outside, everything in the bedroom was mostly black and white, slick where the moonlight caught the shiny paint. You could hardly tell that the walls were painted apple green with tan trim. On a rainy day it made me gag, without the sun to wash out the putrid brightness of that green. When the landlord had given Mama permission to paint, I had wanted white on white, clean and neat like the offices I passed on my way to school, the dentist, the hair salon, the record shop. And like the St. Bernadette School library with the big picture windows over on Stonegate. Everything in those rooms was organized, in its right place. If you worked there, you would never have to waste time searching for anything. No wonder those girls all graduated and went to college. They spent all their time reading and studying in those peaceful white rooms.

But Mama didn't want white paint, she liked colors. She drove all us over to Wal-Mart and dragged us past the other shoppers to the hardware section.

"All my life I been looking at these color strips and I never been able to paint before. We're having colors. Lots of colors. Each you all can pick one room."

When I picked white, Mama looked at me like I was out of my mind. We stood straight on—I was tall as Mama all of a sudden—and faced off in the paint aisle.

"How about yellow?" Mama waved the paint strip in my face. "Like sunshine?"

"I know what sunshine look like, Mama. It glows around us all the day long. It comes through the windows. I want white."

"Oh, no, Mee, you don't really. You'll be bored."

"How you so sure you know what I want?"

"With plain walls in two weeks you'll be falling asleep doing your homework."

"That'd be good. Sleep's good."

"No, sleep's like white, Meeka. It's forgetting, it's dull. It's nothing. You don't want to be stupid and dull."

"I'm not stupid."

"I didn't mean that, baby. But you know God made all these colors for a reason." Her arm made a wide arc taking in the two rainbow displays of paint strips.

"Yeah," I muttered. "So the Wal-Mart man can count his money all night long while the rest of us are having nightmares in purple rooms."

"I never said purple. But look . . ." she smoothed the rack from the bottom up as if the paint had flowed out of her fingertips into those little pieces of paper. She actually looked happy, like the sunshine yellow was flowing right through her veins and making her glow.

Henry Lewis stuck his index finger on a radiant blue. "How about an ocean living room?"

Mama hugged him, then kissed the top of his head. 'Course he was only nine then, shorter and cuter, and he knew it.

"I love it," Mama said. "An aquamarine living room. It'll be like flying on a magic carpet." She rocked him in that hug and smiled over the top of his head at me.

"You pick then," I said, when I really wanted to tell Henry Lewis what a little suck-up he was. If Mama thought it was such a big deal, let her paint whatever colors she wanted.

Then I didn't even get white doors and windows because the paint man convinced Mama that tan trim would set off the green walls better. At least I was away at school during the day and at night you could hardly tell it was green. When springtime came round though, I almost didn't mind it. The leaves outside matched the pale apple-y color and it made the room feel like a tree house. Jasmine noticed it first, one night after school let out when we ended up sharing the room, not long after Rey came to live with us.

Up till then Jasmine usually slept on the bottom bunk in the other bedroom with Henry Lewis on the top bunk. But once Rey arrived, he took over the bottom bunk and we set up the cot at the foot of my bed for Jasmine. On the nights Aunt Ruthie had to work and Liné stayed over, we played musical beds. The little girls had the bunkroom, Rey took the sofa downstairs, and Henry ended up on the cot. That way he could work on homework while I did, or read after the little girls' bedtime.

With Henry Lewis missing, Jasmine and Liné fell asleep in Mama's bed, and no one fussed with them about it. Aunt Ruthie probably let them eat cookies and cupcakes for dinner too. But that was okay, little kids had special privileges. They weren't good at making decisions on their own. They didn't have any practice at it. They hadn't lived long enough to learn much of anything. Just the thought of a little kid who hadn't lived long enough to learn much made my throat thicken. I wished Rey had ignored my bad attitude and stayed.

It was awful what happened to Henry Lewis, but I shouldn't be blaming Rey. Even though Henry Lewis was always telling you what he knew, not to impress you, but just excited about whatever he'd learned, he hadn't lived long enough to know about the current in the creek. I was the one who should have known. I shouldn't have let Rey egg him on about swimming, when I knew he didn't really know how. I was the oldest. Of all of us, I'd had the most time to practice making decisions. I should have told Henry Lewis he couldn't go down that ramp, even up to his ankles. I should have stopped him. Even without being sure where it dropped off or without knowing that the water was freezing cold like the white man had said to the crazy white lady.

Shadows from the moon moved back and forth on the bedroom wall. The wind was blowing harder than it had this afternoon. The branches of the magnolia tree splashed creepy shapes on the furniture. I was alone again, twice in one day, a whole room to myself. It didn't feel like my life.

Through the floorboards the voices of Aunt Ruthie and the women from church buzzed like those awful mayflies. I couldn't hear what they were saying, but it didn't take much to imagine their tongues clicking and their heads shaking over what a terrible sister I was. I imagined that their half-finished sentences were really questions about how had it happened, who had done what. It didn't matter how. How was past. It only mattered that he was gone. I'd been minding him and I hadn't kept him safe.

By the time Ashante came home from the creek, I had cleaned up after the little girls' bath and had balled up their muddy clothes into the laundry basket. I lay on my bed listening to Ruthie who stayed mostly on the front steps. She talked to the people who came by, more and more kept coming, the same people who turned around in church to see who was whispering and who was dancing in the pews. I didn't know how she kept it together to be pleasant and say the same thing over and over again, the words building and falling like they did when she prayed at church. *We don't know anything yet. Thank you. Yes, we'll let you know when we hear.*

When I heard Ashante's voice, I figured he wouldn't have come without bringing Mama. I rushed downstairs. One look at her face though—so frozen, so empty—I wished I'd stayed upstairs. Yet my feet froze and I couldn't leave. As soon as he settled her in one of the kitchen chairs, Liné threw herself into Mama's lap and bawled. For a whole minute, maybe two, Mama set there, no words, no tears, her eyes staring at nothing. Then she bundled up her niece, her arms closing in around her, shushing her with the oddest kind of moans, no words. She didn't shut her eyes though. Over Liné's head she looked right at me and asked that one question, the question that had no answer.

What else could she be thinking with her only boy out there in the dark? She hadn't said more than those few words. Just *Where's Henry Lewis, Mee?* She'd waited to hear the answer, her face scary blank while the metal legs of the table rattled on the floor where she leaned against it, her body all shakes and jitters.

I wanted to be in her arms, all wrapped up safe, but I wasn't a little girl anymore. I wasn't mad at Liné, not really. Everyone felt sorry for Liné. Her daddy, Aunt Ruthie's first husband, had been shot in Iraq when he worked there as an army mechanic. But still, with Liné carrying on in the kitchen, I felt like ordering her to get out of Mama's arms. It wasn't her brother who'd drowned. And Mama wasn't her mother. Even as I thought it, I knew how juvenile it was to think like that. The truth was Rey didn't have a daddy either, least not one that Aunt Antoinette owned up to. And my own father was gone. Maybe not dead, but not around to bring home surprises and wrestle on the floor and take up for us.

Last year when the boys started hanging around the seventh grade girls, Rey had volunteered to fight them off. He was trying to be nice, but everyone laughed when he said it. It was funny. I laughed too, boys being a thing that happened to other girls, not to me. This year now that I was in eighth grade, the middle school held dances. When the first boy asked me to dance—Walter Saunders from church, Wall they called him—Rey was off trading fishing stories or telling jokes, whatever boys did in the far corner of the gym. As if it was important to hang at the fringes of places so they could bolt when no one was looking. His promise to protect me gone completely out of his head.

Even though Ashante told Rey he had to walk me in and out and watch out for me, a cousin keeping track of my social life wasn't cool. And certainly not my younger cousin. I wanted a father to stand in the doorway, to fill up all that light and space so that when a boy walked me home from a dance, he knew I had people to take up for me and make it stick.

Ashante might would stand there if Mama asked him. I was ninety percent sure. So far it wasn't a problem because no boy had tried to walk me home. Maybe it would never be a problem. Maybe no boy would ever try. Most likely I'd never get asked to another dance. I'd be *that girl who let her brother drown.* No one would want to be seen with me, much less dance with me.

As far as cousins went, Rey and Liné weren't half-bad. Some of the kids at school had uncles and grandparents living with them all the time. Family was complicated. They could insist on stuff that might not be anything you wanted to do. Liné stayed over whenever Ruthie had to work graveyard shift at the nursing home, which was pretty regular, one or two weekends a month. But that wasn't the only reason, even though Mama never said otherwise, least not directly. A couple three times I overheard her say bad things about Ruthie's second husband to Ashante. "Liné's safer here" was all Mama told me to my face before she forbid me to say anything to Liné or Aunt Ruthie. "She and Jasmine play good together." And it was true.

As it turned out the whole world knew Ruthie caught Gerald in the back seat of some woman's Grand Marquis. *He doesn't even have good taste in cars,* Ruthie said, and she was the first one to admit he wasn't reliable. Why didn't she kick his butt out? There was no accounting for grown-ups. He didn't come over to Linden Street much, but when he did, he creeped me out with his bug eyes and his fingers always running up and down the neck of his beer bottles. I made a point to stay out of his way.

Cousins actually weren't bad to have around, even if I did have to clean up after them and drag them with me wherever I went. They occupied each other. Henry Lewis followed Rey everywhere, everywhere Rey let him. Jasmine and Liné, ten months apart, were best friends. It was good for Jasmine because Liné didn't act like a baby. She washed dishes like it was a game, and she swept the front steps every afternoon when they got home from school with a broom that was taller than she was.

"It's my job," she said when Jasmine tried to take the broom away from her.

"You're making us all look bad," Rey complained.

I glared. "She's fine. Let her go on and do what she wants, if it makes her feel better."

"Work doesn't make anyone feel better." Rey argued from the yard where I couldn't reach him.

MINDING HENRY LEWIS

"You sure wouldn't know about that."

He stomped off in a huff and dragged Henry Lewis with him. When they didn't show for dinner, Mama was cross with me, like it was my fault Rey was always making trouble.

"I can't work all day and come home to you kids fighting. You gotta help me out here, Mee. You and Rey are old enough to follow rules. If you set an example of what's right and fair, the other kids'll do like you two. Go find those boys now and bring 'em home. And no more fussing between you'all."

That night, for the first time ever, Mama put the little girls together in their sleeping bags on the floor and let Rey have the bottom bunk below Henry Lewis. I had to sleep all by myself as if I had a disease that was catching. It surprised me back then how much I missed my little brother's odd questions once the lights were out. And I missed his peculiar garbled dream talk and how it filtered into my own dreams. After that I tried to get back on Mama's good side by volunteering to be the official babysitter after school. It worked out well. The two little girls entertained each other and Henry Lewis slept on the cot in my room more often.

In the moonlight I analyzed the empty cot. The pillow squashed into the corner and the sheets crooked just like Henry Lewis left them mornings when he got up to pee. Just like he'd left them this morning. How was it that someone could be here one minute and be gone so quickly? In Sunday school classes I'd read the Bible about God giving everyone a second chance. Henry Lewis had hardly had his first chance. And here I was being mean and grouty to Rey when he felt horrible too.

Right from the beginning everyone loved Henry Lewis, grown-ups, kids, even animals. That boy smiled all the time. He was so crazy wild over dogs they never growled at him. Ever since he could talk, he told jokes. Even if they weren't funny, the way he told them, his head tilted sideways, his hands drawing pictures in the air, everyone laughed. He could do his multiplication tables out loud by second grade, practically could do them backwards. And he was never bothered that he couldn't shoot a free throw. Leastways, he didn't obsess over it or spend hours practicing like Rey and every other boy I'd ever met.

Too much to explore in the world, Henry Lewis would say, *to waste time on a ball.* Or sometimes he'd say, *that ball have a mind of its own.* He was worth two of any other boy. He was worth ten of me.

Six, eight years from now when Jasmine was a teenager, she wouldn't remember Henry Lewis at all, the way she didn't remember

Grandpa TomTom because she'd only been six when he died of an infection from diabetes. That didn't seem fair either. People's memories ought to last longer than that.

Downstairs the front door opened and shut and shut again. A flurry of car doors slammed, engines groaned and faded away. I leaned my forehead against the window to see how many cars were left. The glass was chilled when I'd been expecting the moon to warm it like the sun. That wasn't how it worked—I knew from science class—but still the cold smoothness on my skin sent unexpected shivers down my legs and arms. Under the tree our van made a dark blot next to the line of other blots that were the neighbors' cars, one for each assigned space, six for the six townhouses. The neighbors were inside their houses. And each car was where it ought to be. It seemed so wrong. As if the world was pretending to be on course, when it was really upside down with Henry Lewis gone.

In one of the two visitor parking spaces Ashante's motorcycle was all by itself. With those tilted headlights it looked lonely. Moonlight sparked off its grill, and you couldn't see the dents and worn places. It was his hobby, fixing it up, keeping it running. When he'd first moved in, I'd thought obsessing about a motorcycle was stupid. All weekend Mama would sit on the folding chair while he worked. Even with the air-conditioner hum, I could hear them laughing and talking below my bedroom. Whenever he revved it up, the old cycle groaned instead of roared, and no matter how hard he polished the chrome, it didn't shine like the ones at the Harley store outside of town where we stopped some Sundays after church so he could look. When Mama teased him and he didn't get angry, just laughed, I decided he was different. I liked him. He wasn't stuck on himself.

For the first time all night the other visitor's space was empty. I heard low voices and slow footsteps come up the stairs. Ashante was talking to Mama like the school nurse talked to a kindergartener with an earache.

"Rey's okay on the couch, I think. Everyone else in bed," he said.

Although her answer was lost or maybe there wasn't one, the footsteps continued up. I lay back and closed my eyes. The door opened a few inches. When I peeked, I could see their silhouette, his arm around her waist, so close they looked like Siamese twins. Her face hidden, Mama sighed. He drew his other arm around her shoulders until his hands came together. When he pulled her closer, her head fell against him as if it were too heavy for her to hold up all by herself.

I tried to slow down my lungs like a sleeping person. I shut my eyes again. If I saw Mama's face, I knew I would start crying.

"She's asleep," he said just above a whisper. "Thank goodness."

Even with Mama's face muffled in his shirt, I could hear the way her breath caught in her chest. After he backed them out and pulled the door shut behind them, my hands shot up to my face, palms against my eyelids to push back the tears. I used the corner of the pillowcase to block the noise in my head.

I would never sleep again. Mama wouldn't be able to either. The rescue people, were they sleeping? Doubtful. They had their jobs and I had mine. I shouldn't be here when my brother was out there. It was one thing to make sure the little girls got home and to be here for Mama, but Ashante was with her now. He would take good care of her. I needed to be with Henry Lewis.

The magnolia branches had been sending me the message all night, clack-clack-clack against the roof, and I'd missed it until now. What an idiot. It had been hours, at least two, maybe three since I'd left the creek. I should never have left him. I slid open the window, clicked the plastic releases on the fancy new screen, and pushed it up as high as it would go. We hadn't had screens before, not in the trailer and not above the Laundromat.

Legs first? While I considered the options, I tugged the sweatshirt over my head, wiggled my arms into the sleeves. The van was right there next to the tree. In the movies they always dropped onto the car roof. I'd done it on the monkey bars a gazillion times. The van roof was like the ground, only a foot closer than when we first moved in because I'd grown so much this winter.

Once I laid my stomach on the window sill, I stretched out my fingers to touch the branch closest to the window. The bark was colder than the air and the ridges were wet and slippery. I hesitated. It was too slick. My hands might slip. What if the metal roof buckled or made a popping sound when I landed? Ashante would hear. Or the Carson's in the townhouse next door. All Mama needed was a trip to the emergency room in the middle of the night. I pulled myself back inside and shut the window. I'd have to use the stairs.

When I opened the hallway door, a strip of light glowed under the bathroom door. The shower was running. My socks didn't make any noise on the hall carpet or on the stairs. At the bottom I squinted at the couch to see if Rey was awake, but he was curled up like a hedgehog under the quilt from the upstairs cot, his face covered. I hoped he was asleep in there, hoped he'd forgotten my yelling at him.

From the kitchen the radio crooned, so strangled and low I figured Ashante and Mama hadn't noticed it was still on. Maybe the late night songs, quieter with fewer advertisements, would weave themselves into Rey's dreams and block the nightmares, keep him asleep. I didn't want company.

For once the front door didn't squeak. Outside the moon caught on the specks in the concrete sidewalk and turned it into a long sparkling trail like the yellow brick road. I sprinted over to Stonegate. As I raced past the big houses that faced the river, their windows formed glossy caverns of black. Somewhere behind me the deep blur of an idling engine snaked out of the shadows. I shivered at the idea of being out on the water, but made myself concentrate on the pavement in front of me. Between each house moonlight streaks flashed across the river's surface as I ran, faster and faster towards the creek and my brother.

Chapter Six

By the time Jake arrived from the airport, Celie had thought four or five times about taking a shower and going to bed. It was the logical, practical thing to do. She'd even hung a fresh nightgown on the back of the bathroom door and turned down the bedcovers. But she was still in the chair, when Jake's whistle from the back door sounded over the hum of the kitchen television. She'd forgotten to turn it off after she made tea. Tea being her second choice to a stiff drink.

The first idea had been a momentary lapse only. She'd given up alcohol cold turkey after the hospital nutritionist told her it was the number one factor in recurrence. Whenever the idea of the soft edges of a drink snuck up on her, often enough to surprise her, she dragged up the image of one particular patient from the infusion room, a woman dealing with her third recurrence. All bones, in a threadbare flannel shirt, the woman, who was Celie's age, smelled of scotch from across three recliners. Maybe that's how she was dealing with the very real possibility that she wouldn't survive a third time. Celie had to fight to quell the nausea. She didn't want to be that woman.

"I'm home," Jake called. The television drone ended abruptly, the click audible from where she sat in the living room. "Celie?"

In the deep leather chair she struggled up from the haze. "In here," she answered and watched the archway from the dining room where he would appear. The strap of his laptop bag would drag the shoulder of his suit off-center like a disheveled teenager wearing his father's sport coat two sizes too big.

"Hey," he said, his smile a little sheepish and then gone. "I thought you'd be in bed by now."

She shrugged. Her eyes filled.

"Oh, sweetie," he said. Dumping the briefcase, he stepped in broad sharp strides across the rug to her chair, his hand light on her head. "I'm so sorry you had to see that. And I wasn't here."

But even as she wept, the tears in instant streams as if someone had signaled her to cry on cue, she sank back into the chair to avoid his kiss. It grazed her forehead. She was mad at him for dispensing of her just like that, at his assumption she was so incompetent that merely seeing the tragedy would render her ineffective, as if she were completely helpless without him. And she was mad at herself for giving him the opportunity.

He squeezed her shoulder before he collected the suitcase again. It bumped the wall as he moved into the hallway. "Just let me hang up these things and we can talk."

While he unpacked, she stripped in the bathroom and stuffed her clothes down the laundry chute. After she scrubbed her face and neck with the washcloth, she brushed her teeth as vigorously and slid the nightgown over her head. Grunge and aches and shivers despite the day's early promise lapped at a sudden deadpan lethargy. The bed sheets were cold and she wriggled her legs to warm herself.

"Did you want to tell me about it?" he asked once he reappeared in his pajamas.

"No," she answered, not surprised at his sharp intake of breath. "Not tonight."

As he leaned over to set the alarm clock, his face was hidden, but she knew he was hurt. She worked to keep her tone as neutral as she could manage.

"How was your trip?"

"They're going to handle the whole advertising campaign. All their top design people were there. It's a plum for a start-up like them to sign a national corporation like ours." He dumped a pile of newspapers on his bedside table and flung the covers open.

With a tug back for her share of the quilt, she waited for him to decide whether he was going to read or go straight to sleep. He liked to wind down with a book, but tonight the room went dark. He spoke into the void.

"You'll love Curtis. The new guy in charge of the mid-west campaign. He used to be a substance abuse counselor."

She gritted her teeth. With Jake, everything was reduced to the lowest common denominator. Substance abuse counselors were touchy-feely types. She was a court mediator. She and Curtis must be soul mates, never mind that he could have a prison guard mentality and she could be a strident feminist.

"You sleepy?" Jake asked, his hand on her thigh.

"Mmmm," she mumbled to avoid committing, an old mediation trick.

"Did you take one of your pills?"

She held her breath, overcome again with that feeling of isolation. Lately they lived in different worlds. If they didn't make love, he would blame her insomnia medicine, an easy way to avoid acknowledging the widening gulf between them. He didn't understand what was happening with her. More and more she wondered if he really wanted to. Unilaterally he attributed it to their physical distance. He seemed driven to make up for the months of celibacy and expected her to want the same thing. Did he really think a pill could cure everything? Bedroom antics, a good night's sleep, and she'd be fine in the morning. As if that were all that was wrong.

Although she was exhausted, she didn't fall asleep even after he turned onto his side, his breathing almost immediately slow and rhythmic. Her life, which had been inching back to sane, was suddenly off course again. Things didn't fit. When she shut her eyes, the brown head drifted through the steamy sunlight and there was the girl, crouched on the dock, ready to jump. Celie's chest tightened as if she'd just run that same distance in the unusual afternoon heat.

Except she was cold, so cold. She blinked in the dark room. The curtains floated away from the window like piles of dead leaves that rose and sank with each passing car. Jake always slept with the windows open, at home or when they were traveling. It was not negotiable. Above her head the stream of cold air swirled like an advertisement for coffee. The Coast Guard helicopter was long gone and the spring night had fallen to a more seasonal temperature. While she debated whether to get up and close the window, the brightly colored curtain fluttered up and out again, a wide lingering wave and then a sharp deflating return to the wall.

To Jake's snores she slid out from under the covers and shut the window. He didn't stir. She stuck her feet in her slippers and padded to the bathroom. By the sink she felt for the prescription bottle and took one of the pills the oncologist had given her. It had been prescribed for nausea, but she'd discovered early on it guaranteed eight hours of uninterrupted sleep. A nurse friend had warned her it was an anti-anxiety generic, to be careful not to become addicted. Never before the cancer had she taken anything to help her sleep. She'd never needed to. The little blue jar of Melatonin recommended by a friend ten years earlier during menopause sat unopened in the medicine cabinet. She choked on most pills. Even for a headache she hardly ever took anything. But after the diagnosis last winter the idea of waking up alone in the middle of the night was too awful to contemplate. At two in the morning all the possibilities loomed more ferocious and deadly.

Not sure why, she lifted the bathroom curtain and looked out into the night. At the far end of the driveway something moved across the open space, a blur that glinted in the moonlight and disappeared into the shadows. A deer? A person? The rescue people were long gone. She had watched them leave. Who could it be? She opened the window, bristled at the slap of cold air, but slid the screen up to see more clearly.

It was a person. The person—he or she—was climbing the fence. The long shadow moved in and out of the moonlight toward the seawall, more slowly because the ground was rough there. She knew that stretch of ground. Without thinking beyond the mystery of who would be out at this hour, she eased the lock on the side door and stepped out under the portico. Whoever it was lingered on the seawall, just back from the edge, close enough to look down into the water. Instinctively the muscles across the back of her shoulders tightened. That's exactly where she had stood this afternoon.

A single streetlight on Creekside Drive reached down the hillside. It shed meager light on the scene, not bright enough for her to see the person's face. She started down before she remembered she was in her slippers. One slide on the smooth driveway and her body jerked to a halt. After that she inched down, careful to keep her eyes off the water and locked onto the human shape on land.

At the fence, anxious to avoid this afternoon's feeling of freefall, she looked down to be sure she managed to haul herself over in one piece. The slippers dropped away. By the time she gathered her nightgown in one hand, maneuvered each leg over the rail, and replaced the slippers, the shadows had swallowed the mysterious person as if she had imagined it all. Convinced she was dreaming, that psychological trick your mind played during sleep to work through the anxieties of the day, she turned around to start home. That was when she heard the song.

Two steps closer, but still a good twenty feet away, she paused and listened harder. Deep in the night shadows, further back from the water, a human shape took form again. It was the boy's sister, the girl from this afternoon. *Meeka*, Celie whispered to herself. The teenager was sitting on one of the fallen logs. Her long legs were folded underneath her, her head was down. Her face was still hidden, shielded from the flickers of light between the branches that stirred ever so slightly with the breeze. Still, Celie recognized the shoulders, the straps of the ribbed T-shirt, bleach white against cappuccino skin.

"Silent night, holy night," Meeka sang softly, the words graceful and clear, with none of the panic or anger from earlier. When the chorus ended, she started over. Halfway through the verse she faltered, snuffled once or twice, but recovered enough to move right into "Somewhere over the Rainbow," with the key change hardly a pause.

At first Celie was so intent on her footing and on anticipating the words, her recall of the song not as good as Meeka's, that she didn't realize she was singing too.

Meeka shot up from the log, poised to run. "Who's there?"

"It's me, Mrs. Lowell, from this afternoon."

"How long you been there?"

"I saw you from the house. I didn't know who it was."

"Now you know. You can go home."

There was an awkward silence when Celie tried not to stare at the lines of tears that glistened on the girl's cheeks. They stood an arm's length apart.

"I'm not bothering anyone."

"I didn't think so."

"This isn't your land, is it?"

"No, but—"

"So go then. This ain't none of your business."

Celie noted the slide into slang. The girl knew better, but something had changed drastically since this afternoon, maybe in these last few seconds. This girl was no longer in shock. This girl was angry.

"Just leave us alone," Meeka said.

The *us* was like a slap. She scrambled to think how to make the girl understand why she couldn't leave her alone. "I'd like to help."

The look Meeka directed at her made her shrink back. Meeka didn't have to say *just like you did this afternoon* for Celie not to understand.

"Meeka, I'm so—"

"Don't say that. Everyone's so goddamn sorry." She was yelling, the words bouncing off the creek as if there were a dozen people shouting. "Sorry, sorry, sorry. It doesn't change anything." She sank back onto the log, as if the force of the words had worn her out.

Celie choked back the rest of what she had been about to say. She recognized the feeling, not that the girl wanted to hear it from her. But as she turned to go, it struck her she was waffling again, doing exactly what she'd done that afternoon. What she'd done all year. She kept letting herself off the hook because she was convinced she would fail. Celie Lowell couldn't possibly do anything well anymore. She was a cripple, a cancer victim, helpless.

She turned back and forced herself to speak distinctly, hoping for more authority than she felt. "You promise you won't go near the water?"

Meeka glared.

"Someday," Celie worked at her choice of words. She didn't want to sound like a know-it-all grownup. "When you can talk about it, I'd like to hear about your brother."

Meeka didn't answer one way or the other. Celie told herself that was a good sign, though the longer she stood there the less she was convinced. Other sounds filled the night. Water lapped against the boards of the seawall. On the far side of the creek the grain barge, tied two hundred yards upstream, clunked against the wooden dock. Regular thumps of car tires rode over the expansion gaps in the Rte 19 bridge, even at this hour of the night. Somewhere in that lapse Meeka began to sing again, a clear signal that the conversation was over. Although this song was one Celie didn't know at all, it trailed her like an orphan lamb as she started back toward the cottage.

What was she thinking? The girl had just lost her brother. She was hurt and confused. It was the afternoon all over again. There was no walking away. With the deep water right there she couldn't take a chance. She knew better than to leave a child alone by the creek. Slipping into the shadows, she found a spot where she could just make out the line of Meeka's back, a paisley curl, and the darker less defined smudge that was the log. The embankment beyond Meeka was a blue-black blur. As her head and shoulders lifted and fell with the song's cadence, the moonlight seemed to spill down the hillside in the same slow rhythm, wherever there was a break in the tree line, the laces of Meeka's sneakers like white drips on the night canvas. Celie settled herself against the field cedar's trunk—out of sight but with a clear view of those white laces.

A sudden recollection of listening to her mother's songs on long car trips came to her, a memory she had buried, almost forgotten. From the back seat the music had floated back, a shifting shapeless suggestion of all the feelings she had for her mother without the physical connection of sight or touch. Being an only child, she'd observed more than she'd participated, the kid who stuck to the fence when the others chose kickball teams or raced for the jungle gym. It struck her it was the same sense of isolation that had reappeared with the cancer. It fueled her irritation with Jake and with his assumption she couldn't manage without him, when she had managed all her life on her own. And perhaps it explained why she felt so close to this girl, all alone in the night and searching for what she had lost.

Above the cedar an owl's muted hoot jolted Celie upright. She must have dozed. Moonlight flashed through the tree branches, swift as passing headlights, recurring bursts with each breezy intake. Even where she huddled within the tree's shelter, she could tell the temperature had dropped. She hugged her knees to her chest. Time had passed. She had no idea how much. Although she strained to hear above the owl's insistent Morse code, the girl's song was missing.

Her panic was instantaneous. She scrambled up and headed to the boat dock for a better view of the old marina. The log was empty.

She started to run, wildly scanning the surface of the creek for movement, a glint on the water, a bobbing shape. Nothing. The sound of air being dragged into her lungs and the thick thud of footfall after footfall on the hard ground reverberated in her head. She couldn't have slept long, the moon was pinned in the same spot. If Meeka had gone in the water, surely a splash would have awakened her. Except for the owl though, the night was quiet.

"Meeka?" she yelled, her voice cracking.

Behind her the porch light at the cottage flared.

"Celie?" Jake yelled. "Celie, is that you?" He paused, his voice louder the second time.

She moved out into the open, turned to face him, and waved. The moonlight shone around her like a theatre spotlight. "Down here. On the dock."

By that time he was halfway there. The relief on his face flooded with irritation. He stopped a foot from her. "What are you doing down here in the middle of the night? Why didn't you wake me up?"

"I can't go out of the house without permission?"

"That's not what I meant." He was motioning for her to walk ahead of him back toward the house. "I woke up and you'd vanished."

"I came out for some fresh air."

"At one in the morning?"

"What difference does the time make?"

"Okay, okay. You're fine. I don't want to argue with you. If you're going to act crazy, just leave a note next time."

The words were on the tip of her tongue, the whole long story of the year falling apart, her battle to be herself again, and the constant pressure of his expectations.

He spoke more quietly. "I have to get some sleep. I have an 8:30 conference call at the office."

"So go."

"Don't blame this on me. Normal people don't take strolls in the middle of the night."

She was speechless, the insult so clear, the void enormous. He hadn't asked her the first thing about what was bothering her. He simply assumed she was crazy.

He wouldn't give it up either. "You have to see how insane this is."

"First I'm not normal. Now I'm insane?"

"You're getting worse, not better. I can't go off and leave you if I don't know you're safe."

"You go every day and I'm still here. I'm dealing with this, not you."

"That is patently not true. You're not dealing with it. You're avoiding it. And you're not the only one who's affected. Look at me, I'm standing outside in my pajamas at one in the morning."

"You don't need to follow me around. I was taking a walk, that's all."

"There's more to it than that. Something else is going on. Why can't you tell me?"

"You can't fix it."

His glare faded, replaced by a perplexed look. He reached out to touch her cheek, but she stepped away.

"I'm worried about you," he said.

"I know that." But it still sounded confrontational.

"You need to move on, Celie. Let the cancer go."

"And you can make that happen if you stay?"

He looked away. They had crossed a bridge, she felt, one she had meant to avoid. She passed in front of his open hand, the lady to his gentleman, but their retreat to politeness was just as far from the truth. He couldn't hide how badly he wanted to be somewhere else, anywhere else. She realized they should have talked about this before now. There were a lot of things they should have talked about. A hundred arguments whirled in her head, but once his face hardened, she could tell he had steeled himself against any concession. All these years together, there were no real secrets. They knew each other too well. They were both thinking it might be better if he did leave.

The concept widened to encompass more. The word *leave* so broad suddenly that she sucked in air to offset the shakiness, the kind that preceded fainting. She imagined the wary circling in the bedroom, the heft of packed suitcases, the finality of the trunk latch followed by disappearing headlights on the driveway. The sudden clarity of how he really felt stunned her into silence. They climbed the hillside in unison, but without words.

He went straight to the bedroom. While he rattled in the closet, clinked hangers, shoes, she disappeared into the guest bathroom. Over the sound of dresser drawers opening and shutting, she turned on the shower and twisted the dial to the hottest setting. But instead of getting undressed, she stared into the mirror and listened to the water fill the drain, the constant falling away of what was and what had been and what might have been.

She waited for him to leave. If she went out, he would issue pat, well-meant instructions about counseling, maybe even lawyers. She teetered at the edge of an abyss deeper and wider than she'd ever known. She knew what came next. Jake only understood forward action. He would expect her to leap to it. She might not be able to restrain herself from telling him to go to hell. Or from apologizing and asking him to reconsider. With the fingers of one hand digging into the palm of the other, she resisted the logjam of words in her throat. In all the months of fog and this daze of new tragedy, nothing had ever been clearer. If she spoke, if he stayed, she'd never find the old Celie.

Chapter Seven

When the songs had run through me and Henry Lewis didn't show up, I knew he was gone, really gone. It had been silly to think he might be hiding in the reeds, waiting for me to come walk him home. All the phrases I'd heard from Ruthie and Mama and Pastor Ware when bad things happened to other people over the years circled in my head. *People grieve in different ways, it takes time, good things come from bad.* This was different. Nothing this bad had ever happened to me before. It felt like the end of the world. I sang the songs because they needed to be sung and because I didn't know what else to do. It didn't change anything. My brother was lost.

As I trudged up the marina ramp and back to the townhouse, echoes of my complaints over the years crashed around me, all the times I'd belly-ached about Henry Lewis's long-winded explanations and about having to drag around town with the little kids. This was my punishment for being selfish and impatient and spiteful. It made perfect sense. Every action had consequences, Mama had said it over and over. If you started something, you had to live with the consequences. It was the thing I remembered most clearly Mama saying the day my father showed up at the trailer.

"The very first time Latrelle asked me to go riding with him, I should of said no. But I didn't. I was seventeen, always buried in books. He brought me peaches and told me he was going to be mayor someday. He was so sure of himself. I had my diploma. I ought to have known better than to trust someone else's blather about dreams. But I'd been studying hard to get through early and I didn't have a lot of experience with boys. I thought he was going the same place I was. When you're young, you believe you control the world. Falling in love is so easy. It's just about the easiest thing you'll ever do. No one tells you it's harder to stay in love than anything else."

"How can you know if someone's going to change on you like that?"

"He didn't change, Mee. I did. He always liked riding around town and talking ideas with folks. Problem is he needed the whiskey to talk big. And the further he got from being mayor, from all those big schemes, the more he needed the whiskey."

"You wouldn't have us without him."

"Not all consequences are bad. You still have to fit your life around them. They don't fit themselves to you."

Mama had gone back to studying for her exams, but I understood. Good consequences or bad, in the end it meant more work for her.

Back at the townhouse the door was still unlocked, the lights off, exactly how I'd left it. No one had missed me. That was a good thing. I didn't want to have to explain going out in the middle of the night to wait for Henry Lewis. Truth or lies, it would sound as if I'd gone bonkers. I slipped off my sneakers on the porch and slid inside. Before pushing the door into place, I twisted the knob so it didn't scrape, the way I'd seen spies do in the movies.

"Where you been, girl?" Ashante whispered out of the dark cavern of the unlit living room. "Your mama doesn't have enough to worry about without you sneaking out in the middle of the night to meet some boy?"

"I wasn't."

"That door didn't just open and shut?"

I sank down on the stairs. Much as I wanted to, I didn't look away when his eyes drilled into mine. I deserved this.

"I know this a hard time for you, Mee. But it's harder for your mama. Only thing we can do right now is be there for her. Someday when you're a parent you'll understand better."

"How do you know? You don't have kids." It shot out like a bullet, mean and ugly and spiteful, all the things I'd been telling myself were the cause of my failure to keep my brother safe. It was too late to take it back. Ashante had been nice to us all. He didn't yell or complain at the noise or the mess or the extra cousins.

"You're right. I don't know a lot about it, but I'm trying to learn. You three are my kids now."

He didn't raise his voice or tell me how selfish and juvenile I was acting. And he was still counting Henry Lewis. I felt about as small as an ant.

"You gonna tell me who's the boy?"

"No boy. I went to find Henry Lewis. I was thinking he might be too weak to crawl out of the weeds or yell for help."

Ashante came and sat next to me on the stairs, inches between our shoulders. He didn't try to hug me. He didn't lecture. For a long time we sat, his breathing low and steady. I wanted to thank him for that, for being up when I came home, for believing me. I wanted to tell him how the moonlight floated out across the water and formed a path like you could walk right out there and how tempting it was. And how the songs melted into the night until the space filled with music and how I'd been praying my brother could hear the music wherever he was and know how sorry I was for what I'd done, for letting him drown. How it wasn't enough, but it was all I could think to do. But I didn't say a word.

I didn't want Ashante to say it would be alright. I didn't want him to lie to make me feel better. I didn't want him to forgive me. I didn't deserve to be forgiven.

MINDING HENRY LEWIS

Chapter Eight

After Jake's car tore down the driveway Celie continued to stare at the empty yard from the bathroom window. The branches of the willow oak lifted and fell. The shower water ran in a steady swirl of background noise. She thought about what she should be doing, but none of it seemed as important as making sure Meeka was safe. She considered whether the Breedens had a land line listed in the phone book or if she should go down to the townhouse. Although she composed a neutral question that she hoped would yield the information she wanted, whether Meeka was safely at home, Celie couldn't get past how terrifying it would be for Mary Breeden to hear that knock on the front door at this hour.

In her mind she kept rephrasing the question to hide the obvious fact they both had been out in the middle of the night. It made them sound like conspirators and she didn't want Mary Breeden to think she had encouraged her daughter to break rules. Or to think that they were both unstable.

"Damn you, Jake. Now you've got me thinking I'm crazy." Disaster scenarios clogged her brain. After all this time surely someone from the Linden Street apartment would have come looking at the creek if Meeka wasn't at home. She was just a girl. She'd been through a terrible trauma. They would be watching her carefully.

The conversation at the seawall just now, played back, gave her some small comfort. Meeka was angry, not despondent. She was coherent, not babbling. Yet Celie couldn't shake the image of her face. That shocked glare, accusatory and unforgiving, stared back at her outside the window. She grabbed the keys to the Volvo and careened around the circular drive, down the hill, and up onto Stonegate. The creek disappeared in the rear view mirror. Past the unlit windows of George's house, past glimpses of the river between clapboard walls, past the pale wash of the cinderblock gymnasium at St. Bernadette's and the forest green dormitory rooftops. She almost missed the turn for Linden Street.

The townhouse was dark. Mary Breeden's blue van was parked in a neat line with the other tenants' vehicles and one small motorcycle. An old magnolia towered like a vine-encrusted turret beside the building. At the far end of the block Celie did a three point turn and parked where she could see the windows of the Breeden's unit. There were no lights, no voices. After ten minutes of nothing, she eased the car back onto the pavement and drove home. By the time she was back inside the cottage the rush of adrenaline had faded. She was shaking, chilled, and exhausted. From the kitchen she heard the drone of the shower. She'd left the water on all this time. She was crazy.

With trembling fingers, she stripped off the nightgown, the hem soaked and muddy, and stepped under the water. It was icy, but she refused to get out. She let it stream through her hair and down her skin until she could barely stand from the shivers. After she put the soiled nightgown in the sink to soak, she crawled under the covers with the heating pad. It was a long while before the tension in her back lessened to bearable.

When she woke up, the bedroom was so bright she thought it must be noon. She wouldn't let herself look at the clock. It was slovenly to waste time, something the old Celie would never have countenanced. Her mother would be ashamed of her. In a clean pair of jeans and sweatshirt, juice in hand, she started a list on the kitchen pad. She told herself she felt better. A stern voice in her head lectured that busy was preferable to sitting around wishing things were different.

Jake had made a full pot of coffee and left her a note. *Don't forget to call the health insurance people about the counselor.* She was confused. Had she dreamed the conversation about his leaving? Had he talked about leaving before he panicked over her disappearance or after her refusal to explain? If he was not really worried about her, what was the point of saying he was? Counseling would be pointless if he'd already made up his mind he'd had enough. And hadn't his counseling suggestion sprung from the drowning, not their latest argument? It made her angry all over again.

She added the counselor to her own list and chucked his note in the trash. She would call before lunch. Let the insurance people get their desks straight and their mornings organized. Her scribbling made a quiet scritch-scratch of achievement in the kitchen. They needed cream for coffee, salad stuff for dinner, and another box of brownies for Saturday's guests. She wrote those things down on the pad under the heading 'store.' She refused to think it might all be for naught if Jake had left for good.

She wanted to cook something for the Breedens. It took her almost half an hour to decide what would be appropriate. It had to be useful and not too elaborate. Once she finally decided on a baked ham and a dessert that didn't require plates and forks, she added those items to the list. The car keys poked up out of her purse, a relief that there was no harried scramble to remember where she'd left them, something that had become commonplace in the last year. Forgetfulness, a verifiable side effect of the cancer chemicals, was new to her. Although she had finished the list, she stayed on the kitchen stool and doodled on the paper, tiny curlicues connected to open rectangles that resembled a maze. Five or six times she sipped at the empty juice glass.

She should fire up the computer and search the insurance company website for a phone number. But she didn't. She twirled the paper under the pencil eraser, round and round, and thought about what she would say to a counselor about Henry Lewis, a boy she'd never met, whose dying thought must have been why hadn't the woman on the hillside come to his rescue.

When she finally did get up, her purse seemed impossibly heavy. She unloaded several items, including the phone, before she slung the bag over her shoulder and headed outside. But on the back steps she decided she shouldn't leave those things on the counter where anyone could see them through the kitchen window. She gathered them in cupped hands and stuck them all under her pillow in the bedroom. Without thinking she drove to Food Lion instead of Wal-Mart. It was quieter, easier to find things without so many customers. The truth was she'd never seen anyone she knew in this Food Lion.

Half an hour later the man who bagged the groceries carried them out to the car without even asking. She hardly eked out a thank you, she was so busy analyzing what there was about the way she looked that made him think she couldn't manage the bags by herself. He couldn't have known the ham was too heavy. Despite the nurses' repetitive warnings, she often forgot the weakened right arm and the possibility of lymph edema. She was constantly picking something up, only to put it down at the immediate stab of pain and switch arms. Doctor's orders to protect the arm without the lymph nodes. When he first explained that it was subject to swelling and pain if the white blood cells had to compensate for an injury to that arm, she listened like an avid medical student, clinical, focused, yet with an unfamiliar detachment. Although the lecture was interesting, he was talking about someone else's arm.

Every twinge caught her off guard. Every ache reminded her the old Celie was gone. She'd been healthy her entire life. She'd been to the hospital only to have babies and visit friends having babies. Last year's string of appointments and treatments had been her punishment for such an easy life. It wasn't anything she could voice to Jake or the boys, or even to her daughters-in-law as close as she felt to them. It sounded like whining. If she wanted them all to stop assuming she was helpless, she needed to be more like the old self who took every obstacle in stride, the way she always had. No one wanted to hear gruesome details, only that she was on the mend.

In spite of her dismay at the sudden automatic link between her and illness, the details had been all-consuming to her. They still were. The regimen had become her life. Although she only went now for check-ups every three months, she choked up at the thought of driving the hour to the hospital. She hated being so familiar with the building that she knew in advance how the industrial glass door would hesitate a whole second before it slid open to engulf her. It appalled her that anyone watching might think she paused out of fear. She cringed at the idea of giving her name to the receptionist so that everyone in the room knew she was no longer Celie Lowell the court mediator, the tennis player, the world traveler, but this bald skeleton with a piece of plastic and metal imbedded in her chest to allow the infusion of drugs that did what her body had failed to do, keep away disease.

Back at the river house with the groceries she was still fuming. When she flipped open the back of the wagon, the keys flew out of her hand in an arc that should have been funny. Not amused, she retrieved them from the grass. Right there in the driveway she stripped off the sweatshirt. She was perspiring in the already steamy morning, so unlike what springtime in Virginia ought to be. Yet how dare she complain about a sunny day with what Mary Breeden was suffering?

One at a time with her left arm she unloaded the bags. It took several trips. After everything was put away, the ham sat on the counter next to the tub of chocolate chip cookie dough. The ready-made mix was a temporary concession to her inability to mix dough with the weakened arm. She wouldn't look at the ingredient label. The boys would be shocked that their mother, the queen of homemade, had stooped to bad-for-the-arteries prepared dough.

The ham and the cookies for Meeka's family would give her a chance to talk to the girl's mother. She needed to tell Mary Breeden that her daughter had been brave, beyond brave, that Meeka had done what she could to rescue her brother. No child should have to beat herself up about that. It was devastating enough to lose a brother.

After Celie set the oven to pre-heat, she sorted the mail. There wasn't much since their regular bills went to the Middleton house. When she spread Wednesday's newspaper out on the dining room table, there was Henry Lewis's face smiling up at her with the headline, *Local Boy Drowns*. She read the article twice standing up.

After she sat, she read it again. It only listed three children in the family. No second son, and only two daughters, Tomeeka and Jasmine. She'd messed that up too with her assumptions. Rey and Liné were not even half-siblings or that would have been mentioned in the article. Maybe neighbors, but that meant there were other mothers in shock.

And Henry Lewis was not Henry Lewis she discovered, he was Henry Lewis Breeden. She hadn't thought, had just assumed Lewis was his last name, that he had a different last name from his siblings. It was common among black families in Middleton when she and Jake were raising their children. If she were honest, it was just as common among the poor part of the white community too. Many of the mothers she met in court-ordered mediation had two or three children, each with different fathers and different last names.

Many things about the South had been new to her when she married Jake. In the Connecticut suburb where she'd grown up there were no black families and very few Asians. Heddingford fathers rode the train to the city and their wives stayed home and raised the children. And while she'd never before articulated the distinction with poor families, she realized, looking back, that there probably weren't many of those either in Heddingford. It wasn't until college that she'd had classmates and fellow choir members with ethnic backgrounds different from her own. She'd made friends from all over, one Nigerian girl in her freshman geology class and several black girls from New York whose fathers were diplomats or professors. Although they hadn't double-dated or gone to visit each other during break, no one orchestrated that or even thought about it. It just happened. Looking back, she wondered if she had somehow subconsciously maintained the distinction.

When she and Jake first moved to Middleton, the small Virginia farming community they'd carefully chosen to replace their generic suburban childhoods, it happened in just the same seemingly unintentional way that they gravitated to people with their same background. Local businessmen were both white and black, small operations mostly, the five and dime, the barber shop, the dry cleaners. At the beginning the Rotary Club, with those same businessmen, was their social circle. At public events she routinely met black women she liked. Thomas's kindergarten teacher, an attorney, the postmistress, and several of the Social Services people she worked with on court-ordered mediations. They knew each other's children and greeted them at soccer practices and at the grocery store, but they weren't the friends who invited her for coffee or to the movies. She wasn't sure why exactly. She'd never really analyzed it until now.

After she finished re-reading the newspaper article about the drowning, all on page one, she left it on the table and went back to the bedroom to get her phone. If Jake tried to call or told the boys about her 'inexplicable' behavior, they would worry when they couldn't reach her. It was easier to answer than to explain why she hadn't kept the phone with her.

The midday sun made a broad band of discoloration on the old Oriental at the foot of their bed. An illusion she guessed, but blatant enough that she knelt and eyed the rug from a different angle just to be sure it wasn't stained. It was the first thing they'd bought after the wedding, a happy bargain after a long day exploring thrift stores in their newly adopted hometown. A happy memory. But when she stood up, she felt dizzy. She put a hand on the bed to steady herself. Her head felt heavy and off-balance. Sun glazed the room, painfully bright and too warm. Outside the double windows the same brilliant sunshine from yesterday blazed across the river. Here and there sharp tufted whitecaps peppered the channel. Closer to the shore in the shallow water, they faded to pencil-thin ripples like her pen and ink drawings from high school art class. She kept her back to the window that opened to the creek so she wouldn't see the brown spot floating there midstream in the ebbing tide. The off-balance feeling remained.

With one hand on the quilt, she stepped around the mattress to her side of the bed. Perched on the edge, she lifted her feet, one at a time, and let her shoes drop. Once she lay down on top of the covers, her mind went blank.

The muffled sound of tires on pavement filtered through the bedroom window. Panic-stricken, she stuffed her feet back into the boat shoes and tucked in her shirt. If Jake, returning in a fit of conscience, found her in bed in the middle of the day, he would commit her to the mental ward. The clock on his side of the bed read 2:30. That couldn't be right. When she'd come home with the groceries, it had been morning. The power must have gone off the night before. But the light in the bathroom was working fine. And the sun was still shining.

She checked the driveway. A blur of white, not Jake at all. Well, of course, if the clock was correct, Jake wouldn't be here. He never left the office in the middle of the afternoon. And maybe he wasn't coming back under any circumstances. She thought about hiding out in the bathroom again. She didn't want to answer questions from anyone about yesterday. If Tracy Anne Sheffield thought she could weasel out enough to report to the church ladies, she'd better think again.

"Anybody home?" A male voice called from the kitchen door. The knock repeated, two shorts and that expectant pause that meant whoever was there was peering through the screen to see if anything was moving inside.

"I'm coming," she called out, hoping for the mailman who knew nothing of her part in yesterday's horror.

From the back steps Barry Morgan smiled through the screen door. The bill of his cap prevented his nose from pressing against the metal. His teeth gleamed.

"Hey," she greeted him. "My favorite contractor. Aren't you kind to come by and check on an old lady."

"Jake said you had some nail pops in the new ceilings."

"You mean Jake called and told you I was alone today and asked if you'd stop in to see if I was all right."

Barry raised his arm so she could see the spackle bucket.

"Have it your way." She smiled in spite of the jab of irritation at the easy conspiracy Jake inspired. "Come in, come in. You may work on the nail pops to your heart's content."

"Thanks. No one wants to upset the boss."

When he laughed at his own joke, she tried to laugh too, but it came out a garbled sputter. Although he looked at her oddly for a second longer, he didn't comment.

"I didn't realize you had company," he said.

"Company?"

"I thought I saw someone on the hillside steps, by the south side of the cottage, as I drove up."

Celie shook her head. "Not that I know of."

"Maybe a neighbor dropping something off?"

Celie couldn't imagine who that might be. "I didn't hear anything, but I . . ." She stopped herself. Someone at the side door could have looked through the master bedroom window, could have seen her in bed. Sleeping in the middle of the day would surely be reported to Jake as questionable behavior. She would look later, no point in dragging Barry into their mess.

"Maybe just shadows from the trees." He smiled and waved at the air as if it were insignificant.

No matter how hard she tried to put it out of her mind, the image he'd suggested lingered. Trish might be snooping around for evidence of Celie's emotional collapse, fodder for a nice intimate discussion with Jake about his crazy wife. Not trusting herself to

75

speak again, she left Barry to the repairs and purposely headed outside with her gardening gloves. The side door investigation would have to wait.

She wriggled her fingers into the gloves, the ends worn to a muddy gray, the knuckles matted with dried clay from the last gardening session, when she couldn't recall. Her fingernails, lost during the chemo last summer, had reappeared recently, more curved, but subject to odd cracks and discoloration. Although she'd never been one to spend time or money on manicured nails, the gloves were a necessity now to protect what was struggling to grow back. With the bucket and the small spade, she headed for the daylilies where they'd sat overnight in their makeshift carryalls.

But the creek spinning out below her wasn't empty. That same dark head bobbed in the water.

"Stop," she blurted, even as she twisted away and focused instead on an osprey gliding onto one of the fence posts uphill. "You ridiculous woman. There's nothing there. It's over."

But she didn't look again. She decided to weed Jake's vegetable garden where the garage blocked any view of the creek. The daylilies could wait. Twenty minutes later she had accumulated a pile of weeds that overflowed the bucket. By the time Barry crossed the lawn to her shady spot she was repositioning volunteer marigolds along the edge of the raised bed.

"All done," he said.

"Thank you. You are a nice man."

"Sure there isn't anything else? I'm between houses."

"No projects in the pipeline?"

"No."

The regret in his voice made her look up. Last year Jake had pushed the cottage work forward on the theory that the economic mess meant contractors were hungry and prices would be lower. Although the two men teased each other about it, it bothered her. She didn't understand how they stayed friends. Jake explained that it was just business. Women were so different. They hid that kind of thing in all sorts of compliments and would never admit it, yet the grudge would linger. Women had long memories.

"We've talked about redoing the old shed into a guesthouse next," she said.

"That sounds interesting. Get me the sketches and I'll give them to Len."

Len Oncek, the architect Barry had recommended, had been very patient whenever Celie hadn't felt well enough to discuss the cottage plans. He'd been through the cancer regimen with his own wife. In

March Celie had heard at church on the weekend they opened the cottage that Kathy Oncek was fighting a recurrence of stomach cancer. The coincidence, that six degrees of separation thing, struck Celie anew. After her own diagnosis, everywhere she went she looked for women without hair and never saw any. How could she be the only one when it was supposed to be one woman in ten? And then there was one right here in town, Kathy Oncek who sent her Get Well cards and added her to the Methodist prayer list. And yet her relief was tinged with shame.

From her research online Celie didn't think Kathy would live through it this time. Although they knew each other only from the house plans, Kathy had sent several hats along with the cards. Lately Celie had repaid the kindness with cards of her own, but it frustrated her to do something so superficial in the face of the lurking evil that was cancer. The disease had a unique energy and humans hadn't been very successful at doing more than delaying the end result. The same helplessness she'd felt after her own diagnosis dogged her. It made everything in life seem more suspect. It made Kathy's recovery improbable, the Get Well cards an ineffectual gesture.

"How are the Onceks doing?" she asked Barry.

He held up his hand to shield his eyes against the afternoon sun that had circled around the garage to chase the horizon. "They decided to stop this round of chemotherapy. Mostly, I think, because of the side effects. They're talking about what's next."

Her mind stuck on what he wasn't saying, *Hospice, a funeral.* She'd never been good at funerals. Just last fall, before she found her own tumor, she'd gone to a college friend's funeral, Rayne Lyman. She'd left the cemetery before anyone could recognize her. She hadn't trusted herself to talk about it in the appropriate tone. It all seemed so foreign to her, a language she didn't know, as if cancer might be contagious.

The irony hit her again in all its improbability. When they were twenty, she and Rayne Lyman had played afternoon after afternoon of tennis on a maple-shaded campus court where Celie had trouble concentrating, so envious of Rayne's being svelte and rich. All that good fortune hadn't saved her from cancer though. People might not die of breast cancer as often as they used to, but they still died.

"I'll have to take Kathy some of Jake's rosemary bread," she said, more to herself than Barry, before she remembered that Jake had packed and left.

"They'd like that."

"She lent me her hats, you know."

Barry didn't answer. He was gazing at the creek from where he stood at the high end of the driveway. It was one of her favorite views too. It had been, she corrected herself. When the sun snapped and leaped off the dark water, the sparkles were mesmerizing.

He didn't look at her when he spoke. "That boy would have stopped trying to swim within seconds. The water's so cold this time of year."

"Henry Lewis." She said it louder than she meant to. "Henry Lewis Breeden."

Barry continued to stare off into the distance without acknowledging the correction. Apparently everyone knew about the water temperature except her. Until Richard brought it up by the seawall the cold was a factor that had never crossed her mind. She didn't know how long Henry Lewis had been in the water at the point when she heard the voices. While the scene continued to replay for her when she least expected it, it never started before the moment when she first heard Meeka call out across the water. It never included the children walking down the hill to the boat ramp as they must have. Or their teasing and giggling in the sun-dappled yard next door. Celie never saw Henry Lewis take off his shoes, never heard the discussion between the children of what he was doing and whether he should or not. She had trouble remembering her own thoughts before that single moment when Meeka's fear shot across the creek.

While that point in time was singularly clear, the day itself grew murkier and murkier. Why had she taken the shovel out that afternoon? Where was Jake?

Barry coughed. "I'm sorry. I shouldn't have brought that up."

"It's okay. Jake's decided I ought to talk to a therapist. I suppose I should have gone last year with the cancer. This just compounds things."

"You look rested though, like you have more energy."

"Thank you for noticing. Mostly I do feel better." She scraped off the trowel and let the rich fertilized soil fall back into the raised bed that had once been solid river clay. Jake had planted last spring, not her. And again this spring, without even consulting her, he had started the seeds. In the midst of all that time at the hospital and in doctors' offices she hadn't thought about the garden, the threat of frost, the marauding bunnies, Jake's kneeling and working the soil all by himself, the cheerful windowsill of tomatoes. Truthfully she wasn't thinking of any of that when she'd weeded just now. She couldn't quite remember what she had been thinking.

"It's so odd, Barry, how big things become unimportant and little things get to be show-stoppers. Every time I had to drive to the infusion room at the hospital I dreaded it. I didn't sleep the night before. I would sit in the parking lot and steel myself to get out and go inside. But every time I'd hear worse stories than mine and go away feeling infinitely better. I think that's partly what I've been missing, that reminder that my situation is not the worst one."

"I don't think they'd recommend going back just for that reassurance."

"No. No one would ever go there if they didn't have to."

"Listen, do you want to walk me through the changes you're thinking about for the shed? I have time."

She smiled up from where she was kneeling by the bush of wintered-over parsley. "Not today. You've done enough and I have house stuff to catch up on. Really, that's all. Thanks for the nail pops."

After he was gone she sat back and rubbed the dirt off her gloves. This was the part she had trouble explaining to Jake. Her interest in the garden had evaporated. The flowers didn't make her feel better. She couldn't even recall the plans for the hillside. She just couldn't decide what to do instead.

For the rest of the afternoon the obsession with yesterday dragged at her. From the porch, from the bedroom window, as she passed the creek in the car on her way to the post office—she wasn't brave enough to walk and risk the neighbors' inquiries—the images from yesterday repeated and repeated. And the voices too. Again she felt the heat of that April sun between her shoulder blades and the glare that battered the dock, the hillsides, the little houses above and the stick figures below.

She stewed over the other things that had happened after the rescue team's arrival. She wondered if they had really happened. She didn't trust her memory. Meeka Breeden hiding in the place where her brother had disappeared and singing to him in the moonlight, that could have been a dream. She thought about Henry Lewis's mother. She could have imagined the woman in the van. And today, was Mary Breeden alone in the empty townhouse, the children off at school?

No, not today, not the day after. They would have stayed home to be together. With the shades drawn, they would sit distracted and numb. They would stay close to each other, preoccupied with the empty chair, the unmade bed, the missing voice.

When the stove buzzer rang, she manhandled the pan and managed to get the ham for the Breedens out and onto the trivet to cool in spite of her weak arm. It turned out beautifully, crisp browned edges, curled squares centered around pinpoints of cloves. Wrapped in foil, it filled the cottage with its sugar and salt smell. While it had sizzled away in the oven, she had re-read the newspaper article about Henry Lewis. When she tried to read the other headline stories, the words blurred and his easy smile from the school photo beamed up at her. She found herself grinning back at him as if he'd made a joke only the two of them understood.

She hurried through two full sheets of cookies. Leaving them to cool, she showered, then piled them onto a double paper plate, whipped the clear wrap around them, and added a third plate to anchor the whole. It reminded her of the Christmas cookie factory her mother set up every year in the kitchen and her own duplication of it with Thomas and Rory. The afternoon's sense of accomplishment was fleeting.

Maudlin at the idea that those times would never be repeated, Celie took the container of left-over cookie dough to the front porch and sat in the shade on one of the old wicker chairs they'd rescued from a yard sale, now painted a pale blue. Her bare ankles stuck out into the last slice of sun while she spooned cookie dough into her mouth. Gooey and sweet, the chocolate chunks stuck in her teeth. She couldn't stop. When the tub was empty, she leaned back and sighed. She'd read somewhere that small pleasures made life bearable. If you paid attention to small pleasures, the article said, you could store those bits of happiness, one on top of the next until you had enough built up to get through the bad times. It was supposed to make the rest, the bad things, manageable. Since when did she rely on pop psychology?

Now Mary Breeden would have to learn that, whether she wanted to or not. But Celie couldn't move for trying to think what small pleasures could overcome the loss of your child.

Chapter Nine

Thursday morning, once the other kids went off to school and I was alone in the house except for Mama, I took coffee and a plate of Mrs. Carter's banana bread upstairs.

"Mama?" I spoke through the closed door. "Mama, you awake?"

When she didn't answer, I opened the door. She was dressed and sitting in the rocker by the window, her hands folded neatly in her lap, the window cracked an inch. The room was chilly. I pushed the window down into the sill.

"I thought you might like your breakfast up here."

"Ruthie?" she whispered.

"It's Meeka. Ruthie's running errands."

Ruthie had told me not to say she was at work. She wanted it to sound more like she'd be home any minute.

"I can get whatever you need." I set the tray on the extra chair and nudged the mug a little closer. "This is coffee, not too hot, ready to drink. And banana bread. Mrs. Carter next door made it with extra honey from her son's beehive." Honey was supposed to be soothing, according to Mrs. Carter.

I moved over to the window and tried to see what Mama was seeing. Three or four robins fluttered across the little bit of lawn and pecked at the bright green patch of new shoots where the landlord had spread grass seed a few weeks ago. When she didn't pick up the mug, I nudged it again.

"You like coffee. Ashante says you need to stay strong. You gotta eat. Try it."

Still no answer or movement. I waved the plate in front of her nose.

"Ruthie will tan my behind if you don't eat some of this."

No reaction. The doorbell rang, three long bleats like the bell itself was mad and then a repeat knock.

"Please eat. I'll be right back." I flew down the steps with a quick prayer that it wouldn't be the rescue people with bad news or Mrs. Carter sniffing around for the inside scoop.

"Who is it?" I asked through the peephole.

"Detective Staigehurst, Essex County Sheriff's Department."

I opened the door. "Did you find him?" It came out in a rush.

He hesitated. "Not yet. We came for an official statement from . . ." the officer reviewed the paperwork on his clipboard. "Tomeeka Breeden. Is she at home?"

81

My immediate thought was to tell them to come back tomorrow. It avoided having to answer questions without Ruthie or Ashante here. Sooner or later though it would catch up with me and they would know I had lied. There were punishments for witnesses who refused to cooperate. Television detectives were always threatening people who wouldn't talk to them with obstruction of justice. Whatever that was exactly I wasn't sure, but it sounded bad. It hardly seemed like justice to force a person to talk when something awful had just happened to someone they loved.

"Is Ms. Breeden here?" His eyes were hidden behind his sunglasses and he didn't smile.

I ran to the bathroom and threw up the cereal and banana I'd had for breakfast. I was still on my knees when the footsteps came inside and the front door clicked back into place. What if he called out and upset Mama? Scrambling up, I rinsed my mouth and wiped my hands on my jeans.

"Are you alright in there?" the detective shouted.

I yanked the door open and crossed in front of him to the kitchen table. "We can sit here."

"Ms. Breeden is coming?"

"I'm Tomeeka Breeden."

"You're—"

"Yes."

"You're a minor."

It seemed too obvious for an answer. I could hear Rachel's sarcastic *duh.*

"Is there a parent at home?"

"I'm not a baby. My mother is upstairs, but she's not feeling well. As you can understand."

"Another relative maybe?"

I shook my head. "I can tell you what you want to know. I remember it all."

He looked at me as if I might bolt again. "Well, just a few questions then so we can finish the report."

The blue-green edge of a tattoo curled out from under the cuff of his uniform. He wasn't much older than Rachel's brother. I would have liked to ask him if he knew TJ, if they'd graduated from high school in the same class, if they'd played basketball at the elementary school or taken Drivers' Ed together. It would be easier to talk about Henry Lewis with a friend of someone I knew. But all this delay was just avoiding consequences.

"I didn't stop him from going in the water. He'd read about how to swim in a book. He thought he knew. He learned tons of stuff from books. He was the smartest person I know."

The officer opened his pad and started taking notes. I wondered if this was his first investigation. His knee jiggled when he wasn't writing. Every few words he looked up as if he were watching for clues about whether I was telling the truth. He waited though for me to go on.

"That man at the creek said the water was too cold and too deep, that no one could swim in it, but he was wrong. I swam. I jumped in and I swam back to the dock. Not very far, but I did it. But my brother was too young to know how. Maybe the white lady is right and accidents happen. But accidents happen because people make bad decisions. I shouldn't of let him near the creek in the first place. If I'd stopped him, he'd be at school today. It's my fault."

His mouth hung open and he stopped writing, as if I had just confessed to pushing Henry Lewis.

"Don't you have to arrest me?"

He shook his head and frowned. When I didn't say anything else, he capped the pen and stuck it back in his shirt pocket.

"They don't arrest a person for that. And certainly not a kid."

"I've ruined my mother's life. You don't know my brother. He was amazing. He should be alive and I should be dead." My voice came from far away, fading in and out as if I was in a tunnel that curved one way, straightened out, and curved again. I tried to keep my eyes on the policeman's face, to remind myself that he was the one I needed to convince. "My brother was going to build a spaceship to travel to the next galaxy. He knew how everything worked, engines and crystals and solar power. He was smarter than all the other kids in school combined."

The detective put his hands on my knees and held them there until I stopped trembling. "It's going to be alright."

"How can it be?"

"It just will. I know it doesn't seem like that right now. It seems awful. And it is awful, but you didn't do anything wrong. It's going to get better."

"How old are you?"

"22."

"They wouldn't let you be a police officer if you didn't know right and wrong, right?"

He straightened up, as if he'd been called to attention by someone in the next room. The newness of his training rules scrolled across his face in the blinking lids and the lip biting. I could see him trying to figure out where I was headed. Ashante would say he shouldn't play poker.

"It is my fault. There's no one else."

He thumbed the pad. He flipped the cover open and shut. He stared everywhere but at me. I felt badly for him. Interviewing the sister of a dead boy wasn't a great job for anyone. But there was no point in my lying about how it had happened. It wouldn't bring my brother back. Or convince my mother to forgive me.

The policeman had been gone for hours. I didn't think I would ever eat again. My belly tightened into such a hard knot that I just sat on the toilet, my arms crossed on top of my knees, my head down. As hard as I was trying to be quiet, I was sure they could hear my moans. The smell from the kitchen was disgusting. Burnt coffee, reheated tacos, pies with every kind of fruit, and all those flowers people had brought without containers. What did they think? That Mama ran a flower shop and she'd have a hundred empty vases sitting around? When there was no more room in water pitchers and soup cans, Aunt Ruthie stuck the last bunch in a cardboard juice carton with the top cut off. I hated those perky bright flowers.

"Are you asleep in there?" Rey pounded on the bathroom door.

"Go upstairs," I mumbled.

He had lost his mind since yesterday. He'd thrown paper airplanes at Liné until she started crying. When he back-talked Ashante, his punishment was sitting for ten minutes in the hot van. *You need to think, boy,* Ashante hissed. He caught Rey's collar in his fist and walked him out the door, but you could still hear. *People here are hurting. Think about them, not your own sorry self.* When Rey came back inside he was all sweaty and sulking, like he was when the high school boys wouldn't let him join their pick-up basketball games.

At first, when he came in still mad, it ticked me off. I was about to add my own lecture to Ashante's, when Rey just crumpled on the floor next to where Mama sat by the kitchen table. When Mama put her hand on his hair, he leaned his head against her leg. He was only a year and a half older than Henry Lewis, not even thirteen yet. Of course he was upset. He'd lost his best friend and his mother was miles away and not coming home anytime soon, leastways she'd been gone for over a year and she never called to check on him. On the floor big bad Rey just melted away to someplace else. I wished I could do that, sit and let Mama stroke my hair, but someone had to mind the two little girls, keep them busy so they left off bothering Mama. She'd made it clear she wanted nothing to do with me.

"How about a bubble bath, Liné?" Aunt Ruthie said when she arrived late Wednesday afternoon after her day shift. She removed the sixth or seventh cookie from the little girl's hand. "I'm guessing you and Jasmine could stand more than a quick wipe behind the ears."

I told myself she wasn't being critical. She might have forgotten I supervised their bath the night before. Finally free to excuse myself, I escaped to the bathroom. My insides hurt worse than cramps, worse than flu. It felt like someone gutting my insides like a fish. I wondered how long before I could sneak up to bed. It didn't have a thing to do with all these people who came and went. No one asked me a single question. No one said a thing to me. They went straight to Mama, touched her shoulder, hugged her. Ashante stood right behind her, her personal bodyguard. He shook their hands and thanked them for the casserole or the flowers, nodding at everything they said like the church congregation did. No one was fooled. He only wanted the line to keep moving.

Practically the whole town had come, and more still coming. Through the closed bathroom door I could hear the church ladies who had stayed late last night and were back before Ruthie left for work. They called out the first names in a kind of PA blare as the visitors passed through the living room and into the kitchen. They paid their respects and slipped back out in a steady stream. I had no idea how long this was going to keep up. But there was no way I was going to ask and come off sounding selfish.

"Meeka." Rey must have his lips to the crack between the door and the frame. "Please. It's the only bathroom right now with the girls in the tub. I really need to go."

"Okay, okay." It took me a minute to straighten up and wash my hands. At first I wasn't going to look in the mirror, but then I thought I better check to be sure the pain in my gut didn't show on my face. If people saw that, they would be curious. They'd ask questions I didn't want to answer. Except for my eyes all puffed and red at the edges, my face looked the same as it always did. That babyish pudge of cheeks and Mama's full lips in a slightly smaller size. Aunt Ruthie said I'd be pretty some day with those high cheek bones, but that day never seemed to come.

Rey had his back to the bathroom door when I opened it. He let me pass without speaking to me. The murmurs in the living room were gone. Maybe people were finally done gawking. Ashante and Mama were alone in the kitchen. They stood together, and he was holding her real tight. Her shoulders slumped and her arms hung loose, as if she was about to crumple right there in a heap. His one hand rubbed up and down her spine. Over Mama's shoulder he faced the stairs, right at me. But when I looked more closely, his eyes were shut. There were tracks on his face that caught the light and glittered. He was crying.

It was a backwards kind of comfort to see that he cared like that, tears and all. I'd never seen a man cry. I didn't know him that well, maybe he cried a lot. He'd moved in just after Christmas, after he'd been seeing Mama for five or six weeks. He worked overtime at the lumber yard whenever they offered it, so he wasn't there a lot on Saturdays. Sundays we were at church all day. Between choir practice, worship, preaching, and eating, the grownups didn't have much to do with the kids, aside from some of the men showing off how to float ringers over the horseshoe stakes.

Not that Ashante was mean to me or to anyone. He never raised his voice. He wasn't ugly or rude, just so keen on Mama it was like he barely saw the rest of us. I was glad for my mother, glad someone loved her like that, like in the movies. It didn't matter that she spent less time with them and more with Ashante. I liked having that space, even though it meant I had to watch the other kids more. Except now it did matter. Ashante would be working hard to help Mama get over losing Henry Lewis. The space between Mama and me would be greater.

The knife in my stomach twisted again. I leaned against the doorframe while I waited for it to pass. When the cramping didn't let up, I decided a walk might help. Since lunchtime when the policemen showed up to talk to Mama and Ashante, my stomach had been acting crazy. Luckily the officers hadn't asked to speak to me again. The person I most wanted to talk with was my best friend Rachel. With Mama stricken and not connecting to anyone, the longer the extra TracPhone was out of minutes, the longer it would be that I couldn't call Rachel. I hadn't seen anyone my own age in two whole days. I needed to get out. Away from all the voices and smells and eyes, maybe my stomach would settle down. Ashante already had given Rey permission to walk down to the elementary school to play pick-up basketball. Ruthie was watching the girls in the tub. No one would notice I was gone.

When I slipped out the front door, no one stopped me. I walked through the border of trees to the road that led to the courthouse and Main Street. While I waited for the light to change I analyzed the stream of trucks and cars whizzing through town. The headlights formed a blurry line of white blips, and their taillights an identical red snake. As they barreled by, I wondered how my friends and I had been crazy enough to cross here without the electric walking man.

Demeta had dared us the first time. We linked arms and raced together, shrieking and laughing at the thrill of it. Playing chicken with the frenzy of metal and rubber gave me a rush that made my whole body tingle. It was terrifying, as terrifying as talking to Wall Saunders. Yet I couldn't stop herself. Running through that time warp made me feel like the world was all pretend, cardboard houses and painted trees. It wasn't real and any second I would wake up my normal boring self, trailing along behind the little kids where no one ever noticed me. The recollection of the terror and the thrill held me in place on the sidewalk.

When a sixteen-wheeler blasted his horn as if he knew I was thinking about making a run for it, I had to grab the light post to steady myself. The real world was dangerous. I hadn't known that before yesterday, really known it like you knew your multiplication tables.

Breathing hard as if I had dashed across, I waited for the crossing light and then headed down Pleasant Street to Rachel's. Since third grade Rachel had lived in a brick duplex three blocks past the Laundromat, far enough away from the Rte 19 circus that we could play kickball in the street. Rachel lived with an older half-brother and their mother. Mrs. Washington was sick most of the time, holed up in her bedroom. *Sick in the head,* Rachel said as if it was a joke. I didn't think it was funny. When Mrs. Washington called out from the bedroom, Rachel would go see what she wanted and usually took her a glass of water or some crackers. Once Rachel told a bunch of girls that her mother's brain was fried from drugs so they had to keep her locked up.

It wasn't true. Several times I'd seen her wander out, once when we were cooking pizza from the freezer. Even though she was in her pajamas, she asked after my mother and reminded Rachel to wash the dishes, not just rinse them, pretty normal mother stuff. She did hide out though, so something wasn't right.

Rachel's older brother HiTop was in jail. I had never met Homer T. Washington, just seen pictures and heard stories. He was ten years older than Rachel, a half brother by a man who was long gone before Rachel was born. Rumors about HiTop's drug dealing were all over school. From the way Rachel clammed up when his name came up, I was pretty sure the truth wasn't so different. I had no idea how he'd gotten the nickname and Rachel had made me swear never to talk about him where her mother might hear. Demeta was the one who said HiTop had been arrested twice for selling crack in Richmond. The first time he went to juvey, but he wasn't so lucky the second time.

Rachel's other brother was a stepbrother, Thomas Jefferson Washington, TJ for short. TJ was nineteen, five years older than Rachel. His father had been married to Mrs. Washington for ten years, but had died in a car accident. The accident had been the beginning of Mrs. Washington's escape from real life. When TJ was younger, he hung out with Rachel and me. We were his groupies. He taught us how to climb trees, introduced us to Ice-T, and warned us about internet predators. Since he graduated high school, he only came home on weekends, and then only once a month. Some kind of logging job in West Virginia. He always had pockets full of money and nothing to do. He took Rache and me for ice cream or onion rings at the drive-thru in between lounging around on the couch, quizzing us on their homework, and teasing about the boys in our class. He always had a book with him.

Last fall Rachel and TJ had an argument. She wouldn't say what it was about, but she refused to talk to him, ignored him to his face. Since then, whenever he offered to spin us around town in his old rattletrap two-tone Malibu, she made excuses. I hadn't been able to get an explanation from either of them.

As I jogged past the Dairy Korner and the gas station, my throat burned, a combination of running and swallowing all that creek water. *Slow down.* When I twisted around to see who might have spoken to me from one of the yards or the windows I'd passed, I realized I'd said it out loud to myself. There was no one there.

The rumble of the pickup truck barreled behind me before I saw it. Out of the thickening shadows at the corner it crossed under a streetlight behind me, the gears a painful grind. I edged onto the grass to let them pass. Heads in the truck bed shifted up and down like horses on a circus merry-go-round. I tried not to stare.

"Whoa, whoa. Hold up, Franklin," a boy's voice called from the truck bed. The gears whined as they shifted down. The truck slowed. "Something interesting here. A girly girly on the move." The boy with the big mouth leaned out to his waist and swiped at my hair with a tentacled arm. "Sweeeeeet."

"Sweeeeet," the other boys repeated along with a series of long low whistles.

The truck bumped against the curb. Through the windshield I could see the driver twist the wheel off-road toward the overgrown hedge and closer to me. He cursed big time when the hubcap ground against the concrete. Then the front end bounced up and over the curb and into the yard, blocking my path. If only I'd cut through one of these yards ten seconds earlier.

"Got a friend, cutie?" It shot out from the mass of boys in the truck bed.

I edged away, four, five steps backwards on the grass, out from under the streetlamp. It had grown dark without my noticing. Their faces were indistinct, though I thought I recognized two boys from the high school wrestling team. I couldn't have spoken if I'd wanted to. My tongue was so thick I was having trouble swallowing.

"Watch out. Watch out, guys, any minute now she gonna talk."

"The Kewpie doll can talk?"

There were more whistles. Bottles rolled in the truck bed, magnified like footsteps on the grain barge in the fog.

"She gonna say the names of her friends so we can go round 'em up and have a party. C'mon, girly girl, spit 'em out." The boy with the octopus arm grabbed at my hair again, missed, but latched onto a piece of shirt. "A chickie cute as you is bound to have friends."

"Hot friends," another voice called out.

"Where y'headed all by y'self this time a night?" The boy holding my shirt hissed across the side of the truck. His breath was moist, beery, like Aunt Ruthie's husband Gerald. "If you ain't goin' t'see friends?"

When I jerked my shoulder backwards, a button popped, but the material came loose from his fist. I fought the urge to run. If I ran, they'd know I was scared. I walked, as fast as I dared, away from the truck, away from the boys, away. Two blocks to Rachel's house, two mostly unlit blocks. The truck lurched forward and then stopped short again. The wheels chewed up the lawn and spit out chunks of grass and dirt. Bodies tumbled forward. Curses flew.

"Chickie need a ride? Here, chickie chickie."

"Party, party." Shouts erupted into banging on the sides of the truck and hoots of laughter.

I'd never make it to Rachel's. I needed to get back to the traffic and the lights. But when I spun around towards Main Street, my ankle twisted. I stumbled and fell down on one knee. A shape moved onto the open tailgate, his head and shoulders outlined above the others. As he tried to regain his balance, he tipped, swayed, straightened. Then he stepped into the air. I waited for the crash, but feet spread, knees bent, he landed on the lawn without toppling over. Right next to me.

His fingers gripped my arm. He pulled me close until we were face to face in the shadows. "Hey," he said, his voice rough and low, full of unspoken things.

When I struggled, he tightened his grip and his other arm reached up, closer, closer.

"I know you," he said. His clammy hand held my chin so I couldn't turn my head.

"Don't," I said, but he held fast. "Let go."

Behind him the truck rocked. Arms and legs rose and fell. Curse words alternated with laughter and the chanting refrain of hoarse voices. "Party. Party." It was like a giant pig pile and there was no counting how many boys there were or when another one would jump out. A bottle plumed upward and crashed down on the street, glass everywhere.

"Give her here." A loud voice shot out from the mess in the truck.

"Yeah," the boy on the grass whispered in my ear. "I knew I knew you. You're the sister of that little kid that drowned."

When I yanked my arm away, I fell backwards and one flip-flop stuck in the grass. I sure wasn't going back for it. Slipping behind the hedge, I tried to figure the quickest route to outta-here. Sticks from the bush pricked into my shirt. Behind me a scrabble of feet and fingernails scraped on metal, but no rush of air from anyone following me. I edged toward the corner of the house.

Someone from the truck yelled, "Hey, Romeo, you done lost her."

"Have another beer, you fucker," the boy on the grass yelled back.

"Don't go, little chickie."

"Back, back, you idiot. Back the truck out to the road. She's getting away."

"Screw that if she don' wanna party with us."

"Shut up, you freaks." It was the voice of the boy on the grass again, not as close, but angry. "Her brother just died."

I slid along the thicket of overgrown hedge, keeping my eyes on him. He held his ground, a self-proclaimed gate keeper. As I picked my way through a passel of trashcans, I lost sight of him and the truck. Jogging with one bare foot was painful, not that I was going to stop. A thud sounded behind me, the grind of the gears, and the rumble of wheels on pavement sped up and squealed at the corner. I needed to get to the stoplight and across before they rounded the corner and caught up. If those were the boys I was supposed to dance with at school, it would suit me fine if no one invited me ever again.

"Meeka Breeden?" A different male voice announced behind me, older, more confident, as if he were taking roll call in class.

I didn't turn to see who it was. No good came from being out at night, I knew better. Wrong place, wrong time. Aunt Ruthie and Mama had chanted that to us since we were little. I just kept my legs churning forward. To the highway, to the other side of the streaming traffic, to home.

"That is you, girl, isn't it?"

The voice grew louder. Whoever he was, he was getting closer, but I wasn't taking any chances. Running now, I winced every time the bottom of my foot hit gravel.

"Rachel's little friend gone and growed up all of a sudden."

At the mention of my friend's name I couldn't help glancing back. It shocked me that the man had come close enough that I could see the links in the chain around his neck. Just outside arm's length, the grin in the dark turned familiar. Rachel's brother TJ. His shoulders filled the space between the bushes, but he didn't crowd me. The image of my drunk father filling the trailer doorway flashed. TJ was tall and broad like Latrelle, overpowering. Yet he was different from the way I remembered Latrelle, all sour and overheated. Still that hard push behind his words made me nervous for what might come next.

"Where you running to, Miss Meeka, in the dark? Or are you running from something?"

How did he know? I put my hands to my cheeks. "I was just walking."

"Walking's for daytime. At night riding's better. Safer. And riding in a car's best of all. Mine's right here."

That sounded more like the TJ I knew from last summer. When he smiled, I managed a small smile back. He jingled his keys, then tossed them up, ten, fifteen feet over his head. As if he were trying to decide something important—his eyes on the keys, not me—he grabbed them out of the air and balanced them on his palm. I could feel my chest loosen, the tremble in my legs fade.

"I was going to see Rachel."

"I'll take you," he said, back to his library voice. "I'm goin' that way."

I followed him down the sidewalk, what there was of it, crumbling concrete and weeds in between cracks. When we passed the alley other voices filtered out from the shadows, low murmurs, and laughter. The Laundromat gang of old timers was telling jokes and rolling dice. I'd seen enough of them for a lifetime back when Mama rented the walk-up apartment to get away from Latrelle.

TJ stayed just ahead. He tossed words over his shoulder without looking to see if I was still coming. "I heard 'bout Henry Lewis. Tough thing. He was a great kid."

"Yeah." I choked that out, but stopped without sharing the rest of what I'd been about to say. It suddenly seemed too personal. There was too much to say, things I wanted to shout out for everyone to know. He was a great kid. He could describe the entire galaxy, the size and color of every planet, the way they discovered new stars, all the rivers in Virginia, and the Indian legends behind their names. He knew which years they made Corvettes and the way to win at Parcheesi without blockades. My eyes felt hot and prickly. I thought about turning back toward Route 19 and going home.

"Come on." TJ held the passenger door open. It was the smooshed-berry-maroon Malibu he'd driven last July when he dropped us at the carnival, same gash of missing paint on the fender right below the license plate, the last time he and Rachel had been on good terms.

It took me two blocks before I realized he wasn't headed home, not mine or Rachel's. Curb petered out into crabgrass. Ditches grew wider. He drove on. The car wound past houses set way back with windows hazed over in an aqua network blur. Once we reached the airport road the distance between houses lengthened. He gunned the motor and barreled down the black river of pavement, windows wide open on both sides.

"Thought you could use a little air," he said. "Clear your head."

I wanted to believe him. "I'm okay now."

"I wanna show you something."

"Your sister's waiting on me."

"I don't think so. She's at school, wrestling meet or softball conditioning, something."

"You can take me there then."

"Maybe later. You're real down. I can tell. Where I'm taking you is awesome. Big time awesome." He was too old to be talking like Rey.

"Mama'll be upset when I don't call."

"Your mama has bigger problems than where you are right now."

About then my heart started ticking as loudly as the alligator's belly in Peter Pan, Jasmine's latest favorite book. I wished I had insisted Rachel tell me what TJ had done to make her so upset. I thought about all the movies I'd seen with people throwing themselves out of moving cars. But when my fingers felt for the door handle, the darkness sped past the open window too fast for me to even guess where there was an open stretch of field and softer ground. He turned down the radio, though it was already mostly a bass drumbeat echo of my heart.

"All week long," he said. "I work in the woods. West Virginia. I stay up in the mountains with the crew at the lumber camp. Guys from all over, no women. You knew that." He slowed for the intersection even though it was deserted. "Meeka?"

I didn't get what he was gabbling on about, but I got the command in his voice. "Yeah, Rachel told me."

"We sleep in bunks, twenty in room, eat mashed this and mashed that, piss off the back porch, ruin our health. Endless card games at night, movies once a week. Like prison, except guys come and go, quit when they can't take it anymore. I listen to those jerk-offs talking trash day after day. Makes you yearn for something different, something finer." He drummed the steering wheel with one hand in between slapping the dashboard for emphasis. "Do you have any idea what I'm talking about, Miss Meeka?"

"I guess."

"Girl, you gotta pay attention. People who get ahead in this world pay attention. They don't miss a thing."

He had that right. If I'd been paying attention, I would of known about the creek being evil, I would of stopped Henry from going in, I wouldn't of been out walking at night, I wouldn't be here riding with TJ to God-knows-where.

"Anybody there?" He was yelling over the motor in high gear. The wind blasted through the car.

"Yeah, I'm here. Tired, that's all. Can you just take me home?" The words were blown out the window the minute I spoke them.

"Nothing going on at your house. You wanted fresh air, right? You left outta there so you could breathe, right?" He only waited a half second for me to answer. "I understand, Miss Meeka, I know exactly how you feeling."

I thought about our house, the voices spilling out of the downstairs, filling up the stairwell, the upstairs hallway, and how even my room no longer felt the same with the empty cot. I didn't think anyone could know how I was feeling, and certainly not TJ who only had the one stepbrother, one he'd rather not claim.

"Where I'm taking you is gonna make you feel better. Trust me."

I wished I could.

When he finally slowed the rattletrap Mercury and pulled off the road, I had no idea where we were. I'd lost track with all the twists and turns. The car bumped along a sandy lane, following double tire tracks. Right through the middle of a hay field, it seemed. When an opening appeared on the left, he made a wide circle with the steering wheel and swung into what looked like a dirt parking lot. Logs marked the spaces and several tall poles with wide-brimmed lights circled the sandy rectangle. All but one of the bulbs were out. On the eastern edge of the lot was a dark brown sign with painted white lettering, unreadable from the car in the dark. I could barely make out a shape on the sign, a carved outline of the state of Virginia.

"This is not your mama's duplex," I said.

"Damn right. This is way better. Come on."

He yanked the keys out the ignition and was halfway across the empty lot before I decided, no matter what he had in mind, it was safer with him than all by myself out in the middle of nowhere. I hurried along behind him, my one bare foot cold in the sand, the other slipping and sliding despite the single flip-flop. By the time I caught up, he was waiting by a second brown sign. He handed me the lost flip-flop.

"Where d'you find—"

"I don't like bullies much," he said. "I get enough of that all week in the woods."

"You saw? And you didn't stop them?"

" Jeezus, girl. Stop whining like a baby. You were doing fine on your own."

He tapped the sign with his finger. Wildlife Sanctuary, it read along the top, in the same carved letters. A map, covered by clear plastic, showed several creeks with roots coming off their edges like little snakes, all dead ends. The smaller creeks all led into one fatter blue line. Eight or nine straight lines of white dashes ran out like spokes of a wheel to pictures of birds and animals, pinned under the yellowed plastic. I recognized most of them, the bald eagle, the osprey, the chipmunk, the sea otter.

"It's not too far now," he said and grabbed my hand.

While we walked side by side in the ridges made by the tire tracks, a hump of grass between them, he talked about the drive to West Virginia, the way the flat marsh gave way to soy fields, the fields to hillsides of grapevines and orchards, the vineyards to scrub oak and skyscraper pines. He talked about his high school friends who were fighting overseas, a girl he'd dated who'd saved a whole school bus from a suicide bomber by decoding one radio message.

"HiTop never understood he had options. He's smart, but he has no imagination. He couldn't see himself anywhere but here. And now he's not even here, he's in a cellblock with a window two inches square. He can't even see the sky." TJ's arm swung up and he stopped walking. "D'you see that?"

"What?"

"Meteor shower."

I only had a vague idea what that was. In the corner of my eye I saw the afterglow of a sparkle. I'd missed it, whatever it was, but the hint of what it had been lingered like a camera flash.

"It's not dangerous," he continued. "Scientists study the patterns and predict when they're coming. The hour, not the minute. When asteroids break apart, they send icy particles through the edge of the atmosphere. Sometimes they come from outside our solar system, light years away."

I knew light years. Henry Lewis had read tons about light years. They were interesting. The fact that something happened weeks or years before and you couldn't see it until it traveled through time to where you were, give or take a few million miles of space. It was like discovering you had a hidden talent or that someone you thought didn't like you actually did like you. I started to choke up. TJ sounded just like my brother.

"Henry Lewis knew all that stuff. I wish I'd paid more attention."

"It's never too late. Human brains are sponges. Every day, every minute we learn from little things, without even realizing we're learning." TJ swung my arm with his, linked across the sandy roadbed. "But I'm worried about Rachel. She's off track. I don't want her to make the same mistakes as HiTop."

"She doesn't touch drugs."

"I mean the imagination part. You and she gotta help each other. Do like your brother and think about going places, discovering new stuff, making new friends."

He was pulling me along the tire tracks, almost jogging. Sand spray flew off our heels. The wind brushed past us the way it did on the Whirl-a-Gig at the county fair, perfumed with the scent of excitement.

"Is that what you'all argued about when school started?"

"About that guy she's hanging with."

"Willie Sparks?"

"Yeah. He's bad news."

"She likes that he has a car."

"Big deal. If she stays with him, she'll be riding around in that same car twenty years from now. Two black eyes and a backseat full of babies."

"How d'you know that?"

"I seen lots of guys like him. Big talkers. They're always sneaking around, trying to get something for nothing. Why doesn't he take her out to the movies and dancing?" He didn't wait for me to answer. "He likes bossing her, that's why. He's a loser."

"He spends money on her all the time."

"So do pimps."

It took me a minute to choke back my surprise. "She would tell me if they were . . . you know."

"Miss Meeka, you are too good to be true."

I hit his arm with my fist. The idea of Rachel and Willie . . . Rachel wouldn't keep that big a secret from me. We were supposed to be best friends. "You're teasing."

"You're easy to tease."

"I'm not a little kid anymore."

"That's for sure. But you're too nice. You think everyone's like you. You're gonna get hurt, you don't watch out."

He tugged at my hand, pulling me closer. Before I knew what was happening, he leaned across and our faces were just millimeters apart. I waited, sure this was going to be a kiss, the kiss. I imagined the pressure of his lips on mine, long enough for a sweet aftertaste to linger, the shy smile, the way girls in movies smiled after a kiss, a real kiss, not the kind of brush in the dark when we played spin the bottle. But he didn't kiss me. When I opened my eyes, he was grinning.

"Careful, Miss Meeka, wolf's at the door. And you really don't want to let him in."

He sprinted down the lane, and I ran after him, overcome with the surprise of it, the wonder of being that close to another person, feeling safe, feeling happy, if only for those few seconds. I laughed out loud in the silent night, thinking that meteor showers were better than rainbows. They shot out of the dark and painted a gray world with brilliant light. They illuminated a new path. Knowing they existed even when you couldn't see them somehow made anything possible. Nothing had changed about Henry Lewis and yet there was something in that short time that convinced me there would be a future, a time when the pain and the shame would be less.

At the end of the ditched lane I caught up with TJ. He was lounging against a small dock made out of brand new boards. The dock hung over the creek, the same wavery thread of brown water like the creek below Creekside Drive, but smaller and quieter, without as much of a current. The boards had not faded yet to match the mud flats. It still smelled of sawdust. Beyond the railing the creek etched a broad bland scarf across the pale green marsh. The creek and the marsh were all tangled up in the night and each other, hard to tell which was which.

"I thought you'd never get here," he said, that same taunt in his voice.

"Listen, you're the one dragged me all the way down here. What's so awesome?"

He pointed up again. The black sky was speckled with so many stars I felt like I was seeing double.

"Over there," he said.

I blinked and when my eyes opened, a burst of light shattered one corner of the sky and made a long diagonal white flame across the black.

"That's another meteor shower? Looked more like a lightning bolt."

"That's a shooting star. Meteor showers are a whole hour or two of shooting stars. One after the other."

He lay down on the dock on his back and motioned for me to join him. He counted out loud, silent in between the slow chant of numbers. I started counting too. I wished he would kiss me here. I licked the corner of my lips where I could almost taste him. After three more streaks of light, I remembered Henry Lewis jabbering on about his latest science fair project. Scientists in California had discovered a new comet and he couldn't stop talking about it. Rachel and I had teased him about his head being in the stars. Well, he was up there now, that's for sure. He was watching the same shooting stars we were. I imagined a bridge between the dock and the sky, the images passing across time and space like rainbows did from one horizon to the other, the burst of the shooting star at his end and the fading tail of it at mine. Suddenly I wanted to remember every second of this, to explain it all to Mama. If anything could make her feel better, this would.

We counted twenty-three shooting stars, seconds apart, and then TJ sat up.

"I was right, wasn't I? You feel better."

I stayed on my back. I wasn't ready for it to end. Twenty-five shooting stars was a nice round number. "A few weeks ago Henry Lewis was studying a comet, one particular comet that only comes once every 700 years. Something like that. Scientists know how that comet started just like they know how the stars and planets formed. He said they can go back and back to what came before that, and before that. Way far back, before before. Back when no one knew the first thing. That must be God, don't you think?"

"I don't know about God. It would be good if He was really out there, but who can know that? Some things you just have to believe even without being able to explain them."

I liked that he didn't push me to debate, just let me think through what he'd said. "Like Henry Lewis going straight to heaven. I wish Mama would stop thinking about what happened in between."

"People think too much. We aren't supposed to understand every little thing. Like before before and beyond beyond. A human mind is too small to hold all that. It's too complicated. There are too many unknowns. What happened to your brother can't be explained. It just happened. Same thing with shooting stars. 'Least that's what I believe."

I wondered if he was trying to tell me that what happened to Henry Lewis would have happened no matter what Rey or Mrs. Lowell or I had done. Warnings and who dared who and who was brave didn't matter. It could be something in the before before that had sent us to walk the Jessup's dog and made the day hot and the water cold and the ramp slippery.

"TJ?"

"I'm still here."

"Do you miss your brother?"

"Sure. But HiTop was fifteen when he went away the first time. Except for messing around at home, throwing the football and talking trash, we didn't do much together. I miss Rachel more."

"Henry Lewis's only been gone two days and I miss him every second. Everything reminds me of something we talked about or a place we went together."

"You wouldn't want it any differently."

"It hurts."

"That just means it was real. You're lucky. Some people live their whole lives and never feel that way about anyone. Think of it as a gift. Better than a fancy car or a big dawg house."

"At least you get to see Rachel when you come home."

"Not enough lately. The West Virginia job's such good money, I'm saving a boatload, but I'm gone two or three weeks at a time. She's out with the creep when I am home. I'm having trouble keeping up with her. If I were closer, I could keep an eye on her. Her mother's in a bad way. I'm not sure if it started with my father dying or if it was something else."

"She uses crack, Rachel says."

He shook his head. "Maybe back when HiTop's dealer friends were coming around, but not now. I think she's sick from something else. Cancer maybe, and she's decided not to fight it. She won't talk about it."

"She's scaring Rachel."

"It's not that she doesn't love Rachel. She just doesn't have the energy to deal with one more teenager."

"If you came home more, we could count shooting stars more."

"Oh, no. This was a once-in-a-lifetime experience, to celebrate what a great scientist your brother was." He stood and shook the sand out of his hair. "Time for girls to be safe at home."

Of all the things I'd imagined might happen once I was in his car, the wildlife sanctuary was a complete surprise. I hadn't gotten to talk with Rachel. I hadn't figured out a way to bring my brother back. I hadn't been abducted by a truck full of boys who didn't know better. I hadn't been kissed. But when TJ took my hand halfway back, it was enough.

Chapter Ten

In the blackness of the curtained bedroom Celie jolted upright. She'd
been dreaming again. Her chest throbbed where she'd been breathing
hard, running down a hill that never seemed to end. The muscles in
her calves contracted. She felt the beginning of a charley horse in her
right leg. Even in the dark she could see the small brown head bob
against the smooth water. When she realized her hands were
clenching the sheets, she concentrated on making her fists relax.

A cool washcloth would have helped, but she didn't want to risk
waking Jake. He had shown up at dinnertime as if he'd never left, no
mention of the argument or the night before. She hadn't even seen
his suitcase and she wondered if he'd snuck it in the back way as part
of the pretense. Or if it was still in the car? The possibility still
tempting him.

They'd avoided each other and had eaten separately. If he woke
now, he would drill her about being awake. *Had she taken a pill?
Why had she drunk coffee so close to bedtime?* During the treatments
he'd been considerate, forgiving of her irregular sleeping habits. But
this new eagerness to solve what was bothering her seemed less
personal, as if it were one more thing to be scratched off his To Do
list. According to her Middleton friends, not all husbands were that
attentive to their wives and she should appreciate his concern.

All the anxiety of last year washed over her, a tornado of anguish
that circled around in ambush. She held her breath and willed her
heart to slow down. As she settled back on the pillow, she wondered
if Mary Breeden lay awake too, fighting her own wild heartbeat and
unsteady lungs. She had to be struggling to stay sane against the
craziness at this unexpected twist in her life. When you gave birth,
you had no idea how quickly things could change. No one warned
you.

She thought back to the first delivery room moment when the
doctor said it was a boy. Jake had grinned as if he'd produced
Thomas single-handedly, while she was simply relieved that she
wouldn't have to try so hard the next time, that she'd done what
she'd set out to do, have a boy first. Why, she wondered for the
zillionth time, had it taken her months to love Thomas when Rory
had been so immediately hers? She'd been shocked at her first son's
greediness for all of her time and energy, the drain his constant
hunger put on her, his refusal to fall asleep without her presence. As
a child he'd needed her in a way Rory never had. Thomas insisted on

100

sitting next to her. He had to draw her the best picture, buy her the best birthday present, kiss her hello first, and give her the last hug good-bye. Her relationship with her second son had been so natural and easy when being Thomas's mother had been so exhausting.

What if Mary had felt the same way about her son? In the midst of the ache there might be a twinge of guilt that by that first misstep, in not loving him enough, she had somehow contributed to his death. Celie felt another wash of relief that her boys were grown and out of the dangerous part of childhood.

Jake's hand wriggled free of the covers and found her shoulder. "Can't sleep?"

"No." She waited for the questions, amazed at how easily he slipped back into the routine.

"Want to talk?"

"I'm going to try to go back to sleep." Even if she wanted to tell him, she wasn't sure she could articulate what was bothering her because she didn't understand it herself. It was too mixed-up. All of her imaginings had nothing to do with the real Henry Lewis. She didn't know if she'd ever seen him before, ever passed him on the sidewalk. He could have been a horrid bully or a smart-mouthed jerk. He could have been a boy who teased dogs or kicked kittens. Still her grief was hard and clear, as fragile as the most expensive crystal vase. Henry Lewis Breeden was one mother's son and therefore he was her son. It was that simple. At least it was that simple in the middle of the night.

Jake was already snoring.

In the morning it had rained. The cold ground leaked great swathes of steam in the already too warm sun. Sunlight pulsed through the panes and made the house stuffy. On her way to the kitchen she opened windows and paused at each one to breathe in the damp fresh air. She was debating whether to take her breakfast out to the front porch when Jake came and stood shoulder to shoulder by the kitchen windows where she was counting the fishermen hauling in crab pots.

"You're up early," he said.

"The proverbial early bird."

"But you were awake part of last night, weren't you? Or was I dreaming?"

She stepped sideways, away from the heat of his arm against hers, and bent to find the dishwashing soap. She didn't trust herself and after the other night, she didn't trust him.

"You forgot your sleeping pill?"

"I'm trying not to take it every night."

"But if it guarantees you'll sleep, it seems to me—"

"Jake, stop."

When she spun away from him, he began gathering his lunch paraphernalia. Such a creature of habit, she thought, the routine of saving ingrained in him even though they had plenty of money. He still touted the economies of packing lunch to Thomas and Rory, though they'd been independent for years, 'off the payroll' as he liked to say.

"It's just with that boy drowning and all—"

"Jake."

"Okay, okay."

He worked silently. At the opposite counter with her back to him she sliced strawberries for her cereal.

"If you want to talk," she said, "maybe we should talk about what happened yesterday."

"I was out of line. I thought you knew."

She couldn't think fast enough. His concession was too pat and it didn't solve the problem.

"So big plans today?" he said, though they both recognized he was changing the subject to avoid an argument.

She forced herself to reply. "I have those library books to return. And I might tackle the linen closet."

"Painting?" There was that same incredulous tone from the other night.

She ignored it. "No. Just sorting out the old towels and the cleaning supplies. You know how we junked that stuff in there when we first bought the cottage. It's a mess."

Although he was listening, she knew he was preoccupied organizing his own day. That, at least, was the old Jake, single-minded, efficient, goal-oriented. The aftereffects of cancer or even the threat of separation didn't figure into his schedule. If it wasn't actually on the agenda, it shouldn't usurp any mental energy. Even as she let it pass, she recognized how dysfunctional this was, this skating around the issue, tamping their emotions to avoid any display or outburst. Thin ice, she thought, and it struck her as exactly right, the danger hidden, but everywhere.

After she added cream to her coffee, she took the tray out to the porch. She couldn't help the feeling of relief when he didn't follow. It hadn't always been this way. When Rory went off to college, the empty nest had encouraged a new closeness. It gave them both the chance to start over, in a way. Here was this person she'd lived with for twenty-five years, but as a provider, a father, a business partner.

In the absence of all those duties, who was he really? Did he like museums? Jazz? Touring wildlife preserves? They had money and time to try new things, and it was almost like dating again, exciting and a little bit scary. She had to ask more and give him space to experiment. She had to adapt to his reactions. And he had to do the same for her. These were the years they'd become serious art collectors, galleries being something they discovered they both enjoyed. They'd gone to Italy, Turkey, Czechoslovakia, and Spain. If the cancer hadn't torpedoed the whole thing, she wondered if they would have continued in that happy renaissance until they were rocking together on the porch with their pacemakers.

"Celie," he called from inside. "I'm off. I should be back about six." He didn't wait for her to answer.

As she sipped her coffee and tried not to dwell on what they'd lost, the dots that were the local fishing boats drifted along the dark blue slate of the river's unruffled surface. Over the marsh a pair of osprey fussed at each other before they settled onto the nesting platform at the creek opening. Mornings on the river you almost forgot how fiercely the wind could blow up into a storm from nothing.

She re-considered for the umpteenth time her idea to walk the food down to the Breedens. She used to walk to the library in ten minutes. Before the chemotherapy. Still, she needed to return the books and the Linden Street apartments were on the way. But the books and the ham and the cookies might be too much to carry. The more she debated, the more awkward she felt. Yesterday while the ham was cooking, she'd told herself it was only the usual act of neighborly kindness. Southerners did that so well, a contribution to the grieving family. When the word *survivors* stuck in her brain, the guilt rose up and made her stomach flip. She had to work hard to find the thread of her previous thought.

Over the years whenever she delivered a casserole or a cake, she found herself giving silent thanks that the tragedy had not struck her own family. She was lucky, blessed, whatever. But then the shame of such a selfish feeling would crash around her, and she would feel worse than ever. The randomness of tragedy ought not to make one celebrate the missed bolt of lightning, a kind of sick gratitude that it was someone else who had to endure the suffering.

With the Breedens it was more awkward than that. In spite of walking the children home for the police, they weren't friends. Meeka had made that clear. Not only did Celie not know the family until now—although they lived barely four blocks apart—she existed in a very different world. Well-off with two good salaries in the household, she'd never had to leave her children without a sitter. She couldn't imagine having to face that dilemma. The safety of your children was not simply one spending choice out of the many a mother made. It was horrible to think for some mothers it was a matter of having the money to spend. Necessities were food and rent. Once your child was a teenager, you could reallocate money for clothes or school supplies, but when they were dependent, day care was a basic. It was about keeping your children safe.

Especially after last night's confrontation with Meeka, the last thing Celie wanted was to arrive in her shiny Volvo station wagon, her white lady's imported car, and be seen as an interfering do-gooder. The food was a simple acknowledgement of their sorrow, that's all. She didn't want it to be misinterpreted as any kind of judgment about Mary Breeden's competence as a mother or her lifestyle. Still, worrying about Meeka and her mother was the closest Celie had come to getting outside of herself in a long while. She needed to do this.

With one hand she shielded her eyes and watched the last skiff, done for the day, plow up the creek. A lone crab pot bounced against the gunwale. Temporarily out of service, it probably needed mending. As the low boat coasted over the spot where Henry Lewis had disappeared, she set the coffee cup down so hard it slurped coffee over the rim. A pale brown puddle spread across the tray. She stared at the stain.

What made her think she knew anything at all about the Breedens? She could have the whole thing wrong. Mary Breeden might have thousands of dollars in the bank and a Volvo of her own. Without knowing their circumstances, Celie had pieced together a story from her own subconscious, to serve some selfish need to distinguish herself. She only sensed there was no father in the picture. Why jump to that conclusion except that all her life she'd read in her newspapers and magazines that black fathers didn't stick around? Her own experience with court mediation was limited since those families were already in trouble. And even as she admitted the blunt reality that it was poverty, not race, that drove fathers away, she recognized how much her own childhood in white suburbia defined her assumptions.

The only real facts she had were all mixed up in yesterday's barrage. The man who had comforted Henry Lewis's mother had not volunteered to walk the children home. Nor had they gone to him for solace, naturally or otherwise. There was another explanation for what had happened. More than one, in fact. He could be a parishioner from church, a brother, an unemployed boyfriend who hit her, who disliked the children. He could be a work colleague with no connection at all to Henry Lewis. She had assumed the children were siblings, but she'd been wrong about that. The one thing she was sure of was that Mary would be feeling guilty. Working mothers laid their own blame.

She carried the breakfast tray back inside. Standing in her newly renovated kitchen with her stunning view of the river, she felt her privilege like the weight of the world. She had all this and she was alive, the cancer beaten back beyond the castle walls.

But that wasn't the real explanation for her discomfort. It was possible in that stark minute when she saw his head only as an unidentified brown spot, before she knew it was a boy, that he may have looked across the water and seen her looking back. He may have thought, *oh, good, there's an adult who will help me.* Without any thought for whether he knew her or whether she was black or white. And then he sank into that water, not understanding why he couldn't move his arms and legs, waiting and wondering why she didn't come.

The unease that made her question her intentions was grounded somewhere else, deeper than her not knowing the Breedens as neighbors. Deeper than her failure to save Henry Lewis. It had to do with how close death had been that afternoon. To her. It wasn't the collective grief for your neighbor's loss. This was different. Losing Henry Lewis was personal. She had lost something too.

Eyeing the ham in its shiny aluminum pan, slick with melted brown sugar, her stomach clenched. Unsteady all of a sudden, she dodged the dog, asleep on a stripe of sunny carpet, and dashed for the bathroom. She made it just in time. With her eyes still closed, she flushed and pulled herself up by hanging onto the edge of the sink. She ran cold water on the washcloth and held it to her face. After she'd brushed her teeth, she sat on the closed toilet lid for several minutes to be sure things were settling in her stomach.

And there, staring her down, were the one milligram pills in their little plastic bottle, a blatant advertisement for instant oblivion. She shook the bottle lightly like a rattle and let it rest sideways on one palm. She guessed at the number remaining. It was tempting. A chill ran up through the bottoms of her feet as she called back the feeling of yesterday's fully clothed body nestled under the bedcovers. Warm. Safe. Unhealthy.

The bottle popped when she set it down, like a baby's burp. The lid tipped and slid onto the counter. She looked away.

After she sluiced more water across her hands and face, she toweled dry. She kept her eyes focused on the mirror self. Vague

105

beginnings of a tan showed on her forehead and cheeks. Two sunny afternoons in the garden and she looked less sickly, more like her old self. She wanted it to be true. Maybe she would just take a short nap this morning to clear her head. She'd wake up at lunchtime, fully rested, the jumble of last night's wakefulness and bad dreams gone. She'd be primed and ready for the walk to the library by way of the Breedens and the promised warmth of the afternoon. She used nail clippers to slice the pill in half. With a huge gulp of water, she swallowed it and buried the other half in the bathroom trashcan. But when she went to close the container, she changed her mind. She dug through the trash and found the discarded half and put it back in with the others. Then she pushed the whole container to the very back of the shelf.

When Jake telephoned, she was sound asleep. The tune of the ring tone drifted into her consciousness like a hawk riding a header, barely visible above her head. It took her eight repeats to free herself from the sheets and answer the damn thing.

"Sorry to disturb you," he said. "I didn't mean to bring you in from outside."

She didn't correct him, and the lie seemed to stare back at her like a disbelieving juror. The silence lengthened.

"Celie?"

"What's up?"

"Just checking in. Driving in I heard on the news that they hadn't found that boy yet. Are the rescue people over there bothering you?"

"No." The slow motion feeling from her deep sleep lingered. She tugged the curtain pull. Below the bedroom window there were no patrol boats and no yellow vests. "Did the newscaster say where they were searching?"

"I don't remember. But if they're not there, at least they've left you alone."

That was absurd. Rescue workers would go where they had to go to do their job. It was not a tea party where they could choose to avoid some crotchety old lady who objected to uninvited guests. But it sent her brain whirring downstream. Henry Lewis's barefoot body, heavy with that brown water, bumped along the muddy bottom, pulled by the tide, away and away. Two days already. They might never find him.

"Celie? You there?"

"Where else would I be?"

He didn't reply right away and she was forming an apology when he finally spoke. "Sounds like you need a nap."

She laughed, the humor of it almost cartoonlike, the one so unaware of the other.

"Jeez, it's good to hear you laugh, sweetie. Why don't you get some gas for the boat, make a picnic, and we'll eat out on the water tonight? The fuel containers are marked in the garage. Just fill them halfway or you won't be able to lift them. I'll leave the office about three so we don't miss the sunset."

She choked out a good-bye and put the phone down on the dresser like a piece of contaminated rock from outer space. She didn't want him to be sweet. If he was sweet, how would she tell him that she couldn't go out in the boat? She didn't want to fly across the water as if everything were fine and Henry Lewis wasn't down there somewhere, maybe right below the boat, drifting, waiting to be found.

The clock radio blipped to ten-fifteen. She'd been asleep barely an hour. The pictures of family on her dresser glowed. Rory eked out his signature sheepish grin, as if he knew he was stealing time from his next great idea. Thomas's long arms embraced his wife on one side and his mother on the other. Now that both boys were married she needed to add a frame with Lila. She was flush with family. And down the street Mary Breeden and Meeka were having to learn how to do without.

When the dog barked to go out, she was seated at the dining room table, composing a sympathy note to go with the food offering. After two ruined cards, she resorted to the pad for drafting. The most important thing was for Mary Breeden to know how brave Meeka had been to try and save her brother. Writing it down would avoid some of the awkwardness. Maxy barked again while Celie dithered over whether to let him out through the living room so that she didn't have to see the old dock and the creek.

Ridiculous woman, she whispered to herself as she led him through the kitchen. With his usual detachment, though slower than usual, he maneuvered down the back steps and surveyed the yard before he ambled across to the shed and disappeared. Without looking down the driveway in the direction of the creek she stood at the back door with the screen open and let the sun soak in. It must be seventy-five degrees out here. Hot for a spring morning. She could edge the iris bed by the garage with the flat-bladed thingie and not get her knees muddy. She'd work an hour, then shower and visit the Breedens.

Just as she was about to step inside to grab her gardening gloves, she noticed movement on the road above the marina ramp. She blinked and focused. Meeka again? How many times would that afternoon repeat itself in her mind? The girl was really there. It was not a figment of her imagination.

Meeka shifted from foot to foot just the other side of a sparkling new chain that ran across the top of the old ramp. The chain was a surprise. That Richard Widener would rush right out after the drowning and install a chain was like a slap in the face to the Breedens. It was hard to reconcile with the man who had worked so diligently from the rowboat to find the boy. She had a sickening thought. What if Richard had stopped her from going in after Henry Lewis because he was worried about a lawsuit? Unknown neighbors with big city lawyer friends might be more of a risk than a single mother with a passel of children.

Cautious Richard, who had prevented her from jumping in, must have gone straight to the hardware store the next morning, his shoulders still aching from the rowboat. Or even more sickening, he might have gone first to his own lawyer. It appalled her, the idea that lawyers and lawsuits were already part of the language of Henry Lewis's life. Of his death, to be more correct.

She held her breath, but Meeka didn't move past the chain. She spread both hands above her forehead to offset the glare. For a long time she stood like that, her face to the water and the dock. It was still morning. The children must have stayed home from school a second day. But who let Meeka wander off by herself again? Or did they know she was here?

Grabbing one of the baseball caps from her chemo stack, Celie followed the fence between the cottage and George's yard as quickly as she dared to the lower part of driveway. From there the hill on Stonegate Road rose at a steep angle. She was moving more slowly, the beginning of a familiar ache in her chest. She'd never mastered this hill on her bicycle, even before the cancer. She gazed off in both directions to make it seem as if she was out for a random walk, not on a mission. She wished she'd thought to put Maxy on his leash. Most children liked dogs. It would be something neutral to talk about.

When she turned the corner at the top of the hill and started down Creekside, Maxy nosed out of the overgrown hedge of one of the rental houses. She'd forgotten he was out. Tail wagging, he crossed the road to Meeka as if they were old friends. Celie slowed as she watched. With the dog snuffling at her bare ankles, the girl crouched and stroked his back.

Celie stopped ten feet from them. "He loves attention."

Meeka jolted up. Her face was a wrangle of emotions, none of them pleasure.

"I won't say a thing to anyone," Celie said.

"I'm not doing anything wrong."

"No, no, it's natural to want to go back to where you all were last together."

"I was just walking." Her tone was surly.

"Me too."

Maxy yipped and put both paws on Meeka's blue-jeaned leg. Celie drew a dog biscuit from her pocket, a long standing habit to carry them there. She held it out to the girl. With her palm open, Meeka let Maxy lick at it until he worked it into his mouth.

"No school today?"

Meeka gave her that teenager's look of total incredulity that meant adults were totally lame. "My mother can't be left alone."

"Of course."

"Ashante came home for lunch."

"I'm sorry. I wasn't prying. You don't need to explain to me." Celie struggled to think of a neutral subject. She understood a teenager's aversion to sharing. "His name is Maxwell. Maxy, my kids call him. He's a mutt. A little bit Labrador and a lot dachshund."

"Looks like a hot dog dog."

"Exactly. That's an American nickname for dachshunds. Maxy's an old man actually, fifteen. He didn't always have those white hairs."

When Celie bent down to point out his aging physique, Meeka knelt too and let him burrow his nose into her lap. Celie felt in her pocket for another biscuit.

"He's a terrible flirt," she said. "Angling for another treat."

"Mama says we can have a dog when I get a job."

"What kind of job are you looking for?"

"Anything regular. Minding kids doesn't count. It has to be every week or it won't pay for dog food." She let Maxy lick her fingers. "A little dog like this can't eat much."

"One cup in the morning and one at night. And we give him a little cottage cheese or egg in his dinner to keep his coat shiny."

"I could do that. Wal-Mart sells a huge bag of dog food for thirteen dollars. 60 servings, it's printed on the side. I figured it out. If I worked three or four hours a week for six dollars an hour—that's what my aunt Ruthie says they pay kitchen aides at the nursing home—I'd have enough for a collar, food, treats, and a little bit saved for shots. It's twenty for a dog tag and the county won't give you one unless the dog has a rabies shot. Goodwill sells dog beds."

"You've been thinking about this for a while."

"Henry Lewis loves the Jessup's dog and it's so old it can't even fetch a stick."

Meeka stopped rubbing Maxy's ears and glanced down the street. It took all Celie's willpower not to reach over and touch the girl's cheeks where the tears spilled out.

"I keep thinking he'll be back," Meeka said.

"I do the same thing."

Meeka's glare was instantaneous. Celie flushed under her scrutiny. She felt the anger, the confusion, the guilt overtake everything. She wished she knew the girl well enough to hug her. She seemed so alone.

"I don't know how to swim." Meeka pressed one cheek after the other against her sleeve.

"The creek's too deep. And too cold this time of year. It was an accident."

"But I was watching them. I shouldn't of let them go near the water. I know Henry Lewis can't really swim, no matter what he says." Meeka was patting the dog in a steady but distracted way while she glared down at the creek. "That water's greedy. Why d'it want him anyway? There's no point taking a boy like that, who can't hardly take care of himself. He wasn't hurting anything."

"It could have been anyone."

"That water is evil. Little kids can't ever win against that kind of evil."

"It's just water. Knowing more about swimming will help you understand."

"It didn't help you save him."

There it was, the hard truth. Celie wished she could tell Meeka that grownups couldn't always change things, that she felt more guilty than Meeka could ever know, but Jake's cautionary voice sounded in her head. *They weren't on our property,* he had asked right off the bat. And in spite of how badly she felt, she knew that what she'd said to Meeka was true, there wasn't always someone to blame.

Meeka didn't wait for her to finish. "Better to stay away from water altogether. I'm never going to swim. Not ever."

"That's certainly your choice." Celie thought for a minute and chose the words carefully. "But knowing more about it, about anything, helps a person make decisions. The same way you know more about taking care of a dog since you investigated and asked questions."

"It doesn't change the fact that we can't have a dog."

"It will once you find a job."

"Who's going to hire me now? I can't even take care of my own brother. No one will ever ask me to watch kids again." She pushed Maxy away and stood up.

And Celie, who could think of a million reasons why Meeka was wrong, just let her walk away because in the end none of it mattered. Celie knew how to swim and she hadn't been able to save Henry Lewis either.

"Hey," Jake's cheerful voice boomed out of the cell phone. "Listen, there's a mess here at the office with the computer system and I can't leave when I thought. Sorry I couldn't call before now. Did you make the picnic already?"

"I haven't had a chance," Celie said.

"Good. Just skip it. I'll stop and get a pizza. I hope you abandoned that closet and found something to do outside on this beautiful day."

"I've been cooking stuff for the Breedens." She worked at keeping her voice steady.

"The Breedens?"

"Henry Lewis's family. Barry Morgan says the memorial service will be Monday whether they find him or not."

"I don't think you should get involved."

"You already told me that. I'm just going to take the ham down there and leave it."

"Did you call the insurance company about a counselor?"

"On my list." She was being truthful.

"Okay, gotta run. Get some sun. Sorry we can't do the boat ride tonight."

He hung up before she had a chance to tell him the last thing she wanted was to be out on the river.

With the ham in its throw-away pan, cradled against her ribs, crinkling with each step and the cookie plate in a plastic grocery store bag with the library books underneath knocking against her leg, she followed the curb past the houses that backed up to the river. It was not the route she'd taken Tuesday with the Breeden children, but it was one of her favorite walks. Shade from the old oaks blanketed the wide street in cool grays and blues. Glints of sunlight dappled the road.

This morning everything seemed awry, a bit too perfect, as if someone had painted the scene from memory and she was observing the painting instead of the reality. It usually gave her a sense of peace, but today with the stilted perfection it jarred. The bobbing heads of the daffodils were too cheery. The curtains in every window, drawn shut, were too neat. The river was too flat, not a white cap or a ripple. It was all fake, a Stepford movie set. Perspiring and chilled at the same time, she kept looking over her shoulder, not willing to trust the apparent brightness of the stage set.

Out of breath at the corner she stopped and let the weight of the pan and the bag rest on the trunk of a parked car. Although she checked the windows of both houses on that side of the street for an owner who might complain, no one pounded on the glass or reprimanded her. When a car whizzed out of the alley, she heard herself bleat in surprise. Her watch said she'd left home fifteen minutes ago, a long time to cover two blocks. In just a year, the doctor had said, her energy level would return to normal. It was not the encouragement she wanted. She eased the things off the trunk and trudged on.

Outside the Linden Street apartments a string of cars formed a three-sided barricade around the front yard of the Breeden's townhouse. Two nondescript sedans that looked like they'd lost the fight were parked with grills in, along with three shinier cars, all black. The lone red one, in full tattooed decoration showcasing years of repairs, flanked the others, a last minute arrival. She paused by the street and considered coming back another time.

Without the children in tow, she could make a longer appraisal. The townhouses still looked new, though someone somewhere in the melee of the last two days had said they were two years old. She couldn't remember who. The plantings under the gutters were threadbare, a good idea with no follow-up. Clay leaked through the mulch in wavy tan bulges, and the bushes tilted, as if they couldn't quite get comfortable and were on the verge of deciding to depart. Insufficient fertilizer, her mother's voice lectured in Celie's head. New grass seed had been planted recently, but stingily, over wide stretches of bare dirt, the straw scattered in patches like acne. The developer had shorted the landscaping budget. That was obvious.

The Breeden's faded blue van sat in the side parking lot, its tinted windows like guilty hooded eyes. She was relieved that the children's mother was home with them. For whatever reason—Celie hoped it was an understanding employer—Mary hadn't had to go back to work. Celie could say what she'd come to say and not have her message reinterpreted by relatives.

From the window beside the front door a familiar pixie face with bright eyes peeked out from behind the curtain, but immediately disappeared. Liné. Celie swiveled to see if Jasmine manned the other window. Little girls were perpetually curious. They would be intrigued by the stream of strangers, the withdrawal of their older sister's attention, the whispered assurances between their mother and other adult relatives, the intrusion of unfamiliar faces and voices, the unsettled feel of their home without Henry Lewis. They were both too young to understand that his absence was permanent.

When Celie stepped up to the front door and knocked, the bag with the library books and the cookies rocked against the door making a second and third echo of her knock. There was a long moment on the concrete stoop while she examined the painted white door, how it glistened above the handle, but dwindled to a scuffed dingy portion nearer the bottom. The sugary smell of the ham enveloped her like new gardenias. On the other side of the hollow door voices and the scrape of chairs on bare wood filtered through church music. A television perhaps, or a radio. She could envision the interior space: the mismatched chairs, a chipped Formica table, mourning relatives lined up on a sunken couch, dishes stacked in the sink, odd coffee cups on end tables, and the blurred cadence of the forgotten TV evangelist in the background. She shook her head to chase the images away. She was doing it again, jumping to conclusions.

This visit was a mistake. She shouldn't have come so soon. Mary Breeden didn't want to talk to a strange woman, especially not the last person to see her son alive. And Meeka would not want another reminder of the disaster. Maxy aside, they were not friends. Cookies and sugar-coated ham were the wrong things to bring. She should have called first. Maybe Henry Lewis's mother had diabetes. In one of the hospital health magazines Celie had read while waiting for her chemo infusion, she'd learned there was a higher incidence of diabetes in African-Americans. Why had she ever thought the Breedens would welcome her? An oddly tongue-tied white woman, breathless and stuttering, who'd been too late to save Henry Lewis.

She was just about to turn away when a plump woman in an orange warm-up suit answered the door. Her eyes strayed to the things in Celie's hands, but immediately moved back to her face as if embarrassed for her.

"Hello?" the woman raised her eyebrows, a question without words, but not unkindly.

"I'm Celie Lowell. I . . . the children . . . we met Tuesday. I walked them home."

"Please come in."

Once the door shut behind her, the room fell back into solemn gloom. Voices of people from the dim corners halted while the broadcast minister's voice rose over the show choir on the television. She breathed in the close air, the overwhelming helplessness, the shock of unexpected tragedy. Jake was right. She shouldn't have come. She fought back the panic.

"I brought a ham . . . for Mary Breeden." That wasn't what she'd planned to say. "I figured she'd have lots of people to feed."

"That's so kind," the woman in the warm-up suit murmured.

"And cookies . . . for the children. Sometimes they don't like all that heavy food."

When the woman didn't reply, Celie stumbled ahead. "Is Tomeeka here?"

Liné nodded from the background, her face half-hidden, her arm curled about the curtain. Her feet were bare, her toenails a hot pink.

"Mee," she shrieked and all the heads in the gloom turned away from Celie to look at the little girl. "Mee-ka. The white lady's back."

"Liné," the woman who let her in said sharply. "That's enough. Too much, too loud. Excuse my daughter please, Ms. Lowell. I'm Ruth Carter, Mary's sister." She extended a hand, but in the next instant of recognition at the impossibility, she withdrew it. Celie's hands were full. Ruth Carter called up the stairwell. "Meeka, honey, come on down. Ms. Lowell's here to see you."

Without waiting for Meeka to appear, Ruth Carter motioned toward the arched opening into the kitchen. It was just as Celie had imagined it. Seven or eight pairs of eyes from chairs along the living room wall followed her progress toward the kitchen. The woman who had sobbed into her steering wheel stayed seated, next to the same younger fellow from yesterday, casually dressed again in cargo shorts and a sleeveless T-shirt, but with a long sleeve dress shirt unbuttoned and hanging open.

Ruth spoke again. "Mary, this lady brought some food." She put a hand on her sister's shoulder. "Honey?"

Mary's head swung in slow motion to face Ruth and Celie. But her eyes didn't focus and she didn't stand, merely faced in the direction of the doorway between the two rooms, like a blind person on cue. Celie hesitated, the ham so heavy she was afraid she would drop it any minute. Yet she felt reluctant to step fully into the kitchen where it was clear that Henry Lewis's mother was hiding.

"Here," the young man leaped up. "Let me help."

"Thank you. I live down the street, past the corner, by the . . . at the end of Stonegate. I don't want to intrude."

When she realized she was babbling, she stopped herself. He wasn't as young as she'd thought. The muscles were misleading. Late thirties, Mary Breeden's age, she guessed.

"No problem," the man said. "I'm Ashante Green. Friend of the family." He jiggled the pan in Celie's hands as a reminder, and she let go. With his elbow he cleared a spot on the counter among the other plates and dishes of food covered in plastic and foil. He peeled back the plastic bag, lifted the foil on the ham, and sniffed. "Rey's favorite."

"So Rey is your son?" Celie asked.

Hums erupted behind her from the mismatched chairs, a gospel chorus of mourners. Horrified at herself even as she thought it, she wished she could get past the stereotypes from her childhood. As a child everyone she knew lived in a Cape Cod with a picket fence, a father who worked in the city, and a mother who met the children at the front door after school. White families in white neighborhoods. Standing in Mary Breeden's kitchen, she felt out of place and naïve.

Ashante looked confused too. His lips parted as if he was on the verge of speaking again, but he didn't. Meeka saved them. Taller and thinner than Celie remembered from their conversations, the girl hesitated at the bottom of the stairs, then stepped across that corner of the living room to within inches of Celie. For a moment she thought Meeka was going to scream at her to get out. Instead the girl lowered her eyes and shuddered, the struggle to control her emotions even more obvious.

"You . . . came back," she said, her voice shirred and barely audible, no trace of the belligerence Celie had been expecting.

"I wanted to tell your mother how brave you were on Tuesday. I wanted to be sure she knew." Celie's back was to Mary, but she couldn't turn around to face her because the girl's eyes had locked on hers. "How hard you tried to save your brother."

She held out her hand and after the briefest consideration, Meeka took it. When Celie glanced over her shoulder, she saw Mary Breeden sit up straighter. Those dark eyes swam into focus, not on the stranger, but on her daughter. Ashante let his hand rest a minute on Mary's arm, a quiet signal of reassurance, before he reached out to relieve Celie of her other bag. Her first impression of his kindness from Tuesday was reaffirmed.

"Cookies. For the children," she said and squeezed Meeka's hand, but the girl didn't let go.

"Thank you," he finally spoke when no one else did.

"How is Rey?" She directed the question at Meeka.

Before she could answer, Ashante did. "He'll be fine. He's small for his age, but tough."

It flashed through Celie's mind that she wasn't so far off about the family history. Perhaps Rey and the two little girls were his children after all, but only half-siblings to Meeka as the oldest. She'd seen that often enough in mediation and when she'd volunteered in her sons' elementary school classes. Maybe Ashante and Mary were married, and Mary had kept her first husband's name because of Meeka and Henry Lewis. As the possibilities multiplied, it added to her confusion. There were too many variables. Her discomfort must be obvious to everyone.

Without thinking she squeezed the hand in hers again. When Meeka's eyes widened, Celie realized the girl had forgotten they were still connected.

"Rey's at school," Meeka murmured as she withdrew her hand.

"I'm glad to see you again." It took all of Celie's self-control to not mention their meeting early that morning.

Ashante was working at the counter rearrangement as if he couldn't think what else there was for them to discuss. Behind her in the curtained living room the chorus murmured to itself, or perhaps to the aunt who had answered the door. Celie didn't dare turn around to see because she was afraid all the eyes would be examining her, the outsider, the stranger who had appeared in their midst with her curious questions and awkwardness. Mary still hadn't spoken. Her eyes were unfocused, her lips parted, her shoulders slumped, her feet flat on the floor without any hint of life, her hands loose in her lap, as if the trance had been imposed by some otherworldly power. Her whole demeanor was so blank, so inexpressive, so clearly lost that Celie was reminded instantly of why she had come, one mother to another.

"Mrs. Breeden." She took a step closer, hearing the echo, wishing she'd said *Mary*, blank suddenly over what she'd been about to say. "I'd . . . I'd like to teach your children how to swim. All of them, I mean. But Meeka especially."

It came out unexpectedly. She had meant to wait until a third or fourth visit, until she and Mary knew each other better. The last thing the mother of a drowned child would want is to put her other children near water. But Mary only blinked and continued to stare past Celie's shoulder. When she turned to track Mary's gaze, Meeka's face reflected horror. She was backing up, almost out of the room. Ashante stepped away from the counter and lowered himself back in the chair next to Mary, as if any sudden motion would scare her into flight. He wrapped one arm around her shoulders and rocked her closer to him. The hint of a moan from her dwindled and died.

Celie scrambled to think how to explain herself, to fix what she'd started. "I'm so sorry about your son. I have a son too. Two sons. Thomas and Rory." That wasn't what she'd meant to say either.

116

"They're grown." She was instantly paralyzed over the inference that she had somehow managed to keep her own sons safe until adulthood. What a mess. This was more difficult than she had anticipated. "I know this isn't the right time, but someday, when you're ready, I'd like to give the children swimming lessons. One at a time, of course. In the river, not the creek. Where it's shallow by our beach. Their feet can touch there."

The words ran out of her mouth in double time. Meeka was making small choking sounds from the doorway. From the expression on Mary's face Celie might be talking Hungarian.

"Not right away," she continued. "Not until you're comfortable with it." She was making this worse. The words echoed in her head. The idea that a mother could ever be comfortable with her own child's drowning was ridiculous. "What I meant to say, what I came to tell you is . . . I wanted you to know how brave your daughter was, is. She's a natural swimmer."

Her face felt scorched, yet no one objected, no one covered her gaffe with platitudes or hurried her away. As the silence lengthened, Celie studied Mary's face for some hint that at least her sincerity had been conveyed. "She would learn easily." Had she said that already?

She imagined the two of them on the beach, Meeka kicking in the shallow water with her hands on the sand and Celie demonstrating the stiff leg of the scissors kick.

"I'm a good teacher."

The inference that she'd taught swimming lingered in the silence. It was an outright lie and she couldn't imagine why she'd phrased it that way. Of course when Rory and Thomas were babies, they'd paddled in her arms and she'd caught them as they jumped off the edge of the pool. But she hadn't given them formal lessons. They joined the swim team after private lessons at the swim club in Middleton. Privilege came from money, money from education, education from privilege; an exclusive cycle. Mary Breeden's children enjoyed none of those advantages.

It crossed Celie's mind that everyone in the room must be thinking the same thing. *Who is this scatter-brained woman?* The image of swimming might have sent Mary deeper into despair. Celie tried to make eye contact with Meeka, but the girl wouldn't look at her either. Disconnected from Meeka, the only one she halfway knew in the sea of strange faces, perspiration mixed with the odd flush of food odors, she felt like the girl who popped out of the cake. Everyone was looking at her, but no one quite believed she was real. She blurted out an apology, fumbled with the knob on the front door, and fled.

Back on the deserted street she realized how badly she'd botched the whole thing. They must think she was crazy. Certainly Meeka would, after this last scene on top of their midnight meeting and the ridiculous conversation about the dog. Half expecting a crowd on the porch, Celie glanced back at the apartment. The door was shut. The curtain was askew, but the little girls were gone. She was startled when Meeka's face stared out from the shadowed opening. And more startled that Meeka didn't look shocked. Or even angry. She looked curious.

Chapter Eleven

Whatever did the crazy lady want, barging in here and carrying on with all that mess about swimming lessons? She was truly and completely out of her head. And she was totally different from the way she'd been that first day and those other times at the creek. Why did I think she was bossy like the teachers? The woman here today was scared to death. Scared to come here, scared to be holding my hand, scared to see Mama.

"What you got going this afternoon, Mee?" Ashante asked while I was watching her stream down Stonegate.

"Is Mama going to work tomorrow?"

"We'll have to wait and see. I doubt it."He glanced back where Mary sat still as a painting, staring at nothing. "It's Friday, her boss said take all the time she needed. Nothing at the office that couldn't wait."

"Should I keep the girls from bothering her?"

"Probably better to keep to the regular routine. For them and for her." He leaned one shoulder against the wall. "She's worried about you."

"No, she's not." I didn't say, *she hates me*, but I was thinking it.

He hugged me then, a real hug, and I had to get away fast before I cried in front of him and all the church ladies sitting elbow to elbow in the living room. Maybe he did see me and Jasmine and Henry Lewis as separate people, more than just Mama's children. It was clear he understood how important we were to her. I wasn't used to that.

Back upstairs in my own room I dug my backpack out from under the bed. If they were going to keep me home from school, I had to keep up best I could. The book we were reading for Language Arts was very strange. A bunch of boys stuck on an island. Not a single girl so far. Hard to tell where the story was going or why we were reading it for class. Just like the boys I knew in real life, the boys in the book were making fires and building forts. I'd been meaning to tell Rey about it. He would think it was awesome how the boys in the book used the fat boy's glasses to start the campfire. It sounded just like him and Henry Lewis, using leftover stuff to make tools and forts and all. But the further I read, the more I could tell something bad was coming. Probably not a book Rey should read.

119

When they teased the fat boy, it wasn't the least bit funny. Without his glasses he was blind. I tried to imagine what it would be like not to see people when they came close to you. How much scarier it would have been if I hadn't been able to see the boys in the truck. I wouldn't have known how many of them there were. I wouldn't have been able to tell that the one boy had jumped off the truck until he had hold of my arm. It was scary enough when I could see them.

I would have liked to ask TJ why boys did that, testing and pushing each other, even their friends. After the other night I was having trouble sorting out how I felt about him. That was something else altogether. I hadn't told anyone about the boys in the truck or where TJ had taken me. As long as I was stuck at home there was no one I could talk to about it. After he dropped me off, I snuck upstairs and crawled into bed, but I couldn't sleep for thinking about the wind swirling the spring hay on either side of us as we walked under the stars and how the sand silted between my toes, warm and cold at the same time.

All my life I was thinking Henry Lewis was so different from other boys, interested in books and science and how things fit together in the world. TJ knew about outer space too and talked about ideas, but in a different way. TJ made it sound like he wasn't convinced science had all the answers.

And his warning about the wolf, what was that about? He was way too old for me and I didn't want a boyfriend anyway. Not that he'd offered. I didn't have time for a boyfriend. I was going to college, read a bunch of books, and learn how the world worked so I could invent things to make it better. I could kick myself for being so ridiculous over the idea of a kiss, a kiss that hadn't even happened.

It kept coming back around to the way he understood my wanting to escape. I told myself he was just being nice because he knew I was hurting. It didn't mean anything. But I liked how it felt when he looked in my eyes, that he listened and didn't make fun of me or use that closeness to touch me anywhere. It was a simple, pure connection, almost like he knew I needed to talk it through, to hear the words and try to make sense of them. It had nothing to do with the boy-girl thing, only another way to let me know someone understood how I was feeling, how alone.

That's what the island book was really about, how alone people were. The whole island isolation thing. How people act and communicate in difficult times. People weren't always better together. They were mostly not. The pressure of bad things happening made a person forget everyone else and concentrate on saving himself. Scared and worried they talked each other into things they'd never do on their own. Good and bad. Like the boys in the truck. Or the boys in the book when they called the fat boy Piggy. They were being mean to make themselves feel braver.

Piggy reminded me of Birdie Harmony. It wasn't his fault he was fat. Birdie couldn't help her lisp. Rey was stuck with a selfish mother. He had to learn to live with that, like the lady on the creek couldn't change being born white. Some things just were. Like TJ's shooting stars. Worrying it over and over in your head didn't make it easier to live with or understand.

As miserable as I was over Henry Lewis, I didn't want to be alone. I wanted to be at school with my friends, talking about books and people, about anything except what had happened at the creek. If Rachel was hooking up with Willie, I wanted to hear about it. And I had a million questions for Rachel about TJ. My whole life had changed in one afternoon. Things at school could change between History and Algebra, and I wasn't there.

They let Rey go back already because he's a cousin, as if there were some ranking by degrees that said it hurt less for cousins. That couldn't be true. Just because you didn't sit around and cry buckets. Look at Aunt Ruthie. She'd gone right back to the nursing home after Tuesday, a double shift to make up for missing yesterday and leaving early the day before, but every one of her fingernails, her pride and joy, were chewed down to nothing, and she held those little girls on her lap, snuggling in the bunk bed, sitting on the floor next to them doing puzzles, as close as she could keep them.

The world was shifting and everything I knew was slippery, sliding every which way. I needed to get back to school. Even if Mama got better, everything was on me, the oldest. From now on I would have to work twice as hard to invent all the things Henry Lewis would have invented plus the things I wanted to invent. I was trying hard to do what Ruthie and Ashante thought was best and not be selfish, but falling behind in class would only make it harder.

Boys treated smart girls differently, and I didn't want to lose that edge. It was way safer. The dumb girls slinked around the hallways, looking over their shoulders, afraid of being caught by the tough boys who pushed them up against the lockers and snapped their bra straps. Or worse. No one bothered me, except to try and bribe me to give them the answers or write their papers for them. I didn't have to say no. I just looked at them sideways and they backed off, like they knew ahead of time I wasn't the type of girl who would give in. It was a game to them. They saw me as a brain, not a girl. It was definitely safer.

One time this winter when Charles Holmes asked for my science homework, I almost said yes because he was so quiet, not in your face like the other boys. Because I'd never seen him with another girl, I figured maybe he was saving himself, the way God said in the Bible. After Rey told me Charles was gay, I did start to wonder. I still liked him, though not in the same way, because he never trashed the other kids.

With the island book above my head, I lay back on the pillow and analyzed the cover. It only showed the boys in a clump by a campfire, I had to imagine the rest of the island. I liked books that didn't tell you every single detail. The Language Arts teacher was always saying to exercise your imagination like you exercised your muscles.

Maybe someday I'd write a book about Henry Lewis and make up a life for him. He'd have a family of boys—no big sister—and he'd teach them all how to swim so they could race in the Olympics. He could grow up to be a high school swim coach. He'd have a beautiful wife, who was short like he was, but nice. In the book nothing bad would happen and he'd live to be a hundred and ten. He'd get a letter from the President of the United States—maybe it would be a woman president by then—wishing him Happy Birthday.

Rey whispered through the door without knocking. "Can I come in?"

I slid the book under my pillow. "Yeah."

"You better now?"

"My stomach is. Did they let school out early?"

He ignored my question. "I heard that white lady in the kitchen going on and on about swimming. What did your mama say?"

I couldn't help the snort of laughter. Half in and half out of the room, he tapped the toe of his sneaker against the doorframe. He mouthed, *I dunno.* I couldn't believe he was so eager to swim. At the flash of white by his side, I did a double take. He pulled his arm back out of sight, but not before I'd registered ten inches of white gauze from his wrist to his elbow.

"What happened to your arm?"

"What?"

"Come on, Rey-ban, the bandage on your arm?"

"Don't call me that. It doesn't hurt."

"What happened?"

"Brad Potter happened, that's what."

"You fought Brad Potter and you're not dead?"

He let the arm hang down in full view and flexed his fingers where they were stuck out at the end of the bandage. He was proud

122

of himself. He must have been fired up if Brad Potter hadn't massacred him.

"You fought at school?"

"Lunchtime."

"Do Mama and Ashante know?"

"Not yet. Ruthie came and signed the papers after the school nurse wrapped it up."

"They suspended you."

"Two days, no biggie. It would have been more if we'd been inside."

"Did you start the fight on purpose so you could stay home?"

He shrugged, which was almost as good as an answer. He would tell me the rest when he was ready. He wasn't a crybaby. Then I noticed his feet.

"Where your basketball shoes? I thought the guys practiced Thursday afternoons."

"I can't with my hand."

"You love those shoes. You practically wear them to bed. What'd LeBron do now?"

"Nothin'. I'm just wearing these today."

It was a lie, plain and simple. The fancy high tops were the only thing his mother had ever given him. He only took them off to go to sleep and church.

"Have it your way. Where are the ones Antoinette sent?"

"Lots of the guys play in regular sneakers."

I lunged at his knees and he tumbled sideways onto the cot like a lumberjack's tree falls in slow motion, the bandaged arm raised like a signal flag.

"Tell me . . . what happened . . . to your shoes." I rubbed his head with my knuckles. "Or I'll say you lost them and you'll be in more trouble."

"You can't. Not on top of the fight. Please." He squirmed loose.

"So, spill."

"I gave them to Henry Lewis."

"What?" I didn't believe him. "When?"

"Today. After Ruthie signed me out. She let me walk down to the . . . the funeral home. Mr. Thatcher said he had a locker for each . . . ah, person. He put them in the locker for Henry Lewis."

"My brother does not have a locker at Thatcher's Funeral Home." I could hear myself yelling, but I couldn't stop. "You are so lying."

"No, Mee, it's true. Mr. Thatcher says there's no way he'll be alive when they find him. It's what the man with the rowboat said too, down by the creek. The water's like ice."

"They don't know everything." I curled over on my side. It was horrible to think of Henry Lewis in a funeral home, in a casket.

If Rey wanted to give him something, that was okay. It was his way of dealing with what had happened. Just like Mama hiding inside her head and not talking. She couldn't help how she felt. Rey couldn't help how he felt. You dealt with things in your own way.

"I found his hat," Rey whispered.

"What hat?" I asked, even though instantly I could see the blue hat on Henry Lewis's head when he started down the boat ramp.

"His Braves hat, from when the Cub Scouts went to the ball game in Richmond."

I began to flip the pages in *Lord of the Flies*. "I don't want to talk about it."

"It's an important clue. Ashante thought so too because he called the Sheriff right away. It must of floated to shore after the rescue people left. It was there that first night when I went back. They took it for evidence, but they said they'd give it to Mr. Thatcher when . . . when . . . it was the right time. That's what made me think about the shoes."

To hell with funeral lockers and baseball hats, all I could think was that Rey had gone back to the creek by himself and I hadn't known. He could have fallen in and drowned, the same thing happening all over again. Something was really wrong with me. I should've never let him out of my sight. Any idiot could figure he would go looking for his best friend.

"You can sleep on the cot," I said. "But only if you promise not to go back to the creek without me." The metal springs squeaked when the cot bumped the wall, but I didn't turn over. "Promise."

"I got basketball practice."

"You didn't promise."

He was crashing down the stairs before I remembered that I'd been the one to grab the hat off Henry Lewis's head while he unlaced his sneakers. I must have dropped it later. What could he think except his big sister was giving him permission to go in the water, when she should have been dragging him back and telling him no.

When the front door rattled the whole house, I realized Rey was leaving. I grabbed my sweatshirt. He couldn't play basketball with the bandaged hand. And he'd already gone back to the creek once.

Outside Mama's room I paused for a minute, my head next to the closed door, and listened. Ashante was talking about work, the traffic coming home, the weather report. He listed the food in the kitchen with funny descriptions about who brought what. Mama didn't laugh, but every once in a while she hummed a little as if she heard what he said. I tiptoed down the stairs. They wouldn't miss me, and Rey already had a head start.

As soon as I was outside I tore down Linden toward Creekside. The streets were deserted. Too early for the school buses and most all the neighbors worked. From the top of the marina ramp the dock was empty. No Rey. He might have taken the long way around to see the black lab that lived in the house with the miniature white lights on the bushes. I ran to the corner and checked in both directions. No Rey. The crazy lady's hillside was empty too. No lady in a hat staring out at the horizon. I sprinted down the last stretch of Stonegate for a better view of her house. There was no car in the driveway. Without thinking I slipped into the shadows under the oak trees and started up the hill. I wanted to see what she was always looking at from the house. At the top I turned at the exact spot where she usually stood.

Looking back across the creek toward the old marina, the view was amazing. All the way to the Rte 17 bridge. Past the falling down ice house, past the public boat ramp the grain barge bobbed up and down at the dock, the gray towers peering down above it. Spinning halfway around, I could see two loops in the river. Beyond the last spit of the farthest marsh—toothpicks of green and brown—the river twisted right and then left in a thinner and thinner stream of silver. It looked like strands of an old woman's hair in a giant comb. No wonder she stood here. The tugboat captain must see the same thing from the little glassed-in house on the top deck as he chugged into the channel. Out there was the rest of the world.

At the top of the hill a brick path wound around the fence to the gate. Inside the fence was the house. And a swimming pool, dark blue and sparkly. I'd never guessed. I pushed and pulled at likely places on the gate and the metal frame around it. No luck. The knob at the top looked like decoration, but, as plain as the fence was, it seemed a little too frilly not to have some extra purpose. When it popped, the gate opened.

Careful to stay a good foot from the edge, I walked all the way around the pool. The tiles along the inside edge were painted with fish in flashy colors, orange and yellow and lime green. Two shiny ladders, two sets of steps, and an underwater bench built into the side of the pool. A big dolphin grinned up from the bottom. If you swam here, you would be able to see your toes. Anyone outside the pool could see you wherever you were. If only Henry Lewis had decided to swim here instead of the muddy creek.

Barks from inside the house made me jump. Her dog. Maxy sounded frantic. Maybe he needed to pee. I tried the handle and the door was unlocked. When I opened it though and called him, he didn't come out, just gazed at me where he was lying on the kitchen floor with those sad black eyes. It wasn't like I'd planned to go in.

"Lonely?" I knelt next to him.

He pushed his nose into my hand, still didn't stand up.

"Maybe you're hungry."

After I filled his water dish, I analyzed the cupboards. Where would they keep dog food? I found a plastic tub under the sink. Maxy sniffed at the nuggets in my hand, but he wouldn't eat.

"Sorry, buddy. I know how you feel."

The kitchen window ran the whole length of the counter. Across the river you could see the big bridge that went north. In the dining room through another long window, you saw the same bridge. Behind the couch and the television in the next room there was a whole wall of books. There must be a thousand. Two big chairs lounged with a table between them, a book on each side of the lamp as if the people reading them might return at any minute. I turned to leave—how would I explain being inside—but there was Maxy right behind me with those sad brown eyes. Just as I bent down to pat him, he ambled away and climbed into a faded dog bed by the fireplace. With his tail dripping over the back edge, his tummy bunched up, he looked a little bit like a turtle against the light wood floor. I laughed out loud. He groaned.

"You're right, not that funny." I shouldn't be here. If Mama knew . . .

Still, the rooms were cool and smelled like lemon-lime soda. The hallway was wide and dark. I bet the crazy lady could play music in every room, and not just from a scratchy old kitchen radio either. The hall led past two bedrooms and a bigger square room set up like an office with a three-legged triangular desk in one corner. The big bedroom at the far end was painted the palest blue I'd ever seen with white trim and white doors and windows on three sides. It was like being on a cloud. If you woke up here, you would see the river and the creek at the same time. You would think you were flying.

One dresser was a mess. Bits of paper and toothpicks in plastic wrap and half-opened packages of Tums. A man's plastic comb, pennies, a crumpled handkerchief. So she did have a husband. The other dresser was much neater and a funny little wooden doll with a pole in her head and several hats on the pole. Behind a bright yellow ceramic dish with a jumble of earrings and rings, there were two photo frames. The first one showed two boys about TJ's age, one in a black robe like English judges in the movies. The other picture was one of the same two boys slightly older. He had his arm around a woman in a wedding dress and his other arm around the crazy lady. These must be the sons she'd mentioned to Mama. I couldn't remember their names.

I didn't open the tall carved box at the back of the dresser because the tray in front of it was more interesting. A circle of flat black stones wound around an arrangement of shells. The shells were mostly white, some with pink edges and some with milky orange insides. When I ran my index finger along the edge of one, tiny grains of sand stuck to my skin. I picked up one of the black stones, but put it right back down. It was warm. I chose two of the smaller ones. Warm too and smooth.

There were so many and they were so beautiful. I knew it was wrong. But she had everything and I . . . I put the two small ones in my pocket and re-traced my steps. She wouldn't miss them is what I told myself as I passed through the big room with all the books Maxy opened his eyes and groaned again. Not much of a watchdog, but that was partly my fault. I had confused him with biscuits and dog food. I made sure the screen door shut fully before I popped the pool gate and hurried down the driveway and back to Creekside Drive. Still no Rey on the marina dock or the seawall.

The stones stayed warm in my pocket. I didn't know what I'd been thinking. I'd never stolen anything in my life. But she had a bunch more. She wouldn't know they were gone. And if she did, well, that was okay too. I wasn't really thinking straight. Let her see how it felt to lose something.

Chapter Twelve

In the post office line on Thursday Celie heard about the fight not long after it happened. She overheard it actually from Richard Widener's wife. Missy Widener was ten years younger than Celie, a few years younger than Richard. She stayed busy with their one son who was in fifth or sixth grade. They'd been introduced at one of the farmers' markets. Celie could not remember how long ago or by whom. They hadn't had any other conversations. Sometimes she heard Missy calling Tripp in from the yard, their voices crisscrossed in exasperation. The arguments were broadcast at a volume way too public. Missy would insist he be polite and obey the rules or she'd call his father. Tripp talked back and refused to conform no matter what she asked. It created a constant war. Without permission he left the yard. He would show up lounging outside the post office, kicking his soccer ball on St. Bernadette's lacrosse field, strolling downtown with an ice cream cone at eleven on Saturday morning as if he were the mayor. For a twelve year-old to wield so much power unnerved Celie. Not that her boys hadn't broken the rules. But they'd never been openly disrespectful like Tripp.

Although Missy nodded hello when Celie took her place at the end of the post office line, she turned immediately back to her friend, a woman Celie didn't recognize and didn't think she'd ever seen before. The characteristic volume of Missy's voice grated, and Celie pretended to be checking addresses on the letters she was holding.

"The older boy got cut." Missy's eyebrows peaked in exaggerated concentration.

There was an indeterminate shuffling of feet as other people in line discreetly repositioned themselves to hear better.

Missy seemed to grow an inch taller. "Rey . . . Rey Davis, they said his name was."

The other woman pounced. "Davis? That can't be right. The boy who drowned was a Breeden, Henry Lewis Breeden. The obituary says the mother's name is Breeden."

"Different fathers. It happens all the time with those families."

Celie bristled. She knew just what they meant by 'those' families and she was embarrassed. For them and for herself.

Missy's friend continued in a sharp, overly dramatic voice, like an actor reciting lines on stage. "But cut? How could that happen? Knives are banned from schools."

"Some of those kids have no supervision. They bring any old thing from home. Who knows where they get a knife like that? If there's a drug dealer in the house . . ."

Celie put a hand over her mouth. She had to cough to stop herself from shouting them down. No one could possibly believe that the gentle man comforting Mary Breeden was a drug dealer.

"Was the Davis boy hurt badly?" Missy's friend asked.

"Luckily . . ." Missy paused for dramatic effect. "Mr. Carpenter was walking to his car and saw the flash when the other boy pulled the knife out of his backpack. Laura Singer said Mr. Carpenter box-kicked the knife out of the boy's hand before he could swing properly."

"I think it's kick-boxed, not—"

"Whatever. Can you imagine Mr. Carpenter, mum as a gravestone at St. Mark's every Sunday, having to deal with flashing knives in the middle of class?"

"I heard it was lunchtime. They were outside by the picnic tables."

"Whatever, poor kid. Horrible thing to lose your brother, but to be attacked over it—"

"Poor kid, nothing. Betty Ann Pachinko saw them from the cafeteria window. She said the brother threw the first punch." Missy was enjoying the audience.

"Maybe the other boy said something to upset him, maybe accused him of . . . ah . . . pushing his brother, rough-housing."

"Well, some kids are born trouble-makers. They were all down there together on the dock. They had to know they were trespassing."

"No, no," Celie interrupted, though no one turned around so she wasn't sure they'd heard her. Her ribcage closed around her lungs and she squeaked out the words when all she could think about was Rey with a severed hand or a gaping wound on his cheek. Shell-shocked Rey, who had run for help and been too late, like her. Celie waved one hand in the air to get Missy's attention, to emphasize the error of what they said. The other customers shifted again ever so subtly to bring this new actor into their line of vision.

"Rey wouldn't attack anyone. They're a nice family," Celie said.

Missy and her buddy swiveled on their heels and stared at her as if she were the rude one for eavesdropping.

Missy hissed over the line of heads. "You know the Breedens?"

"I know Rey isn't a thug." Her voice was at half decibel compared to Missy's.

Missy turned back to her friend, as much as announcing that Celie's unreliability was a known fact.

"Next, please." At the postman's signal Missy and her friend moved up to the counter together.

A sour taste filled Celie's mouth, the orange she had eaten for breakfast. With the muscles in her abdomen cramping, she headed for the door, bumping past a Latino woman, a baby's downy head on her shoulder.

"Sorry," Celie mumbled, desperate to remember the Spanish word. Rory's wife Lila had given them several lessons in simple Spanish. Diplomat that Lila was, the word for 'apologize' was high on her list.

"De nada," the mother murmured as her arms tightened around the chubby baby.

"De nada," Celie repeated. Outside by the loading dock she threw up the entire orange and her coffee into the cornflowers. With one shoulder against the brick wall, she stayed bent over at the waist until her stomach muscles unknotted.

Small town gossip drove her wild. If only they would consider how it sounded before they spoke. But they were so starved for something, anything to happen that they exaggerated and then the damage was done. It wasn't malicious. Missy Widener was a pleasant enough woman. Still, Mary Breeden and her children did not deserve to be held up to this kind of scrutiny when they were already struggling to learn how to live without Henry Lewis.

Celie went home, anxious to remove herself from further inspection and unable to face the waiting line of curious faces. She found her cell phone in the pocket of her shorts, on the closet hook where she'd hung them before she'd changed for her morning walk to the Breedens. Although the phone was almost out of juice, she tried Thomas's office number anyway. Talking about something as mundane and non-controversial as weekend plans would be a relief. If he and Caroline could come down, it would be a much needed distraction and a buffer with Jake. The recording said the lines were busy, please leave a message.

Even Rory's gentle spaciness would be welcome, but his phone reported that he was out of the calling area. Although it was two hours until dinnertime, what Celie really craved was a stiff gin and tonic.

The desire for the sharp tang of lime and fizz and the thought of that zing sliding through her chest surprised her. Her last drink had been the night before her examination by the breast surgeon, before any of the tests, when the discovery of the hard place in her breast had finally been admitted after weeks of worrying it with her fingers.

A year had passed. She had no idea whether there was a lime in the refrigerator. Jake kept track of all that now.

While she sipped at a tall glass of water by the sink, she stared at the wind curling the river surface into whipped cream. A breeze had sprung up from nowhere. Her head thrummed with a deep repeating throb that matched the snap of the flag on the pole outside the kitchen window. She had to get away from the river, the creek, and the images of a quiet morning turned to disaster. She telephoned Caroline.

Thomas's wife of six years was a great listener. Raised by a single father, she had embraced the Lowell's as her new family wholeheartedly. She spoke often of how much she liked their matter-of-fact approach to life and to family differences. She took the grandmothers to tea and to the movies. She remembered everyone's birthday and each one's favorite dessert. She knit constantly and loved to watch old movies, an enormous bowl of popcorn within easy reach. Caroline's father, affectionate and pleasant enough, had been preoccupied with running a regional corporation. He hadn't had much time for his only child. Maybe Caroline had been starved for attention. But Celie thought she just enjoyed being in the middle of all the activity and discussions, neither the ringmaster nor the princess riding bareback.

As an only child herself, Celie felt a special bond with her first daughter-in-law. Caroline was a gift, the daughter Celie had always wanted. Lunch with Caroline, a little shopping, that's what she needed, not a gin and tonic at all.

Caroline answered on the second ring. Over background music another female voice was counting in rapid repetitions of one to ten. "Hi, Mom."

"Is this a bad time?"

"Oh, no. I'm doing an exercise tape. Truly dull."

"Any chance you're free for a late lunch? I was thinking of coming to town for some sewing supplies. Thomas's office lines were all busy."

"He's training a new receptionist. I'm not sure she knows what she's doing."

"That's not good."

Caroline laughed. "What time do you think you'll be here?"

"I'm flexible, sweetie. I'd just like to have a visit and hear your news."

"How about one of the salad places in Central Park?" Caroline always had an idea. "Or would you rather avoid that traffic?"

"Downtown might be less busy."

"Okay, let's meet outside the Monroe Museum. We can leave the cars in the shade and walk from there."

"You're sweet to make time for me."

"Mom. Don't be silly. I'd love to see you."

As Celie hurried through a shower, she told herself Caroline was actually right, she was a silly old woman. They all humored her. But today, haunted by the sad faces at the Breeden house, she wasn't going to analyze too much.

Once she drove past the *Thank You for Visiting Essex County* sign she was amazed at the relief she felt. With the hard symmetry of sidewalks and boxwood borders and gabled roofs behind her, replaced by soft pines tunneling on either side of the highway and pale green leafy canopies overhead, she let her shoulders sink back against the seat. It was hard to believe only two days ago she had flown through here in the opposite direction with wind blasting through open windows, in eager anticipation of that first view of the river.

The road to Fredericksburg swayed right and left, bordered by hay fields and rows of energetic winter wheat ready for harvest. These were old farms, third and fourth generation farmers. They lived on hope. It was the ultimate act of faith to plant seeds, invest your time and money, and then depend on God to send the rain and sun at the right moments. In a way it was the same thing you did with children. Only with children you had more input, more chances to provide the sustenance and the example that educated them for the life you envisioned for them. She and Jake had been lucky to have the resources to make that training easy, not that they hadn't made some of the luck themselves. Along with their share of mistakes.

One dinnertime when the boys were little, Jake told the story of how he and Celie moved to the country when they were first married. He described how everything they owned fit into a four by six U-Haul truck. Although it was the truth, by the time the children heard it, they had a houseful of furniture and Rory had challenged the tale.

"All this stuff fit in one U-Haul?" he asked.

While she and Jake laughed, Rory must have thought he'd caught his father in more than a slight exaggeration. Thomas, though, had understood immediately and, after that, he began to hoard his savings. His more cautious personality, so like Jake's, was transparent early on. After all his angst over establishing independence in high school, the similarities to Jake reemerged. It became a family joke. Thomas, the clone, born old and wise. Penny candy had been his only downfall until high school when he discovered girls.

After driving through the Rte 301 intersection, Celie eased the old Volvo back to the posted speed limit. She had been caravanning behind a single line of cars, but reached open road on the final stretch of undivided highway before the city. In the last year she had schooled herself to drive more slowly. She knew her reactions were off. Her mind wandered. Often she had to pull over under a shady tree for a nap, even if she wasn't actually falling asleep at the wheel. She could feel her concentration slipping. She hadn't argued when Jake insisted that she close down the mediation business.

"You can't push yourself so hard," he said. "We have to concentrate on the treatments."

That all-inclusive team captain 'we' came so naturally to him. And to be fair the whole family had worked hard those months to make her life as easy as possible. While the isolation she felt as the patient was unavoidable, she never once doubted that any one of them would have taken that burden from her if they could have. It didn't make her feel less afraid. It didn't make her feel better physically. But it did make it easier to want to get better, for their sakes, so they could stop worrying over her and get on with their own lives.

The grief she felt, though, over losing the life she'd had couldn't compare to what Mary Breeden must be feeling. Without knowing Henry Lewis at all, Celie had no trouble imagining the vacancy of Mary's days without him. The mad crush of loading five into a car for church or the grocery store, the decibel level of any dispute between them, the sticky closeness of all those jostling elbows at the dinner table, and the rank smell of so many dirty socks at the bottom of the laundry hamper, Celie knew that intimately, if on a smaller scale.

The rhythm of the Breeden household would be off. The missed beats would be cymbal crashes in a familiar cacophony of children racing for the school bus or drawing straws for bath time or beating each other to the van's front seat. Like an orchestra without a drummer, the other notes might be just as sweet, but they wouldn't fit the same way and nothing would balance properly.

She didn't notice the repeating waves of red strobe until she pulled up for the stoplight by the downtown train station. A patrol car pulsed directly behind her. Because her mind was on the order of one way streets in the historic section, she only saw the revolving lights when she turned to check the roof rack in the driver's side mirror. The rack had a tendency to slip its screws on any big bump, like railroad tracks or potholes. The car was almost fifteen years old. Whenever it happened, the black frame lurched sideways and hung crookedly over the back seat window. One bang too many on the glass and it might crack the window. She and Jake and even Thomas had all tried to tighten it at one point or another. It refused to hold. Rory, though, who didn't pay any attention, had no trouble with it during his entire three years of grad school.

A very stout policeman tapped one knuckle on the window. "Excuse me, ma'am, did you not see my lights?"

She lowered the window, eye level with the buttons that stretched across his belly. "Well, yes, of course, just now."

"It's been two and a half miles." He flipped open a very official looking black notebook and began to write.

"Two and a half miles? From before the airport?"

"Back by the driving range."

"What is it? Do I have a taillight out?"

"No, ma'am. You were speeding, 60 in a 45 mile an hour zone."

"That can't be right. I don't do that anymore." But of course even without his pursed smile, she knew instantly that was the wrong thing to say. *Play the C card,* she could hear one of the infusion center patients suggest. Celie smiled back inadvertently. "The cancer last year made me so—"

But he was into his routine and not interested in her excuses. "Driving is serious business, ma'am. We had three fatalities on this stretch of road last year." Without waiting for her to respond, he recorded something on his pad. After surveying her up and down like a race horse, he barked in that same chilly tone. "Registration?"

"It's in the glove compartment." *Why hadn't she retrieved it immediately, before he asked. She knew the drill.*

"I'll need to see it, please."

For an awkward moment she reached for the handle, then hesitated because he hadn't given her permission. He watched her confusion as if he were enjoying it.

"I'm sorry," she said. "My brain is still so fuzzy from the chemotherapy. Is it all right to open the glove box to get to the registration?"

"If that's where you keep it."

The whole incident took thirty minutes. Caroline, as businesslike as Thomas, would be waiting at the designated meeting place. She wouldn't call because she wouldn't want to make an issue of her mother-in-law being late. Since the cancer Celie was late often, what with the roadside naps and the forgetfulness. Although Caroline meant her patience to be a kindness, Celie felt the reprimand in it, as

134

she did in Jake's commentary on her constant naps or her failure to finish her dinner.

Once the officer had driven off, she stuffed the speeding ticket in her purse, tapped through her phone contacts to Caroline, and sent the order to connect out into the airwaves or satellite waves or whatever it was that made the damn cell phones so ubiquitous and so useful.

"Mom, are you okay?" Caroline's voice was warm and concerned. "Where are you?"

"I'm two blocks away. I'll be there in a minute. I got a speeding ticket."

"Oh, well. You're alright then. That's only money."

Just like that Caroline put it into perspective. The tension that had been building inside Celie since the trooper's appearance at her window fell away. Great sheets of anxiety slid off and crashed around her like the wake on a water ski ride. Just money, not health or peace of mind. Or the life of a child.

Chapter Thirteen

By the time Celie hugged Caroline good-bye and stopped at the fabric store for curtain lining and hooks, it was after four. Even without the summer beach crowd, the Fredericksburg rush hour traffic clogged the single-lane road headed east. At this rate Jake might beat her back to the cottage. Still she drove under the speed limit and didn't turn on her music for fear of losing track of her speed. She'd sworn Caroline to secrecy about the ticket.

"Jake will think I'm losing it. He already wants me to see a counselor."

"Counseling's not a bad thing, Mom. It gives you an outlet. A safe outlet, where you can say how you really feel without hurting someone's feelings or worrying them."

"I know. It's on my list to call."

"It might be easier on Dad if you did talk to someone."

Celie let a minute pass. The last thing she wanted was an argument with her daughter-in-law. It was logical that the kids would see it more neutrally, be concerned for both of them, but it irked her that *easier on Jake* received the same priority as her well-being, considering she was the one with the life-threatening illness. But even as she thought it, she knew how self-centered and whiney that sounded. From what they knew and saw, she was cured. They were ready to move on. She needed to follow suit.

"You know, Caroline, I'm so glad you call us Mom and Dad. Jake and I are forever saying how lucky we are to have such a strong family. And you add so much. You and Lila."

But she wasn't fooling anyone. Caroline must know she'd changed the subject on purpose. She'd never needed counseling before the cancer. If she started now, she was conceding failure.

When she arrived back in town, it was close to five o'clock. Cars still lined the Main Street parking spaces in the old part of town. She slowed the Volvo at the bakery and pulled into a parking space out front. The bakery window shade, painted with a folksy string of boats and a Van Gogh circle of sun, ran ceiling to floor. They were closed for the day. She sat in the car and stared. Her mouth had been watering for a lemon poppy seed scone. Foolish, really. At lunch she'd eaten like a death row prisoner hours from execution. When Caroline commented on her appetite, they laughed about it like schoolgirls caught whispering in the back row. Celie could still feel the flush of embarrassment she'd felt at having her eating habits analyzed by her daughter-in-law. But Caroline wasn't being snide, only pleased that Celie was interested in food again.

Neither of them mentioned the drowning. At the least Caroline would report Celie's lunch performance to Thomas, who would tell Jake and he'd be reassured. His Italian ancestors equated food, and lots of it, with stability and well-being. His wife was on the mend. He could get back to business.

There she went again, critical when she should have been comforted by their concern. The enjoyment of the drive and the lunch and Caroline's amusing story about Thomas trying to hang pictures with the yard stick and the level evaporated. Eyes shut, she pressed her fingers into the corners and pulled against the lids to squeeze out the sting. She was a mess. She couldn't even go four hours without falling apart.

She heard the children's voices before she saw them. They rounded the corner, a loose gaggle of gangly limbs and brightly colored T-shirts. Meeka herded the little girls behind Rey who was walking backwards and motioning with his arms, the drum major. He crossed in front of the hood of Celie's parked car without seeing her. The gauze bandage on his hand blazed white in the sunshine. So it was true, there had been a fight.

"No, you are not, Miss Jasmine Frasmine," Rey said. "Aunt Ruthie said no and that means no. You think she talks for her health." He tapped Jasmine on the top of her head with the index finger of his good hand. "I told you two times how it's gonna be. I don't want to hear nothin' more about it. Understand?"

Liné ducked to avoid a similar tap. "But, Rey." She drew out his name in a long whine. "We'll be quiet. Jasmine and me can look at the picture books while you and Meeka—"

"No." He glared. "You're staying outside with Meeka." For a second or two Celie received his stare through the windshield before his eyes blazed with recognition. Once he connected her with the woman by the creek, he frowned and turned away, herding the others away from her car. She felt silly sitting there with a smile on her face, waving like they were best friends. She disengaged the seatbelt.

Meeka's head dropped to whisper something to the girls. Her arms draped around their shoulders. With two quick steps Rey moved closer to form a tight knot with the others, an instinctive shield against the looming reminder of that awful afternoon. Celie scrambled for what to say. She hadn't meant to upset them.

"Oh, dear, I missed the bakery," she said. "Where are you'all headed?"

No one spoke. It was Liné's head poking out from the clump of arms and legs that made Celie smile again. The little girl grinned back.

"Rey's going to the libery," she volunteered. "The libery lady's gonna let him use the computer to check on something."

"Shush up," he said. "She doesn't want to know all that business."

Celie noticed the look exchanged by the older two over the heads of the little girls. When he looked back at Celie, he was still squeezing his lips together, trying hard to mask his irritation. Meeka loosened her hold on the little girls and they spilled out across the sidewalk like marbles.

Meeka spoke first. "Ruthie says thank you for the food."

Jasmine grinned and twirled on one foot. "We awready ate all your cookies. Rey had the most."

"Well, good. That's what they're for. I'll make you some more."

"Can you make orange ones?" Liné bounced back and forth from the grass to the concrete. As her arms swung up and down in an exaggerated march, her skirt flicked from side to side. "I love orange."

Meeka popped her eyes at Liné as if she had done something so inappropriate that no one could forgive such a lapse.

"Please, please, please.." The little girl ignored Meeka. "Orange is my favoritest color in the whole world."

"Mine's watermelon." Jasmine put one arm in front of Liné and usurped the first place in line.

"Watermelon's not a color," Rey said. "It's three colors." He tried to stuff his hands in his pockets, a gesture of disgust in the face of so much disobedience in the ranks. When the bandage hung up on his jeans, he gave up and let the hand fall.

Meeka spoke above their heads. "You don't need to worry with more cookies, Miss . . . ma'am. Everyone's brought so much. Brownies, fried chicken, sweet potato pie—"

Jasmine interrupted. "Ashante says it's a regular grocery store at our house."

Rey punched her between the shoulder blades and she started to whimper. Meeka gathered her in again. As she pressed the little girl's face into her stomach, she shot a sideways frown at Rey.

"They're just being kids," Meeka said to no one in particular.

"It's all right. My children used to talk all at once too," Celie said.

Meeka waved her free arm in the direction of the townhouse. "You left your library books at our house by mistake."

"My library books?" It took her a minute to fit the image of her books into the Breeden's overstuffed kitchen. The whole day came back to her, the baking and the walk and the bags. But she was fuzzy about whether it had been yesterday or the day before. Time had slowed to a crawl.

Meeka continued to talk without looking at either her or Rey. "It's not a problem. We can take them back next time we go or I could bring them to your house. Only reason we didn't bring them today is we weren't sure if you were returning them or had just gotten them to read."

Liné sang out. "Banana cookies would be okay too. Yellow's my second—"

Rey interrupted. "The libery's gonna close while we're standing here." His voice cracked in that painful way of boys growing up, despite his attempt to restore order with a tone of authority.

She understood he meant to dismiss her as a useless adult. There she was talking about bakeries and cookies when he had something important to do at the library. She wondered if Meeka conceded to him regularly or if this was something new, realignment of responsibility in light of Tuesday's events or of Rey's becoming the only male in the group. Meeka looked pained, but that could have been her reaction to seeing Celie again.

As she watched the children move down the sidewalk, she wished she had bumped into them at the library. She could have read a book to the little girls while the teenagers checked whatever they needed to look up on the computer. She could have done something helpful and positive.

For several minutes before she started the engine she sat in the car and tried to shake her mood. All in all the children looked well. They had each other, a good thing. Even a little bickering would keep them distracted. She envied them that. As an only child with parents who worshiped healthy living and books, she had missed out on the Tom Sawyer kind of mucking about of larger families. When Jake suggested they stop after Thomas—his much desired boy child—she argued for at least one more. Feeling guilty, she prayed for a sunnier, easier baby. Secretly she had wanted a girl. Then with Rory she'd been surprised at how different the two boys were. Their personalities, their likes and dislikes, their talents.

Still siblings had another level of communication between themselves, beyond words. Although they were inseparable as little boys, Thomas could always tell just how far he could push his little brother. When they were in college, Rory was forever explaining to her not to worry about a certain girl Thomas was dating, that she wasn't *the one*. Even now that they both had wives and weren't together as often, they had an uncanny ability to anticipate what the other one would want for dinner or for his birthday. At Christmastime Caroline and Lila had joked about it with her when she'd bought the boys sweaters and they had switched colors without a word.

Christmas, even Christmas from four months ago, seemed a long distant memory. These last three days the clock had moved backwards. With Henry Lewis gone but always present in her mind, her life felt narrow and intense. Every detail related to the next detail, the next moment or the last. She felt manipulated, as if a puppeteer were running her through a script that didn't allow for diversions. A world with no free will. She kept hoping she'd wake up and it would be over. Except there were so many familiar things around her she couldn't really be imagining all of it. If it were an illusion, it must be some kind of psychological construct to protect her from the minefield of reality.

Now there was a question for the counselor. How did the human psyche cope with trauma? It seemed to collect the smallest details, to fill the brain until the imagination had no space to move. Emotional gridlock. Intellectually she knew it didn't work that way. Her imagination roared into the void without regard for the details or the truth, like a locomotive in a one-way tunnel.

The rattle of the car's passenger door handle yanked her back to the present. George, in his pressed white dentist jacket and hot pink bow tie peeking out below the collar, motioned for her to unlock the passenger door.

"Hey, neighbor, having trouble with your car?"

She popped the door lock and waited as he slipped his long torso into the empty seat next to her. She hadn't seen him since that night. He smelled like cinnamon and she wondered whether her subconscious hankering for the bakery was affecting the here and now.

"The car's fine," she said. "I was just thinking."

"Rodin has nothing on you. You look terribly serious. Would coffee help?"

"I thought dentists had office hours."

"I'm done for the day, out looking for a damsel in distress."

She had to laugh. Knights in armor didn't wear lab coats or administer Novocain by needle. "I haven't been a damsel for twenty years."

"Actually you're much too capable for rescuing. But I need a strong dose of caffeine after the last little old lady and her dreaded root canal. And I hate to drink alone."

"You don't really drill into little old ladies with those monstrous machines."

"Sadly, yes. Not my favorite thing either."

"Yet you've been doing it all your life?"

"Well, I usually don't admit what I did before dental school."

She couldn't help laughing. When a shadow passed over the windshield, she looked up to see the outline of a woman paused on the sidewalk. It took a second for Celie's eyes to focus and realize the woman was staring through the windshield at her. And at George. She turned her face down, but too late. The woman, vaguely familiar, issued a telling nod after taking in the two of them laughing, in the throes of an inside joke. She rushed off followed by the slap of her shoes in double time on the sidewalk.

"I know that woman," Celie choked out.

"Sure, Ness Porter. She's the local busybody."

"She was in the post office this morning with Richard Widener's wife."

"Ness and Missy went to high school together. St. Bernadette's. Fifteen years ago maybe."

"Is she always that obvious?"

"You didn't grow up in a small town, did you?"

She shook her head with a silent instruction to herself not to break down at the sympathy she heard in his tone.

"She's harmless," he said.

"That's easy for you to say. You were born here. And you're a respected local businessman. You can probably blackmail them all. Dentists hear everyone's secrets."

"Some. It's how I fund my gambling habit."

"It's not so funny when you're the new meat in town." She fought the giggles.

"Don't be afraid of Ness. In the long run it means nothing. Today you're a half hour of conversation at the bridge table. Tomorrow they'll walk right by. Or offer to share a newer tidbit with you about someone else." He was laughing, laughing at her.

She bristled. "I think you ought to go now."

His eyebrows formed a dark fret line across his forehead. Even when he frowned, he was so casually handsome. She wondered if he had any idea. She wondered again about the woman at his house. Most definitely his wife didn't seem to enjoy his sense of humor, she'd concluded as they sat there. It bothered her even more that she noticed how good-looking he was, as if she had ever chosen friends or boyfriends for their looks, such a seemingly superficial criteria. But even in his ridiculous cliché of a white coat, even when she had been so rude, it was hard not to stare at that classical jaw line and the deep chestnut eyes, so warm, so gentle.

"I mean it," she growled. "You should go."

"Let the coffee be reparation, my treat. I can tell you all about Ms. Ness Porter's curious habits in regard to Sunday church offerings."

"I'm not interested." But even she could hear how harsh she sounded. "I'm, I just . . . I still have an errand or two left."

He sprung himself free of the car, lowered his head back down to the open door. "Then I will make it up to you another day." The door slammed and he was trotting down Washington Street like a speed walker before she could say how unnecessary that would be. Yet she watched him all the way to the corner. And she felt as if she'd lost her last friend in the world.

How and why she felt as she did about George was too complicated. It was easier to go back to worrying about the Breeden children, already on their own again barely two days after the drowning. She drove the back route to the library and parked at the elementary school, far enough away that they wouldn't spot her car. She only wanted to be sure they made it across the main road safely.

Perhaps Mary Breeden was napping and had shooed them outside to give herself some peace and quiet. Holed up in those darkened rooms with the ghost of her dead son, she couldn't be sleeping very soundly. Celie wished she'd bought the newspaper from the box outside the bakery. Details about the search and the memorial service might be listed. Although she wasn't at all sure she would go—the children didn't need her there as another reminder of the time lapse minutes of Henry Lewis's disappearance—it felt like the proper thing to do. Neighbors supported neighbors. And Meeka, so prickly and guilt-ridden, might need Celie's presence as someone who had been there, someone to stand with her against the speculation that would be dogging her from the gossip-mongers. That same speculation might explain the aunt's prohibition against public places like the library.

The raggedy huddle—Rey still in the lead, Meeka holding one hand of each girl—appeared on the far corner by the traffic light and stopped. Good for Meeka, they weren't trying to run across ongoing traffic. Between the corner convenience store and the library, Celie lost sight of them again, but they reappeared in marching formation in the library parking lot. The little girls were swinging their arms, their mouths wide. Singing, she guessed. Rey led the group like a sergeant at arms, primed for an imminent attack, with Meeka protecting the rear.

At the front steps of the library he circled around Jasmine and Liné. At his hand motion, they sank down cross-legged on the grass. Meeka sat too, with a world weary shrug of shoulders that said she was too old to be sitting on the ground. When he reached the library door, he must have called back to them, because all three heads turned and they waved. Celie felt better. They could find their way home.

The cottage, shuttered all afternoon from the sun, was cool and peaceful. She gave Maxy a welcome pat where he lay curled on the hallway rug. He barely raised his head. Although he had been Thomas's dog as a puppy, with the insurance office on the opposite side of town, Thomas's work schedule ruled out a dog at home. Caroline kept hinting about a puppy, but if he wouldn't take Maxy after their fifteen years of shared history, he wasn't going to take on any kind of pet at this point in his career. He had inherited Jake's single-mindedness.

Celie switched to jeans and an old linen shirt. The bed looked inviting, the pillows askew, the covers gathered together haphazardly this morning on her way to the shower. In an effort to talk herself out of that trap, she drew back the curtains with a ruthless flourish and left the upended dust motes to settle in the sunshine. In the living room she put on one of Lila's CDs. Lila collected wild music from her mission trips. Steel drums and chanted foreign words repeated and repeated like an empty hammock in a steady breeze. It was hard not to feel the energy. She ought to call and thank her again.

On the drive home from Fredericksburg she had planned dinner. Although she craved pasta, warm, cheesy pasta, she tried to think of something else. Last year with her iffy stomach they'd eaten so much macaroni and cheese Jake had imposed a ban on noodles. The idea of the buttery scone had temporarily distracted her, drawn her to the bakery. And then she'd caused all that disagreement. At least the children had stuck to their plan in spite of her. Who knew if George would give her a second chance?

The anticipation of the pained look on Jake's face dissuaded her from spaghetti. Salad with roasted chicken seemed safer. While she defrosted the chicken in the microwave, she sprayed the pan and pre-heated the oven. She stuck four breast pieces in the pan with little pats of butter perched on top. It was too early in the season to grill outdoors. Once she pulled everything from the vegetable drawer, she lined up the ingredients by the sink next to her favorite pale blue bowl. Across the river a fisherman tossed his crab pot back in the water and glided toward the next one. When she recognized the boat, she let herself be distracted. The old trawler needed paint badly. He was one of the few crabbers who collected twice a day. She was so busy watching him work his catch that she wasn't paying attention to what her hands were doing.

When the knife sliced into her finger, she shrieked from the pain before she looked down. The white line was already gushing red. Luckily the fingernail had stopped the blade before it went all the way through.

"Damn." Wrapped in a wad of paper towels suspended over her head, the finger throbbed while she tried to remember whether the band-aids were in the medicine cabinet in their bathroom or the guest bath or the linen closet. "Damn, damn, damn."

Jake would be upset with her. *You move too fast. You need to concentrate on one thing at a time. Slow down.*

Last year she'd had enough slowness for a lifetime, though it was hard to make anyone else understand the sense of time lost forever while she'd been stuck in that chemo chair. Second by second, hour by hour, her life had spun away from her. Those hours would not, could not be replaced. Now she had a finger that needed medical attention—another doctor, another hospital—when she had been happy making dinner and watching the fisherman after a relatively uneventful day. For those few minutes she'd been at peace, and that didn't happen very often lately.

Chapter Fourteen

Rey was doing his vocabulary homework in front of the TV when I came in. The little girls had lined up the stuffies on the back of the couch and were toppling them over one by one, great shrieks of delight as they flopped on the floor.

"Where have you been?" I tapped the top of his head.

"Basketball practice. I told you before I left."

"You didn't play long."

"I only watched." He held up his bandaged arm.

A white unicorn sailed over the couch and nipped his shoulder.

He yelled. "Jasmine, Liné. Cut that out. You'll wreck my homework."

Liné popped up from behind the couch. "So sorry."

Jasmine's head appeared like a second Sesame Street puppet. "So sorry."

The two girls giggled and their heads sank out of sight. More giggles.

I slung myself down on the couch next to Rey. "They need to go outside and run around."

He kept on, writing, flipping pages in the dictionary, mouthing the letters, and scribbling away.

"Rey. I have to check on Mama. You need to take them outside."

A matching pair of Beanie Baby squirrels flew and knocked a teddy bear off the couch. Jasmine squealed. I swept the rest off the couch.

"Rey," I repeated with more emphasis. "Before they break something or we'll all be in trouble."

I left him on the front steps with strict instructions to keep his eyes glued to the girls. They had already forgotten Beanie Baby target practice and were drawing hopscotch squares on the sidewalk. Scattered around the kitchen were mugs and plates with half eaten pieces of pot roast and cake. The living room chairs were backed against the wall as if everyone had gotten up in a rush, a pile of crumbs in front of each chair like the church kneelers. The stove clock said five-fifteen. Ruthie must have gone on to third shift at the nursing home.

"Ashante?" I called up the stairs. It amazed me how quickly I'd adjusted to my mother's silence.

When he didn't answer, I wiggled off my sneakers and went up in my socks. They might be taking a nap. I was debating whether to knock, but the bedroom door was ajar.

"Ashante, are you in there? Is Mama awake?" I pushed the door an inch or two, just enough to see her side of the bed. Although the covers were drawn down, the bed was empty. "Mama?" I pushed harder and the door swung wide, hit the rubber end of the wall stopper, and bounced back. I stiffened my arm and held it open. The room was empty.

I had no idea where they'd gone, or where they might have gone. Pastor Ware and his wife had been here twice yesterday. Mama's supervisor at work came after dinner. The church people finally left at bedtime. Who else? And then it hit me. The rescue people must have found Henry Lewis. There was nothing else that would make Mama leave the house. When she came back, no telling what she would be thinking, but it was bound to be worse. Her family needed to be waiting.

From the window in my room I scanned the parking lot. The van was gone, but Ashante's motorbike was there. He'd come home from work. He would have driven her. She wasn't in any state to drive. I raced downstairs to ask Rey. If he had disobeyed me and let the girls leave the yard, I was going to kick his butt all the way to China. They weren't in the front yard where they were supposed to be. Two pairs of pink roller skates lay like dead fish on the beach of pale clay between the lily pad patches of new grass.

"Jazzy? Liné? Where y'all hiding?" I squeezed my feet into the sneakers. "Come out right now. This isn't a game." I sucked in air. "Rey, you're a dead man if you don't show yourself this minute."

Nothing moved. I ran around to the street side of the townhouse, though we were all forbidden from playing where the post office traffic was heaviest. The narrow strip of grass there was empty too.

"Rey Davis. You're in deep, deep you-know-what. Front yard. I told you. Front yard." I muttered and cursed as I ran toward the creek. "Please don't be near that water. Please."

But before I made the corner of Creekside Drive where it ran along the water, I saw the three of them bent over something on the shoulder of the road. From here I couldn't see what it was. Swerving away from the loose gravel and the odd pine cones, I ran as fast as I dared. I came up behind Rey at a half-run and yanked his shoulder back to see what they were hovering over. At the last minute I had to grab onto his shirt to slow myself down. We both ended up falling sideways, a tangle of arms and legs.

"Get off me," he yelled. His bandaged arm shot out in self-protection.

"I told you not to come down here, Rey."

"He said he was Jazzy's father. Once she heard that, she wouldn't stay with me. I had to go. And I couldn't leave Liné all by herself."

I whipped my head around where the little girls were kneeling in front of a grungy mess of a man. His legs stretched out in front of him on the grass, ending in black lace-up shoes with no socks, the toes brown from wear or mud, I couldn't tell. His jacket was three sizes too large, wisps of fabric frayed at the collar and the ends of the sleeves. The front of his shirt was pocked with stains. Coffee or ketchup, I hoped, not blood. A crumpled black felt hat perched on his knee, the ribbon hanging by a thread from one side. Every few seconds his hands patted the hat into place on the wobbling knee. Still I recognized him immediately. Latrelle.

But he was an ancient deflated version of the angry man from that long ago afternoon at the trailer. What did I expect? Eight years come and gone. I was fourteen instead of seven. This Latrelle had dirt buried deep in the creases of his forehead and something crusty by the corner of his mouth. He was missing two teeth, who knew how many where you couldn't see. Jasmine stared, her eyes wide. While I untangled from Rey, she scooted away from the man, closer to me.

"He doesn't look anything like Henry Lewis," she blurted. "He can't be our daddy."

Latrelle's answer was garbled, the mumble started long before her question. Rey's eyes flashed back and forth as he took in the stains, the missing buttons, the gritty fingernails. I flicked the hat off Latrelle's knee.

"How dare you come here? Mama has enough to deal with right now without trash like you. Go back to wherever you've been hiding."

"We're family."

"Oh, no, we're not. You didn't want us all this time, you don't get to claim us now."

"I done lost my boy."

"He's not your boy."

"Yeah, Henry's my boy too."

"No, he isn't. He's ours."

I tightened my grip on Jasmine's hand and pulled her along the street towards home. It was all I could not to scream at the top of my lungs that if he'd been a real father he would have taught his son to swim years ago, if he'd been a real father he would have been working and paying for a real babysitter so we wouldn't get into trouble, he would have been paying attention, instead of drunk in some corner, not remembering or caring that he had three children who needed to be protected from a greedy creek and all the evil in the world.

When I didn't hear the other kids, I glanced back. Rey and Liné hadn't moved. Latrelle sat in the same position, shoulders hunched forward, his hat on the grass where I flicked it. His hand batted at the empty air above his knee.

I yelled then. "Rey. What you looking at? Bring Liné and move it. Nothing but trash down there. We're supposed to be home."

Back at the house Mama sat in the kitchen chair as if she'd never left. Ashante dug stuff out of the refrigerator for dinner, slapped it on plates, and stuck them one by one in the microwave.

I dug out the silverware from the dish drainer. "Where did you and Mama go in the van?"

"I thought a drive might help, get her outside, sunshine."

He seemed resigned to this new zombie Mama. I felt terrible for him. He hadn't signed on for this kind of tragedy. How long would he stay if she didn't snap out of it? I guessed it wasn't the kind of thing you snapped out of, not really.

Why I didn't say anything right then about Latrelle, I had no idea. When Rey didn't bring it up either, I was grateful without understanding why exactly. It was not something I expected a boy to understand, an unexpected kindness. Latrelle's condition disgusted me. I was shocked he was alive and furious he would come here. It made me so angry that he claimed any part of Henry Lewis. The selfishness of saying he cared when his actions showed he didn't, that made me even angrier.

Of course he must have been drunk. That seemed the worst, that he would show his sorry self in that condition. Still when I went over the scene again in my room after dinner, I flushed at how quickly I'd let him get to me. Long ago I convinced myself he was dead. For years I told myself I didn't care, that he wasn't worth thinking about. I didn't want Rey or anyone else to read any shred of feeling into the way I lost my temper. I especially didn't want Latrelle to think I cared. I hated him, loathed him, despised him. The entire Thesaurus entry for *hate* spun out in my head like a ribbon of type. There was no perfect word, but they all fit. I had no father.

After dinner Ashante came upstairs and knocked on my door. "We thought maybe you should go back to school on Monday."

"Sure." I didn't ask him who 'we' was. It couldn't include Mama. She didn't want anything to do with me.

He glanced at the island book, touched it with his fingers as if something about the cover connected with him. "You know, Mee, people will be curious. They don't mean anything by it. You should be ready though. Some of the kids will ask questions, get up in your face. You should go on about your business. Don't be rude, just ignore them, walk away."

I hummed agreement. I could tell he had more to say.

"They'll find him soon."

I recognized that voice, *everything will be fine*, a grown-up's way of smoothing over the uncomfortable truth. I'd caught myself doing it with the little girls.

"You sleeping okay?" he asked.

"Yeah."

"Did something else happen today? All you all were so quiet at dinner."

I couldn't think how to explain it. I wasn't sure how much Mama had told him about Latrelle.

Ashante forced a smile. "You promise you'll tell me or Ruthie if something's bothering you?"

I nodded, but kept my eyes on the book.

"Mee?"

"I'll be fine."

He went to the window, his back to me. "Everything's so green. I keep forgetting it's springtime. And then when I go outside, I'm surprised at the new leaves and the flowers. It seems like it ought to be winter."

I had no idea what he expected me to say to that. He sounded so sad. I tried to think of something positive to say, to thank him for sticking around, for noticing how we were at dinner, and for doing all the things he was doing even though he didn't have to do them, but I was afraid I'd cry if I tried to talk.

"Your mother's working through this. She's like you, she's a fighter. Once she's over the shock, she'll be better."

Better seemed a long way from the mother I knew, but it wasn't his fault. It was mine. I had caused this and I needed to make it right. I just didn't know how.

Sarah Collins Honenberger

Chapter Fifteen

Jake called from the car, halfway home. Celie heard him turn down the radio as soon as she said hello.

"Rory called me when they couldn't reach you on your cell this morning," he said. "They want to come up this weekend and I couldn't think of any reason why not. Is that okay? Phyllis and Sam won't mind another couple at dinner Saturday night."

It was easier to ignore the implied criticism in his comment about the phone because she was so relieved at the idea of Rory and Lily coming. The McCallenders were Jake's college friends, not hers, and Sam McCallender monopolized every conversation. The kids would change the dynamics of the whole weekend for the better, not just the dinner. They'd bring all kinds of goodies. Lila baked when she was feeling creative. Rory and Jake would find a project and fix something with Jake's tools. Male bonding, good for fathers and sons. A project like that could keep Jake occupied for hours. The four of them might take a boat ride together and she'd hear all about the kids' latest travel plans. They didn't sit still long. Celie tried to remember if she had changed the sheets in both guest rooms, in case Phyllis and Sam decided to stay over too.

"You still there?" Jake asked.

"Sure. I mean, sure, the kids can come. I tried to invite Thomas and Caroline, but I'm not sure he got the message."

"But you left a message?"

"I tried."

"Either you did or you didn't?"

She tried to remember the sequence of the phone calls, the receptionist hanging up by mistake, the recording because she'd forgotten to mention it to Caroline at lunch. She wasn't sure what she'd said in the message. Lots had happened since then. But Jake didn't wait for her answer.

"Never mind. We can talk more when I get there. Rory said they'd arrive about eleven tomorrow. And they'll leave Sunday after dinner. That work for you?"

"Eleven, yes. Great." She wrote the number eleven on the pad and "L & R."

Out the window the dilapidated trawler chugged down river to its next set of traps. Every once in a while a flash of neon buoy would strike a bit of lingering sunshine or a sudden golden froth of wake

150

would spray the dark hull with rainbow sparkles as the boat slowed. When she and Jake were out in the pontoon boat, she looked for those orange markers and tried to imagine the fisherman's life beyond the boat routine. From this distance she couldn't tell if he was young or old. His body was only a squarish blot against the gray planks. She'd never seen him up close. Still, her imagination videoed calloused hand over hand on the wet line.

She shook her head, that wasn't right. He would wear gloves to remove live crabs from the pots. The men unloading their catch at the marina all wore heavy gloves with striped canvas cuffs, boots too, and thick rubber aprons. A bright red drop appeared on the counter. And another. She'd forgotten the cut.

The paper towel was soaked through. She let the whole hand rest on the edge of the sink and ran the cold water again on the finger inside the wrapped paper towels. Ice? That might stop the bleeding. It occurred to her that maybe she was light-headed and should sit to avoid fainting.

"Cee, what are you doing?" Jake's voice blasted from the phone wedged between her shoulder and ear.

"Thinking, sorry. Dinner'll be ready when you get here."

"Great, see you then."

He sounded pleased, his earlier impatience with her forgotten. Why not? His wife was where she was supposed to be, doing what she was supposed to be doing. Routine restored, life on course. With a little bit of luck, he wouldn't notice the bandage on her finger.

The thick, buttery odor of roasting chicken made her stomach roll. When crackers didn't help, she went out and lay in the hammock to get away from the smell. Her finger throbbed and she debated whether she'd wrapped the tape too tightly over the thick gauze pad she'd found in a crushed box under the bathroom sink. Below the hammock the last of the afternoon's unseasonal heat rose from the bare hillside, silting in around her already warm limbs. The field cedar blocked her view of the marsh where the rescue workers had stood their watch on Tuesday evening. Feeling like a traitor she relaxed and faced the sky to catch the breeze on her face.

As the hammock rocked, she gazed past her toes where high tide displayed the stalks of marsh grass and plumed phragmites like the Beefeater helmets outside Buckingham Palace. Their muddy roots were hidden below the water line. Long shadows stretched onto the narrow strip of beach that edged the lower lawn. Those fingers of washed out dun and ginger extended out to where the current ran deep, stronger at the creek's mouth. The triangular sign there was faded, the neon painted edges battered and chipped. It was intended to remind visitors and boaters familiar with the river about the sandbar, a warning to steer wide, closer to the mudflats on the creek's swampy island. On this side of the marsh one determined egret stalked the beach, a peck here, a peck there.

As she lay on the woven ropes with the hot air below her and the cooler air above her, the solution came to her. She should take pictures, photographs of the empty river, the stippled current like a piece of floating burlap, almost separated from the water itself. No rowboat, no uniformed people, no brown head bobbing mid-stream. If she took enough pictures and studied them long enough, eventually the pictures would substitute themselves in her brain for the reality of Tuesday's horror.

When Jake found her, she'd left the pillow on the hammock and was on the beach. She'd snapped three dozen angled shots of the reeds and the ripples, using her middle finger on the shutter button. The bandaged finger stuck out like an extra piece of equipment.

"What are you doing down there?" He called from the patio. Even at this distance she could hear disapproval in his voice.

"Hi." She stopped long enough to register he was still in business clothes, his tie loose, the folded newspaper in hand. "Hungry?"

"Anytime."

She shut off the camera and slogged through the sand in her bare feet. It was already ten degrees cooler than when she'd started. From the way he stood above her, his hands moving to keep mosquitoes at bay, he must be perplexed at not finding her inside, waiting for him with the promised dinner. There would be more questions. Her idea about the photographs was so experimental she wasn't sure she could talk about it without sounding a little ridiculous. Halfway up the steps she called up to him.

"Why don't you change while I fix the plates?"

He didn't answer.

"Would you rather have a drink first?" she asked.

"That sounds good. Let me change then."

He hadn't even been listening. He must be distracted with work issues. Maybe he truly wasn't interested in what she was doing on the beach. Or maybe she'd only imagined the disapproval. The patio was empty when she reached the top step.

While she was setting two places at the dining room table, she noticed that the bandage had soaked through again. She put her good hand under it in case it started to drip. Luckily Jake had his back to her, fixing himself a gin and tonic at the bar.

"I can't believe we're drinking gin already. It's only April," he said. "Rushing the season." And when she didn't answer, he continued. "Eighty degrees, they said on the radio. That's gotta be a record for April 8th."

She was too preoccupied with her finger to dwell on his lumping her into the gin drinkers. With the cut hand across her chest to keep it higher than her heart, her shoulder turned so he couldn't see, she hurried down the hall toward their bathroom.

"Did you want a glass of tonic, Celie?"

"Back in a sec." In the mirror pink spots blossomed on her shirt. "Damn." She picked at the bandage while watery red stripes dribbled down the white porcelain. When she finally worked the medical tape free, the cut flowed in a steady crimson stream as if it had just happened.

"What the heck?" He yanked her shoulder back to get a better view. "Celie? How did you do that?"

"Making the salad. It's just a little cut."

"Just now?" He spread her palm open and examined the finger. "You need stitches."

"No, it'll heal. You know how skin is. The bandage holds it together, it grows back. I just won't be able to garden for a bit."

"We're going to the emergency room. Right now. It's probably already infected."

"I washed it out. I know how to do that."

"You're supposed to be careful of that arm."

She hadn't thought of that. It had never crossed her mind. For the last hour, in the hammock, on the beach with the camera, she hadn't once thought about the bad arm, or the cancer. She started to laugh. Giddy with the surprise of it. Amazed.

Some months ago another patient, a woman on her fourth or fifth recurrence, so thin she and her husband shared a recliner in the treatment room, had told Celie there would come a time when she didn't think of the cancer for a whole day. It had seemed impossible. But here it was. Almost three hours and the cancer had been absent.

"What the hell is so funny?" Jake was pressing a clean inch of gauze to her finger. He scrabbled with his other hand for the tape. After affixing the tape, he wrapped her hand in a dark towel, the finger buried in the awkward bundle. "Come on."

All the way to the hospital she laughed. She choked on the burbling, uncontrollable hiccups of laughter that kept spilling out. When Jake pulled into a ten minute space by the double glass doors for emergencies, she was still laughing. She refused to let him help her out and elbowed him away.

"I am quite capable of walking by myself." But it came out garbled with the sputtering laughter. She held up the arm like a boxer's mauled glove. "I'm going to live. It's just a cut." She grinned at him.

Why couldn't he laugh? It was funny. The whole thing struck her as hilarious. The overly concerned efficient husband, the huge green terry cloth paw at the end of her arm, the high speed rush to the tiny makeshift emergency room, her own cackles of joy. Didn't he see how funny it was? How wonderful?

"My wife's in shock." A frowning Jake announced to the receptionist at the admission desk.

The girl couldn't be more than seventeen. In the over-lit room her gum smacked to music from a tinny overhead speaker. He didn't seem to notice her lack of concern.

"She cut herself earlier this afternoon. I don't know how much blood she's lost. She should have come sooner, I know. But I was at work."

Celie couldn't even get upset at him for making her sound like an imbecile because the whole episode was like a sit-com. The girl punched buttons on an intercom or phone as if none of it mattered.

She spoke with a cinematic southern accent. "Follow that black line to the second cubicle on your left. Your wife needs to change into a hospital gown. Pants can stay on, but she should sit up on the gurney. Someone will be right with you."

Flurries of machine hums punctuated the frozen air of the waiting room. As an afterthought the receptionist called out to them when they were halfway down the hall.

"Insurance card?"

Jake pivoted like a snow globe angel. He ripped his wallet from the back pocket of his khakis. Another cartoon image struck Celie as hilarious. She tried to control herself, to keep from giggling. She didn't mean to embarrass him and he was clearly embarrassed. He was being ridiculously sensitive. They didn't know the girl, had never seen her before, not even dashing around the local Wal-Mart. His concern over what a stranger might think struck Celie as overly sensitive. But then she was used to having to detail the most minute personal bodily functions to perfect strangers and he wasn't. His furtive glance from side to side reminded her of the old movies where a fedora hid the detective's face except for the cigar. And so the laughter was impossible to stifle after all. Even the sterile cubicle with its wall of futuristic blue and silver machines and the twirly piano stool for the doctor seemed cartoonish and funny.

"What is wrong with you?" Jake's voice was distant and fierce, the way he'd sounded when he used to reprimand the boys for taking tools without putting them back or for eating a bowl of cereal right before dinner. He pushed away her good hand and undid the buttons on her shirt. While he held the gown, she wriggled into it.

"I'm fine. The finger will be fine. Truly, Jake, it's alright. You can stop worrying about me. Please." She put both hands on his arms, even the swaddled hand. "Please." It was her most serious voice. "I need you to stop worrying about me." Then she burst into tears.

In stepped the doctor, looking younger than Rory, dreadlocks and unlaced boots and a wide smile taking them both in as if they were rapidly dividing paramecium under a microscope. He extended his hand, palm open, creamy skin outlined in black, and signaled hello to her over Jake's shoulder. Although Jake shook the doctor's hand, his eyes stayed on hers, a warning to behave. The doctor spoke with an accent. She had to concentrate to decipher what he said.

"I understand you cut your finger. Want to show me?"

When he motioned for Jake to move aside, Jake hesitated before he stepped back as if protecting her was more important. He continued to look only at her and he did not return the doctor's smile. At the doctor's repeated directions she climbed up on the gurney and stretched out her hand to let him work his magic. He arranged her arm on a moveable stainless steel tray table.

After an hour and four stitches and a typed sheet of general instructions they drove home in silence. Jake made her sit while he cut the chicken off the bone and served the dinner. When she saw the tiny bite size pieces on her plate, laughter bubbled up and she had to keep her head down so he wouldn't see. They ate silently. Her bandaged finger waved up and down as she speared lettuce and tomatoes with the fork between her thumb and third finger. It made her want to giggle again, but when she saw how drawn his face was, she swallowed the laugh.

They were not quite done with dinner when there was a knock at the back door.

"I'll get it," Jake hopped up.

Over the murmur of voices, the screen door opened with its familiar squeak. When it didn't shut, she strained to hear the conversation, unsuccessfully. Once he came back, he took a long swallow of his second gin and tonic before he spoke.

"That was Tracy Ann."

"I wondered."

"Worried about you."

"Nosy."

She was still working through her surprise that he'd left off Tracy Ann's last name. Suddenly the woman was a best buddy, instead of a mere acquaintance. Or maybe the two of them had had numerous whispered conversations that he hadn't thought to mention, private conversations between close friends.

"That's ridiculous. People are concerned about you. It's natural. They're not doing it to offend you."

She folded the napkin into a neat triangle and laid it by her unfinished plate. "Well, thanks to Henry Lewis, I'm not the latest curiosity. She can stop inquiring."

He started to stand, but must have changed his mind. She wondered if he had been going to leave to avoid an argument or if he had simply had enough and needed to have it out.

"This has to end, Celie. The cancer's gone. You survived. It's time to get on with your life. Not everyone—"

"I take special vitamins. I can't sleep. My arm is almost useless. I have no right breast and barely an inch of hair, and you're worried about offending Tracy Anne Sheffield." She pushed herself back from the table. "The cancer was never supposed to be there in the first place and I'm supposed to believe it's gone. Who are they kidding?"

"It is gone. The tumor cells they took out in the operation were dead, every single one of them."

"It's not gone. It's lurking, hiding, slinking around inside me until it can find a way to come back, stronger, bigger."

She noticed the tightness in his lips, the way he slipped backwards in his chair ever so subtly as if she were a little bit crazy. He probably didn't even know he was doing it. As he ran his eyes over her face to assess whether the rant was over, the muscles in her own neck tightened. Instinctively she put her hand on her throat where the vein, connected to the infusion port, pulsed. The man-made implant in her body was an alien reminder that she was incapable of living on her own.

"Sure, Jake, you go ahead. Live your life as if the cancer never happened. There are no more stacks of medical bills to sort through. Your wife doesn't need you to feed her macaroni anymore. It's not quite that easy for me. My life will never be the same. And I don't hear anyone offering any guarantees."

She didn't need to look up to feel the shock in his eyes. She knew him too well, could feel the flair of anger and sense his immediate mental command to calm down and not let the anger take control. Yet she couldn't stop.

"All your friend Tracy Ann Sheffield wants is insider information so she can spread it around town what a wimp I am."

"No one thinks you're a wimp. You're trying to do too much. The doctors told you to rest. Just because some woman you don't even know can't supervise her kids properly, you're going to shoulder that blame too? You didn't cause the cancer, and you didn't cause this drowning."

"I didn't even try to save him."

She was wrapped in an old Army blanket on the porch when he found her later.

"Looking for shooting stars," she started so he wouldn't think she was brooding, though that was exactly what she was doing, as hard as she'd been trying not to.

"I'm sorry," he said, after he positioned the wicker rocker closer to the edge of the porch where he could see the same slice of sky.

"I'm sorry too."

"You're right, I don't understand how it is for you." The wince in his voice was obvious. "I'm trying, though."

"I know that. You didn't ask for any of this. I shouldn't lash out at you."

"The books say it's normal."

"Nothing about it feels normal."

"Typical, I should have said typical."

"God, that's worse. I feel as if someone else has taken control of my body and my mind. I say things I never would have said before. In thirty years how many times have we ever argued like this? It's so pointless. And I'm so tired of it."

"Of course you are. You need rest, even in remission."

"I didn't mean the cancer. I meant I'm so tired of arguing."

He stuffed his hands in the pockets of his jacket and tilted his head back to see the stars. She hadn't left him any room for compromise and that was his specialty. Poor man. Five minutes later he excused himself and went in, their overlapping murmured goodnights through the screen door like echoes of invisible bats on a close summer evening. Civility was restored, yet it felt more like defeat.

With the blanket bundled around her legs, she focused on the sparkling patches of night sky to the east, 80 degrees above the horizon. She'd moved out to the steps because the porch overhang blocked her view of the North Star. It was unusually quiet. This early in the season no wayward motorboats zipped by on their way home. The new leaves on the maples and oaks, still curled tight like nautilus shells, barely stirred. The evening's stillness soaked into her body, heady perfume of sorts, everywhere and nowhere she could touch.

In the cooling air she recalled other Friday nights when Thomas and Rory recited ghost stories by the bonfire pit with overnight friends. Their voices would float up from the beach, their tanned muscular bodies hidden from view below the hillside. Despite the six years between them they had been best friends all along. Even as little children Thomas, ever the entertainer, would bring Rory snacks and make up bedtime stories. There was something magical about listening to children confer when they didn't think adults could hear, the sweet simplicity of their view of life, right and wrong, unconditional love. Everything was defined in terms of affection—I hate pudding, I love the jungle gym—because simplicity was all they knew. Celie wished she could go back and live that time again, knowing what she knew now.

"Just one," she whispered to herself. "Just one shooting star and I can go to sleep." It was as silly a wish as she'd ever made, but she forced herself to stay awake until she saw one, the stark blaze there and gone so quickly that she would have missed it if she'd blinked. "Thank you," she said to no one in particular. Jake would be sound asleep. He'd missed it.

Chapter Sixteen

Saturday was laundry day. But by nine o'clock when Mama hadn't gone downstairs, I figured we weren't doing laundry this Saturday. I fiddled around in the bedroom. I dumped my backpack and repacked for school on Monday. I looked through my closet for my old sneakers. The new ones were muddy and I didn't want to risk a trail of tiny clay rectangles all over the living room with all the other comings and goings. Until I was lacing my sneakers I didn't notice that I'd put on the same jeans I'd worn all week. Mud on the bottom hem. Too late. And who cared anyway?

And then I thought of TJ. He wouldn't head back to the mountains until Sunday night. I dug out my favorite pair of black jeans and picked a clean shirt from Old Navy with snaps instead of buttons, kind of cool, but not outrageous. I didn't actually own anything outrageous because Mama thought fashion was a waste of money. One of her many opinions on clothes, books, friends, and most everything. Sometimes I argued back, but like the paint colors, when she was on her high horse it was easier to go along and get along.

How she was acting since Tuesday, it looked like there wasn't going to be much arguing or even talking anytime soon. Henry Lewis's passing was like a huge empty corridor. I was at one end and Mama at the other.

Early as it was, outside the bird orchestra was already geared up. They raged back and forth, long notes, sharp tweets, wild fluted trills, as if the night without any noise had driven each one mad to be heard over the other. I gathered up the clothes scattered under the bed and on the floor. After I stuffed them into the plastic laundry tub, I shoved the whole thing in the closet.

Henry Lewis's things were mixed in with mine, but the idea of sorting through them horrified me. I had no idea whether Mama might want to save them. But I wasn't going to ask. Wherever she was in her mind, the sight of them might be too much and she'd sob again like she had in the kitchen that first night.

My stomach was churning. I should go down and eat breakfast but somehow going down before her seemed wrong. My whole life she'd been in the kitchen drinking coffee when we kids came down for breakfast. Every single morning far back as I could remember. I wasn't ready for that to change. I didn't want to be the one in charge of breakfast. I didn't want to be in charge of anything ever again.

Let Rey supervise Liné and Jasmine for a change. Boys had it easy. They didn't have to help with laundry or dishes, only once in a while take out the garbage or clear the table. They didn't have to carry around a baby for nine months or rip their bodies apart getting it out. Everyone expected guys to have hot cars, drink beer, and watch TV so that's what they did. Boys could hook up with a different girl every day of the week and no one called them sluts. Men could touch girls and comment on their bodies whenever they felt like it and laugh afterwards as if it were a great joke. And then the ones who did get married sat there, waiting to be served dinner, and complained about their kids' grades or their wives talking too much. Or they didn't come home at all, but spent their paychecks in bars or at the race track.

In one lunge of the broom I swept the cobweb down. I pushed the collection of loose dirt around the bedroom floor and all the way down the stairs. The little pile of dust and hairs was sprinkled with tiny edges of notebook paper where Henry Lewis had torn a page out of his school binder Monday night. Hardly enough of a pile to bother with since we'd cleaned last weekend, still. Sweeping up was a small thing to help Mama. One less thing for her to worry with when she was barreling back and forth to the office. Her last promotion meant a bigger paycheck, but more meetings. One more way to show her I could take good care of a puppy.

After I tipped the dustpan into the kitchen trash, the tiny squares of paper stared back at me. Henry Lewis had touched that paper. I pinched a few and stuck them in my pocket. I pinched a few more.

"Mee-ka?" Jasmine could never seem to get her whisper soft enough. "Mee-ka, can I come down?" She balanced, on the top step, on the tips of her toes, poised to twirl.

"Don't you dare, Jazzy. You'll fall."

"Can I come down?"

"Who said you can't? Get Liné. Get Rey. It's breakfast time."

If Mama wasn't up, then fine. I'd see to breakfast. The two little girls couldn't get into but so much trouble here in the house. Rey could pour his own cereal like he did every other morning.

"Where's Mama?" Jasmine asked.

"How I'm supposed to know that? I'm down here and she's up there, last I knew."

Jasmine finished the stairs two feet on each step, still on her tippy toes. From the last step she whispered. "She's not. She's gone."

Tapping her chin, I played the game. "She must be hiding. From that humongous purple dragon in the attic. She's allergic to dragon fur."

"She is not lergick to dragon fur."

"Yeah, she is. She's allergic to Ruthie's cats, isn't she?"

Jasmine hooked herself to my forearm with both hands and swung off the step, her toes pointed up and her knees bent to avoid scraping the floor. "Wheee."

I held my arm as steady as I could for a few swings, then lowered her to the floor. "What about Liné?"

"She gone too. And Ashante's boots and jacket. Did they go to get Henry Lewis?" She started to sniffle.

That took the wind right out of me. I sank down onto the bottom step. She waited for me to say something. Maybe this was more punishment. Life would never again be normal. Unexpected things would keep on and on because I had upset the balance of the universe by letting my brother die.

Jazzy wormed herself between the wall and me. She was stroking my slippers. "It's all right, kitty. Don't cry, kitty. Poor little kitty."

"Stop that." I pulled my feet back under my knees. "Are you sure Liné isn't in the bathroom? Let's go see."

But before we started up, Rey came bouncing around the corner at the top of the stairs. "Where the heck is everyone? It's like a crypt in here. Are you guys eating that blueberry pie for breakfast?"

I couldn't believe he'd said *crypt*. Boys were morons. Truly. Jasmine slipped under my arm and danced up the steps, twirling and twirling. When she started to tilt, she clutched the rail, steadied herself, and started in on the twirls again. She probably didn't know what a crypt was. Good thing. No way I was explaining that to a six year-old.

"Jazzy. Never mind 'bout Liné right now," I said. "Come back and eat."

Rey thumped down in his stocking feet. He turned sideways as he passed Jasmine. His eyes were puffed like marshmallows, and he'd put on his same clothes from yesterday; his faded Magic Johnson T-shirt and cut off sweatpants that were so loose everyone could see his grippies. Mr. Tough Guy, except someone ought to tell him that plain white Ts were in and hero worship was out. If he was trying for cool.

"We're having cereal," I said. "But go ahead and eat pie. If you want to get in trouble."

Jasmine scraped the chair across the floor toward the cupboard. "Nanas too. I want nanas on my cereal."

"Sit." I tapped her head and steered the chair with her on it toward the table. "You could help here, Rey. Pour her some Frosted Flakes while I find the bananas in this zoo."

"That isn't my job."

"Tough. It's your job today."

Henry Lewis usually set the breakfast table because three girls took so much longer in the bathroom. I willed Rey not to speak again. I wasn't keen on another argument, but if he wanted a war, I'd give it to him. Just not so early in the morning and not this morning when he needed to show a little respect.

He skulked around me, but stayed clear of my feet. As he collected the spoons and bowls, I rearranged the towers of casseroles, triple layer cakes in plastic domes, and zucchini bread wrapped in foil. I moved everything, searching for the bowl of fruit that used to be right under the dish cupboard. I was still looking after he'd set both boxes of cereal in the center of the table, opened the Frosted Flakes, poured half a bowl for Jasmine, splashed in some milk, and nudged it across the table.

"Thank you, thank you, thank you." Jasmine trilled from the chair where she stood and swayed to her own music, the bananas completely forgotten.

"You're a crazy girl." I patted her head and smiled. It would be nice to be like Jasmine and be excited about breakfast or twirling on your toes. "Sit down 'fore you fall down." I tipped a plate with sliced bananas over the bowl of Frosted Flakes and we all watched them plunk one by one into the milk. "Eat slow. You don't want it going down the wrong pipe. No school today so you can take your time."

"Seriously, Meeka?" Rey asked. "They cancelled school because of Henry Lewis?"

Boys were so ignorant. "It's Saturday," I smirked.

He swallowed and took another bite. "Where is everyone?"

"You see a crystal ball here?"

"Where d'your mama go?"

"My guess, if she wanted us to know, she'd of left a note. No note." I reexamined the piles of food people had brought, trying to remember if there was any peach cobbler in that mess of pans. Rey's suggestion of pie had given me a sudden craving for cobbler.

He didn't get it. "Maybe we oughtta call Aunt Ruthie."

"Go ahead. That's probably where Liné is and Ruthie just forgot to let us know." I cut a piece of the zucchini bread and took a bite where I stood. "Call her." I took another bite. "Oh, yeah, I forgot. You don't have a cell phone."

He took his bowl of Cheerios off the table, cupped it in one hand, and moved toward the living room window. "Van's gone. Maybe Aunt Mary had to work."

162

MINDING HENRY LEWIS

"On a Saturday?" But still I rose up from the chair just enough to see the parking space where Mama usually parked. No van.

"She could have." He was running out of steam like always.

Whenever he was losing at Mancala or cards, he complained that I was smarter. It was almost as if he knew sooner or later he'd lose. Sometimes I let him win to show him that he could. How did he ever expect to be smarter or succeed at anything with that loser attitude? Anyway, older didn't mean smarter. Look at Antoinette. But I couldn't say that to him.

"When has she ever gone off without telling us or leaving a note?" I said.

"She might if it was an emergency."

"She probably had to see someone . . . about . . . about what happened." The idea of my mother leaning over Henry Lewis on a stretcher, his fingers all puckered, his skin puffy, made me gag. I shoveled the rest of my breakfast into the trash.

"What should we do?" Rey asked.

"'Bout what?"

He gave me the evil eye.

"Stay put. Wait for Mama and Ashante."

"Boring." He shoveled the last spoonful into his open mouth.

"Yeah, well, more excitement like Thursday's fight with Brad and you'll be stuck inside a long time. Or underground."

"I won."

"Does he have a bandage halfway up his arm?"

He wedged his bowl into the pile in the sink. "Maybe I'll go see if the guys are playing ball."

"Another great idea."

"What?"

"Go. Take your anxious self down there to school without the bus, take that big fat history book and your saxophone too. You never can tell. They might be having a special band practice on Saturday. Or a history test you can join in on. In the parking lot. Jazzy and I can take care of things here. Go on."

She had lined up flakes on the table and was talking to them in her tiniest mouse voice like they were pets. When I signaled to Rey, he frowned.

"Yikes," he yelled. "Stop doing that."

With the side of his hand he wiped the little puddles into his empty bowl and dribbled the whole mess into the trash. Jasmine started to whine, gearing up for a serious cry, but he was quicker. He made a quick swipe of the table with the towel off the stove handle and shook out a handful of dry cheerios from the open box. All

163

smiles, she went right back to her game, spooning wet flakes out next to the dry cheerios and making whispery introductions in her own special sing-song chirps.

When I shrugged, he rolled his eyes back and smacked his forehead in mock disgust.

"Your mama mighta forgot to write the note," he said. "A lot on her mind, you know. She prob'ly meant to, but got distracted. I think we oughtta call Ruthie. Lemme borrow the cell phone."

"If we need to call anyone, I'll call. It's my phone."

"Your phone, your room, your brother. You are in a pissy mood."

I lunged for him, but he was too fast. One leap and he was past Jasmine, through the living room, and out the front door. One of my shoulders hit the kitchen doorframe, and I let myself slide to the floor. "I hate you, Reynaud Jones. You're a disease."

Still holding her dripping spoon, Jasmine slipped off the chair and rushed across the room. A trail of milk, soggy flakes, and smushed bananas trailed behind her.

"Don't cry, Mee. He'll come back. Mama too. Liné. Ashante. And Henry Lewis." She stretched her arms around my shoulders. "They're all coming back and we'll all be together again. You'll see."

By the time they came home, I had run through my ideas for entertaining a six year-old. I finally stuck *Beauty and the Beast* in the VCR and tried to drown out Jazzy's sing-along by humming my own monotone version of Lady Gaga as I wrote in my journal about the island boys. The due date of the Language Arts paper had gone completely out of my head—last Friday, next Friday, everything was all jumbled up—but at least my ideas would be in some kind of shape when they let me go back. If I didn't get to class soon, I'd go crazy thinking about all the ways last Tuesday could have ended differently.

The sound of the ball bouncing against the side of the apartment stopped and Rey yelled that he was walking over to the middle school to look for a pick-up game. The minute he left I ransacked the house for the cell phone, even though I was pretty sure Mama had it in her purse. I hadn't dared to ask outright to borrow it. The TracFone was out of minutes, useless on Mama's dresser. I was still pawing through stuff when I heard the van tires on the gravel. Rey had been gone half an hour.

"They're here, they're back." Jazzy shrieked over Teacup's cheery little welcome where she was bouncing on the couch.

"Let Mama be," I said. "She might not feel like singing and dancing if she's been talking to the . . ." I thought better of saying

164

police. "To official folks." I pushed Jazzy's shoulders down until she was sitting and then I sat next to her, an arm across her lap like a seatbelt. "Let's see how she's doing first. Can you sit still and wait? Please."

She curled into me, her hand patting my tummy. "Did you see Liné? Is she with Mama?"

"Just wait until all them come in."

When the door finally swung wide, Mama stood beside Ashante. She hesitated as if she couldn't see for the dark. She blinked at the two of us on the couch.

He nudged her from behind. "It's your girls, Mary. Waiting on you. You're home now."

Mama murmured something that sounded like *home.* When she still didn't move forward, Ashante nudged again.

"Jasmine, Meeka, give your mama a hug. She needs a big hug from her girls."

I unwound Jasmine and set her on the floor. "Hey, Mama. Here's Jazzy."

Jasmine stretched up on her toes. "Aren't you hungry as a caterpillar, Mama? I am. We been waiting and waiting for you to come home so we could eat lunch. Meeka made me wait for you." When Mama didn't lean down or pick her up, Jasmine let her arms down slowly until they were circling Mama's legs.

Mama let herself be hugged, her arms limp by her side. Her eyes darted around the room. "Jasmine?" she asked, looking into my face, as if she'd forgotten which of us was which.

"Did you bring Liné?" Jasmine asked.

"She's with Ruthie," Ashante said. "Maybe tomorrow."

I didn't want them to think I'd neglected the kids for my journal. "I fed her breakfast. Rey too before he went to play basketball."

Thanks, Ashante mouthed over Mama's shoulder. He looked ridiculous, her pocketbook hanging from his arm and her sweater draped over his other arm like a drag queen.

While Mama didn't speak to Jasmine, she didn't let go of her either. Jasmine spun the bottom button on Mama's shirt round and round until the material was all jammed up. One of her games that no one could figure out. Mama scanned our faces again.

"Now where has that boy of mine got to?"

Even Ashante looked surprised. I bolted. Past Mama, past Ashante, out the open door and down Linden Street, running as fast as I could. To nowhere. To anywhere but where Mama was still waiting for Henry Lewis to come home.

Chapter Seventeen

Lila and Rory arrived mid-day Saturday, on time for a change. From the basement where Celie was ironing the tablecloth for dinner with Phyllis and Sam, Jake's college friends, she heard him teasing the kids about their watches being set on daylight savings time.

"Okay, okay, Dad. If you're not ready for us, we can leave and come back in an hour," Rory teased back.

"Just kidding. I'm thrilled you're here. It's been a hard week for your mother."

He just had to set her up like that. There would be more interrogation. More cautious discussions of what she was doing with her time and how she was feeling. And no acknowledgment that he was part of the trouble. She fumed. Rory had enough on his plate—new job, new wife—without an emotional wreck of a mother.

"Where is Mom?" Rory asked.

"I'm not sure. Inside, getting ready for tonight's dinner, I guess."

"You go ahead." Lila's voice. "I'll unload."

The screen door banged. Rory's sandals slapped the floor over Celie's head. Maybe they wouldn't think about the basement. They might assume she'd gone for a walk and get distracted with something else. If she slipped out the bulkhead door, she could go down to the lower patio and slide the kayak onto the beach. Out of sight, out of mind. They would never think of the kayak because she hadn't had the strength to paddle it since before the cancer treatments. She could disappear for a long explore in the marsh and miss lunch altogether. That would serve Jake right.

She made it as far as the beach and had to sit down. Dragging the kayak across the grass and over the driftwood pile, across the sand, had made her dizzy. The boat was half in and half out of the water before she remembered Henry Lewis was still out there. The policewoman had explained it took three or four days sometimes for a body to surface. He could be in the marsh, caught in the weeds. With the paddle in her arms, she sat on the sand. At every curve she would worry he was going to float into sight. There was no way she could cruise along the surface of the creek, pretending nothing had happened, pretending life was the same as the last time she ran the kayak up those narrow fingers of water, sun on her shoulders, breeze at her back. She just couldn't do it. She couldn't even remember when that was.

"Here she is, Dad." Rory yelled over his shoulder as he straddled the crest of the hill like a mountain climber, his boat shoes edged into the upside of the slope.

Jake appeared beside him. Caught, Celie waved at the two of them above her. When Jake started down the steps, Rory touched his arm and he stopped. After a brief conference, their two heads together like generals over the map table, Jake headed back to the house.

"Hey, Mom," Rory said as he bounced off the bottom step. "Going out or coming in?"

"It was just an idea, but now that you're here . . . How are you? How's your gal?"

He sat down on a piece of log that had washed up on the beach. "She's great, amazing, really. How are you?"

She ignored the long look. "I'm fine."

"Kayaking again, that's great. I have so many memories of you skating along the top of the water like the crew team. Up to the bridge and back before breakfast. You made it look so effortless."

"I always thought you were asleep."

"Nope, spying on you."

She dug the paddle into the wet sand and made a slow smooth circle at the tide line. It disappeared almost as quickly as she drew. "I'm glad you're here to run interference for me with your father."

"Interference?"

"He thinks I'm falling apart."

"Thomas said the boy was only nine. It had to be horrible."

"Eleven." But she was stuck on the idea that her sons had been conferring about their mother.

"What was his name?" Rory asked.

She burst into tears.

Sometime later, when Lila trotted down the stone steps and called them for lunch, Celie was surprised they had been talking for over an hour, not just about Henry Lewis, but about Rory's new client, the assignment Lila had at work, a foster family at their church with a pair of Romanian twins, and Caroline's design for the nursery. Celie hid her resentment that Caroline had discussed the project with Rory and Lila, but hadn't mentioned it during their lunch meeting yesterday. After the initial sting, she realized, to be fair she had asked questions mostly about Caroline's job, not the baby, and too, Caroline probably assumed, from whatever Thomas had told her about the drowning, that she should steer the conversation away from children.

Lila leaned down and kissed Rory, then hugged her mother-in-law. "Did you remember sunscreen?" she asked him.

He shook his bowed head, but rolled his eyes where only Celie could see.

"My oh-so-competent and learned daughter-in-law." Celie pushed herself onto her knees and leaned on the log for balance. "She's right, you know."

Rory stepped over the kayak toward her, but stopped when she shook her head.

"I can do it. It just takes a little longer because I'm old."

"You are not old," Lila blurted.

After a momentary hesitation, he looped around the end of the kayak, took Lila's hand, and started up the steps. "So what did you and Dad concoct for lunch?"

It amazed Celie all over again how perceptive her younger son was despite his brain working overtime on engineering concepts more complicated than everyday things like laundry and meals. Before anything else he had wanted to know Henry Lewis's name, and he understood that old ladies with creaky knees did not want to be observed when they had to stand from a sitting position.

Although she volunteered to clean up after lunch, the kids insisted on doing it. When Jake suggested a nap in the hammock, she knew he meant her. It was too nice to stay inside. With her book in hand, she went in to grab a water bottle from the fridge.

"You two should use the bikes," she said. "Dad put air in the tires last weekend."

"Maybe later. Rory's writing a report for work," Lila said. "And I'm in the dead zone of Follett's new book."

"I wish my book was as captivating. The characters are so self-centered. And so mean to each other."

Lila turned her head sideways to read the title under Celie's arm. "Never heard of him."

"Oprah's latest pick."

"Isn't he the one who complained publicly about her readers not being the type to read his books?"

"Yes, a very stupid man. So many reviewers say he's the new Tom Wolfe, writing the truth about American society. I hate to think people are as petty as his characters. But if the queen of life-altering optimism recommends him, I thought I should try this second book of his."

Rory looked up from his paperwork. "If you give me a half hour, Mom, I can help you with the garden."

"What's the matter with the garden?"

"I noticed the bags of plants. I could dig the holes for you."

"I'm not sure where I'm going to put them."

"Well, they were down there by the hydrangeas. I thought—"

Celie gazed out in the opposite direction, at the river. Two sailboats seemed stuck on the canvas, and a few weekend fishing boats, gunwales too close to the water with too many passengers. What was it about boats that attracted people who lacked basic common sense?

"Go and do your reading," she said. "I'm going to work on the marinade for the chicken."

They went off, shoulder to shoulder. A good team, affable, smart, kind. Despite all that affection and pride, she felt as if she'd avoided a war, though that was hardly fair. Rory didn't realize the daylilies were part of Tuesday's disaster. She was relieved though. She had dodged having to explain why she didn't want to work the garden that overlooked the creek.

Chapter Eighteen

When two policemen showed up on Sunday afternoon, everyone was still in church clothes. They knocked loudly and announced their news as loudly, enough that Rey and I heard the whole thing from upstairs where we were playing a very slow game of Scrabble while the little girls colored. Once I heard an officer say Henry Lewis had been found, I coughed like the television ad for Nyquil to drown out the details before Jasmine or Liné overheard things they shouldn't. Rey went out to spy from the top of the stairs. I stood guard by the door. In between coughs I pieced together that a man thirty miles downriver had called the station early, but they'd had to do a bunch of official things before they came to tell Mama.

"You go," Ruthie said to Ashante once the deputies had gone back outside.

"They need a relative."

"I can't do it." Her voice broke.

"Well, Mary can't do it."

"You think I don't know that?" Ruthie started to cry.

It was the first time I ever heard Ashante raise his voice. Usually when he was upset with one of us, he lowered his voice and spoke more slowly to make his point. Even that hadn't happened very often. All this mess and Mama so out of it, maybe he'd hit a breaking point. No matter how he acted or what he said, he wasn't blood. And he must be feeling like this wasn't his problem. Blood wasn't much if Latrelle could abandon them like he had. If Ashante left now, it would all be on Ruthie who was already stretched with the extra shifts and corralling Gerald. One person could only handle so much. I hated for Mama to hear them arguing, but it might snap her out of it if she thought she was going to lose Ashante. Everything was connected and everything was so complicated.

I shut the bedroom door and put on my headphones. I'd bought the yard sale CD player with leaf raking money. I'd been so thrilled at the idea of having my own music that I didn't think to try the machine until I got home. It cut on and off, the lid popping up every time the disc stopped spinning. I'd been ready to return it and ask for my money back. Henry Lewis had taken it apart and cleaned it. It had played perfectly ever since. When the motorcycle started up a minute later, the music didn't block it out. I rushed to the window. The motorcycle was trailing behind the police cruiser like a parade.

170

MINDING HENRY LEWIS

Ashante hadn't come upstairs to consult Mama. And he'd gone off without telling her what the policeman had said. Neither he nor Ruthie had asked her if she wanted to go. Even though she was still not right—in spite of all the praying and carrying on by the church ladies—she might want to hold him, her only son. She might want to say good-bye. But no one gave her a chance to say what she wanted.

It only proved how bad off she was. For three days she'd sat in that chair and stared into space or laid on the bed with her eyes wide open. Jasmine would say things four or five times before Mama blinked and then she'd say, *what's that, Jazzy, what you saying*? Ruthie held Mama's face in her hands to get her attention, to get her to eat, to lie down. Ashante kept repeating that she'd be better soon. I thought it sounded like one of the things adults say to children because they think they can't understand the real explanation. I wished I had the first idea how to fix what was wrong with my mother.

When he came back from the station, he called us all to the kitchen.

"They found Henry Lewis. They're taking him to Thatcher's." He seemed to be stuck, but somehow started again. "Thatcher's Funeral Home. They'll bury him Wednesday."

Although Mama stared right at him, she didn't say a word. Her face blank like she'd been doped up with the same bad stuff the grungy old men behind the Laundromat used, gone to another world. Ashante stood with his back against the wall as far away from all of us as he could get. Ruthie hugged us one at a time, but not Mama. With her hand on Mama's shoulder, she cried quietly.

"We gotta pray for your mama to get through this. All of us." She looked at Ashante. "Did they say anything else?"

"What? What else is there? He's gone. I told them it was him. I did what you wanted me to. It's over."

Ruthie went outside on the steps. He followed her out, after a sharp jerk of his head, which I took to mean *stay put*. He shut the door even though it wasn't cold outside. Rey shooed the little girls upstairs. Once they were out from under foot, I fixed hot tea for Mama and I held the mug to her lips until she sipped some. I wanted so badly to run away, hide anywhere. I couldn't sit much longer and watch that face, cold and dead as Henry Lewis. Half our family gone in one fell swoop.

Outside Ruthie and Ashante continued to argue in short bursts of words and long silences. When he came inside, he bundled Mama up in a lap robe and rode her over in the van to the police station to sign the official papers to end the investigation. Afterwards he walked her up to bed where she stayed for the rest of the day. She didn't speak, didn't cry, nothing.

At dinnertime the rest of us sat around the kitchen table with our food on paper plates and listened to him try to coax her to come down and eat, but he came back alone. I wondered how much longer he would try.

As soon as I could manage to sneak out without anyone noticing, I did. With no plan in mind, just to get away, I found myself veering toward the old marina ramp. As if I had no free will of my own, like Henry Lewis was calling me back. Crazy, because that wasn't where they found him according to Rey's version of the policeman's report, not even close. From the corner of Creekside and Stonegate I could see the top of the ramp that led down to the creek, but not the water itself.

The new chain at the top, right by the road, rocked in the breeze. I ran my fingers across the silver chain. It shocked me how cold that metal was even though it was sparking in the sun, practically humming with electricity. I'd expected the chain to be hot. I wondered if things would've been different if the chain had been there all those times we had passed by to walk the Jessup's dog. If the chain had been there warning us, Rey would have known not to dare Henry Lewis.

The white lady insisted it was an accident. She couldn't mean, could she, that it would happen no matter what anyone did to prevent it? Warnings were supposed to make people stop and think. No one would waste time putting up signs if they didn't work. And if knowing things, thinking about things ahead made a difference, then accidents weren't completely random. I took that to mean that if I'd been doing my job the best way I could, I would have found out about the creek and the ramp and not let my brother and the other kids go down there.

Since the other night, someone, Mr. Widener maybe or the police, had hung the chain. Then later, this morning maybe, they'd wired on the black and white 'No Trespassing' sign to the chain. A warning on top of a warning. It was meant to make people stop and think. Kids could still sneak down the ramp. It was just a chain. They could still dare their friends to swim when they were hot and the water looked cool. They could still fall in or slip or go out too far. But now that the chain and the sign were there, they would have to think about it harder. And they would have to make a bad decision. It was more than just not paying attention.

With so much happening, I saw how easy it was to miss things, important things. In school you didn't learn anything unless you paid attention. If you didn't pay attention, you would repeat sixth grade like Clarence Littleton. I'd always thought not moving up to middle school with your friends had to be the worst. About then I looked up from the chain and saw Henry Lewis's head disappearing in the creek. Just like that afternoon. And I knew there were worse punishments than not being with your friends.

I turned away and broke into a run. The idea of being in the water again and feeling that awful terror when your feet didn't touch the bottom horrified me. Swimming lessons were a really bad idea right now. The next time I saw the white lady I'd tell her so.

Back at the apartment Aunt Ruthie was trying to locate Antoinette. She telephoned three or four numbers in Baltimore and finally reached her. Ruthie explained quietly, then listened with her hand on her forehead. She was so quiet I almost forgot she was on the phone.

"God damn it, Antoinette. Shut up. Just shut up. For once this is not about you. Mary's lost her son, and you're her sister. She needs you to come for the funeral. Your son needs you to come. Pull your sorry self together and get down here before Wednesday. Don't hang up. Rey wants to talk to you."

"Is she coming?" I asked once Ruthie had passed the phone to Rey.

"Who knows?" Ruthie whispered. "She said she would."

I didn't believe it. Antoinette talked to Rey for less than a minute and all she did was yell at him to stay away from the *fucking* creek. You could hear every word through the phone. Rey didn't even flinch. He kept on smiling like it was Christmas and Easter all rolled into one. I felt awful for him. He didn't have a clue how unlikely it was that she would come all the way from Maryland for a dead nephew she hardly remembered she had when she hadn't come in a whole year for her own son, alive and well.

In the van I found a map of the Eastern United States. I explained to Rey—with a ruler and the map key—about inches being so many miles and how far it was from Baltimore to here. Then I explained how expensive bus tickets were and how you had to go to Richmond or DC to catch the bus to Baltimore. If he knew all that, I figured he wouldn't be so broken up when his mother didn't show.

I wasn't trying to be mean. He hadn't seen his mother's high heels and the way she wiggled her butt when she'd left the year before, prancing out to that muscle man's car and never even waving back at her only kid. I'd seen it. I remembered. And I remembered a lot of other things about Antoinette that Rey may not have ever known.

Before he was born and even sometimes after, Antoinette used to babysit for us because she didn't have a job and Mama did. Although I was barely two when "it" happened and didn't remember it myself, I'd overheard Mama and Ruthie talking about their sister and how wild she was. One particular story, about the last time Antoinette babysat, the sisters repeated and repeated. It was like they were pinching themselves, the story a way to remind them how different they were from her. Like, if they kept reminding themselves, her bad karma wouldn't touch them. Every time Antoinette did something crazy, Mama and Ruthie would rehash that same old story. They ranted about it so often I knew the details better than if I'd been old enough to remember it myself.

Antoinette's friends, two or three men, had stopped by the trailer to visit. They brought a lot of beer, a lot of bottles. Someone stepped on one and didn't bother to pick up the pieces. Two year old me cut my foot. Mama was at a training session for work. Although Latrelle was still around, he wasn't living with them. He dropped in when he felt like it, drinking, talking big, a worse babysitter than Antoinette. It might even have been some of his friends who'd been visiting that day. With all the visitors, no one, not even Rey's own mother, changed his diaper. His butt was raw skin. When Mama came home to the mess and her little girl's foot wrapped in a towel with duct tape, she'd said a lot of bad things to Antoinette.

"We had words," was the way Mama described it. "Uh-huh, sure, you know what kind of words."

Aunt Ruthie would uh-huh right back. She did know those words. "With all that beer, that woman were walking crookeder than a bent paperclip. She slid right off those show-off heels of hers ten, twelve times."

Mama would shake her head. "And when I asked her why she treated the children that way, she slammed the door hard enough to let everyone know she was hot. Like she was the one wronged. Something the matter with that girl right from the start."

"She's still working against herself, thinking it's everyone fault but hers. Some people make their own trouble."

"That's Sister. That's her for sure." Mama did not tolerate people who didn't keep their promises.

I knew better than to repeat the story where Rey could hear it. I just left the map there on the coffee table so he'd understand come Wednesday when Antoinette didn't show. Women shouldn't have babies if all they thought about was their make-up and what kind of car a man ran around in. It didn't make any sense to me that Antoinette and Ruthie and Mama, as different as they were, could be sisters. Before Ashante Mama hadn't had a boyfriend since Jasmine was a baby, and that was a lot of years. Good years once Latrelle stopped coming around.

When it was just the four of us we'd had so much fun. Sometimes Mama made pancakes for dinner. She let us camp out in the living room with scary movies on Friday nights. Even before her latest promotion, she had to bring work home from the office. We knew to be quiet when she was working.

With Ashante here it was like Mama was lighter, not all tangled up in work. She still worried over how many people passed through her office and needed more help with not enough money to make a difference. But she left most of that worry at work. Ashante could make her laugh if Henry Lewis dropped his pizza on the floor or if Jasmine tied everyone's shoe laces together under the table while we were eating. I especially liked to watch when Ashante and Mama danced to the radio. Once Mama slipped off her shoes, her stockings made a whispery noise on the vinyl floor. When Ashante kissed her neck behind her ear, she'd shiver and smile huge, her eyes closed tight, squeezing out everything but the happiness.

Like Aunt Ruthie said, Ashante was a kind person. You could tell he was glad to be with Mama, the way he let her drape her legs over his when they sat on the couch, the way he let her talk all about the idiot things people from her office did. He didn't shush her or complain about hardly anything. He didn't talk that much, period. And he'd never yelled, until today. Plus he wouldn't give the time of day to Ruthie's Gerald, which showed what a good judge of character he was, to my mind. I wanted people to say that about me when I was a grown-up.

After Antoinette hung up on Rey, Aunt Ruthie called the nursing home and switched to late shift. She and Ashante worked without talking, as if they hadn't argued earlier. She cleaned up the kitchen, pitched half-eaten pies, scraps of chicken, and some of the droopiest flowers. He rearranged the furniture and mopped the kitchen floor. When Ruthie called us for dinner, it was almost eight. I collected the girls from the bottom bunk where they were playing with finger puppets. We ate in silence, even Jasmine and Liné somehow understood there was nothing worth saying. Rey gobbled it all, but boys were always hungry. Mama didn't lift her fork.

"I'll be at the nursing home until seven tomorrow morning if you need me." Ruthie was looking at Ashante. "You leave for work at seven-thirty?"

"Seven-fifteen."

"I'll try to get off a few minutes early, make sure they get off to school."

"I don' wanna go to school," Liné fussed.

"You gonna let Jasmine ride the bus all by herself?" Ruthie said. "Mee, you'll have to help in the morning."

I could just tell from Ruthie's tone of voice that she wasn't going to change her mind about school, no matter what she said to keep from having to listen to the whining. Ruthie showed me how to change the coffee filter and measure for a new pot. Pushing past Ashante with the laundry basket, Ruthie cut him off in the middle of his offer to do it. "I can run it while I'm writing up charts. You have Mary to deal with."

It was hard to listen to them treating my mother like a sack of dog food, a burden to be moved from room to room. Except for the horror over Latrelle and her bad days at work, she had been fun, better than most of the other mothers. The radio always on, her feet tapping and her arms swinging. She liked sunny days, trumpet players, being pregnant, Christmas, rainy days, bright colors, everyone she ever met, ghost stories, and kids. Her kids, especially.

When Aunt Ruthie got ready to leave for the late shift, I was so cross I couldn't even hug her good-bye.

"Go on, now and get some sleep, grouchy girl," Ruthie said. "You'll feel better once you get some rest."

I didn't see how rest would change anything.

Although Ruthie came upstairs to check on us one last time after she'd packed the laundry into her dented wagon, she didn't speak, just stood in the doorway like she was counting heads. Rey was on the cot, already zonked, his basketball shoes right there on the floor by his head, as close to under the pillow as he could get them. He didn't look like the old Indian medicine man tonight. He looked like a baby being rocked, his arms splayed every which way, his lips open, safe. When Ruthie's station wagon chugged out of the parking lot, Meeka didn't have to get out of bed to know that the muffler was coughing smoke like a cartoon. Mama called it Ruthie's Roadrunner. She'd mimic the cartoon sound of the beep beep and they all laughed. I lay there wishing Mama would joke about it again.

In the morning just as Ashante washed the last breakfast dish, Ruthie arrived in her uniform. She hustled Rey onto the school bus, never mind all his fussing and carrying on that he wanted to stay, Henry Lewis his soul brother.

"Meeka needs me."

It was as close to true a thing as he'd ever said and I was surprised a boy could figure that out. To fight off the crying, I packed the island book in my backpack with my journal and laced up my sneakers.

"Where you think you're going?" Ruthie stood in the doorway.

"Ashante said I could go. I thought he talked to you about it."

Ruthie shook her head. "It's too soon to leave your mother alone."

"Mama doesn't even see me."

"It's shock, girl. It'll pass. When it does, she gonna want family close. Anyways, you're smart. You miss a few days, you can catch up."

"I'll have to make up the science test and the Language Arts paper."

"Next week's soon enough, honey. Mr. Johnson's waiting on me at the funeral home to make the arrangements, and I work second shift. We gotta get your mama through this first week, past the burying part. Someone has to be here when Rey and them get out of school. We're a team. We stick together."

It didn't feel like a team. Where were the cheerleaders? Ahead of me was a long day in the apartment with zombie Mama in bed and folks from church and all over coming to say their piece and gawk at me, the big sister who let her brother die. Aunt Ruthie was going back to work, Ashante too, and Rey to school. When the little girls disappeared up the bus steps, I would be alone, all the responsibility on my shoulders for the stranger my mother had turned into. No matter that Ruthie didn't mean it this way, it was part of my punishment for not keeping Henry Lewis safe.

Once Ruthie left, the old car sputtering down the street, I felt under the mattress. The white lady's stones were smooth and cool. They must have come from the ocean, way down where the river spilled out to the Atlantic. Rolling over and over in the sand, all their rough edges worn down. I drew a circle around the smooth edge, round and round, and thought about all the places the stones had been, the things they'd seen. How amazing to be carried past islands and cliffs and continents to end up in the hand of a girl in a little town in Virginia.

I had to return the stones. I'd never stolen anything before, even when Danielle had dared us to shoplift at the 7-11. I wasn't a thief. Every time I passed the creek, I thought about the white lady standing there and watching Henry Lewis disappear. How easy it would have been for her to jump in, and if she had, Henry Lewis would still be here.

Sure, I'd gone to her house, wanting to ask her why, why hadn't she just saved him. I was looking for trouble, Mama would have said. Not that I had any idea what I would have done or said if the white lady had been home. But her car was gone and the back door was open. When I called through the screen, the little black dog hadn't complained, almost as if he understood I needed to be there. I hadn't gone there to steal, just to look. But when I saw the stones on the dresser, stacked so prettily in front of the photographs of the lady's children, the urge to make things even overwhelmed me, to take something of hers, to make her hurt too, to make her pay for not saving Henry Lewis. .

It wasn't logical. It was ridiculous really. But with the stones in my pocket, it felt like the world had tilted back a little closer to straight.

Chapter Nineteen

By Sunday night Celie could hardly keep her eyes open while they finished leftovers with Rory and Lila. Jake's voice wove in and out of the drone of conversation. She didn't even try to follow it and the three of them continued to talk as if she wasn't even there. Once their car finally glided down the driveway, she went straight to the bedroom and changed into her pajamas.

"Celie?" Jake called from the porch, his voice coming through the bedroom window instead of down the hallway. "Come out and sit on the patio. The sunset's spectacular."

She was too tired to debate. Bundled into sweatpants and a fleece jacket over the pajamas, she shut the window with a resounding thump and joined him on the patio.

"It's not that cold," he said.

"I'm freezing."

"Don't stay then."

"No, it's fine. I have two layers on."

He pointed to the sky above the cottage. She nodded. It was something to see the array of colors streaming across what had been a nondescript pale blue all day.

"Sam was wild last night, huh?" Jake said.

"How many Manhattans did you make for him?"

Jake frowned. "Only one. Why would you say it like that?"

"Like what?"

"Like I got him drunk."

"We shouldn't have let him drive home."

"It's not far."

"That's irrelevant. Something like eighty percent of accidents happen within twenty miles of your residence."

"Where did you read that?"

"It's true. It's in that ad about seatbelts. Well, not really an ad. A public service announcement. From the State Police maybe."

"Sam wasn't drunk." Jake wouldn't let it go.

"You're the one who said he was wild."

"I meant the stories he was telling."

She concentrated on the sky. The long horizontal bands of deep turquoise and orange were mesmerizing. "Is this still the effect of that volcano erupting out west?" she asked.

"Mt. St. Helens? Maybe." He scooted his chair four or five feet toward the creek in order to see the actual sun itself. "I'm going down to the dock. We're missing the best part up here."

She couldn't seem to get her legs moving. He paused where the walkway met the driveway and glanced back at her. She was still in the chair.

"You're not coming?"

"Too cold."

He went down without her, didn't even turn around again. He wasn't feeling so protective that he didn't mind leaving her alone. Although her first response was negative, she realized it might be he had taken what she said at the emergency room to heart and was trying to give her space. There had been no shoulder pats, no squeezing her arm when he passed. She tried not to think how prickly and unlovable she'd been these last few days. Like any marriage, they had times when they didn't click, when conversations seemed strained and irritation came more quickly. It was a miracle that any two people could stay married for three and four decades. Something about the weekend, seeing the kids, Sam and his wife, made her think this too would pass. She almost got up to write it down. A counselor would see it as a step forward.

From the porch she could see the sunset just fine, let him have the creek view. There would be other nights, other sunsets. The sun was low enough that the sky around the house had turned solid cobalt. Any second the color would drain away and it would be black. The only light would be the North Star and maybe Venus if it were the right time of the month. She'd read the paper, but couldn't recall what it had said.

For another two or three minutes, she sat there shivering, trying to remember if he had opened two or three bottles of wine on Saturday night. Not that it really mattered, but Sam had not been able to stop talking about his investments, a personal subject she felt ought not to be shared outside family. His volubility was characteristic, most definitely alcohol-related. Neither of their kids drank, a coincidence she attributed to Caroline and Lila's preferences, not an adverse reaction to growing up around a cocktail hour that she and Jake followed religiously on weekends. So at dinner it would only have been Jake, Phyllis and Sam drinking the wine. A bottle apiece, that was a lot.

The conversation had been one-sided. The two men traded stock market stories one after the other, then moved on to college tales. At first Phyllis and Lila managed a side conversation about movies and books, which Celie listened to in a pleasant haze without adding much. The kids cleared the dinner things before dessert.

Leaning across the corner of the table, Rory had whispered to her when Phyllis slipped out to the bathroom. "Are you feeling okay, Mom? You've been staring out the window the whole dinner."

She examined his face to see if this was a tease. "Not the whole dinner. Sometimes it's nice just to listen. Lila's so lovely to entertain Phyllis." She meant it, it had been easy, and drifting had been a nice switch to the tension with Jake.

"Should we put on coffee, Mom?" Lila asked.

She laid her hands on Rory's shoulders in an ownership kind of gesture, more typical of a long-married spouse. An oddly aggressive expression from Lila who usually deferred and deferred, to Rory, to her in-laws, to Thomas and Caroline. Celie hoped she hadn't offended her by not engaging more actively in the discussion. She had been tired all weekend. It must be all that time in the sun.

"Who wants decaf?" she asked. When no one raised a hand, she lifted her shoulders to Lila in mock disbelief. "Make whatever kind you want, sweetie. You two will be up solving the problems of the world long after we old folks are zonked."

And then, as if a celestial hand had zapped Jake with the realization the men were monopolizing the evening, he mentioned the kids' honeymoon trip to Nicaragua. She smiled at him in thanks, and he smiled back. There was the old Jake, her conspirator. Before either of the kids could answer though, Sam jumped in and described his experience there decades ago. It didn't upset her. It just made her glad she was married to Jake who had twice the social awareness. Energized, she scooped ice cream onto the apple cobbler in record time.

Lila and Rory did get to talk a little when Phyllis asked again about the honeymoon. Once the kids excused themselves after dessert to take a quick walk before retiring, the party dissolved. Jake saw Sam and Paula to their car as Celie listened to the voices blur and dim. There was a time when she and Jake walked every night before bedtime. Maxy actually liked the leash and he certainly needed the exercise. During her treatments though, Jake had gotten into the habit of excusing her from the dinner table for an early bedtime. He was a wizard at recognizing exactly when she was incapable of staying awake a moment longer, almost before she realized it. She had been grateful. When had that changed? When had she changed? He still took the evening walks with the dog; he just didn't ask if she wanted to go.

Without talking, she rinsed the plates and filled the dishwasher. He cleared the rest and repeated some of the conversation she'd missed. When she reached for the dishtowel to dry the pots, he elbowed her aside. "That's enough. You're exhausted. You cooked. The least I can do is put stuff away. Go ahead and get ready for bed. I'll be in in a minute."

Undressing in the dark bedroom by herself while Jake wrapped up the leftovers, she tried to recall those easy evenings, thirty years worth before the cancer, times she had been eager to pace herself next to his longer strides, to hear his ideas for the company, about the kids. Mostly she remembered the feeling of being energized by their discussions. They'd been a good team, like Rory and Lila. It had been too long since she'd felt that way. She blamed the damn disease, but it was more than that. He still had the power to change his world, and she had lost that somewhere. The sickening feeling of hopelessness that she'd felt standing on the seawall with Meeka washed over her again. Twice in one day she'd admitted that she needed help. She would find a counselor and fix this. Tomorrow.

On Monday morning Tracy Anne Sheffield was at the kitchen door at eight-thirty with a plate of scones and her fancy initialed coffee mug. The hot pink matched her windbreaker.

"I thought you might like some company," she said, the screen door propped open with her elbow.

"That's very kind."

Celie did not move backwards until Tracy thrust the plate into her hands and stepped up over the threshold. It would have been awkward not to invite her in after the screen door shut behind her. They stood on opposite sides of the kitchen while Tracy sipped from the miniature opening in the lid of the plastic mug.

"I guess you heard the body washed up yesterday," Tracy said.

"No." She hadn't heard. She'd had guests all weekend but she wasn't going to give those details to Tracy Anne to broadcast all over town.

"Steve Markham said they couldn't put the picture in the paper, the body's too bloated after that much time. At least it's been identified. And they interviewed the guy who found it, so they have the story."

Each time Tracy Anne uttered 'body' and 'it,' Celie cringed internally. What was the matter with people? Did they have no imagination that they couldn't comprehend how awful it must be to lose a child and to hear him described in such chilling, clinical terms?

"You made these yourself?" Celie changed the subject. "I've been looking for an easier recipe." She ripped off the plastic wrap and chose one.

"Oh, no, they're from the coffee shop. I don't bake anymore." It sounded like a boast. "Actually I never did bake much. Freddie's always on a diet. It wouldn't be fair to him."

She smiled in a way that made Celie want to poke out her eyes. Thin people didn't understand how hard it was not to gain weight. With the blandest smile she could muster, she composed a socially acceptable thank you.

"I don't eat many sweets either. But fresh blueberry scones . . . that's a real treat. I'll have to get myself down to the coffee shop more often."

"The girls go on Tuesday mornings."

"The girls?" The look of insincere sorrow on Tracy Anne's face made Celie feel like she was back in middle school again.

"My bridge club. The eight of us have been playing for years."

"My father warned me about bridge before I left for college. Such a waste of good reading time."

Tracy Anne laughed. She didn't even catch the dig. "You probably haven't heard about the funeral either."

Much as Celie hated to prolong the conversation, she wanted to know about the service. "When is it?"

"Wednesday morning. At the Baptist Church in Farnham. The black Baptist Church."

Celie was sorry she had asked.

"I could swing by here and pick you up." Tracy Anne said.

"No, no thanks. I'm sure Jake will want to be there."

"I thought he had a business trip."

Celie turned her back to hide her surprise. How the hell did Tracy Anne know Jake's schedule? They had been having secret conversations about her.

She bumbled her way through an explanation about riding to the funeral with a neighbor. When Tracy Anne left finally, Celie pitched the scones into the trash, after putting one in Maxy's dish for spite. She couldn't think why she had said that about Jake wanting to go to the funeral. He would be in Raleigh for his quarterly board meeting and he wouldn't have gone to the funeral in the first place. *You don't know those kids*, he'd said right off the bat.

She didn't need a ride. She could drive herself to a funeral. She was used to driving. She'd driven herself to most of the treatments. And if she decided it would be too emotional, George might be going. Or Barry. Either one of them would take her if she asked.

Right after Tracy Anne left, it started to thunder. The air, which had been hot and heavy after five days of unseasonable sunshine, hung weighted down with moisture in spite of the rain overnight. Charcoal clouds from the north careened across the river and plowed up against more charcoal clouds stuck on the southeast horizon. The approaching sound of the thunder sent her racing around to shut windows. She was out of breath when the rain hit, great opaque sheets of sideways drops that struck the panes with enough force to rattle them in their frames. She could hardly see to the north through the storm. The bridge was obscured completely. In the bedroom she checked to be sure the windows were secured and put on her slippers. After a few minutes of watching the tree trunks turn black and the new green spriggy leaves twist in the wind, she shuffled through the papers on her dresser for her list.

As she reached out to stroke the pale sleek half-shell of conch she'd brought back from one of their family cruises, she noticed the things on her dresser were out of place. There were only three stones from the beach in Rockport. Three were missing.

When she had first unpacked boxes from the Middleton house at the cottage, she'd discovered a bag of beach finds from their summer travels. She'd made a small arrangement on a piece of pottery her mother had made in one of her art classes. The turquoise raku tray in front of the photos was just large enough to hold six black stones and two white ones and a few of the smallest shells. She had selected the smooth flat stones herself on her beach walks on Cape Hedge Beach, a favorite haunt for the boys who had belly-surfed for hours there. The homemade altar reminded her of how short a lifetime was compared to the eons of time that had smoothed the chips from rougher granite veins in mountains far from the sea.

She must have knocked them off in the night by mistake. On her hands and knees she looked under the bureau, the nightstand, the bed. Nothing but a few floating cobwebs on the baseboards and the list she'd come in to find. It was odd. Besides her, only Jake came in the bedroom. Neither he nor the boys would notice the rocks. And she knew she hadn't moved them herself. At least she didn't remember moving them. Was she that fuzzy that she could have forgotten something like that?

The linen closet clean-up at the top of last week's list didn't seem as necessary as it had when she'd written it down. Still it was manageable and mindless. She removed all the sheets and towels from the three shelves, discarded the ones that were stained or worn, and refolded the rest in neat piles. She fingered the lace on two of the ruined pillowcases. Handmade. Miniature blue and yellow stitches blossomed into a posey on the ivory linen. Some woman had worked on that project for days, probably with children playing at her feet. Not here at the cottage—it wasn't old enough—but in front of a window for extra light or under an oil lamp. Perhaps with a friend or sister stitching alongside, they had talked about where to get an extra ration of butter or when their husbands would get leave. Women had their own history, different from the machinations of men's politics and inventions and war-mongering.

The continuity of women's history appealed to her. There was a comfort in knowing earlier generations had experienced what she had, as a mother, a wife, a member of the community, the church. Before her, in the thirties and forties, women had died of cancer, even though there had been no extended treatment regimen back then. They had just taken to their beds, curled up with the pain, and died weeks or months later without explanation. In the late forties when they started actually calling it cancer, it had been an automatic death sentence. While she was in high school, she remembered one of her mother's friends had been diagnosed. Her husband left within a week. Flat out, four kids, no support. He signed over the house as if it were a great gift though she had no income to pay a mortgage in addition to the oil bill or the real estate taxes. Seventeen and a blatant feminist, Celie had vowed never to let a man put her in that position.

When she and Jake started to date during her last year of college, the world was different. He already had his business degree and worked with plenty of women who had theirs. She loved how much he enjoyed his female colleagues. He raved about their diplomacy, their ability to compromise without letting egos clash. He'd been so proud of her when she set up her own mediation practice.

Although he had never completely understood the incredible juggling act of motherhood and proprietorship, he did help. He *babysat* when she had conferences or evening meetings. Much as he loved the boys, he'd never been the one in charge of the children. At five o'clock he didn't look at his watch and shut down his computer so he could go home and feed them dinner. It was a huge disconnect, one she hadn't had time or energy to explain to him when she'd been in the middle of child-rearing. She'd just done what had to be done.

She smoothed the lace on the old pillowcases, folded the edges inside the wafer-thin fabric, and shoved them into the trash box. But when she saw them there, bunched up and discarded, regret overwhelmed her. Fine-boned fingers had worked a tiny needle through the weave of the bleached material and created the delicate patterns. Those same hands had pressed out the wrinkles and pulled the handiwork over feather pillows for someone to dream on.

Whoever that was, they must have dreamed away happily for years to wear the cloth so thin. Who was she to discard them so cavalierly simply because they had discolored with the years, threads given way, lace no longer quite so perfect, stitches lost in the weft of use and those passing dreams?

Jake's voice sounded in her head. *Move on, move on.* She stuffed a stained towel on top to hide them and left them in the trash. The overflowing shoeboxes of mouthwash and motel soaps would have to wait for another burst of energy. It was only eleven-thirty when she gave it up and made herself a second cup of tea. Although the thunderstorm had passed, the sky remained blanched and iffy. A ruffled breeze trailed in off the river. Cooler.

As it turned out Kathy Oncek called and offered her a ride to the funeral. Jake emailed to tell her he planned to leave for Raleigh a day early. If he arrived Tuesday afternoon, he would have time to meet with the Chairman of the Board before the afternoon board convened on Wednesday. He would drive back to the Middleton office on Thursday, and the cottage on Friday after work. Since he would be away all week, there was no reason to mention the funeral or Kathy's offer. If he started in again, she might lose her temper and that would only contribute to the distance between them. She wanted to be there for Meeka. It sounded simple enough. She was trying not to overanalyze it.

Holding the hot mug in both hands, she worried about whether she should have said no to Kathy. The funeral might be too much for someone with active cancer cells. There was the drive to the church, somewhere across the river, the service itself, and then the wake afterwards, a long day for anyone, even without considering the emotional toll. Kathy hadn't said what her connection was to the Breedens, only that she knew the family, and had heard that Celie did too. Maybe she'd taught Henry Lewis or one of the other children. She could have worked with their mother at some point. On the ride over Kathy might explain the details. Celie imagined the stories. She'd been thinking it would help her understand Meeka and Mary, but it would make Henry Lewis more real as well. Jake's voice in her head echoed her own doubt. The more real Henry Lewis was, the harder it would be to put behind her her failure to save him. The more she thought about it, the more she wished she had not agreed to ride with Kathy.

Barry's ambiguous remark about the Onceks ending the chemo early was all she knew about Kathy's cancer. She had no idea of her real condition. She might not be strong enough to be out, but in her sympathy for Celie, a fellow cancer patient, Kathy might be over-extending herself. If she had heard from someone, maybe even from Barry, that Celie was down at the creek that afternoon, she might have offered to drive out of sympathy, ignoring her own physical limitations. Too many what ifs. Celie could feel herself bogging down again in minutiae.

Thomas's perpetual advice was to stay focused on the big picture. Her big picture lately was her list. Not very big really. To disperse the blue thoughts she took off the kerchief and shook out her hair, such as it was. The scrapbook project, that was the next thing on her list.

With the steaming tea mug in hand, she went to the study. After she set up both card tables—one for organization and one for actual installation—she dragged one of the cardboard boxes over to the first table where she could reach it from her chair. Scrawled letters on the flap in permanent marker said "Thomas." The box held things she had saved for the last twenty-odd years. She stared at the jumble inside. It was off-putting. Loose photographs, play programs, drawings from kindergarten on paper so big it had been folded four ways, Hard Rock Café napkins, and scribbled Mother's Day cards. A box for each boy that required her memory to sort and display in the proper order.

While she'd been accumulating the things, it had been fun to think about a time when the boys would be grown and would share the collection with children of their own. Now that the time had arrived, the impossibility of coming close to the truth of those experiences struck her head on. How insignificant some of the treasures were, when they'd seemed so important at the time.

She rifled through the photos in Thomas's box. Every Christmas, every Halloween, every Easter, but how old had he been when he was Darth Vader? Eight, twelve? In one picture the costume covered even his shoes. She could have mixed them up. It might be Rory, adorned in Thomas's costume from the year before. She spread the photographs out on the table, overlapped slightly so she could see the entire series. A lifetime on a card table.

No, only a childhood. Not even that, nothing really. The childhood was inside Thomas, inside Rory. Inside her, in her memories, and in the tightness of her throat every time they hugged her good-bye and went off to their new lives, their lives without her.

She was crying again, sloppy splatters on her hands and on the pictures. She shoved the chair back. It caught on the carpet, knocked the back of her knees, and pitched her forward. When she put a hand out to steady herself on the table, one of the retractable legs—she must not have extended it fully—collapsed. The photos slid, a pool of cascading color on the beige carpet. How she managed to keep from falling, she wasn't sure, but as she surveyed the mess and the open waiting box, the sobs rose in her chest and she gave in, gave up. Whatever this was, it wasn't who she wanted to be. It wasn't who she had been.

With the hand towel from the bathroom against her face, she gulped air between sobs. She bumped around the living room furniture, the towel pressed to her burning eyes, and fumbled for the screen door handle with the unbandaged hand. On the north end of the porch she sat in the Adirondack chair, her legs splayed out, her head in her hands. She couldn't stop crying. And she couldn't stop berating herself for being so emotional.

"Ma'am?" The voice came out of the blue.

She swung around, madly swiped at her cheeks, ready to blast Tracy Anne for bothering her again. At the opposite end of the porch Meeka Breeden held out the baking pan from the donated ham. Shiny. Clean. She had on running shorts and that same sleeveless undershirt from last week. All legs and arms, she looked much younger than Celie remembered her.

"Aunt Ruthie said to bring back your pan." The girl half-turned and eyed the brick walkway by the lower side of the house, her escape route. "But you have three doors."

She surprised Celie by stepping between the bushes, reaching through the pool fence, and setting the pan down on the edge of the porch.

"You hurt yourself?" Meeka asked, and when Celie didn't answer, she pointed.

"My hand? Oh, no, no, it's just a little cut. My husband insisted on the bandage. He overreacts."

"Mama's like that too. She blows up over the least littlest thing. Usually. It doesn't last."

Celie stuffed the towel behind her and watched Meeka back out of the bushes and start down the hill. She admired how confidently the girl moved, the paralyzing hesitation of Tuesday absent.

"Don't go," she called out. "I'm done crying, really."

Although Meeka gave her a long hard stare as if she didn't believe her, she came back, followed the fence line toward the gate, and popped it like a pro. She stepped within an arms' length of where Celie sat.

"Mama always makes us drink water when we've been crying. She says it refills your tear ducts for the next time. Like that's a good thing." With one flip-flop she scuffed at the landscape pebbles between them. "Funny thing, just when things get settled, it always seems like there is something else to cry about."

The girl went on and on. Maybe she was nervous with the pool so close or talking to a strange adult. They hardly knew each other and their other meetings had not been easy. She wasn't making much sense, but she was trying hard. She'd hardly taken a breath. Celie rubbed her forehead to make the ache go away. Crying hard always gave her a headache. Somehow she didn't think Tylenol would help this headache.

Meeka babbled on. "I cried yesterday when they found him. I mean, I wanted them to find him. I hated him being out there by himself. But Mama hasn't cried at all. Not when she came back from the creek, not all those nights he was out there alone, not when they came yesterday to tell us." Her hands stroked her own forehead, a mirror image of Celie, as if she was considering subconsciously what Celie might be feeling. "She isn't talking either."

"Different people—"

"I mean not at all. Basically she hasn't talked since Tuesday. Six days."

"Maybe—"

"You might of just heard they found him. Is that it? Is that why you're crying?"

It was easier to nod, even though it wasn't exactly right. Celie had no idea why the girl had chosen to come to the creek yet again. Neither of them seemed to be able to stay away. They were both trying to make sense of an inexplicable event. Meeka was too young to have much experience with tragedy. No point in adding to her burden with the idea that you lost children in other ways. Life, despite all those wondrous things that happened to you when you were young, could be so cruel.

"We don't have to talk about it," Celie said. There was a long awkward pause while she checked her pockets for a tissue with no luck. Meeka seemed to be holding her breath.

"I don't mind. No one at my house is talking at all. Rey said it right, it's like a crypt."

"It won't always be like that." It didn't sound as positive as Celie would have liked. She leaned her head back against the porch post, searching for better words.

Although Meeka tossed her head, revealing a glimpse of that earlier anger, primed to debate right here and now, she didn't disagree. They were both silent as the echo of the platitude sank away.

Meeka started first. "I can get you a drink of water. If that's okay? You should rest."

When Celie didn't answer, Meeka stepped past her and went inside. The kitchen cupboards opened and shut, the tap water ran. She was gone a long time, but it was pleasant just to sit and not think about anything. With the snap of the screen door, Meeka was back, holding out a juice glass full of water. Once Celie had taken it, Meeka pointed at the river.

It seemed the most natural thing in the world to be talking with this girl on her porch, as if they were old friends catching up. She wondered if Meeka was still fighting the anger or if she'd already begun to heal, the fury of the drowning buried in the intensity of the aftermath, like a rocket burning up at re-entry.

"When I came up the path," Meeka said, "before you came out, I was looking at your river."

She spun around neatly, surprisingly graceful for the gangly legs, setting her face to the river, her long back to Celie and the porch. Celie had to lean forward to hear what she said next.

"It goes on forever and ever and ever. I mean from here you can see all the way to the ocean. That is the ocean out there, isn't it? The Atlantic?"

"Well, yes." Celie said. "It's there. You can't really *see it* see it, but that's where the river leads."

"Oh, I can see it. I can see the waves pushing themselves downstream. And way, way out there, all the way down the river, I can see beaches like they show on TV, *Virginia Is for Lovers*, those beaches." Meeka spoke with heightened conviction as if Celie had denied the earth was round. "When I look out on that river, past those beaches I can see the Nina and the Santa Maria riding the waves like surfers do. And past them there are submarines with their snarky periscopes checking out everything."

Celie wasn't crying anymore. She was fascinated with this girl's imagination. But Meeka wasn't finished.

"You can see the ocean really good, I bet, with that." She pointed through the living room window.

Celie leaned forward and glanced into the house where Meeka pointed. "The telescope? That belongs to my son Rory. He's the scientist in our family."

"Where is he?"

"Oh, he doesn't live here. He's married now. They live in Washington, D.C., Alexandria actually."

"Does it work?" She jabbed a finger in the direction of the telescope.

Celie saw the instant disconnect and it made her laugh. Being married put him in the class of boring adults. It would make him a lot less interesting to a teenage girl. She motioned for Meeka to follow her. With the screen door open between them, the girl stopped just shy of the threshold.

"I was only returning the pan. I should go." Her withdrawal was almost visible and made Celie want to look behind her to see what in her living room could have made the girl change her mind so instantly.

"Don't you want to see how the telescope works?"

"They showed us at the Richmond science museum."

"But just now you asked?"

"I was only making conversation. I thought maybe if your son had it when he was a kid, it might be broken. That's why I asked. My brother liked to fix things and when he took things apart, you could learn stuff. But you're not feeling so good . . ." The screen door wobbled a little in her hand. "Ashante's prob'ly wondering where I got to." The girl was nervous again suddenly, when she'd been fine as long as the focus was not on her.

"You're welcome to use our phone and call," Celie offered. "If you want to stay and try the telescope."

"I'll just go on home, thank you. I mean, thank you for the ham. We picked at it all weekend and it's almost gone."

"Come back another time then and try the telescope."

Meeka's flip-flops slapped the porch floor as she retreated. As she disappeared around the corner of the house, Celie let the screen door fall softly against the frame. It clicked shut, leaving her on the inside. The house was quiet except for the muffled drips of rainwater from the roof outside. Maxy padded in from the other room, cocked his head as if considering whether his mistress was busy, and then, gave up the idea of a pat and climbed into the dog bed without crossing the room. What a practical little dog he was.

She took the cover off the telescope lens. With both hands she slid open the window screen and repositioned the telescope for a clear view down river. One eye closed, she leaned over. She hoped those periscopes would be peering back at her.

Chapter Twenty

Monday afternoon when I left Mama's room to be on the lookout for
the school bus, someone was already sitting on the front steps.

"Rachel." Too late I realized the noise might upset Mama.

She jumped up and hugged me. "Where you been, girl? I left a
zillion messages."

"Trac's out of minutes and Ashante says we have to save the
other phone for official stuff."

"You're being punished?"

"No." I bristled. If she assumed I'd done something wrong,
everyone else must be thinking that too. "A bunch of people calling,
that's all."

"About Henry Lewis?"

"Yeah."

She sank back onto the steps. "We didn't hear until Wednesday
night. My mother forbid me from coming over. She said it was
family only. I couldn't get close to you at church yesterday."

"Ruthie and Ashante thought it was better if we sat in the balcony
and left early."

"We've been praying for y'all. All the Washington's, uncles,
aunts, even Granddaddy Jefferson took himself to church for Sunday
evening prayer meeting when he hates sitting in his Sunday clothes
through two services."

Rachel hugged me again. This time she pounded my back like I
was choking on something and needed to shake it loose. I let her
pound. Two weeks ago, the last time we talked, we'd argued over
Demeta. Since the start of eighth grade it seemed like all we did was
fight over who was whose friend. Demeta was always trying to cause
trouble. This last time she told me that Rachel copied my answers
from the test, and she told Rachel that I stole deodorant from her
gym locker. Demeta's favorite game was passing out candy or gum
and leaving somebody out on purpose. She picked a different girl
each time, and then acted all surprised, when what she really loved
was starting trouble. I was fed up, especially with the way none of us
called her on it. We let her get to us.

Rachel's apology, muffled in a longer embrace than the first,
included Henry Lewis, and the argument over Demeta, how she was
going to make it up to me for missing my birthday during the fight,
and how sorry she was for calling me a pighead.

"I thought you said pinhead." I was choked up on tears.

"I'd never call you that. You're too smart. You don't see me getting any A minuses on my report card, do you? I said pighead."

"What's a pighead?"

"You." She ran the zipper on her backpack up and down. "Stubborn, hard-headed."

We were deep into it on the front steps when Rey came around the corner from the bus stop. Over Rachel's shoulder, I saw him slow down as soon as he saw her. He let the book bag slide off his shoulder like he didn't want to own up to it as his. With a quick *shut up* glance at me, he focused on Rachel, circling her until he was right in front of her. He was working hard to swallow a smile. He wanted to be cool, but he just wasn't. Not yet. Maybe never.

"Hey," she said.

"Hey," he answered. With a jerk, he shrugged the bag back onto his shoulder and raised his shoulders to his full height. No matter how hard he tried to stretch himself, he was not tall enough yet to be messing with an eighth grade girl.

"I heard about the fight," she said and reached out to touch the bandage.

It was a little grayer around the edges than it had been this morning. He shrugged again. This time the smile came loose and he was grinning and trying to lower his head to hide it. That wasn't working either.

She kept on and on looking at him. "Everyone says it wasn't your fault, but they haven't said a thing about whether you're suspended."

"Only in-school suspension, two days. I didn't start it."

"Fistfight's what they're saying." She was really asking.

"He had a knife."

"No way."

"A bunch of kids saw it."

"Inside school?"

"Outside, by the picnic tables."

"But they suspended Brad too, right?" I asked. I wondered whether anyone at school had called his mother in Baltimore.

"Duh." He put one foot on the bottom step next to Rachel's leg and leaned in. It was so Hollywood. He'd been watching too many movies. "Three days."

"Brad's a pinhead," I said.

When Rachel and I burst out laughing, Rey looked back and forth at the two of us. He didn't have a clue what was so funny.

"Inside joke," she said when she could finally talk.

When we laughed even harder, he gave up and brushed past.

193

"See ya, dude," she said to his back.

It was okay for him to stew a little bit. I'd fill him in on the joke later. He'd have to give me something in exchange, maybe explain the sudden crush on Rachel. Although it was a really bad idea for a zillion reasons, it looked like she wasn't going to discourage him—who knew what that was all about—so I'd have to, before his feelings were hurt.

For months Willie had been hanging around Rachel. Least he was before the Demeta mess when I lost track of what was what. With the three days of school I'd just missed, anything could have happened. If TJ was right, Willie was still in the picture, but I wouldn't know for sure until Rachel and I had more time to talk in private.

Willie was in tenth and he had his learner's permit. He had a job and a brother who played college football at VCU, totally famous, at least in their part of Virginia, maybe farther. Rey didn't have a horse that could win that race. I was just relieved he'd gotten through school, cut hand or not, without more injuries. If Brad Potter, the meanest, skinniest, white boy in the middle school, was throwing insults at Rey over what happened to Henry Lewis, then the trouble wasn't over. Not by half. I wasn't keen on going back to school and being in the middle of all that.

Rachel was halfway through her jumbled version of the class discussion about *Lord of the Flies*, about Simon dying, and the boys on the island turning into savages, when I couldn't wait any longer.

"When were you going to tell me about Willie?"

"What about Willie?"

"TJ said—"

She snorted. "TJ's running his mouth where it doesn't concern him."

"Never mind TJ. I thought we were best friends. You should have told me about Willie."

"What about him?"

"Are you—"

She stood up in the middle of the sentence and shook her head, just as a police car cut the corner and pulled up to the curb. "I gotta go." She bent down and hugged me. "Just start bawling, they won't bother you. That's what my mother always does when they come looking for HiTop."

The cruiser window rolled down. "Pardon me, ladies, we're looking for the Breeden residence. Mary Breeden."

"This it," Rachel said from where she was, halfway across the lawn.

I moved to the top step, my back to the door. "My mother's lying down."

"Would you tell her Deputy Wawner from the Sheriff's Department is here?"

Upstairs Mama wasn't lying down at all. She was sitting on the edge of the bed with a book on her lap. It was the family bible that Grammy Breeden, Latrelle's mother, had passed on to Mama for safekeeping after I was born. The white cover had indentations to make it look like real leather and a painted picture of Jesus in a big square edged with gold.

I'd heard the story about the bible a hundred times. Grammy Breeden must have really liked the girl her son married. More than she liked her son apparently because she didn't give the Breeden family bible to Latrelle. She gave it to Mary, even though it listed all his relatives, from 1840 right on up. Grammy's curly-cued handwriting listed *Mary and Latrelle Roan Breeden, married July 4, 1995* after the list of his brothers and sisters and their birthdates and marriage dates. Latrelle was the baby, the last one to get married. The entries for Meeka Emeline, Henry Lewis, and Jasmine Tyner were in Mama's writing. The rest of the Tyners, Mama's side of the family, weren't listed because it was the Breeden family bible. Deaths and divorces were written in the big book too. Nothing more about Latrelle though because Grammy died while her youngest son was still living, and the bible wasn't the right place to record that he and Mama didn't live together anymore.

When I saw my mother's hands folded neatly over the open cover of the big book, I hoped she hadn't gotten it out to write about Henry Lewis. It made things so final to think of a second date by his name and no more entries coming for his wedding or his children.

"Some policemen are here," I whispered close to her head. "From the Sheriff. I can tell them you're asleep."

She shut the Bible and lifted it for me to take. After I took it—it was heavy—she let her arms drop slowly through the air, her hands returning to their folded position.

"D'you hear me, Mama? The deputies asked to talk to you."

She let one hand rest on my arm and used it to pull herself up to standing. Just then the cruiser radio crackled out a stream of words and numbers ending with ten four. She flinched as if she'd been slapped. She placed her free hand on the wall and stepped closer to the window. Without showing herself, she fingered the curtain. I caught a glimpse of Rachel at the end of the block, her backpack bouncing against her back. Rey was in front of her, walking backwards, talking and waving his arms, deep in some story.

Whatever was going on there, Rachel and I needed to talk about that too. The cruiser pulled away, its tires spit gravel, dust everywhere like smoke from a leaf fire.

"Maybe they had to go to an emergency somewhere else," I said.

She stayed by the window until the gray cloud had filtered back to the ground. I wished she would turn around. I wanted to see her face, to see if she'd been crying, then I'd know for sure if she'd written the end date for Henry Lewis. Seemed like if you lost family, writing that end date would be a hard thing.

If she had written it though, maybe she was getting better, already was better than they thought, dealing with it at least. Ashante said she had to get past denying it before she could accept it. I knew enough to know that no one but a mother could understand fully how it was to lose your child. Still all those times of minding my brother and sister, I understood a small part of it, the everyday part of being there and not always being able to do what you want when you want, but not caring so much because of the way they loved you back.

"You coming down, Mama?"

She let go of the curtain and sat back on the bedspread, crumpled from where she'd sat earlier. She didn't straighten the pillows like she normally would have done. She didn't lean back or lie down. One hand touched the cover of the bible. Her fingers traced the indentations around Jesus' face.

"Can I get you some iced tea? A piece of pie? Lunchtime come and gone."

She shook her head and lay back. And just like that I knew I'd been dismissed. My mother still didn't want anything to do with me.

It was an hour later that Ashante came home. He brought pizza and he was moving fast. After he twirled the stove dial to 300, he didn't wait for it to warm up, just stuck both boxes inside the oven.

"She get up at all?" he asked to the air.

I raised my eyes from my book and shook my head. Jasmine and Liné were busy with their crayons under the kitchen table. Without asking they'd taken the blanket off my bed and draped it over the edge and across two chairs. Because I'd snorted at them when I saw it being dragged down the stairs, they were careful to ask before they borrowed my desk lamp. I wanted to say no. I used it for homework and it was a birthday present. Desk lamps, according to Mama, were not in the budget. But when Jasmine asked all nice and polite, I remembered how I'd refused to let Henry Lewis sit at my desk to do his homework Monday night.

196

"Fifth grade homework is just as important as eighth grade homework," he'd argued. "And you're only reading. You could read on your bed like you usually do."

"This book is homework."

"*Lord of the Flies*?" He read off the cover and grunted. "You hate bugs."

"It's not about flies. It's about boys on an island."

He tugged the book loose and rifled through the pages. "It doesn't have any pictures." He handed it back.

"It's a novel. You have to use your imagination."

"But what happens?"

"Right now they're deciding which boy is going to be in charge of which job."

"The grownups don't tell them?"

"No grownups. It was a plane crash."

"Awesome."

"It's getting a little scary because they've discovered wild animals on the island and one of the boy's—Jack—is really into hunting. They're building a big fire with war paint and all."

"Cool. I wonder if we'll read that when I'm in eighth grade."

"Probably. It's a classic."

"What's a classic?"

"Like a car that stays around a long time and people talk about it. A classic book is about something that really matters in life and about how you decide stuff when you don't know if you're going to live or die."

"Can I read it after you?"

"I have to turn it in. It's a school book."

"You could pretend you lost it."

"They'd make me pay for it."

"I'll read real fast. You can just say you lost it in your room and you'll bring it in as soon as you find it."

"Right."

"What? The teacher would believe that. Kids are always losing things in their rooms."

"You're too young to understand it."

"Mee."

"If I finish this week, you can read it over the weekend."

"Thanks. So it's okay if I do my math problems at your desk?"

"No."

My desk was about the only thing in the house that was mine only. But after he'd gone down to the kitchen table to work, I switched over to the bed and he was right, it felt less like homework.

I would have gone to tell him I'd changed my mind but once I'd read a little further, I could feel something bad building and building. It was hard to put it down. Plus I was more and more sure eleven was too young to read it and I would have to tell him no. Except now we wouldn't have that discussion ever. About *Lord of the Flies* or any book. I'd been grouchy about the desk for nothing.

So I let the little girls borrow my desk lamp. I carried it down and set it where they wanted it underneath the kitchen table. It made the whole fort, cave, castle, whatever they thought it was, glow like an alien landing site. Ashante whispered and pointed.

"The girls?"

I nodded.

"So." He boosted his voice about four levels. "I guess you and me and Rey'll have to eat that whole cheese pizza ourselves since it's just us three. You hungry, Mee?"

"I'm so hungry I could eat a whole pie myself."

"How about Rey?" He yelled over the television buzz from the living room. "Feel like pizza, boy?"

The TV died and Rey shot into the kitchen. Ashante punched his shoulder lightly. When Rey put up his fists to fight, funning and all, Ashante spun sideways and Rey hit air. The bandage waved like a giant white lobster claw on the end of his arm. I smothered my laugh in the book.

"You are something, boy." Ashante put his hand on Rey's head and held him a straight arm away so Rey's swings flew wide. "You are tenacious."

"What's that?" he asked.

"Mee knows," Ashante said.

I was pleased that he noticed how I paid attention to words. "It means you keep on trying. You never give up."

Rey ducked and twisted away. With his good hand he pulled plates from the dish drainer, stepped back and forth to spread them one at a time on the table. It was obvious he was feeling better. It made me wonder if Rachel had anything to do with it.

"One of these days," Ashante said. "You're gonna have to learn to use your words, Rey. Fighting's not your future." He was sorting through the mail. "Hey, boy, you hear me? Truly, fighting's not anyone's future. But especially not you. You're too small."

Rey was frowning. "Everyone grows. Soccer coach said my feet's so big I might end up six feet tall."

"Don't bet money on it, kid. Some things are out of your control." He tapped my head. "What do they call that, Professor?"

The boys in the book had just started dancing in the firelight and I was too engrossed to pay attention to the confusion around me. "What?" I didn't look up.

Ashante put his face down on my level. "That system, that scientific thing that gives a kid the same eyes as his parents, the same shoe size?"

"Genes."

He didn't look convinced.

"The science is called genetics," I explained, one finger on my place in the book.

"That's it. Genetics. Rey's small 'cause Antoinette's small."

"What about my dad? I could be as tall as he is." Rey's eyebrows fell. "Was."

"Well," Ashante stopped. He must be stuck on how not to say what they all knew, that Antoinette had no idea who the father was of her one and only child. "I don't think anyone ever measured how tall your daddy was. Anyway, gen-e-tics doesn't work for everything."

Rey drummed on his plate with a fork, his eyes full on Ashante. "Exactly. My mama's a girl. I ain't."

"Aren't, not ain't," I said. "But you're wrong again. Antoinette is no girl."

"Ain't that the truth," Ashante said.

"Not ain't. Isn't. Isn't that the truth." I corrected him.

Ashante laughed. "Lucky for me, not my kind of woman. No offense, Rey."

"Can we eat the pizza now?" He shot a quick fist into the blanket at knee height with his good hand.

"What's the matter?" Ashante asked.

"Rodents."

"Right there? Under the table?"

"Big fat rodents. So fat they don't have any room for pizza or they'll pop."

With that Liné came slithering out on her belly from one side and Jasmine right behind her. "Pizza, pizza," they chanted.

"Go wash your hands." Ashante pointed to the bathroom. He bowed his head in the same direction and pretend-growled at the girls. "Wash. I'm going to check on Mary. Back in a sec."

"Your hands too, Rey," I ordered.

"Why are you so bossy all of a sudden?"

I slapped the book closed. "None of your business." When people refused to understand things for their own good, there wasn't much you could do.

Sarah Collins Honenberger

"You too, Rey," he mimicked the high-pitched squeal of the minister's wife.

With the book under my arm I marched past him and up the stairs. Little kids were a lot of trouble. They could wear you down. Boring. Not Henry Lewis, of course. He had a million ideas a minute and was never afraid to try anything. I missed that about him. But it was what had gotten us all into trouble.

I thought about the cottage and the white lady and the telescope. I'd forgotten again to ask her name. And that was half the reason I'd gone down there with the pan, 'cause Ruthie wanted to write a thank you note. I hadn't told anyone I'd been invited to use the telescope. Even though it had always been Henry Lewis who was interested in telescopes and outer space, I was excited. Using the telescope would be like Henry Lewis being right there with me.

Whenever he was into an idea, like he had been about space and stars, he talked constantly about it. Before that it had been cavemen and their drawings. And before that it had been beehives. Every week he borrowed different books from the library. He couldn't help himself. He would talk to me from the cot about how the sun formed from trash particles and how moons circled around planets. He'd get up and use the flashlight and draw sketches to explain gravity and the solar system. Endless questions that he answered for himself by reading and then talking to anyone who would listen.

I had to find a time to go back and try the telescope. The more I thought about it, the more I liked the idea of a place where I could be with Henry Lewis that no one in my family knew about. It would be our secret.

MINDING HENRY LEWIS

Chapter Twenty-One

Although Meeka had gone and Celie didn't feel as sad, she didn't return to the study. The scrapbook project, though, lurked in the back of her mind. Before Jake came home she would clean up the mess and start fresh another day. She drank a whole glass of water in the kitchen, a leftover habit from the chemo when doctor's orders were eight glasses a day. After she retrieved her windbreaker, she went back out to the front steps. She'd forgotten to close the window screen and the telescope extended like an elephant begging for peanuts. It felt good to laugh.

She replayed the conversation with Meeka. The girl was prickly, so quick to be sure people didn't think she was stupid. From vague recollections of Thomas and Rory at that age, Celie remembered they'd been touchy too. But Meeka's hot and cold was more than the typical teenage conviction that adults didn't understand them. If she was truly nervous or—what was more likely—still upset over Celie not jumping in to save Henry Lewis, then she would have refused to deliver the pan. Or she would have left it on the steps by the driveway door and raced away. She wouldn't have come around the other side of the house looking for Celie. That girl wanted something. But what?

She sat with her eyes closed, her back against the porch column, and listened to the trees shake off the morning's rain. There were lulls and there were crescendos. When the spatters hit the concrete walkway or the roof, a rush of cool air like birds' wings filled the air. As it died down, the normal sporadic cries of the osprey and the lap of the waves below her on the beach took over. Never before had she noticed how private the cottage was, how it was its own universe. Of course until last spring when she'd stopped doing the mediation work, they had been here only on summer weekends. Those Saturdays and Sundays they stayed busy, catching up on chores. And they almost always had friends visiting or the boys.

Meeka's curiosity was charming. Much like a child fascinated with the supernatural. The cottage was a different world. The girl wanted to know more. Yet she didn't want give up too much information about herself, or let anyone get too close. Brave and scared at the same time. A child's curiosity easily overran her sense of self-preservation. It was only as you aged that self-preservation became more pronounced. It was logical that it grew in direct proportion to your exposure to the realities of life. The more you learned about the world, the more you understood the risks, the more you held yourself back from the edge.

She wondered if Meeka recognized her curiosity. A week ago she hadn't known this girl and now she could hardly stop thinking about her. Often when people asked her about the cancer, she said it had taught her that life could change in a split second. Here she was less than a week after Henry Lewis drowned and her entire life seemed encapsulated in these six days. As if the lesson of the last year had crystallized out of the smoke and air in that single instant when Meeka had cried out to her brother.

When Celie realized how chilled she was, she stood up to get the circulation going. The trees were dripping on her, she thought. Yet when she rubbed the sleeve of her windbreaker across her face, it wasn't rain at all. She was crying again.

She didn't know how long she stood on the porch and cried. When she was sufficiently cried out, she picked up the clean baking pan and went inside. She washed her face and blew her nose. After she located the insurance card in her wallet, awkward with the bandaged finger, she used her left hand to punch in the number for Customer Service. She waded through the recorded menu until a real person came on the line.

"This is Brittney, how can I help you today?"

"I need the name of a qualifying counselor. I live in Virginia." Her voice sounded stuffy and she wondered if Brittney could tell she'd been crying.

"Would you mind answering a few preliminary security questions?"

Celie nodded and waited. The rep cleared her throat. Celie waited. The rep repeated her question.

"Please answer with a yes or no. This is being recorded."

"Oh, yes. I mean, no, I don't mind." Celie felt stupid.

After the woman asked for her birth date, the last four digits of her social security number, and her mother's maiden name, she outlined a procedure for the remaining questions which required Celie to select 'Always, often, sometimes, rarely, or never.'

"Lately I have trouble choosing what to eat," the phone rep announced.

"Always." Celie was surprised that her answer came so quickly.

"I take more than one nap each day."

"I do."

"I'm sorry," the rep said. "You have to select from the menu of answers. Always, often, sometimes, rarely, or never."

"Oh, sorry. Can you repeat the question?"

"It's a statement, Mrs. Lowell, not a question. I take more than one nap each day."

She hesitated. "Sometimes."

"Lately the projects I used to participate in don't interest me."

"Often." Another surprise, given that it had taken her months to see the pattern.

The insurance woman rattled on. "I plan events with my friends."

"Rarely." But she knew going back and forth to the cottage contributed to that.

"I feel that my life has no direction or purpose."

"Oh, hmmm. Sometimes . . . No, often."

"I feel that it would be better if I were dead."

"What?" It was outrageous that they would let a perfect stranger with no medical training ask that kind of question over the phone. "Can you please just give me the names of the participating counselors? This is really none of your business."

"It helps us make the correct placement, ma'am. Did you need me to repeat the last statement?"

"No." Her voice had grown louder. "Never. I never wish I were dead." That was the whole issue, wasn't it?

"Thank you," Brittney said. "And thank you for your patience. Please hold."

Celie fumed while a version of Frank Sinatra's *New York, New York* blasted across the air waves. She'd never liked the song. What an awful little man. He thought he was 'king of the heap' all right. How did someone as egotistical as that end up with a voice like an angel?

"Ms. Lowell?" The woman with the movie star name was back.

"Yes." Celie wondered if her tone conveyed the irritation she felt.

"Do you have a pen and paper handy?"

She bit back the rude and obvious answer. She had initiated the request by telephoning. Of course she had paper and pen. "Yes."

After jotting down three names, all female and all with Fredericksburg addresses, Celie issued a more neutral thank you. She punched the red 'end' button in the middle of the rep's programmed "Have a good day."

People were so imprecise with language. It was inane to tell someone asking for a depression counselor to have a good day. If you could have a good day merely by someone else wishing it for you, you wouldn't need counseling. That same laziness was rampant in all kinds of communication. It accounted for the success of her mediation business. Most disputes, whether between business people or married couples, stemmed from saying too little or misinterpreting what someone else said. People didn't articulate what they meant. Or they made assumptions without asking the right questions.

It drove Jake crazy when she asked a second or a third question to be sure she understood the plans for a particular event. "Of course" was his favorite expression, as if she could read his mind and should have, instead of pestering him for more details. Yet in every conversation between them this last week she had not corrected a single one of his conclusions. She'd let him think she agreed with him when she didn't. If it misled him into thinking she was fine, all the better. But it misled her too, hiding the growing distance between them. And she'd always been such a stickler for honesty.

With the pen she traced the words scribbled on the pad. First and last names, street names, and telephone numbers. She wondered if the voice of each counselor would be enough for her to sort them out and choose one. Maybe you weren't supposed to call all three, but simply make an appointment with one and see if that worked. They were all females. How random could that be? She tore off the page and slipped it into the outside pocket of her purse where she kept her keys. If she hadn't made the appointment by the time she next drove, the note would remind her when she took out her keys. She would call them later, after whatever she was going to do next. That was the problem. She had to make that decision first.

MINDING HENRY LEWIS

Chapter Twenty-Two

The day of the funeral I woke up way too early. After lying in the dark for ten minutes, I took Aunt Ruthie's advice to think about something else and finished *Lord of the Flies* in bed. Those British boys were more than cruel to each other. They were evil. Although they knew what was right, they still did those terrible things. I wanted to think it was just boys, being tough, but girls could be as bad. They were jealous, greedy, afraid of being left out. I'd seen it when Demeta was at her worst and I'd felt it myself. Hard feelings to fight.

While I was still crying about the boys on the island, Jazzy came in. She snuggled under my arm and pressed her cheek next to mine. "Don't cry, Mee. He's in heaven. He has all his favorite books and models and he's eating chocolate cake and ice cream for breakfast."

I blotted the tears on my sleeve. "Who told you that?"

"Mama."

"Mama did not say that."

"She told me when people die, they go to heaven. And that's what heaven's like."

"She said that this morning?"

"A long time ago."

"Oh, well."

"Heaven is safe too. Jesus is there. Henry Lewis never has to swim again if he doesn't want to. And if he does, he'll know how without any teaching."

"Mama told you that too?"

"No. I knowed it."

"That's great. Wonderful. Thanks, Jazzy. I'm gonna get dressed now."

She crawled over me and picked up the island book. With two or three wiggles of her behind, she arranged herself like she was the big sister reading in bed with the book held up to the ceiling. She turned the pages as if she was reading, but way too fast because she couldn't read yet, and she kept on giggling. When I moved from the dresser to the closet, Jasmine's head rotated with me.

"Jazzy, I'm changing clothes. You gotta leave."

"I'm not bothering you, I'm reading."

"You can't read."

"Can too."

I pulled the slip up from my ankles over my pajama bottoms, and then stepped out of the pajamas. "I think I just heard Aunt Ruthie's car."

As soon as Jasmine scrambled out, I slipped the black dress Aunt Ruthie had lent me off the hanger. Shapeless with floppy sleeves, it hung like a sack from my chest. It made me look like a barrel. I tried to find a tear or a seam coming apart so Mama would say I didn't have to wear it. When I told Ruthie I'd rather wear one of Rachel's dresses, Ruthie said they were trashy. She brought over two 'appropriate' outfits and ordered me not to bother Mama about something so insignificant.

Except it was important. Everyone would be looking at me, the big sister, the one who'd let her brother drown. I already felt awful enough.

"You're supposed to try these on." Ashante had laid the pile on the bed yesterday.

"Rachel gave me—"

"Ruthie said she already talked to Mary. Let's not rock the boat."

"But Aunt Ruthie's old. Her things won't fit me right."

"It's just easier to get along." He left before I could finish explaining.

I knew how lame it sounded for me to care about the kids from school seeing me in an old-fashioned dress. What I wore wouldn't bring my brother back. It wouldn't make Mama feel any better. All the eighth graders would point fingers anyway and talk behind my back. It was just that, with the right dress, they'd see how I wasn't a little girl anymore in hand-me-downs, and they might not be so quick to say he drowned because I was ignorant. That's what I would have said, if Ashante had let me finish.

I cinched the black belt from the church yard sale around Ruthie's dress. It was better, even if it still covered my knees and halfway to my ankles. I put on my Sunday shoes and tried to ignore the fact that they were too small and rubbed my little toe. In the top drawer I'd hidden one of the lipsticks Mama had thrown away. A nub of red showed, enough. The bracelet Rachel had given me for last year's birthday glittered around my ankle, even though it wasn't real gold. To think I had almost thrown it out when we had our big argument over Demeta. All along Mama had said that girl was trouble. But I had gotten so roiled up, I'd almost lost my best friend over it. Seemed like the older you got, the more complicated life was, no matter how much you thought you'd learned.

If Demeta tried to get to me at the funeral, I wasn't sure what I'd do. One evil whisper and it would be hard to ignore. Demeta was a puzzle. She had three brothers. She ought to understand and cut me some slack. Trouble was, having brothers also made her mouthy. When the oldest one bragged about his years in juvey, Demeta took it one step further and boasted he had connections in New York. She didn't say drug connections, but any other kind of connections— political or Hollywood—didn't make sense either. It was hard to figure why some kids fell for that jive and some didn't. Rachel and TJ were embarrassed over HiTop. Rachel's mother was so embarrassed she was bombed all the time, though it was hard to tell which came first.

I wished there'd been another chance before the funeral to talk to Rachel. I felt all bottled up. With working and trying to be relief for Ashante, Aunt Ruthie had been too busy for anything except random pats on my shoulder. Mama floated from her bedroom to the kitchen and back with Ashante or Ruthie leading her like a cow. No words, no eye contact after that first awful *what happened, Mee,* which repeated over and over in my head. The unlit-empty-store look that begged me not to answer, not to add details and make the horror worse. It was almost like she understood how much better it was not to know, not to be able to see Henry Lewis as he sank out of sight or to see me as I stood on the hard ground unable to do a thing to stop him.

"Mee," Ashante called from downstairs. "Everyone's waiting on you."

As I tugged one last time at the ugly black dress, I imagined the sad line of family in the living room, fixed in place, faces frozen, hands hanging useless, nothing to say while the clock ticked down the minutes before we had to walk out of the dark cocoon of the townhouse and into the bright hard sunlight. I was glad my shoes pinched my toes. It would get worse. My feet would swell. The skin would rub. The blisters would break. Small trials, nowhere near what I deserved.

In the unlit living room the front door already gaped wide. The open van waited. Ashante wrapped one arm around Mama's waist and tugged her forward. When her feet stuck, he bent his head to hers, the words indistinct, but constant.

"Mary." Aunt Ruthie stood by the side of the van. "Come sit with Jasmine, sweetie. Come on now."

"Jasmine?" Mama asked without moving from the doorway.

"Jasmine's here in the van," Aunt Ruthie repeated.

"Where's Meeka?" Mama said in that same monotone, her glazed eyes straight ahead but unfocused, a step behind Ashante.

"Here. I'm here, Mama." I tripped on the bottom stair tread, but caught myself with the wall. I slipped my hand in hers, thinking this was it, she was getting better like Ashante said she would. When her fingers did not close around mine and she didn't answer, panic squeezed my ribcage. I gulped for breath.

"Why didn't you bring Henry Lewis?" Mama said to the air.

My knees buckled. If Ashante hadn't caught me under the arms, I would have crumpled there on the floor.

"He's already at the church," Ruthie said as calmly as if she were talking about an usher. "Come on now or we'll be late."

Watching my aunt guide my mother into the van and settle her into the back seat next to Jasmine, I tried to pull myself together. This was no time to be a baby. Aunt Ruthie and Ashante had their hands full. Mama might never forgive the daughter who had let her baby drown. Who knew how long it might be until she would be able to think beyond that single fact, until she could talk or go back to work? In the meantime someone had to deal with the little kids and keep the apartment halfway neat. Ruthie had her own job and her own rent to pay. Ashante had to work because it looked like he would be stuck paying the bills. Someone had to mind Mama.

As soon as Ruthie slid the side door shut, the van bolted onto the roadway. In the front passenger seat where Ashante had steered me, I snapped the seat belt and concentrated on the white line in the center of the road to keep from bawling. I tried to remember the feeling of walking back from the dock with TJ under the moon, nothing in my head but the idea of the whole big universe out there waiting on me to discover things.

In the back seat Ruthie talked in a steady drone to Mama. Mostly I heard, *sweetie* and *just rest* over and over, nothing from Mama. Once we turned off the main highway Ashante looked over at me.

"You okay?" he said.

"Yeah."

"She's gonna be fine."

"When?"

"I don't know."

"So how come you know the other?"

"I love your mother. I know."

That seemed like the lamest excuse I'd ever heard. I loved Mama too. I'd loved her a lot longer than Ashante, and I had no idea right now what my mother was thinking or feeling.

"How do you know when something's temporary or when something's going to last?" It was as close as I could come to asking about TJ without upsetting everyone.

208

"You talking about your mother?"

"No."

"Love? You mean love?"

"Yeah."

"It's hard to tell. It's complicated. And different for different people. I'm not sure anyone knows for sure." He kept his eyes on the road. "It's why so many people make mistakes. But there's a right time for each part of your life. And if something's going to last, it has to take root when it's the right time. Like corn won't grow in December."

"How d'you know if it's the right time?"

"First off, you have to be older." He laughed, not at me, but still.

"Grown-ups always say that. They're avoiding the question."

"You think you're in love?"

I couldn't help the smile. "I don't know."

"He better be someone special. You got a lot ahead of you, girl. High school, college, maybe more school after that. Your mother thinks you could teach college, math maybe."

"She won't even talk to me."

"You gotta give her time. Burying a child's not supposed to happen. You understand, I know you do."

"I wish I could be as sure as you."

"If we keep remembering how she was, she'll come back to us."

Too bad that wouldn't work with Henry Lewis.

At the funeral home Ashante parked the van in the back lot, around by the basement door, where a man in black motioned for them to park. He must work for Mr. Johnson, the owner, who always donated masses of Easter lilies for the shut-ins. Mr. Johnson rushed out from the basement in his black suit and shook Ashante's hand. He tried to shake Mama's hand but she didn't even notice him. He raised his hand, pretended he'd been signaling our group, and led us toward a long black car. As Ruthie walked Mama over, the rest of us trailed after without talking. We all crowded in the back on two seats facing each other. Jasmine crawled over Liné and Ruthie and wedged herself in next to me. As big as the car looked from outside, once we were all in, there were too many people for the space.

I felt like I'd puke any minute. First I was hot, then I shivered. Gerald sat next to me, his arm on the back of the seat behind my shoulders. It wasn't two minutes until he'd let it slip down. I shrugged and shrugged until he finally moved it. He tucked it between his suit jacket and his shirt and rubbed his chest. It meant his arm was still next to mine and even closer to my chest. Rey glued himself to the far door and stared out the window.

"Everyone all set?" Ashante asked.

"We're all here," Ruthie said.

He leaned in and kissed Mama's cheek before he shut the door. The car didn't move, though, and they sat in the dark waiting. Because the glass was smoked a bottomless gray, I couldn't see much outside. No one spoke. Drops of sweat on Rey's forehead glistened in the window reflection. Gerald's sleeve rubbed against me and I could feel the heat. When his other hand touched my knee, I rammed an elbow into his side.

"I want to sit next to Meeka," Rey shouted, startling us all.

Ruthie looked up and stopped whispering to Mama. "Sure, hon. Gerald, scoot over to the window so the kids can be together."

Once the switch was made and Rey was on my left, he whispered by my shoulder. "Hey."

"Thanks," I whispered back, wondering how the heck he knew about Gerald's wandering hands since we'd never talked about it.

"You're welcome."

As soon as the driver shut his door, the radio crackled for a minute, then Mr. Johnson's voice came through the walkie-talkie. The driver repeated the numbers. I thought he said *go,* but it could have been 'o' for *zero* at the end of a longer number. Through the small back window I watched the road wind out behind us like yarn. The cars that followed us stayed way back as if they didn't want to catch the same disease. I imagined the hearse in front of us cruising down the open road and cars turning off wildly when they saw the big black car approach.

Ashante had warned us the hearse would come out of the basement garage of the funeral home building and lead the procession. I'd never liked the word *hearse* and I was trying not to think about Henry Lewis in there by himself in a closed box where he couldn't see the sky. I was glad Ashante was riding in the hearse, though I didn't know if he was in the back with Henry Lewis or if he was riding up front with Mr. Johnson. Our car mimicked Mr. Johnson's turns in the hearse, an exact three car lengths between them. It felt like gliding on ice, the turns so smooth and steady. No accounting for how my stomach kept flipping.

The church parking area was already jammed. Cars overflowed onto the grass and the side yard, like they had at Rachel's grandmother's funeral last year. Men in dark suits and ladies in hats had formed a line up both sides of the front steps. Everyone had talked back and forth across the steps about everything except the dead person as they waited for Rachel's family to find seats. It seemed wrong to treat it like a party and yet it was a relief to know they would all be busy and not staring in silence at me.

Pastor Ware's grown sons in their double breasted suits waved people along and handed out cardboard fans with Johnson Funeral Home in red on one side and 'The Lord is with you' on the other side. Once the funeral home driver parked the black limousine, Mr. Johnson came over and helped us out, one by one, his hands moist with perspiration. He repeated his instructions, something about the front pew. His expression never changed, serious, but not cross, nowhere near a smile. I had only a vague idea of what he was saying, but was very willing to be steered.

"Jasmine, honey, stay with Meeka." Aunt Ruthie maneuvered Liné on the other side by Gerald and whispered something in his ear. She had to concentrate on Mama, who had balked at the sunlight. Covering her face with her arm, she was refusing to climb the stairs to the sanctuary.

I was relieved when I saw Ashante climb out of the back of the hearse. The little seat snapped shut behind him. He helped Mr. Johnson's men slide the casket out. In a group they carried it around across the lawn to the back door of the church, their dress shoes swallowed in the thick carpet of spring grass. Henry Lewis hadn't been alone. I was feeling better until I saw Rey dart back from the side yard. His tie was crooked and his shirt had come untucked.

"D'you see my mother anywhere?" he whispered.

I'd forgotten all about Antoinette and her promise to be there. "Maybe she's in the church already."

"Come on now, kids," Aunt Ruthie whispered. "Stay close."

As the people on the stairs parted to let us pass, I noticed my mother's slip showed below the hem of her dress. I wished everyone was already seated inside so I could tell Ruthie and we could fix it before going in, before everyone else noticed it. No one would criticize a mother for such a small lapse at her child's burial, but they might blame her family. I stepped closer to hide the edge of white.

"Wait up," Rey said, one step below.

Halfway up Rachel and the girls from school were bunched together on one side. Most of them were already crying. "Love you, Meeka," one girl called out.

Rachel grabbed my hand and squeezed. "Hang on, girl. See you after."

And then the girls were below me, and I was at the church doors, the sun hot on my back, and the heat from the congregation rising up all around me. The pastor's wife hugged me hard and pushed me into the sanctuary. It seemed like every pew was already filled with people. The organ pumped out hymns I recognized from Sunday service, *A Mighty Fortress is our God, a bull work never failing*, whatever that meant. Jasmine pasted her hot little body next to my hip. She was all damp and sticky like the arm cast she had in fourth grade. Rey kept catching the heel of my flats with his church shoes, two sizes too big. I didn't dare turn around and complain because so many people might hear and think I was a selfish person. We moved down the aisle in a fog of music and murmurs to where another one of Mr. Johnson's men flicked his fingers toward the front in repetitive jabs.

Ruthie waited with Mama outside the first pew for the kids to file in, and then she pushed her in and sat by the aisle. Ruthie's hand reached across Mama's lap to hover for a few seconds over my knee, then she laid it in her own lap as if it were the signal for the service to begin and no further delay would be tolerated. Jasmine squirmed and strained to see the altar, so different from every other Sunday, with flowers everywhere and the empty stand for the casket. We didn't need to sit this close to each other. The pew was huge, but somehow with Henry Lewis by himself in the coffin, it seemed better this way, and right. Someone had set up photos of him on tables surrounded by flowers. It looked like the flower store downtown with all those different kinds and colors.

"There he is," Jasmine said. "In his Cub Scout hat and scarf."

"Shhh," I whispered.

"That's my brother."

"Yeah, that's him."

All the time I hoped Jasmine would be quiet once the service started because I didn't want everyone thinking we hadn't taught her how to behave in church. After Ashante and Gerald and two of the funeral home men in their shiny black suits positioned the casket on the wooden stand, Jasmine said more loudly. "What's in that box?"

"Jazzy," I whispered. "This is church. You gotta be quiet in church."

"Mee, what's inside that box?"

"I'll tell you after. Be still. Pastor gonna pray." I was surprised when she shifted back down in the pew and was quiet.

The service was a blur of Pastor Ware praying and preaching and the choir ladies singing and dancing and the congregation carrying on, in the pews, in the aisles, and up in the balcony. The red cardboard fans flashed like butterflies all over the church. When tears overflowed onto my cheeks, I didn't wipe them because I was afraid Jasmine would notice and ask why. And wiping was pointless.

There always seemed to be more. Wherever Henry Lewis was, I hoped he couldn't see me. He would be scared enough.

In the second pew Ashante sat behind us, his hands on Mama's shoulders most of the service, steady and motionless while rivers of perspiration trailed down his face and darkened the collar of his blue shirt. It crossed my mind that he was holding Mama down so she wouldn't float away to be with Henry Lewis in heaven.

She didn't say any of the prayers. She didn't sing. She didn't cry either, just sat with her head bent back like she was memorizing the ceiling, except her eyes were shut tight. Jasmine stood on the bench and raised her hands to clap like the other ladies. Although she didn't know the words to the hymns, she kept on repeating her own little hum of a song.

When the singing ended, while the pastor prayed, she sank back onto my lap, pulling my head down close to her face. "Henry Lewis isn't lost anymore, Mee." She pointed at the pictures. "He's right there."

Why Jazzy spoke only to me, and not to Mama or Ruthie, I had no idea. She whispered though and she didn't fuss, not even when Pastor Ware laid his arms across the casket and cried out for the Lord to save his son Henry Lewis. And she never once asked for Liné, who Ruthie had left in Gerald's charge in the back of the church to avoid any chance of the two little girls misbehaving.

Once the pastor called out his big Amen for the hundredth time and the dancing ladies went back to their seats, the funeral home crew led Ashante and Mama out, with Ashante corralling the rest of the family along the aisle and down the steps. We walked in sad slow single-file across the grass to the little green tent. There was barely room for two lines of chairs. It wasn't until we were under the tent's shade that I noticed the grave. The hole was opened up, the dirt piled all around, and the edges padded with green carpet. We sat in that same order in squeaky plastic folding chairs and watched while the casket was lowered into the hole.

I held Jasmine on my lap with both arms wrapped tight, even though it was already way too warm. Sweat trickled down my throat and Jasmine's hair stuck to my chin. When Rey didn't sit with us, I worried the whole time if he was off howling somewhere or if he was searching for Antoinette in the throngs of people all around the tent. The idea of Henry Lewis in the metal box, in the dark again, made me sick to my stomach. Even with my eyes shut, still I could hear the crowd's breathing, the collective sighs after each phrase about going home and being with your Father in heaven.

It was ridiculous, all those words made it sound like a happy homecoming. Even if you knew about heaven for sure—and who did know, none of them had been there—it could never take away the sadness of not being together with your family.

After another round of hallelujahs and amens, Pastor Ware left us alone with the casket and went to greet the guests. People, in tight bunches you couldn't see past, hovered just outside the tent. A slow steady stream made their way in to Mama in the middle of the front row. Each one repeated how sorry he was. After Ashante and Ruthie thanked them, Mama stone-faced, there was nothing else to say, and they turned away awkwardly. Some of them put their hands on my arm and said things like *we're praying for you, take good care of your mother, God's watching over you'all*. Mama didn't speak.

When the white lady from the creek turned up in the line in a straw hat with a pale yellow ribbon, I couldn't help staring. She was one of the few white people there. She didn't talk to anyone, maybe didn't know anyone. She switched her purse from one arm to the other, rubbed the toe of one shoe on the back of her leg, fiddled with her scarf. While she waited her turn she kept her side to the coffin with darting glances toward the family. Her face was paler than normal, like the people on TV ads with the flu. When she reached Mama and Ruthie, she repeated her name, Ms. Lowell. Mama didn't reach out, so Ms. Lowell shook Ruthie's hand instead. She stood with her lips parted to speak, but for a long minute she didn't speak after all.

"It's a great tragedy. I'm so sorry. I wish there was something I could do."

I was bursting to say how stupid it was to apologize at this late date. Ms. Lowell should have done something that afternoon at the creek. But her face showed that she knew all that and that's why she was so sorry. It was like looking in a mirror.

She had come anyway. She had come when she didn't know anyone here except me. That was brave. All our silly conversations about the little dog and swimming and the telescope, was she thinking that if we forgave each other, things would go back the way they were before? It would be like death row murderers getting to be friends and letting each other off the hook. The only thing I had in common with Ms. Lowell was we'd both failed Henry Lewis. We would always have that failure.

"Thank you for coming," Ruthie said to Mrs. Lowell, echoing Ashante.

Mama began to rock back and forth in the folding chair. I was desperate to get away, from Mrs. Lowell, from the open grave, from this strange silent mother, from the whole terrible day. If I could find Rey, I could convince him to take over with the little girls. But he wasn't anywhere I could see. I burned at the idea that Aunt Antoinette hadn't come. It was selfish and mean not to understand how much Mama needed her sisters to stand with her, how hard it would be to lose your baby all over again to the cold earth. And that didn't even count that Antoinette's own son Rey might be wanting his mother close.

"Meeka," Aunt Ruthie said. "Why don't you take the girls up for some lemonade. Something to eat. Don't let them get chicken all over themselves."

"Where's Liné at?"

"Gerald's supposed to be watching her. He's probably off drinking beer."

Meeka shot a look at Ruthie, but she was already bending to whisper to Mama. Ruthie must have lost her mind to leave him in charge. What was the matter with grownups that they didn't see how dangerous the world was? I wanted to yell and scream at Ruthie and my mother and Ashante and all the rest of the people standing patiently in line, being polite and proper while bad things piled up all around them.

Clear of the line, we streamed across the lawn toward the basement parish hall. I pulled Jasmine through the crowd, ignoring the hands and the murmured greetings. They could think I was rude if they wanted to.

"Come on, come on, Jazzy."

"I can't go that fast," she whined.

"It's like hide and seek. We gotta find Liné."

In the shadow of the church I caught a flash of Gerald's bright blue shirt, but the next second I lost him. I wasn't sure if he'd gone inside or around the back of the building. I was perspiring so much that the sleeves of the dress clung to my arms, the loose part flapping like bat wings underneath. Jasmine broke loose and threw herself down on the lawn.

"I don't wanna play hide and seek. I'm hungry."

"We're going right to the food table," I said. "Please, Jazzy. Please get up. I can't carry you and run too."

"I don't wanna run."

Halfway to the church a strangled voice cried out behind us.

"Meeka? Where's Meeka?"

It seemed as if the whole churchyard froze, like in a game of SPUD. I had to tell myself not to look up at the sky for the ball. I tapped Jasmine's head.

"Okay, you can wait here, right here. Don't move, not even a squiggle. Not until Rey comes. I'm gonna bring Liné, then you'all can go eat."

Before I'd taken the first step, Rey magically appeared and sat down beside Jasmine and started to talk to her about fairies and fireflies. He nodded at me, as wise and sure of himself as he'd ever looked, though his face was splotched and not quite right.

"I'll watch her," he said. "You go ahead. Your mama's calling."

I pointed across the lawn where Gerald had been moments before. "Have you seen Liné and Gerald?"

Rey shook his head.

"We have to find her. He's being weird again."

"But what about your mama?"

"I gotta help Liné first."

Ignoring Mama's cries was almost as hard as watching Henry Lewis sink into that muddy water. Mama was grown, though, and Liné was in trouble, too little to help herself. I passed right by Mrs. Carter and my Sunday school teacher. I jogged, swerving right and left to avoid clusters of people, people I'd never seen before. Out of the blue I heard Liné.

"You are not my mama. I want Ruthie."

And as I rounded the corner of the church I saw Gerald sitting on a bench in the prayer garden, Liné squirming to get off his lap. He was pushing her shoulders down and moving her from side to side across his private parts, his eyes closed and a slick smile on his face. Liné was crying, trying to get loose. The man was a scourge, the way the Bible talked about locusts.

"Let her go." I grabbed her under the arms and yanked her free. "You are sick."

"You need to mind your business, missy. She's my stepdaughter, not yours. She's just loving on her stepdad, aren't you, girl? That's all, just a little loving."

"That's disgusting."

"You're jealous. Someday you're gonna come begging for it. Someday." He reached for my leg.

"Not ever." I twisted away. "You keep away from her, or I'll tell Ruthie and she'll divorce you so fast you'll be sitting on the curb with your suitcase before you can count to three."

Liné was whimpering, her head buried in my neck. We started back toward the tent where Mama was still calling my name. Liné was heavy, heavier than Jasmine, but she wouldn't let me put her down. Smack in the middle of the church yard Rey was right where I'd left him, sitting in the grass with Jasmine.

"Okay, time to eat. Rey's gonna take you. I'll meet you in there."

I set Liné on the ground next to Rey. When Liné started to fuss again, I tucked her shirt into her skirt and kissed her forehead. "You're fine. See if you can find the cupcakes. Save me a pink one."

Jasmine hopped up and danced around Liné. I bumped Rey's shoulder with mine.

"Don't let them out of your sight. And stay clear of Gerald. I mean it. Don't let him near them."

At a fast walk I headed back to the tent, my head down to avoid conversations. When I was almost there, I glanced back. Rey had a little girl in each hand and was walking them into the parish hall like he'd done it a thousand times before. The buzz of voices around me grew louder. People were talking, talking about us, about how my mama was grieving and my Aunt Ruthie was so constant, and about Jasmine calling out to her dead brother in the church. I knew exactly what they were saying. They were saying that Henry Lewis wouldn't be in that hole and all this wouldn't be happening if his older sister had been doing her job, minding her business, and keeping those kids away from that water. But they didn't know what it had been like. They were just talking to talk. They didn't know. And it wasn't any of their business.

"Where's Meeka?" Mama called out above the people talking.

"Hush," Ruthie's voice carried too. "Hush, Mary. She's coming. She's walking right on over here to you."

"Meeka." Mama shouted at full volume.

When I started to run, one shoe flapped against my heel where it was too tight. Every person in that churchyard fixed on me making a fool of myself running to my mother, but I didn't care. Mama was calling for me.

Just before I reached the tent Rachel came out of nowhere, with Demeta and six or seven other girls. They surrounded me, hugging and crying, closing in around me and walking with me so I was invisible and there was nothing for all those staring people to see.

"Here she is, Ms. Breeden, here's your girl," Rachel announced as the clump of teenagers edged under the tent with me in the center.

Her words didn't make a dent in the buzz, still I was grateful I didn't have to try to talk myself. My throat was too tight. My eyes blurred. All I could see was the dark square of shade under the tent like a black hole. I let the group carry me in, so many hands and shoulders and feet moving together. At the first chair she pushed me forward. Mama was standing, coming out of her fog, looking right at me. I spread out my arms.

"Here I am, Mama."

Her arms were clasped together. Her head began to shake, no, no. She seemed to look right through me. Ruthie took my hand and laid it on her arm.

"Here's your girl. She come like you asked."

Mama brushed away my hand like it was a crumb. Her voice was hard. "Where's Henry Lewis gone off to? You shouldn't have sent him on some wild goose chase."

Ruthie sputtered an objection, reached around to pull me into a hug, but I was already backing up. The thicket of stunned girls blocked my escape. All except for Demeta who stepped clear and raised her voice as I tried to slip past.

"Oooowee, Meeka in big trouble now. She can't hide no more. Her mama knows the truth."

"Shut up," Rachel yelled and stepped between Demeta and me. "Shut up, you witch."

I didn't even turn around. Mama's eyes were focused on me and I couldn't look away. She batted at Ruthie who was trying to get her to sit down.

"Wherever did you send that boy, Mee? He missed church."

"He's gone, Mama. Henry Lewis gone for good. He's not coming back. It's my fault. I tried, but I couldn't save him."

It seemed then as if the girls melted into the air. They were there and then they were gone. Ruthie too, out of reach. It was just me and Mama, eye to eye, unbelieving and unyielding. We both shivered under the tent, each of us an island in a green-black sea of shadow, the valley of death. I yearned to feel her arms cinch me close, to feel the weight of her chin on my head, to inhale the familiar scent of her lavender hand cream.

What broke the spell was Jasmine's wail from across the wide lawn. "Meeka. I want my Meeka."

As the keening repeated in thin waves, I lowered my eyes. Painful as it was to hear, I welcomed it. It drowned out everything else. Ruthie motioned for me to go. That thirty feet seemed the longest I had ever walked. The shoes bit into my feet. The hand-me-down dress clung to my legs below the slip. I moved past Rachel and Demeta and the other girls from school like a wind-up toy in jerky steps. Jasmine struggled loose of Rey's hand and flung herself at me, still repeating my name.

He shrugged. "You know how she is."

I gathered her up until she was resting on my hip, her arms fastened around my neck. "Shhh," I said. "Shhh. I'm here. I'm not going anywhere."

When it came time to ride back to the funeral home, Jasmine and Liné had eaten way too much cake and they were whizzing around in circles, their socks bunched into their shoes and their hair matted with icing. Aunt Ruthie asked me to steer them to the car while she thanked the minister. Rey had gone missing again. We sat on the stiff leather seats, face to face, with the doors open on both sides to let the breeze through, while the little girls chattered nonsense. Ashante and Pastor Ware stomped off to find Rey. After twenty minutes both little girls were asleep and he was still nowhere to be found. When Ruthie came back, she was muttering about Gerald. He had decided he wasn't ready to go home and Ruthie had told him that was fine with her, he could find his own way. *Find his own way to hell,* I thought and vowed to tell Ruthie the first chance I had, once this awful day was over. Ashante leaned in to speak to her.

"You take them home. I'll wait here. The pastor has to lock up after the ladies finish cleaning the kitchen, so he can drop us at the apartment. You know boys. Rey's probably gone with them into the woods to drink the beers they snitched."

Once the heavy black doors closed in on us, the churchyard disappeared. This time I didn't watch out the back window. Leaving Henry Lewis there by himself was harder than anything I'd had to do since climbing out of the creek without him.

Chapter Twenty-Three

Rey wasn't drinking beer in the woods. He hadn't simply lost track of time. I knew exactly what had happened. He'd run off on purpose. Without saying anything to the grownups, I looked through the plastic tubs under the bunk bed where he kept his stuff. Nothing big was gone, not that there had been much to start with. Everything he owned except his everyday clothes were buried in one tub underneath socks and underwear, his ingenious way to discourage any snoop. I pawed through it, his notebook of newspaper clippings about his sports heroes with an action shot of LeBron James taped to the cover, a few photographs of a Breeden family reunion when he was a baby on Grammy Breeden's lap, and a slew of his team pictures from the Rec Dept league. His backpack, though, wasn't anywhere.

I closed my eyes and thought about Rey in the limo on the way to the funeral, to see if my brain had registered anything he might have been carrying. His hands had been empty, he hadn't taken the backpack. But if he'd planned this, he could have hidden it anytime anywhere. The other night he'd snuck out to the creek without anyone knowing.

I looked under the doormat where he sometimes left me a note if he didn't want the grownups to know what he was doing. We had worked out the system after he disappeared the first time, last summer, not long after Antoinette tripped off to wherever.

I remembered that argument. I'd worked to keep the screech out of my voice because I couldn't let him see how scared I'd been. He was gone overnight that time and came home on his own when he tried to hitchhike to the bus station but no one stopped. Mama banished him to the second floor, no TV, no lunch, no phone calls, no outdoors.

"How do you think Mama would feel if she had to call Antoinette all the way in Maryland and tell her that you'd gone and got yourself lost?"

He'd grumbled and stalked off to the other bedroom, but twenty minutes later he was back with the doormat idea. "It's for you and me only. You have to promise to keep it secret. I might have to tell you things I don't want anyone else to know."

"Like you some magic disappearing spy?"

"You aren't in charge of me."

"I don't want to be. But Antoinette is loony tunes when she's angry. She could do something to Mama and then where would Jazzy and me and Henry Lewis be?"

"I won't use the damn doormat then."

"Cussing doesn't impress me."

"Damn isn't really cussing."

"Like hell."

"Exactly."

"Okay, leave your crumby notes. Just don't disappear again."

He'd only used it twice. Once when he didn't make the final cut for the middle school basketball team and he didn't feel like answering questions at dinner, and once when he thought he'd seen his mother at the Wal-Mart and he wanted to ride his bike back and see if it was really her. His pain was so obvious it hurt me to see him like that when there was nothing anyone could do to fix it except his mother and she was too busy to be bothered. She probably never thought about him and how he was feeling. What a piece of work she was. Why'd she go to all that trouble to have a baby if she wasn't going to stick around to see him grow up?

Ashante came back from the church an hour later without Rey. After setting up a movie for the little girls, I went outside to think where there was less noise. Ashante caught up with me on the front steps. I'd gone over and over the possibilities of where my cousin might have gone. I was on the verge of running up and down the street and yelling his name.

"Aunt Ruthie inside?" Ashante asked.

"She's gone back to the nursing home, said she had paperwork to finish from last night's shift."

"If you know where he's at, girl, you tell me right now. This isn't the time for more trouble."

"I don't know."

"He talks to you. He trusts you. He must have said something."

If I told him about Rey going back to the creek that first night, then he'd know I'd snuck out too. And it didn't prove a thing about where Rey'd gone off to now. Although the pit in my stomach said the creek wasn't totally out of the question, now that Henry Lewis was buried this had more to do with Antoinette not showing up at the funeral. Rey had confused me though. When we traded off Jasmine, his face hadn't given me the least hint he was getting ready to disappear. I supposed I should have figured it out when he took the whole funeral business without complaining, very unlike him. Particularly odd when he didn't like crowds or church. He'd barely said three words total, more like someone who was preoccupied.

221

Preoccupied with a plan. And I'd been feeling sorry for him for having to deal with the funeral. The worm.

'Course I hadn't given him the first chance to talk over everything that had happened in the last week. As I thought back on the two or three conversations we'd had, I realized I'd been cross with him every time he'd tried. He had to have gotten the message that he was bothering me and I didn't want to have anything to do with him. Still, just because that was how I felt didn't mean I should have let him see it. I was older, almost in high school.

Ashante kept peering down the empty road as if Rey might come tripping down the street any second. His voice dragged out the words. "This is serious, Meeka. Mary's on the verge of a breakdown. The doctor gave her some pills, but Ruthie and I can't be here every minute to make sure she takes them. You kids are all she's got. Rey disappearing is too much on top of everything else. He must have said something. Think."

"He wanted to talk. I didn't let him. Ever since . . . he's been pushing to talk. I just couldn't."

"It has to be more than that."

"He was expecting Antoinette to be here. I mean, at the funeral, and then she wasn't, and I should've—"

He took her shoulders and held her so she'd stop talking.

"Never mind. You couldn't know."

"We have to do something."

"I'll handle it. He can't have gotten too far."

"Trouble tracks Rey. He won't be thinking how to be safe, only how to get wherever he thinks he needs to go. He's convinced I don't care, that no one cares."

"You're a good friend to Rey. He knows that."

But I could tell Ashante was worried big time. I'd blown it again. Things kept happening too fast for me to be ready. I was supposed to be paying attention. I kept missing all the clues.

"I'm going to call back to the church," he said.

"And the funeral home?"

"Yeah. If you think of anything else, any little thing, come tell me right away." His voice wavered and dwindled until I could barely hear it. "And don't you go looking for him. I need you here with your mama and the girls."

He didn't shut the front door tight and I could hear him upstairs telling Mama to close her eyes, get some sleep. It was like Mama was the child, little and scared of the dark and wanting the grownups to promise not to leave her alone. That wasn't my mama. Mama, who had gone to school nights for four years to get her degree.

MINDING HENRY LEWIS

Mama, who argued with the teachers to let me start Spanish early in seventh grade, who taught me how to knit after working all day, and who changed two flat tires by herself punctured by the Starner boys just to be mean back when we lived in the trailer park.

Ashante came back out on the front stoop with his cell phone. "Sheriff, this is Ashante Green." There was a pause. The Sheriff must be talking. "Thank you, yes, saddest thing I ever did. But now there's Rey. Mary's nephew, who lives with us. Reynaud Davis."

He held the phone closer and scanned the street while he listened to whatever the Sheriff was saying. "Your guys on patrol haven't seen him, have they?" There was a pause. "No, he's not in a gang." And another pause, after which he kicked at the railing. "Of course I'm sure. He's a good kid, a good student. His mother? Antoinette Davis . . . sure, sure. No, you can't call Mary . . . The truth is she's not dealing with much besides losing her son, but I can get it from Ruthie. Right, Mary and Antoinette's other sister, the boy's aunt." Ashante's eyebrows arched as if he couldn't believe the sheriff didn't know all this. "He didn't come home after the funeral. We needed to get Mary and everyone home, he was nowhere. Reverend Ware and I stayed and combed the church. I've asked everyone and no one knows where he's taken himself off to."

Ashante's head circled from one end of the street to the other. He nodded and murmured to whatever the Sheriff was saying while the muscles on his arms tightened into darker ridges where he gripped the porch rail. "Yes, sir. We appreciate whatever you . . . You'll call?" His eyes blinked several times. "Yes, sir. Twenty-four hours? Thank you, sir." The hand with the phone slid away from his ear and he kicked the rail again. "They can't start looking officially until he's been gone 24 hours."

"Have you talked to Antoinette?" I asked.

"The number's out of service."

Rey couldn't have known that because he didn't have a cell phone. And I hadn't let him use ours. Even if he had known, would it have stopped him? Not as long as no one here was willing to listen to him.

I talked Ashante into letting me use my mother's cell phone to call Rey's school friends. After shutting the door to my room, I called Rachel first.

"Rache, can you come over?"

"What's up?"

"I need to talk to you real bad."

"I'm not sure—"

"What is wrong with you? You're supposed to be my best friend. My brother is dead. If you don't want to come, just say so. I have other friends." But that wasn't really true and Rachel knew it.

"It's not a good time for me to leave. My mother's gone ape. TJ called and read her the riot act about her drinking, but that didn't stop her. Since the funeral she's finished off a whole bottle of wine. And he told her about Willie. I'm not allowed out. There are gazillion new rules. I only get to ride the bus to and from school. If I'm not in the house on the dot I have to call and tell her exactly where I am, with the house number and the street. Like she's even going to answer the phone."

"You were here Monday."

"She thought I was at cheering practice."

"So lie again. This is an emergency."

"Let me get this straight. Is this the Tomeeka Breeden from Patogansett, Virginia telling me to lie?"

"You know what I mean. Fib, for a good cause."

"You don't know how bad off my mother is. She'll call the police on me."

"Please."

"Okay, I'll try."

Hard to believe that was the best Rachel could do as long as we had been friends. I called two boys on Rey's basketball team. They said he hadn't mentioned anything at the funeral about a trip. I looked up the telephone number for Mr. Oliver, the coach, because Rey had talked to him at the funeral, but his wife said he wouldn't be back until dinnertime. Mrs. Oliver had gone on and on about what a sweet boy Henry Lewis was, so much potential, not in basketball necessarily because she didn't really understand that as well as her husband did and she didn't know all the boys on the team, but still, such a cheerful little fellow.

I was close to losing it. Mrs. Oliver didn't seem to catch on that it was hard to hear all that about my brother, especially with Rey missing. She just kept talking and talking. I was so confused and upset I couldn't decide whether to leave a message for Mr. Oliver or just blurt out the whole situation. Finally I just said good-bye and snapped the phone shut.

The message light immediately blinked back. Fumbling with the buttons, I prayed it was Rey. But it was Rachel calling back to say she was heading over, that she had to be home before eight.

"Any luck?" Ashante asked when he got back from checking the neighborhood.

"No."

He went upstairs and came down two minutes later with his leather jacket and his helmet. "She's taken a sleeping pill. I'm going to ride by the elementary school and along 19 and see if he's there. Call me with anything. I'll be back by seven at the latest. And I'll stop and buy minutes for the cell phone." He hadn't changed from his church clothes, just loosened his tie, but now he shrugged out of the suit coat and put on the jacket. "You have to stay inside to listen for your mother." He pressed his fingers into my shoulder for emphasis. "Don't leave her by herself."

I nodded. As worried as I was and as awful a week as it had been, I liked the way he treated me. Not like I was a stupid girl who had let my brother drown, but a person he could rely on. If only I could find Rey and stop the whole thing from sliding into an even bigger mess.

I was still ticked at Rachel when she showed up red-faced from jogging and breathing hard. Even as I reminded myself of all our time together, this new rift was a potentially permanent change in our friendship. She was the baby in her family, she was used to getting away with stuff. HiTop was a mess and TJ was difficult to pin down. It made her a funny combination of street-smart and goody-goody.

This year as high school loomed closer she'd started acting differently. All of a sudden she paid way too much attention to the girls who slept around and the boys who didn't study. She snuck make-up into school and she skipped class a couple of times. She wore a cami under her shirt and stripped down to it once she was at school, hanging the other long-sleeved shirt in her locker until it was time to go home. And there was Willie. She didn't seem to need our friendship anymore.

"So what's the big emergency?" She said once we were upstairs in the bedroom, away from the big ears of the little girls.

If she was going to be flip, my first inclination was to tell her to get lost. But I needed help. First Henry Lewis, now Rey. It was too much. Three hours he'd been gone. It was dark, and I was worried.

"First off we gotta get something straight. You never answered me the other day about Willie?"

"It's none of your business."

I felt like I'd been punched in the gut. We'd been friends since first grade. We'd sworn to tell each other everything. Every Halloween we climbed over the fence at St. Bernadette's and walked along the river at midnight. I'd taught her how to do a cartwheel, and she had taught me the pretzel dance. We'd sworn not to marry until we were done with college. We were going to go to JMU together because she loved the mountains.

"You should go," I said.

"We can't be friends just 'cause I fell in love before you?"

"We said we'd wait."

"We were so dumb when we said that."

"You got that right. I was dumb to have believed you." My eyes were burning hot. "Why do you want Willie anyway? He's had two girlfriends already. You're just standing in line for someone who doesn't care about you."

"He does too care."

I didn't have time to explain to her that he had been in the back of the truck. I'd been trying to convince myself it wasn't him, but now, with Willie crowding out all our good memories, about to split us apart, the leer on his face loomed. I hadn't even had time to tell her about that night, and here we were arguing again.

"It's not what you think, Mee. He asked, that's all. I haven't decided yet. He loves me, he said he'd wait till I was ready. And I can keep him happy other ways . . . you know . . ."

"Whatever." Since last Tuesday things looked a lot different to me. Willie didn't want Rachel, he wanted a girl, any girl, he wanted sex. But I didn't have time to sort that out right now. I had bigger problems. I needed someone practical to help me think through the possibilities and I couldn't talk to the grownups.

"Rey didn't come home after the funeral. And the map to Maryland is gone."

"The map? What map?"

"I was trying to prepare him for his mother not coming to the funeral."

"Antoinette didn't show?"

It was worse to hear Rachel say it out loud than to think it. Rey must have been devastated.

"Does he have any money saved?"

"I guess. He cut grass all summer."

"Where does he keep his stash?"

"He can 't have much. Henry Lewis would've known, but . . ."

"What about his clothes and all?"

"Under the bunk beds. I already looked."

"His sports junk, his basketball, his glove?"

I hadn't thought of that. "In the closet downstairs."

We raced down and pulled the cardboard box out into the middle of the living room. Jasmine and Line were asleep on the couch. Their heads lolled on the arm rests. Their feet dangled off the cushions.

"Shhh," I motioned to the couch.

Inside his Orioles baseball glove Rachel discovered two letters, folded into small squares that fit neatly into the space for his palm. They were both signed "A," without dates and without envelopes.

"What made you think to look in there?" I asked, kicking myself for not thinking of that.

"I'm an expert at hiding things."

"Like Willie?"

"No, just stuff."

"You're piling secrets on top of secrets, Rache. You used to trust me."

"It's not you, it's my mother. I have to hide her pills so she can't find them. And the vodka bottles. TJ does it too." She reached over to hug me, pouted a little when I wiggled free. "Don't look at me like that. Willie made me promise not to say anything."

"That oughtta tell you something about what kind of person he is. If he won't let you talk to your best friend. And he wants you to sneak around in secret."

She shrugged. "I know. It was part of why I was thinking I shouldn't . . . you know, give it up for him."

"Now you're being smart." I started folding the letters back up. "Rey never mentioned that his mom had written to him."

"What are you doing? We have to read them for clues."

"They're his private letters."

"Then he shouldn't have run off. He's only twelve, remember?"

"He's almost thirteen."

"This is an emergency. You said it yourself. The Maryland map is missing. He's missing. If his mother's secretly been communicating with him, those letters might tell us where she lives. Maybe they arranged a meeting and he's perfectly safe."

"Ashante called her cell number. It's dead."

"So the letters may be the only clue."

Rachel spread them out on the floor, smoothed the creases, and we read together, but the words were messed up and hard to decipher. In each letter Antoinette had sent him twenty dollars. In the first letter she said the hair business was lousy, that she was looking for a new place. In block letters she'd written DO YOUR HOMEWORK in one letter and DO WHAT AUNT MARY SAYS in the other. That was it. No mention of a town, a company, that she missed him, or when she was coming to visit. Her initial 'A' at the end, no *Love, Mom*.

"No wonder he left the letters here."

When I heard tires on the gravel outside, I rushed to the window, but it wasn't the motorcycle or Ruthie's station wagon. I dialed Ashante's phone. He answered on the second ring.

"It's me. I found some letters from Antoinette. Nothing helpful, but she did send him money. Can you get to Maryland with forty dollars?"

"Not on a bus or a train." In the background I heard trucks and a lot of fast moving cars.

"Where are you?"

"I drove out 19, stopped at a few houses to ask if anyone's seen him. I thought if he was hitchhiking, someone from town might have noticed him."

"Do you need me to read the letters to you?"

"No, but is there a return address? Are they dated?"

"No, nothing like that."

"Her writing him would make her not coming today a bigger disappointment."

"Should we call the Sheriff?" I asked.

"Yeah, yeah, yeah," Rachel yelled from the living room.

"Who's there?" he asked.

"Rachel."

"Don't let her talk you into anything crazy. I'll call the Sheriff from here. How's your mother?"

"Still asleep."

"The girls go to bed?"

"Yeah." I wondered if Rachel and I could move them upstairs to the bottom bunk.

"You can always call Aunt Ruthie at work if you need help."

"I'm okay."

"I knew I could count on you. Any more information from Rey's friends?"

"No, but I'll keep trying."

"Good girl."

I made a quick list of Rey's other buddies and started the calls. Rachel cut us both a piece of pie and spooned ice cream on top.

"Dinner," she said.

"You go ahead. I'm not hungry."

"You are way too quiet. Are you thinking about Henry Lewis?"

"No."

"What then?" She cut off a tiny piece with her fork and dipped it in the ice cream.

"What's that all about?" I pointed to the fork on its way to her mouth, more to avoid talking about my brother than anything.

"I read it in a magazine. If you eat little bites, you lose weight."

"I don't think they mean pie."

"I lost eight pounds in two weeks." She twirled the fork like a wand. Pie and ice cream sprayed all over the floor. "Two and a half weeks."

"Mopping the floor uses a ton of calories." I put my untouched plate in the sink.

"Where are you going?"

"I want to check one place Ashante wouldn't think of. You have to stay here with my mom, ten minutes. I'll be back."

"I wanna go too."

"Your job is to hold the fort here. Mama's not right and if she wakes up, you can distract her."

Rachel's mouth opened for another objection. Time was getting away from us. It had been almost four hours since the funeral. In four hours Rey could get in a lot of trouble.

"You saw how she was at the funeral. She doesn't hear me. She doesn't see me."

Rachel tried the hug again, and I let her this time.

"Go, go. Just tell me where the mop is before you disappear."

I pointed to the tall cupboard by the refrigerator. "I'll be ten minutes. If Ashante calls, tell him I'm in the bathroom."

"You mean lie?"

All the way down the steps I could hear her laughing.

Chapter Twenty-Four

After the funeral Kathy Oncek drove Celie back to the cottage. Etiquette said it would have been polite to ask her in for a cup of tea, but Celie couldn't muster the energy for more conversation. She didn't think Kathy was disappointed. She looked as exhausted as Celie felt. The ride over and back had been full of stories about the Breeden family. Kathy and Mary had worked together for five years at the local Social Services department until Mary finished her masters and left for the Fredericksburg promotion. During those five years she handled intake and Kathy ran classes on parenting, anger management, financial planning, whatever they'd needed. Mary's sociology background made her valuable in a rural county where it was hard to entice full-fledged counselors to live.

Kathy drove Mary to the hospital when Meeka was born, and again with Henry Lewis after she divorced Latrelle. Although Ruthie had taken over in the delivery room, Kathy had been one of the first to hold the Breeden babies. Neither Celie nor Kathy brought up cancer.

In the steady southeast wind the awnings flapped like fighting starlings. The metal frames knocked against the side of the house. After she changed into sweatpants and a long sleeve T, she turned on the cell phone and listened to the messages. Thomas and Caroline had called separately and promised to call back. Jake had left three voicemails and three texts, all identical. *Just checking on you.* There was one number her phone didn't recognize and another message from Dr. Ladd asking her to call back, but to a different number than his office. She'd forgotten all about the tests from two weeks ago.

In their first conference last year with Dr. Ladd he had assured them he made it a point to report test results personally. His explanation, it saved phone tag if the patient had questions. She knew better. When bad news was delivered, patients wanted their doctor on the line, not some nurse without authorization. She took the quilt out to the porch, but not the phone. If it was good news, it could wait. And if it wasn't, she wasn't ready to hear it.

She couldn't sit still though. The wind had blown in an almost transparent layer of clouds. White and filmy, the dome of sky melted down into the palest green above the trees and the bridge, like watercolors bleeding on fresh paper. Draped in the threadbare patchwork, she walked along the river edge and back, the cottage a shield between her and the creek. She had made her appearance at the funeral, been a good neighbor. No one had asked how she knew the Breedens or why she was there. She hoped no one there knew besides Kathy and the Breedens. She thought it unlikely, but guessed they'd simply been too busy observing to ask.

There had been no conversation, overheard or otherwise, about Meeka's part in the accident. Meeka herself had been reserved. Except for Mary's outburst at the tent and the other teenager's rudeness, the afternoon had been peaceful. It had been easy to let the crowd move her, up the church steps and down, across the lawn to the family, through the prayers and hymns, a steady pallor of sadness over them all.

Like a small child learning bedtime prayers Celie repeated to herself the assurances she'd been composing all day. With Henry Lewis laid to rest, his family could begin to heal. It was the kind of mantra she recited to mediation clients after a particularly emotional session. Comforting, bland, universal. She knew the lingo. But as she walked and turned and walked and turned above the dark river, she heard how impersonal and cold it sounded. Not one instant of the ceremony had been specific to Henry Lewis. She knew him no better than she had last Tuesday when she watched the bubbles from his last breath sink and disappear. If she was going to find a way to accept her own failures, she needed to understand his legacy, beyond his peripheral appearance as a typical baby boy in Kathy Oncek's memories. She needed to have his life mean something. And if she was having trouble, Meeka could hardly be expected to do it on her own.

For distraction she went back to organizing the papers in the study. An hour into it she'd pasted every last one of Thomas's drawings and certificates and mementos into place, the photos half done. Despite aching shoulders and a stiff neck, she vowed to finish one album before she went to bed. But the longer she worked, the slower she moved and the more she recognized the classic avoidance. She was being childish. She had put off calling Dr. Ladd long enough.

Even though it was after office hours, he took her call. She knew before he said the words what he was going to say. He sounded as weary as Atlas. There was a second tumor. Not as big as the one they'd removed. Rare for it to show up in her other breast, but better than in her liver or her lungs. Another round of chemo, another surgery, more radiation. Although most patients carried doubts about their cancer's eradication, it couldn't be easy for a doctor to admit that the first set of procedures had failed.

Back when the first lump was diagnosed, she remembered her immediate conviction that she was going to die. Within a matter of hours that changed. Hope, like the cancer itself, was one of those unquenchable things that sprouted where it chose. It was a story she had repeated a dozen times to show the mindset of a cancer patient; how once she'd accepted the truth of the cancer's existence, she knew she would be able to get through the treatment. Of course she'd always ended the story by saying anyone could do it once.

Confronted now with the dreaded recurrence, she knew as immediately as before that she had been wrong. She would do it all again. You always chose life. What an odd twist that failure bred that kind of courage. Still it raised the question, when did you say *no more, not again, enough*? If the first round did not eliminate the bad cells, how could you ever be confident in a second round?

This day had been dedicated to the Breedens and their grief. She had embraced the funeral as a way to give finality to the loss. In some small way that was comforting. There would be no more aftershocks or surprises about his drowning. She had purposely put off the call to Dr. Ladd until after the funeral, a skill the counselor had recommended as healthy. "Compartmentalization," they called it. The waiting, though, made it feel more ominous now that she knew for certain the cancer was back.

The wind followed her around the house. Not loud enough to be a howl, the eerie extended sighs rose and fell, as human and as lonely a sound as she'd ever heard. At every pause she felt as if it were waiting around the corner. She was trapped. Dr. Ladd expected her to soldier through the next round, to follow orders. Jake would marshal the troops. Rory and Thomas would chauffeur her to the hospital and back, laden with offerings of another round of soup and snacks from Middleton friends, from Lila and Caroline.

With the wind whining as it was, she yearned for escape. But escape from what? The horror of watching a child drown? The smoldering frustration over Jake's distancing? The burden of her guilt over not being able to help Meeka? The oncoming train wreck of yet another medical battle? In hindsight the idea of the cottage retreat seemed childish. Trouble, if it were meant for you, found you wherever you were. Star-gazing from the front porch seemed pointless. Hoping for a shooting star was pitiful. It wouldn't fix anything.

The solution came to her when she passed herself in the mirror, between the living room and the dining room on her umpteenth trip from the bedroom to the kitchen for something she couldn't remember once she arrived. The mirror image showed the beginning of a tan, her hair sprouting, her eyes bright points of light in the dim house. She looked healthy. She wouldn't go through the treatments again. Like her attempts at escape, it hadn't worked the first time either. It would be easier on everyone. And she had better things to do. If she had limited time left, she didn't want to waste it at the hospital with strangers.

Without making a conscious decision about leaving or staying, she slippered down the hallway and admired the paintings they'd collected over the years. Like a slideshow on fast forward the memories of where and when they'd bought each one, how in sync she and Jake had been, the quiet happy conversations about where to hang them, all rolled past her catalogued troubles. When the phone chimed its ringtone of church bells, it brought her back to the present.

"Why didn't you call me back?" Jake asked. "Cell phones are supposed to make communication easier."

"I was busy."

"Your cell phone was off all day."

"Just during the funeral and while I was driving over with Kathy Oncek."

"So you went anyway?"

She chose to misinterpret him. "It was fine. Kathy wanted the company."

"Thomas couldn't get you either."

"Or Caroline. Or Rory. Or Lila. I didn't really feel up to talking."

Jake would never understand that concept. Things were so black and white for him. She wondered if that was why he found his version of God so easy.

He cleared his throat. "I know long distance isn't the best time to talk about this, but I am really worried about you. You used to want to solve problems."

"Not when you think I'm the problem."

"I'm not the one who hides out from friends or family all day."

"I'm doing the best I can."

"You say that, but it's not healthy."

"Whose definition of health?"

"Can you please call the counselor and set up a session? I'll take you if you want. At least that way you'll have a neutral third party's opinion."

While it sounded fair and logical, it assumed she was the only one who needed help. And it assumed the counselor could cure what was wrong.

"I'm not the kind of guy who walks away from a sick wife."

"I get that. But you're the one who keeps telling me in the next breath that I'm not sick."

He didn't answer right away. "Let's not play games. We've never done that. When were you going to tell me about Dr. Ladd?"

"What about him? He did some standard follow-up tests two weeks ago." She could imagine Jake, sipping the gin and tonic in the hotel bar, the sports broadcast in the background, his jacket over the back of his chair, his tie in his pocket, his business done for the day, except for this last item on his list: *check on Celie*. Or worse, *straighten out Celie*.

"He called me too, Celie. Did you think he wouldn't call your husband? He has treatment ideas he wants to discuss. I switched my flight so I could meet you there. If you can't manage the drive in, I'll call Thomas to come and get you."

She agreed that she'd meet him there and eked out a neutral good night, but that was it. If Dr. Ladd had called Jake, that was more evidence the prognosis wasn't good. Her husband, her son, and her doctor had already conferred and decided what was best without consulting her. When the phone battery blinked that it was out of juice, she set it down on the table, though she felt like flinging it across the room. The unlit corners of the room, the piles, the boxes, it was too much suddenly. She had to get out, away from everything that she couldn't fix, but especially from the temptation of the pills in the next room that offered oblivion.

She snapped the down vest, grabbed a baseball cap, and turned on the driveway lights before slamming the door behind her. Maxy was right there by the back door, lying in the ivy. It was a funny place to nap with the temperature dropping.

"Oh, dear. You patient little doggie. Why didn't you bark?"

She must have let him out when she came home from the funeral. Or was it before she left? When she stooped to pat him, he whimpered and picked up his head, but he seemed to be having trouble with his legs. He couldn't stand after all. She kneeled and put her fingers on his nose. Dry. She gathered him in her arms, an awkward limp bundle. Although she did it as gently as she could, he yelped in pain.

"Sorry, sorry." She managed to get close enough to the car door handle to wiggle her fingers under and open the passenger door. Once she laid him on the seat, she checked his belly and her sleeves for blood, but there were no open wounds. "Poor puppy. Something's not right. Let me get the phone and we'll go straight to the vet's." But before she'd gone three steps she remembered the battery was dead, and they hadn't chosen a local vet yet. As she eased the car down the driveway, her brain scrambled for ideas. Maxy whimpered continuously. She put one hand on his head.

"George," she said as the car sped past his driveway. She backed up, pulled in, and ran to the back door, the door they used with the kids, near their cars. By the time he came, she was calling his name and pounding with her fist.

He pulled her inside. "What do you know? A damsel in distress."

"It's my dog," she said.

He yelled into the house. "Joanie, bring me a short glass of whiskey, would you?" He was holding Celie up around the waist and walking her to a chair at the kitchen table when his wife appeared in bare legs and an over-sized shirt. "Joanie, meet our neighbor, Celie Lowell. Celie, this is my good wife. Especially good when her mother has taken the kids overnight."

Celie blushed. "I'm so sorry to bother you."

"Your dog, you said?" he asked.

"I'm not sure what's wrong. He's very old, in pain, not moving his legs. My phone is dead. And I don't know the veterinarians here."

"Easily remedied. And I owe you anyway. The car, the busybody, remember?"

Joanie returned with a cell phone, already dialing. "Doctor Van Ness. He's on Marsh Run Road, you'll like him. Very direct." She handed the phone to Celie, who bobbled it at first, but recovered and put it to her ear while it was still ringing.

"Vasili Van Ness here." His voice was calm, none of the expected irritation at a late night caller.

"Is this the veterinarian?"

"The same."

"I'm sorry to call you so late, but—"

He cut her off. "You have an emergency with your pet?"

"Yes, my dog. He's a mutt, dachshund mix, fifteen. Something's wrong with his legs. He's in distress and his nose is dry. No blood that I can see. He was fine this morning." But as soon as she said it, she realized that might not be correct. She hadn't paid any attention to Maxy this morning. She'd been preoccupied, and she'd been gone all afternoon. He'd been outdoors all day. He could have eaten poison or been hit by a car.

"Bring him straight over to the office. I'll meet you there. You know where it is?"

"George can tell me. George Fletcher. He recommended you."

"Bring George too, if you like."

After George gave her directions, and she declined his offer to ride along, she ran back to the car. Even from the opposite side, she could see that the passenger door was open. She didn't remember leaving either door open, but the dome light was on. A dark head showed through the windshield. She peered in from her side.

"Meeka?"

"I heard him crying. He's hurt."

Maxy lay in exactly the same position, his head to the side. His tail beat weakly, but he didn't raise his head. Meeka stroked him behind the ears.

"I'm on my way to the vet's," Celie said.

Meeka passed her hand over the quivering black body. "Will he be alright?"

"I'm not sure. Come if you want."

Doctor Van Ness had all the lights blazing and the door unlocked in the cinderblock one-story office when they arrived ten minutes later. A bell jangled when Meeka opened the door for Celie, her arms full of Maxy.

"Back here," he called with that slight hint of a Slavic accent she'd heard on the phone.

She had wrapped Maxy in a towel from the trunk because he was shivering so badly. Meeka hovered, her head close to the dog's head, murmuring something.

"Up here." Doctor Van Ness indicated from the other side of the examining table.

Maxy didn't object to the stainless steel as he always had at the Middleton vet's. With one hand Meeka stretched the corners of the towel out and kept her other hand on the dog.

"You're okay," she whispered. "We're right here."

The vet ran his hands over the dog's belly. In several spots he listened with his stethoscope. "Obstruction somewhere. Lots of gurgling. Sounds like internal bleeding."

Meeka started to cry. Celie rubbed her shoulder. She could see the doctor had slowed down too, a sign she didn't want to interpret.

"He's definitely getting weaker," she said. "He tried to stand at the house."

"How old did you say?"

"Fifteen."

"On any medications?"

"No, but I think he's deaf."

"And blind too, I'd guess, or close," the vet said. "Too old to operate. Even if I thought we had a chance of finding the leak."

"Hit by a car?"

236

"Could be, but sometimes it's just mechanical failure. Dogs are not unlike humans. Their organs fail with age."

"But you can do something for the pain?"

Meeka had pulled herself together and was whispering again to the dog, her lips close to his ear, almost a steady hum.

"He can't hear you," the doctor said.

Celie made a wide circle on Meeka's back with her open palm and hummed a bit herself. "It's alright, sweetie. Sing away, you never know."

The vet hung the stethoscope on the wall. "He won't last long. Do you want to wait or put him to sleep?"

She spoke over Meeka's gasp. "Whatever will stop the pain."

Doctor Van Ness pulled a clipboard off a hook on the cabinet. After making several notations on the top page, some kind of pre-printed form, he handed it to her and indicated where to sign. She signed. Unsure of the date, she left that blank. With his back turned he opened and shut cupboards and drawers. She assumed he was collecting what he needed. When he turned back to them, he laid it on a small pull-out shelf below the examining table; a razor, a small glass bottle with clear liquid, the syringe, a thickish square of sterile bandage. Meeka gasped as the collection grew.

"Does your daughter want to wait in the hallway?"

"My . . ." Celie stumbled. She wasn't thinking. No doubt Meeka had never had to euthanize a pet either. Seven days ago she'd watched her brother sink and disappear. She shouldn't be here, witnessing another death. "Come on, I'll take you home. You don't need to see this."

Meeka ripped her arm free. "She's not my mother. I can do what I want."

Celie saw the doctor's eyes widen. Maxy struggled to breathe.

"It's up to her," she said.

After it was over and Maxy lay warm and still against her stomach, the doctor explained she could pick him up for burial the next afternoon and take care of the bill then too. When she finished thanking him, she found Meeka in the waiting room, her hand jiggling the door knob as if she had advanced Parkinson's disease.

"You're just leaving him?" she said once they were alone outside, slogging through the pine needles to the car.

"Dr. Van Ness will take care of him tonight. I'll come back tomorrow."

Meeka ground her teeth, started to say something, but it never came out. She whipped the passenger door open and sat where Maxy had been. Celie fumbled with her purse, the keys, the ignition. Still silent, the girl stuck her flattened hands between the car seat and her thighs, as if it was taking all her control not to leap out and rush back inside.

"Does your mother know you were out again tonight?" Celie asked.

"She doesn't care."

"Why were you out? Is it the creek?"

"Why do you care where I am, what I'm doing?"

"Your mother might be worried. When my boys were teenagers and living at home, they had curfews. I worried less, and it kept them safe. And out of trouble."

"That's the whole thing, isn't it? From the beginning. You think I'm trouble. Is it because I let my brother drown? Or because I'm black?"

"That's not . . .that has nothing to do with it. I wanted . . . you tried . . . It's just . . ." Celie felt like a spotlight was shining down, exposing the innermost hidden corners of her mind and heart, tumors erupting from years of assumptions, ingrained generalizations, preconceptions. "It's just. I've had enough." Her voice had grown louder. "Henry Lewis is enough. I don't want any more pain. For you, for anyone."

Meeka rubbed her shoulder against her cheek, though it was too dark in the unlit parking lot for Celie to tell if she was crying.

"Too late. Rey's run away."

"Run away? Where? Why? He couldn't have saved your brother. He's too small."

"It's not that. I think he's gone looking for his mother, my aunt, my other aunt. She didn't come to the funeral, just like I tried to tell him she wouldn't."

"Some people can't handle funerals."

"That's not her excuse. She's just lame."

"He knows where she lives?"

"I don't think so. But he's sure he can find her, just like he's sure he can make her love him. Only . . . she only cares about herself. He won't listen to anyone."

"Maybe once she knows how he feels—"

"She's not going to change. She hasn't been back in a year. She's not coming back. But you can't tell him that. You can't tell boys anything. He's gonna have to figure it out for himself."

"When you came down to the creek tonight then, you were looking for Rey?"

Meeka nodded.

"Do you think he might . . . hurt himself?" She had started to say jump in the creek, but she could see from Meeka's face that was exactly what she was afraid of.

"I told him he shouldn't have dared Henry Lewis about swimming. I was mad when I said it, but I shouldn't of. I thought Rey was okay—he's a toughie—but this thing with his mother, on top of Henry Lewis. . . It's too hard."

"I heard there was a fight at school. That wasn't over Henry Lewis?"

"Nuh-uh, it was Antoinette. His mother. They know how to tease him."

"Any idea where she is, where he might have gone?"

"When she left out of here she said she had a job interview in Baltimore."

"She visits? Calls?"

"Sure. Three maybe four times in a year." Meeka snorted in disgust. "When Aunt Ruthie phoned her about the funeral, Antoinette yelled at Rey for a whole two minutes, that's all she said. No *how you feeling, need anything, I love you.* She's not coming back for him. What's she gonna do with a teenage boy when the next man knocks on her door? And the next? How's she gonna explain that to Rey?"

Celie swallowed her shock at the girl's bluntness. She hated to think how a fourteen year-old girl knew about men in that way. For the first time she was glad she hadn't had a daughter.

"What kind of job interview?"

"What?"

"Your aunt, did she say what company gave her the interview?"

Meeka tossed her head, but it crossed Celie's mind that she might not be avoiding the question, just disgusted at her aunt all over again.

"What jobs did she have here before she left?"

"Jobs? Antoinette? I don't think so."

"Your mother and aunt both have specialized training beyond high school. It's logical that their sister—"

"Beauty school. Antoinette was supposively taking classes to cut hair and that kind of . . . stuff."

"Rey knew that? Did he talk to you about her?"

"I wouldn't let him. I didn't want to hear all those excuses. He sounded just like her. He was better than that."

Celie was composing a careful answer, sure that this guilt should be defused before Meeka did something crazy too.

Meeka didn't wait. "I shouldda let him talk. He must of felt like I was blaming him."

"But it was an accident."

Meeka closed her eyes and slumped against the car door. "Can we go home now?"

In reverse Celie eased the car out. Without talking she drove down the winding road headed back to Rte 19. They passed the trailer court, more cars than trailers, mostly dark. A lone security light blazed above the parking lot of one worn-out warehouse. The sign hung crooked. Last fall's weeds, gone to seed, feathered the vinyl siding and pocked the gravel lot like Holocaust survivors. The houses pinned to the far ends of the rutted lanes they passed were shuttered, unlit. Woods spread out behind them like an endless ocean of black. She was relieved to emerge from the dark into the jittery neon glow of the corner convenience store, though it was locked and dark on the inside. The store sign blinked at odd intervals. It must have a faulty connection. Through the window the Lottery sign gleamed slick green one minute and disappeared the next. Each nervous gasp of chartreuse poked fingers of light out across the paved parking lot that disappeared almost as soon as they appeared. The neon jabs intersected with the gray cones underneath the hooded pole bulbs, making a dancing pattern. Even with the store shut tight, it meant they had returned to civilization.

When the red light at the intersection didn't turn green after two rotations in the other direction, Celie turned left anyway. "Don't even think about doing that when you're driving."

"I'm not old enough to drive."

"Soon enough. Trust me, whenever a young person does that, there's always a state trooper right around the corner. It's a sixth sense they have. Troopers love to pick on . . . kids."

"You mean black kids."

"No, I . . ." She was back in the Breeden's kitchen, awkward and embarrassed all over again. "Yeah, okay, that does happen. But it's too easy to stop there. Not all policemen are like that."

"The 911 ones who came last week weren't."

"No, they weren't. You're right."

"So how can you tell?" Meeka asked.

"You want me to say there's a way to predict by looking at them?"

Meeka sputtered a little and Celie was immediately sorry to sound confrontational. Without talking they rode past the elementary school and the library. Maybe the distance between them was too great, the color difference too convenient, too easy to hide behind. It felt a little like swimming against the current to push those automatic assumptions to the back of her brain and to try and stay open-minded. Underneath though, she and Meeka both wanted the same things. Like Rory and Thomas when they were in school, Meeka wanted respect from the people around her. She wanted to be independent and recognized as capable. Celie understood.

She tried again. "It's so much easier to judge by past behavior or stories you've heard, general reputation, than to wait and see, to risk putting yourself in danger, opening that soft underbelly of the porcupine to the horn of the rhinoceros."

Meeka laughed. "Only you could get to zoo animals from mean white people."

"At least you understood I wasn't saying you were a porcupine."

"I could be. Brown enough."

"And prickly." Celie smiled when she saw Meeka smile. "What's so funny about that?"

"That's 'zactly what my Aunt Ruthie says about me."

Once they turned onto Stonegate Road, the dimmed lights of St. Bernadette's greeted them. After hours everyone was asleep, dreaming of tomorrow and a better world. Meeka sat straighter, her hands finally at rest in her lap.

"I'm sorry about your dog."

"Thank you." Celie stopped herself from saying more. She was still adjusting to this more comfortable place.

"I'm not going to get a puppy."

Celie wanted to argue with her, explain what good company a pet was, how much you learn from having an animal depend on you. But this wasn't the right time, and she might not be the right person to make the pitch. "There'll be plenty of time for that later."

"Grownups always say that, but it didn't work for Henry Lewis, did it? And now there's Rey."

Chapter Twenty-Five

When she dropped Meeka at the Linden Street townhouse, every light was on. Whether you believed in shadows or night noises or ghosts, the Breeden's schedule was bound to be off-kilter. It made her wonder if the Jaspers across the street from the cottage or George, her curious and kind neighbor, noticed when her lights were on after midnight and worried about her.

He had left a note about Maxy inside the screened door, an offer to help in a wild, erratic scribble that made her laugh because it was so in character for the caricature she'd created of a happy-go-lucky sailor stuck in a white coat in a dentist's office. But the laugh felt disloyal to Maxy. She didn't call George.

In the morning she would dig the hole herself by standing on the wobbly step ladder and dropping the posthole digger a dozen times. It would save her bad arm from a fight with the shovel and the hard clay. She could sort through Jake's wood scraps and find a piece wide enough to chisel out the four letters of his name and the years, skills she'd learned in high school art class when they'd studied woodcuts. If the arm started giving her fits, she would use a garden stake and wait a couple of days. It was a good thing it had happened now while she still had one working arm.

The house was stuffy and overly warm with the gas logs, though she'd turned them off the minute she arrived from the vet's. There was no point even in putting on her pajamas at four-thirty in the morning. Sleep was impossible. She clicked through the internet protocol on her laptop and Googled Baltimore. There were three Antoinettes under hairdressers, three different last names, no Breedens, but then Breeden would be a married name for Mary. God bless the Yellow Pages for recognizing the future was in the switch to online postings.

She printed out the page. And four more pages of maps with a wider version of the downtown streets that included the three beauty parlor addresses. She did an internet search for the names and found that only one Antoinette had a home phone. It seemed unlikely that the mother Antoinette who had skipped out on her teenage son could afford both a business and a home phone, but she tried it anyway. No answer and no recorded message. She shut down the computer without checking her email. After she stuffed a shirt, clean socks, and her toiletry bag into a discarded backpack of Rory's they used for day hikes, if she drove anywhere now she'd fall asleep at the wheel. Stretched out on the couch with the old quilt tucked around her for a quick nap, she closed her eyes. Sleep was instantaneous.

She hadn't meant to sleep long, but woke with a jolt to brilliant sunrise, that abundant sunshine the weather channel touted as if they had summoned it themselves. The morning was chilly finally, as April should be, that crisp air of spring that captured the sunshine in the spaces between trees and buildings. The triangles of intense color and light formed an impervious surface over a more malleable, less striking undergarment of sky, like a red cocktail dress over a pale silk slip, the hint of a warmer afternoon.

Angry at herself for wasting so much time with sleep, she moved fast, brainstorming and collecting the things on a mental list. By six-forty-five she had deposited on the Volvo front floorboards a cooler filled with water bottles and granola bars. She unplugged the cell phone, fully charged, and stuck it in her purse with her mad money, still in the retrieved envelope from her sock drawer. Bundled in a wind breaker over her sweatshirt, she laid everything else on the back seat of the car: a flashlight, two sleeping bags, her down vest, a plastic laundry basket with towels, and the backpack.

As she worked, she reviewed half a dozen possible scenarios. She discarded the first; that Meeka would still be at home, waiting for the police to find Rey. Surely though, she would not go looking for him before daylight. But the longer she thought about it, the more she realized, as Meeka might have, that by waiting she would lose the cover of night and Rey's lead would expand, dangerously so. Celie didn't want to misjudge her. The girl was smart. Trains and buses didn't run when people were sleeping. They ran when people needed to travel, during rush hour and business hours. Patogansett was an hour's drive away from the closet stations if she was going to be there for the commuter runs. Meeka had a four hour head start.

When the cell phone lit up with Jake's number, Celie slid it back in her purse without answering. Talking to him at this point would only complicate what she was planning. She didn't want to be practical. She wanted to do something that would help, something positive. And she didn't want to lie about what she was doing.

Outside the Linden Street apartments, the county school bus had stopped traffic. It was just after seven. Although she was four cars back on the side street, she could see Jasmine and Liné, their hands linked as they hoisted themselves up the steps. No Rey. So he was still missing. In rural counties one bus picked up students from all the grades within each neighborhood. It worked the same way in

Middleton, though her boys had not ridden the bus. Scenario number four—leaving from school—meant that Meeka should be right behind the girls, but she wasn't there. When the apartment door shut and the bus gathered itself, chugging forward, Celie had a clear view of the empty yard. The van was gone too. Only the silver scooter remained.

While she waited for the bus to turn the corner, she examined the map again. Her hand-drawn arrows showed three possible routes north. Baltimore would be the obvious choice based on what Meeka had told her in their bird-shot conversations. The other question was whether Meeka had enough cash to buy a bus or train ticket. A friend's older brother or sister might be driving her. Or she might hitchhike.

Celie shot a silent prayer into the stratosphere, *please don't let her be hitchhiking.* If only during their ride back from the vet's, she'd been gutsy enough to ask Meeka what she was thinking about her cousin. One of those anonymous car conversations where faces are invisible and kids reveal more than they would in a well-lit kitchen.

When a black-and-white pulled into the apartment parking lot, Ashante came outside almost immediately. Dressed in a blue dress shirt and dark slacks, he looked like he was headed to work. The officers met him on the walkway. He handed them a paper—a note from Rey? Or Meeka?—and the three men cobbled together, their heads bent in a strategy huddle if ever. When they separated, there was more conversation, hand motions, and some toe scuffing by the uniformed men in the sandy edge of the walkway. Ashante rushed inside. The door swung wide in the breeze. Both policemen glanced around, up into the overhead green canopy, across the neighbor's yard, down the street. Celie tensed when one of the officers seemed to be staring right at her. But when he turned back to the apartment, she realized he had to have heard the door opening or someone must have spoken from inside. Ashante stepped out into the daylight and squinted. When he held out a small piece of something dark in each hand, the younger deputy took them and slipped them together into the breast pocket of his uniform.

After the cruiser drove off, she rotated her neck to loosen the muscles and edged the car through the stop sign and out to the main road. The motorcycle engine chugged off in the opposite direction. Kathy Oncek had told her Ashante worked in the business office at the lumber yard on the Richmond road. Even if he wasn't the father of any of the children, it didn't seem likely that he would abandon them in the middle of this new crisis. Without scrolling through the next dozen imagined scenarios, she concentrated on the road. She hoped Mary wasn't alone.

The Volvo practically drove itself to Fredericksburg. She scanned the shoulder for a drooping teenager. At each of the three gas stations she stopped and stalked through the aisles in hopes of finding Meeka curled asleep in a corner. She asked the bored clerks if they'd seen a teen-age boy or girl on their own, but their answers were non-committal. If they had seen anything, asking what time would have been a joke.

Night-time traffic from the boonies might not have yielded a ride, but Meeka wasn't the kind of girl who would sit down and wait patiently with her thumb out. She would be walking, hell-bent on action. Which meant she'd still be east of Port Royal if she'd left the instant Celie had dropped her off from the vets. But there was no one.

On the outskirts of Fredericksburg the speed limit slowed to 45, too fast to see into the passing store windows. At one traffic light, a convenience store on her left, she noticed a backpack disappearing inside on the back of a kid about Rey's height. She veered across oncoming traffic into the store lot, horns and an outraged driver's voice behind her. She braked hard against the yellow curb and raced in.

"Where's that kid?" she asked the elderly man behind the register.

He blinked and looked down the aisle and back at her. "Kid?"

As she turned to check the aisle with the soda machine and the coffee bar, her shoe caught on the newspaper wire rack below the counter, a jumble of newsprint and advertising flyers on the floor. The attendant muttered in a steady stream. Celie kept on going.

"The boy with the backpack?" She called over the shoulder-high shelves when the last aisle turned up empty.

Just then the bathroom door opened by the back freezer, and she shrieked, "Wait."

"Can't. I'm late for my science test." Grinning and very Latino, the boy sprinted past her.

"I am certifiable," she muttered as the shop clerk shook his head in confusion. "Thanks anyway."

Just as she pulled into the loading zone for the Fredericksburg train station, the loud speakers announced the arrival of the DC-NYC northbound train. With a lethal punch of the flasher button on her dash, she left the car and raced up the ramp. She scanned the platform. A dozen men with briefcases, two soldiers in fatigues, and a tightly entwined couple in the middle of a Hollywood good-bye kiss. No Meeka. Celie waved to catch the attention of the conductor who stood guard above his plastic footstool.

"Anyone board already? I'm looking for a girl, a teenager, tall, thin?" When he didn't answer, she added, "An African-American girl?"

He shook his head. The quizzical rise of his eyebrows hit her like a sucker punch. She'd made an enormous error. She had no photo of Meeka. A black teenager might be noticeable in Fredericksburg with just a short physical description, but by DC, where there were thousands of black teenagers, a photo would be critical. That's what Ashante must have given the policemen, pictures of Rey and Meeka.

She could call Mary Breeden about getting photos sent through the local police, but that would depend on whether the Breedens had a home number available through Information. And if Mary had gone to work, she might not listen to a message until evening. Assuming Meeka had left a note and Ashante had given it to the officers, the police already might have put out an APB. That meant another crisis for Mary. A fourteen year-old girl out there on her own. And a further ten hours delay on the missing boy who had been entrusted to his aunt.

When Celie left the cottage, she was hoping to locate Meeka before any of that happened. She wanted to catch up with her, find Rey, and deliver the two children home before it turned from a crisis into a tragedy. She wanted to be the savior. But she'd left it too late. Immediate action was required to avoid disaster. And she'd hesitated. Again.

Sitting on the metal bench, she stared through watery eyes as the train crept off. The whistle built with the engine's momentum until the tracks were two diminishing black scratches against the pale lavender canvas of early morning sky. The station was quiet. She was a useless person. A mess of emotions and ideas, she burst into people's lives, churned things up, and left confusion and conflict in her wake. The minute Meeka mentioned how worried she was about Rey, Celie should have called Mary or Aunt Ruthie. Of all people she should have known the girl would feel responsible. It was, after all, exactly how they both felt about Henry Lewis.

When she returned to the car with its flashers blinking red, a yellow flutter sparked against the windshield. "Damn," she said. "Three minutes. Fredericksburg must be hard up for revenue if they couldn't wait three lousy minutes with the train in the station." The imposition of a parking ticket, when there were five empty spaces further down, seemed particularly unfair. She stuck it in her purse and pulled out the maps with her notations.

She analyzed the bus route, the location of the downtown Baltimore train station, the intersection of the interstate and the hand-drawn stars that stood for the beauty shops. If she drove without stopping, she could be there in two and a half hours, with plenty of time to visit the salons before lunch. It wasn't a foolproof plan, but at least she would be in the city where Antoinette had gone, the most logical place for Rey to start the search for his mother, the place where Meeka assumed her cousin was headed.

And if she struck out, then what? Drive around Baltimore in hopes of passing either child on the sidewalks? It was absurd that she had thought this could work. Mary might have other information about her wayward sister, information she didn't want to share with a fourteen year-old, but would readily tell the authorities. And the Baltimore police were already in place, within minutes of the bus and train, with a network set up to find missing children. If they'd been notified as soon as Rey went AWOL after the funeral, he might be on his way back already and Meeka still safe at home. This whole attempt could be a wild goose chase. She wasn't only useless, she was stupid.

She drove north anyway, unwilling to go back without them. The green signs with the neat white lettered names of familiar towns passed regularly, a reminder that an ordered world existed, just not for her. Whenever she approached an exit, she slowed and stared into the shadows. Hitchhikers always seemed to appear on exit and entrance ramps. Pedestrian bans might not be enforced on ramps. Today, though, the curved silver barricades displayed no teenagers.

When she remembered the cell phone—which she'd set on vibrate, but left in her purse—she considered calling Kathy Oncek for the Breeden's telephone number. At least she could report what she did know and where she was headed. But once she opened the phone, it showed her the inevitable string of messages from her own family. She couldn't call them back or they would try to talk her out of it. She drove on, unwilling to lose time by stopping to deal with their doubts. She stuck the phone back in her purse. There were places outside of DC that banned the use of cell phones while driving. She'd read about it in the paper. It was safer not to use the phone, though she recognized her own attempt to justify not calling. Time wise she couldn't afford being pulled over and falling farther behind Meeka.

The ache in her left breast tightened, an odd twinge very like what she'd felt with the first tumor. She tried to ignore it. After the first diagnosis she'd read all the materials they'd given her and studied hours more on the internet. None of the official medical sites mentioned twinges. Jake had been the one to ask, at the second scheduling conference. Her "team" explained how the bad cells moved into the ducts, why the twinge made sense. But the treatments had taught here that a day or two wouldn't make a difference. Experience was such a grand teacher.

The first I-95 sign to New York City whizzed past, the tangled DC traffic a comfortable distance behind her. She drove like she was at a tennis match, her head swinging from side to side on the off chance that Meeka was on the shoulder between rides. When a siren blasted past her, the first of a trio of speeding cruisers, she fought the urge to pull out and follow them.

"Please let that not be anything to do with us," she said out loud, surprising herself at the automatic linking. And as if they'd heard her, the siren wails were swallowed in the curve of an exit ramp, gone as if they'd never been.

As the old Volvo rose on the northbound ramp over the port of Baltimore, she maneuvered into the right hand lane, eager to descend into the city grid and try to find the internet map locations. From the ramp she admired the view of a thriving city, cranes cantilevered over tankers, rows upon rows of different colored containers waiting for transport, a stunning loose weave of concrete pathways and sports stadiums and flashing billboards, and a wide margin of glass-encased high rise office buildings along the sparkling harbor. Many times they'd visited friends from college who lived here, strolled along the docks, explored the aquarium with the boys, cheered an Orioles home run. Despite the city's reputation for its failing schools and its widespread unemployment, a committed group, their friends included, championed the historic neighborhoods and worked to bring art and education to the more disadvantaged, mostly black, citizens. She'd always liked Baltimore's energy, and open acceptance of who they were. Baltimore didn't put on airs.

But liking it and knowing it were very different things. The roads familiar to her were the thruways leading in and out of the city. Sure, she'd driven around Camden Yards enough times to understand the six block tourist area and how it linked to the waterfront commercial section. She could use the GPS for the hairdressing salons, though it would not tell her which neighborhoods were safe for an older woman. She tried to ignore the sinking feeling that she had the wrong color skin for this city. Residents might or might not respond to her questions about two black kids on the run. Demands from a white woman wouldn't inspire a sense of cooperation. A fool on a fool's errand, her own translation of Richard Widener's words.

Chapter Twenty-Six

The only empty seats on the bus to Baltimore were the pair right behind the driver, one of each side of the aisle. Disgusting scars of hardened gunk crisscrossed the worn material. I didn't want to think about what it was, what it had been. With my backpack as a pillow, I arranged myself on the window seat behind the driver. I was careful not to touch the fabric or the metal window frame with my hands.

In a faceless mass the other passengers and the whole back end of the bus sighed and murmured and coughed and sneezed behind me. After that first glance into the cavern of unfamiliar faces, I refused to look back. In front of me, just over the driver's padded seat, a huge clear window let in light from the station overheads, nothing like a school bus. The fluorescent tinge and its reflection on the grungy gray cinderblock wall turned everything a sick yellowish-green. The engine idled with the door open.

At the bottom of the bus steps a grizzled old man with a paper bag in his arms appeared, a permanent grimace on his face. As he swayed in place, his jaw worked away at something. Twice he spit sideways with so little energy that the long dark streak fell onto his shadow and splashed his shoes. Although I couldn't see the sidewalk, I knew it was decorated with tobacco juice. I was glad I was already on and didn't have to step across it to board. I hoped he wouldn't ask me a question.

When he didn't get in, I wondered if he was looking for the Baltimore bus. But if I volunteered it and it was the bus he was looking for, the only available seat was next to me and I didn't want him there. Trying to look busy, I analyzed the dashboard instead. After several more squirts out of the other side of his mouth, he shuffled off with the paper bag squeezed tightly to his chest like a favorite teddy bear.

Although I'd forgotten the exact departure time, I didn't want to dig into my backpack for the ticket because I'd have to set things down on the icky seat. While I was debating how else to figure out the time, a short square man in a gray and blue uniform with a matching blue baseball cap leaped up the steps. Finally, we were going. He had a routine. He draped his jacket over the back of the driver's seat and tucked papers in different cubbies along the bottom of the front window. He climbed up on the seat, stood on the cushion, feet apart, with one hand on the ceiling to steady himself.

"Baltimore home for you, missy?" He asked without turning his head as he fiddled with the mechanical box above the windshield. Metal squeaked on metal. "Wassa matter? You Helen Keller recarnatated?" He turned and nodded at me as if he were the teacher giving me permission to speak.

"If I were, I wouldn't of heard the question."

"A smarty-pants too. Hope that don't mean you're going to talk my ear off, telling me a bunch of things I already know."

He snapped the cover of the overhead box shut before he twisted his torso, put both hands on the back of the seat, and pitched himself into the air like a circus performer. Although he landed with both feet on the top step, he wavered there long enough that I worried the tilt might send him falling down the steps.

"I got a girl 'bout your size," he said after another ten second inspection of me.

"She taller than you?"

"Almost everyone's taller than me, missy. If I wasted my time dwelling on that, I'd go crazy."

He was rifling through a fistful of tickets like the one the lady at the ticket window had sold me. Mine was in pieces since the sleepy attendant at the gate had ripped it apart, returning the wider end to me. Every fifth or sixth ticket the little man tugged out of the pile and lay down on his right leg. In order to see what he was doing, I inched forward. He turned around and shot me a quick wink. I couldn't help staring. His face was blurred with freckles. I'd never seen a grown-up with freckles. Only kids in Disney movies had freckles. And not nearly as many.

"Trouble is . . ." He looked right into my eyes like he was trying to hypnotize me. "My kids all think they're smarter too. A person's in a bad way real quick if she jumps to conclusions before she knows a person."

It was a nice way of telling me not to underestimate him. I was figuring fast on how I should answer his earlier question about Baltimore when he sprinted down the steps and disappeared. A blur of blue motion appeared in the oversized rear view mirror bolted onto the outside of the bus. In the mirror the gray and blue jacket took up a position next to a stack of boxes higher than his head. One by one he pulled them off, peered at the labels, and fed them into the belly of the bus. When they were all gone, he arched his back, bounced up and down in place with his arms swinging, and trotted back to the front door.

250

"Faster than a speeding bullet," he said as he wiggled into the seat like a dog settled into his bed.

"You are quick. For a grown-up."

"I wasn't talking about me. I was talking about Greyhound freight delivery. Faster than planes. Faster than trains."

I knew that line from the movie, one of Henry Lewis's favorites. "It's a plane, it's a train, it's a Greyhound Bus."

When he laughed, I felt better for the first time since . . . the night TJ had rescued me. My little brother was a huge Superman fan. He had watched the movies endlessly from forever. He might have been in diapers when he first saw it. "Pooperman" he'd say when he was little and couldn't pronounce the S, and we'd all crack up.

One time when we were in Richmond and he saw an old-fashioned telephone booth, he'd gone in and ripped off his shirt. He happened to be wearing a Superman T-shirt underneath, one of many he'd scarfed up from Goodwill with his allowance quarters. When he slid back the glass door so hard that it crashed against the frame, everyone on the sidewalk turned around to see. There was Henry Lewis Superman, leaping onto the bench with his hands out in front like he was flying, the big S on his chest. No fear, that was my brother.

If only he were here to help me find Rey. This was his kind of adventure. He loved to explore. Without him all I could think was that when I got off the bus in Baltimore, it would be a big city. I only had the one idea of where to find Antoinette. Rey better be there or I'd be SOL. Rachel's phrase, one I couldn't repeat at home or my mother would ground her forever.

When the driver cleared his throat, I noticed him watching me in the rear view mirror above his head.

"I'm Liam," he said. "Liam Sullivan. Should have introduced myself first off. Once upon a time from Dublin, lately of Stafford. Not the one in Britain."

I'd never heard of Stafford in Britain, but I knew Dublin was in Ireland, an island across the Atlantic. In school we had talked about wars, and Ireland was one of the saddest ones because they had killed each other for years and years over religion before they finally figured out that it wasn't solving anything. War was the hard way to learn that different didn't mean you couldn't live as neighbors in the same place.

Maybe I would see Ireland from Ms. Lowell's telescope. When I got back, I would ask her. Ms. Lowell would be lonely without Maxy, and she might like the company. When Liam Sullivan cleared his throat again, I realized he was still waiting for my answer.

"I'm Tomeeka Breeden from Patogansett. That's in Virginia."

He seemed satisfied, a quick nod in the mirror before he yanked the door shut with the handle attached to a crooked pole, all built in to the dashboard, the same as the school bus handles in Patogansett. Very clever because the driver didn't have to get out of his seat.

Over the beep-beep of the bus backing up, he said, "So if you aren't from Baltimore, why are you going there? If you don't mind my asking? Isn't every day I get a spring chicken like you on my route."

"I'm not so young as you think."

"I didn't ask you that, though, did I? My girl, the one your size, she don't travel by herself quite yet. So I'm thinking you ought not to be on your own either."

"I bought a ticket. It means I can go where I paid to go."

"You're right about that, Tomeeka Breeden. But city's different from country, and Baltimore's different from other cities you might know."

I did know that. From the internet pictures Rey had opened up at the library computers months ago. Rey insisted on library visits over and over, top of his list for after-school activities on rainy days when there was no basketball or baseball. He must of been thinking about finding his mother for a lot longer than I'd realized.

It was a relief to talk about it. "I'm going to Baltimore to find my cousin and bring him home."

He didn't ask the next question, the one I expected, about where exactly the cousin was. I'd already practiced my answer to avoid a lie. He was like Mrs. Lowell, interested in me, but not critical. He hadn't said I couldn't ride because I was too young. He hadn't refused to take me without a custodian's permission, things I'd read earlier on the poster of regulations in the station. The bus coasted along, up the ramp in a steady powerful glide and onto the much busier highway. As the cars and trucks parted to make room, the bus took over the middle lane in one easy swing. For the third or fourth time Liam Sullivan jiggled the lid of his hat looser, then he disentangled a walkie-talkie from the dashboard.

"Good morning, sons and daughters of this bright, beautiful world. Welcome to Greyhound # 107, the Baltimore Bullet. With stops in Alexandria and DC. This is the express. If you meant to take the local, you bought the wrong ticket, but . . . you'll get the smoothest ride to the wrong place you'll ever have." He waited for the grumbles and laughter to die down. "The good news is there's a Greyhound headed back to where you meant to go. Tomorrow." He laughed at his own joke. "Estimated arrival in Old Town Alexandria, seven forty-eight A.M."

As he talked, I watched the wheel slide through his hands and catch, slide and catch. I could feel myself fading out. The images from the long afternoon at the church faded too; Mama in a panic calling out my name, Demeta yelling her ugliness, Rey searching the crowd for his mother, Ms. Lowell's white face in the black sea, and the slow journey of the shiny steel casket across the church lawn.

When I woke up, I'd be in Baltimore, or maybe only Alexandria. But I was doing something, not waiting for permission or for the grown-ups to take care of it. Maybe I was letting in the wolf, that real world TJ warned her about. But at least I was swimming out into Mr. Green's big, beautiful world to save Rey, and I'd figured out how to do it by myself.

Chapter Twenty-Seven

At the first red light on Pratt Street Celie laid the maps out on the front seat and put the one with the closest address to downtown on top. Camden Yards and its vintage streetlamps created a fairytale effect, as if she'd traveled back in time. Once she passed the fancy waterfront with its brick crosswalks and outdoor sculptures, she followed East Pratt for blocks. As the buildings deteriorated, the pavement reverted to potholes. It was impossible to avoid them all. One bounced the Volvo into the air and it landed hard on tires she was not sure would take that kind of treatment. She slowed down. She didn't have time for a flat tire.

She muttered to herself as she paid more attention to the potholes and crawled through intersections to check the street signs. The left hand turn onto North Patterson came up sooner than she expected. She was so busy watching the street signs that the hood of the Volvo was halfway into the intersection when the light changed. She had to gun it to avoid the crossfire traffic. She had grown rusty with city traffic. Down blocks and blocks she bumped and shifted, past row houses and crumby corner stores and overgrown vacant lots.

She drove through the stretch of North Bradford where the first salon was supposed to be three times before she saw the sign. Sideways, propped up behind a row of shell-shocked trash cans in the alley. No wonder no one answered the telephone. Months of debris littered the stoop in front of the storefront, layered like a bird's nest. A split piece of plywood was nailed across its broken window. Someone had spray-painted in day-glo orange 'JESUS LOVES YOU.' Haste or stealth had landed the last three letters on the old brick. Later would-be prophets had added the 'F' word in smaller black letters, different handwriting, above the YOU, as if it were a two way conversation.

She parked anyway and walked back to see if there might be a referral sign or a telephone number for a landlord or a realtor. No such luck. The street was deserted, not even one old woman hobbling along with her walker or a kid on a skateboard. She balled up her first computer print-out and chucked it over her shoulder into the back of the car. In her head she checked off that address, but she didn't feel any better.

To get to the next salon on her list, she had to find Martin Luther King, Jr. Expressway. Every city in America had one of those. She could only imagine how horrified King would be to know, fifty years later, people still lived in places like this, depressed and depressing. How did a kid grow up in this kind of neighborhood and believe in escape when so many didn't?

Like Henry Lewis, there must be some who dreamed of what was at the other end of a telescope. They rode the fear of the unknown like a wild pony, sitting straight up, squeezing their knees as tight as they could, and looking ahead instead of down. Was it courage, confidence, or foolhardiness? Or was it because the other options simply were not bearable?

Of course each person brought his own character traits and experience to any challenge. Thomas and Rory hadn't responded in the identical way to the things she and Jake had tried to teach them. Thomas was generous to a fault, but dispensed that generosity like a pharmacist, in controlled doses, on his own schedule. Rory reacted more spontaneously, without forethought, without consideration for his own needs. That meant he was more at risk of going overboard or being preoccupied. He might miss seeing the need in one person because he focused so intensely when he did see a need.

With time she could see that it worked for each of them in his own way. She liked that they were living deliberately, not making rash decisions, and definitely not hamstrung by ego. Like a lot of families, Thomas was more like Jake, and Rory was more like her.

With all her worry over Meeka feeling responsible for her brother's death and carrying around that guilt, she saw the positive side of it. Those feelings distinguished Meeka from the masses. She was someone who'd learned early that actions had consequences, a crucial adult concept. Something many of Celie's mediation clients sadly lacked. Meeka would be better able to plan ahead as she grew up, more willing to make the hard choices to execute those plans the next time. The shame was that she'd had to learn it the hard way.

The GPS directed Celie twenty blocks west, crossing over or under MLK. As she merged left into the lazy mid-day traffic, she was still immersed in her thoughts about King and what he'd wanted for the world. To the west the clouds had thickened into a dark band, way beyond the 'partly cloudy' weather prediction offered up on the radio. A storm would complicate the search. The kids would have to go inside. But maybe Rey was already with Antoinette, safe at least from unknown predators. In the short term, Celie reassured herself, his mother couldn't do much damage beyond what she'd already done by abandoning him.

Raindrops splashed on the hood, fast and furious like a summer thunderstorm instead of an April shower. Immediately the windshield was opaque. She signaled and pulled over, not sure if she was in a no parking zone or not. All she needed was to lose herself in this wrangle of unfamiliar streets or hit another car and be marooned in a questionable neighborhood while she waited for the police. The Volvo rocked like a life boat in the wind, surrounded by drumming waves of rain. Although the clouds had piled up quickly, the storm didn't seem to move east as fast. It sat overhead and drilled the roof.

There had been a river storm this fierce not long after she'd had the breast removed. The bandages had been off three or four days, so it had to have been two weeks after the surgery. Everything was painful, though she'd left the hospital without any restrictions. What hurt the most was where, without any warning, the surgeon had yanked out the drain during the follow-up visit. She had been following the printed post op instructions by applying a special cream to that spot and to the hard line of stitches three or four times a day to keep the skin supple, help the healing. Although anything to do with the wound made her woozy, she didn't want to ask for help from Jake or her daughters-in-law. She wasn't ready to share the scars. When the thunderstorm caught her napping at the pool, she grabbed the towel and her book and ran barefoot.

Before she reached the gate, lightning struck the tree directly above her head. The flash of white light, the thunder slap, the crack of the trunk splitting, combined to paralyze her in the downpour. She'd been afraid to touch the metal fence for fear of being electrocuted. So she stood there, drenched, unable to move, even when Jake came out on the back steps and yelled to her. The wind swallowed his words. His arms waved in pantomime. When she still didn't move, he ran over and led her inside.

Without saying a word, he stripped off her bathing suit and ran the shower for her. When she was done, he toweled her dry and put her to bed. She'd been speechless with gratitude. But there had been a minute, while she stood naked in the shower stall after he'd turned off the water, when he had stared at her chest. He couldn't help himself. She knew he hadn't meant to be cruel.

Since then, when she was dressing he made a point of turning his back to give her privacy. Six weeks later when they made love for the first time after the surgery, he massaged the other breast and kissed the other nipple and she hadn't felt anything. She knew from how mechanical it was that he was thinking about the scars and the missing breast. She'd gone into the bathroom afterwards and run the water in the sink full on to hide the sound of her crying. She'd expected, like a veteran with an amputated leg, that the missing breast would ache. But she'd felt nothing at all and Jake hadn't even noticed.

A rap on the passenger side window startled her out of the reverie. The sky was brightening. The rain had turned to drizzle. The blur outside was blue from head to foot. Another policeman. She lowered the opposite window.

"Are you alright, ma'am?"

She wasn't sure what to say. When he frowned, she understood he only wanted the short answer.

"I saw the Virginia plates," he said, "and wondered if you were . . . if you needed directions." He was peering at the scattered maps and the laundry basket with her supplies. "You visiting overnight in Baltimore?"

"No. I'm looking for a girl. And a boy. Teenagers."

"Your kids?"

"No, no, mine are . . . older. A neighbor's children." She heard how vague it sounded, scrambled to think of details that might allay the suspicion she saw in his face. "From Patogansett, Virginia."

"Runaways?"

"Not exactly." That sounded evasive too.

"Can I see your license and registration, please?"

Twice in one week. At least this time she hadn't been speeding.

"Rey is looking for his mother. He left after the funeral, last night. Meeka came to find Rey. She's only 14. Her mother's in a bad way. I thought if I could bring them back to her then—"

"Whoa, whoa. Slow down. You're confusing me." He took the documents from her, but didn't look at them. "We'll get it all straightened out here in just a minute. Sit tight and I'll be right back."

Like she could go anywhere with the flashing lights and the cruiser angled in behind the wagon. Noon already, and she hadn't found either of them or Antoinette. She couldn't wait much longer to return Jake's calls. She had wanted to report good news, but she didn't want to be the subject of an APB herself.

The policeman was back. "Okay, Mrs. Lowell. Want to fill me in?"

"I don't want to keep you from a bank robbery . . . or something more serious."

"Missing kids are pretty serious."

"I think so, but my husband says I should mind my own business. He doesn't want me to feel guilty about the drowning, I get that. It's just that—"

"Maybe start at the beginning." He flipped open his pad and freed the pen from its plastic clasp. "Names and dates."

She started with the funeral, explained about Henry Lewis, listed the members of the Breeden family, and repeated Meeka's version of Rey not coming home afterwards. She kept it succinct, trying to remember exact times when she could, explaining simply that Antoinette, Rey's mother, was a hairdresser in Baltimore. Her mediation training kicked in and she delivered the summary in clear declarative sentences, with as few suppositions as possible. She didn't sound quite so frantic.

"Outside of hitchhiking Meeka could have taken the train or the bus, but neither one arrives in Baltimore until late morning. There's a long Washington layover because it's a hub. All the connections north and south run through DC. You probably know all that." She was wasting time, with Meeka and Rey out on the street, potentially in danger.

"What's the mother's full name?"

"I only know her first name, Antoinette, though her son's last name is Davis so I assume hers is too."

"Work or residential address?"

"I don't know where she works. I just used the internet—"

He jammed the pencil into its holder and closed the notebook in slow motion as if he were purposely giving himself time to quell his immediate and more knee-jerk response. He must hear wild stories all the time. To a person who dealt in facts, not theories, the internet wouldn't count as a reliable source.

Overhead the blacker clouds were sliding off to the east. The sky was brightening. Even with the storm moving out, she needed to find the kids before dark. She put her hand out for her license. Maybe it wasn't the internet reference, maybe he sensed her own impatience.

"Tell you what," he said. "I'm due back at the station. I'll see what I can find out and if you strike out at the other two addresses, call me there."

He pulled out the pen, scribbled something, ripped the page from his pad, a string of numbers and *Sergeant Todd Gilhooly* in careful block lettering. He handed the note back to her with her license and registration. Great, he was anal retentive and she had chemo-brain. Never mind, she told herself, it was comforting to know she wasn't out here totally on her own. Police stations had access to all kinds of information. They might turn up something useful.

"Do you want my cell number?" she asked.

"I have it."

So Rory was right, Big Brother knew all about them. If that was true, why wait 24 hours for missing persons before running the super GPS and locating them? If they were not in any trouble, they could simply dump the information. Some people might argue violations of the right to privacy, constitutional due process protection against governmental intrusion, but every time it saved a child, it would be worth it.

Officer Gilhooly's police car eased into the intersection and swerved sharp right. Halfway down the block the overhead flasher blinked once and then spun seriously. The dispatcher must have called with a 228, or whatever, in progress. The kooky woman from Indiantown, Virginia was no doubt forgotten.

She folded the note with his telephone number and stuck it in the pocket of her windbreaker along with the other documents. She'd lost another thirty minutes. Still thinking about what else she should have told him, she almost missed the turn. The remembered exit number glistened in the rain. She'd forgotten to turn the GPS voice back on after their conversation. Gilhooly was an Irish black man, as broad and square-jawed as the lone football player she'd dated in college. Brave and blunt. But she wasn't hung up on stereotypes, oh, no. That long ago defensive end, Matt something-or-other, had turned out to be depressed, struggling over disappointing a father who wanted him to be a doctor to elevate the family image. Matt wanted to talk and she wanted to dance. Once the band quit they ended up sitting on the frat house roof all night and watching the sunrise. Not at all the strong, silent type she'd imagined football players were, but they stayed friends and only lost touch after graduation.

At their tenth reunion, when she'd been pregnant with Rory, Matt's name showed up on the memorial list, with MD after it. She overheard another classmate say he'd taken an overdose. It shocked her, as full and happy as her life was, with a busy toddler, a solid career, a reliable husband. Mostly she wondered how his father felt, to lose him early, and whether the doctorate was any solace at all. It was something she remembered when Rory was deciding on grad school. She'd used the story to convince Jake to back off when Rory had no interest in business school.

"See," she muttered to the absent Jake. "There's a reason for everything."

Still thinking about Officer Gilhooly, she pulled over again at the light rail station, into the loading zone, and reactivated the Garman. Sporadic bursts of people exited the down escalator from an overhead platform, streaming in front of the car. And similar clumps crossed the other way to ride up. While she waited for the GPS to download the maps and spit out its next instruction, she watched passengers cross in front of the windshield. She almost missed Meeka in her rain slicker. The wind flipped off her hood when she stopped at the transit map.

Scrabbling with the unlock button and the door handle, Celie was already calling her name before she was out of the car. "Meeka, Meeka Breeden."

Meeka swung around, the surprise obvious. "Ms. Lowell? How—"

"I figured you would come here looking for Rey."

After an anxious scan of the sidewalk and parking lot beyond Celie and across the road, Meeka slipped behind a passing group of students and disappeared in the jumble.

"Wait, I'm not trying to stop you, I came to help," Celie cried out. When she spotted her again, she was shooting up the escalator three steps at a time. Except for the single second of realization that the distance between them was growing, Celie didn't hesitate. She elbowed past a mother with a stroller and climbed the escalator even as it carried her up and closer to the rumbling tracks. "Excuse me, excuse me." She zipped past the last rider and burst onto the platform just as the buzzer sounded. The doors slid shut and the train rolled away. Meeka had turned her back.

"Damn," Celie said. "Damn, damn, damn."

"There's one every seven minutes." The young man standing next to her rolled his eyes, the cords of his IPod hanging from his ears like earrings. "You can't leave your car there anyway. They'll tow it."

But it was worse than that. As she negotiated the down escalator from the top of the platform, two scruffy-looking fellows closed in on the open driver's door and peered inside. Their heads bobbed in hurried conference. The second one stood back up and surveyed the empty sidewalk. By the time she reached the pavement, still forty yards from the car, they had piled into the Volvo—with her purse, her credit cards, her cell phone, her maps, and the key in the ignition. They turned out of the station at a speed she hadn't known the Volvo had in it after fifteen years and over 250,000 miles. With the wild turn, the jerry-rigged overhead luggage rack swung wide. When the car swerved back into the lane and shot forward, the faulty metal section snapped back, hit the stanchion, and flew off into the gutter. She surprised herself by laughing. The remedy was right there, a little extra speed and a sharp turn. They could have fixed it years ago.

She teetered on the curb and cursed cell phones for putting old-fashioned phone booths out of business. She had Officer Gilhooly's phone number in her pocket, for all the good it did her. As she jogged toward the address for the second beauty salon, etched in her mind because she'd just plugged it into the GPS, she realized this salon might very well be the right one since Meeka was here in the same neighborhood. Meeka had looked surprised but not shocked. Still, running away was not the reaction Celie had expected.

What was so threatening about a Patogansett neighbor following her to Baltimore? She'd thought, after Maxy, they were getting to be friends. As much as any fourteen year-old girl could be friends with a woman older than her mother. It would be an unusual teenager though, who would share with any adult her plan to leave home without permission and travel by herself to a strange city. This girl was complicated, the situation more complicated. Her own boys and their friends hadn't been so hard to read. But Meeka was independent to a fault. She worried about her image. She wanted people to see she was smart and responsible. And she was hurting. That hurt, whether she liked it or not, bound them together.

Right from the beginning Celie saw she had misjudged the situation. She'd thought when Meeka talked about Rey and his issues with his mother, she was considering how best to help her family. But now it looked like her decision had already been made before their discussion. When Celie, trying not to interfere, was neutral, Meeka read that as approval.

So far Celie had counted eight blocks since the light rail station, all due west. There was no sign of Meeka. She had slowed to a fast walk. Jogging had never been her forte, but the burst of adrenaline that had propelled her up the escalator and down had completely abandoned her. Every fourth row house had boards over the windows and a condemnation notice stapled to the front door. Some stoops had piles of yellowed newspapers, moldy in their plastic sleeves. Some had folding chairs and strings of miniature Christmas lights. She said hello to the wizened old ladies and plump younger ones who leaked sideways out of their lawn chairs. Most harrumphed back. If she'd had a picture of Meeka, she would have taken the time to ask if they'd seen her. But without it, she just hurried along, hoping that, despite the station confrontation, Meeka was headed to the same address.

At Number 431 the door was locked, the blinds drawn. The sign in the window said *Closed*. Someone had scrawled *temprari* across the bottom edge with a bright blue permanent marker. Taped to the window between the glass and the broken Venetian blinds was a handwritten list in oversized letters, the names of four women with days and hours next to each. Antoinette Jervais was the third name. The blinds jiggled against the glass to a deep visceral drum beat from music inside. Over the music a man's voice repeated the rap two beats behind. Celie put her ear to the door.

"You can't sing worth shit," a woman's voice wheezed.

"Shut up, Mash."

Celie maneuvered herself to the edge of the step to peek through the blinds, but the room was too dim to make out anything in the half inch of air the between yellowed plastic strips. She didn't know what to do next. But from the look of it, whoever was inside didn't want visitors.

The lot to the left was a wreck. Three walls of foundation stood only four cinderblocks high, only one corner remained standing. The masonry was crumbling. Rotted clapboards were scattered across the waist-high grass. In the center of the ruin an old stove rose from the weeds. The door, blackened and lopsided, hung from one hinge. Scraps of paper and plastic bags had glued themselves to the cornflower stalks. Compared to the wild looseness of the rundown salon building and the adjoining abandoned lot, the brick townhouse across the street with last year's leggy geraniums in a crooked window box looked like a maiden aunt, disapproving and staid.

When Celie raised her hand to her forehead to see better from this distance, the front window curtain shifted back into place. Someone was watching. She toyed with going across and asking the spying neighbor about the salon. Whoever was inside the brick house lived some semblance of normal if they planted flowers. She could feel the eyes still on her and instinctively lowered her face. In the cracked concrete front steps of 431 she noticed the bottom half of a syringe. If the children were here, she needed to get them away as quickly as possible. She knocked on the door, listened with her head turned sideways. When she heard voices, but no footsteps in the direction of the door, she knocked harder.

"Meeka?" she called with her mouth close to the peeling wood. "Are you in there?"

Yelling ensued. Over the singing man's voice, the woman said, "Oh, fuck. The bitch across the street called the police again."

"Put the stuff out back."

"Hey, hey, where you going? I ain't done yet."

Celie tried the door knob again, though her hands were slick with perspiration. Her chest tightened as she tried to steady her breathing. Over the general pandemonium she thought she heard a girl's voice.

"Please," the girl was yelling to someone, "Please stop. Please leave him alone."

Not surprising that no one came to the door. Celie rattled the handle and pounded with her fist. "Open the goddamn door."

Seconds ticked by. The yelling inside continued. Something heavy fell and a door slammed. A fourth voice, another man, cursed and ran his mouth, but no one came to let her in.

Chapter Twenty-Eight

Locked in that tiny bathroom, I didn't know how long I could keep out the angry men I'd seen in the second room. I shook the bars on the little window above the bathtub. I screamed for help through the paneling on the outside wall. Why hadn't I paid more attention to Rey from the beginning? I should've left home sooner. And I shouldn't have run away from Ms. Lowell. I needed her now. I needed someone, anyone.

It was incredible how messed up Antoinette was, and how Mama and Ruthie had no idea. In a year she'd gone downhill fast. She was barely recognizable. Crusty old mascara streaks on her cheeks. Her hair, which had been straightened and styled when she left Virginia, looked like a Slinky gone bad. Whatever she was wearing on top had lost its strap on one side, so half her chest was uncovered. Under the ripped top she had on panties, bare feet, nothing else. I thought it was probably a good thing her sisters didn't know. It would make them so sad, when they were already sad.

Antoinette had barely raised her head when I came in.

"Hey, honey," she'd stared for a good minute. "You heard 'bout my party all the way down there in 'ginia? Damn." She laid her head back on her arms. "Ain't my niece looking fine?" She was talking to an empty room.

I had stepped closer, but not too close. "Aunt Antoinette? Is that you?"

"The one and only." A shirtless man stumbled out of the back room. "You the next trick?"

When his hand grabbed at me, I backed up to the wall, but he lurched past to the front door. It was swinging open. He clawed at the handle and pulled it shut. The lock slid into place.

"Now, sweetie, it's your turn." He turned around and lunged.

I ran in the opposite direction, past my aunt hunched over the table. I tripped over clothes and shoes, bottles and trash, ran through a second room and through the only door. Smack into a bathroom, smack into a dead end. I shut the door behind me just in time. Barely locked it before he was pounding on the other side.

"Come out and meet your auntie's friends. Honey? That your name, Honey from Va-Ginny-A?"

Six people I'd counted in the cramped two room space as I replayed my run to the bathroom. The 'salon' with its single mechanical chair, its cracked mirror, and the sink full of liquor bottles, was hardly a thriving business. One man and a second woman, both weasely and skinny, half asleep, hung off folding chairs on either side of a card table in the corner. The table was covered with candles, ash trays, and stained paper plates. Droopy Antoinette sat in the salon chair, tilted sideways with a broken hinge. Bad looking stuff all over the place. I almost tripped on the bare mattress in the back room.

There was Rey in one corner trapped behind a beat-up recliner, just outside the reach of one of the biggest men I'd ever seen. He looked worse than drunk. Rey was screaming and pushing and pulling the chair to keep it between him and the man who spit out a string of curse words that didn't make any sense. Another man lay on a bare mattress. He was naked, half asleep. The smell was awful. The bathroom was worse.

I wasted too much time getting here. When the bus had arrived ten minutes ahead of schedule, the passengers had cheered. In the terminal Liam bought me a can of Lemon-Lime and a package of peanut butter cheese crackers from the machines.

"If you're going back on the bus, I'm the six-forty run tonight. I'll save that front seat for you." He was really asking.

"I'm not sure."

"Well, I'll be here tomorrow night too. And the next, and the next."

He was being cheerful on purpose, I could tell. My dread must have showed on my face. The sidewalks in the city were crowded. People rushed along without looking where they were going and cursing if you got in their way. What if I was wrong about Rey and he wasn't here? Or maybe I was wrong about Antoinette, and Rey would be better off with her. She was his mother.

The sound of more scuffling outside the bathroom brought me back. I had my answer about Antoinette, too late. There were minutes when Rey wasn't screaming and that scared me even more. I had to get out and get help.

"Rey, hang on. I'm gonna figure this out."

The man who chased me was still banging and cursing on the other side of the door. "She's right there, nice little titties, smooth skin. Come out, come out." He coughed a horribly gummy kind of cough. "I could take off the hinges. If I had a screwdriver."

Unlikely, you creep. But it was only a matter of time until he beat through the stupid door. Nothing here looked very permanent. Another male voice, sloppy but loud, maybe the man who had Rey cornered, started to argue with him.

"Screw it. We got little titties right here. S'good enough for the time being."

A deep-throated scream, not Rey this time. "Goddamn bitch, he bit me."

"If you hurt him, I'll kill you," I yelled from the bathroom.

"A wily cat. I like dat," the first man slurred through the door. "You gonna have to come out if you want to save your little friend. Come on out, now."

He must have thrown his whole body against the door. The frame shook and part of a ceiling tile above the door dropped and nicked my shoulder. A big piece off the medicine cabinet's mirror, already cracked, jiggled loose and shattered in the sink. Startled, I backed up and fell over the lip of the tub. I sat there, stunned. But it gave me an idea.

In every tub there was a drain. At home when it clogged with hair, Mama showed me how to pull it up and clean off the clog. Part of the drain piece was plastic, but part was metal. A piece of metal might be able to dig out around the window. The sill was black with mold. It had to be rotten. After I freed the drain contraption, I ripped off the plastic part and the chain. The round piece that let the water drain through was a hollow cylinder. Metal, with a nice sharp edge. I jammed it into the window sill and yanked. A six-inch piece of wood popped loose, the ends ragged and black with rot. The opening would have to be ten times that big if I was going to fit through it. I stabbed into the sill again.

Another scream penetrated the door. Rey's words were pitched high, impossible to understand, the pain very clear. And then I heard a smack, and he stopped screaming. God, don't let him be dead. I prayed out loud, repeating the words as I dug into the soft wood and tore the loose pieces out with my fingers. "God, don't let him be dead. God."

His mother, where was his goddamn mother? She should be protecting him, but she was worthless, stoned out of her mind. Could a mother sleep through what was happening to Rey? I wondered if I was strong enough to knock out a man with a chair. I tried to think if I'd seen an empty chair in the second room, the room with the mattress on the floor. Even if the men were as drunk or doped up as Antoinette, I had to move fast. There were three of them and only one of Rey. Kicking and biting, he hadn't been able to get away.

The man who was hurling himself at the door still had strength, even if his mind was all muddled. I would never be able to stop them by myself.

"Please," I cried through the door. "Please leave him alone."

If I promised to come out, would they let him go? I wanted to be brave. But I wasn't going to be stupid. It wouldn't help either of us. One of us needed to go for help.

"I called the police with my cell phone. They'll be here any minute. You hurt him and they'll arrest you for sure."

But I wasn't sure they believed me, or even heard me. This wasn't something I could solve by myself, no matter how much I wanted to. I needed the police, adults at the least. I plunged the metal drain into the wall an inch outside the window frame and started ripping away the bad wood on the left side.

Chapter Twenty-Nine

Before Celie's knuckles hit the neighbor's door, it opened with a painful whine. The woman who answered wore dreadlocks past her shoulders, gray and white intertwined. She stood a full head taller than Celie, resplendent in a lime green tunic and matching skirt. "I already called the police." Her tone was polite but clear. It said *there's nothing you can do about it.*

"How long?"

"How long what?"

"How long did they say till they get here?"

"They didn't say. But they know me. I don't call over nothing. They've raided that place where you were just knocking." She jabbed in the direction of the street. "Twice before. Always haul more men out of there than I ever see going in. She must conjure them up out of voodoo."

"She?"

"The salon lady. It started out well enough, four women, doing hair, nails. That was last fall. But lately, you can't believe the stuff that comes out of that place."

"You mean Antoinette Jervais?"

"That's what they call her, singing to her at midnight, let me in, let me in. Why do men always fall for that kind of mirage?" She straightened her shoulders and craned her head back until she was staring at the ceiling, directing her words heavenward. "They don't recognize the devil, that's why. The devil, he's way smarter than any man."

While Celie had no trouble believing this woman had talked to the police, she was less sure that the police were really coming. If they'd heard the devil explanation before, they might discount her reports of real danger.

"May I use your phone?"

"You may, of course you may. People don't think angels need human technology, but God sends the lifeboat and we shouldn't turn away just because we don't recognize Him."

Celie dialed the number from Officer Gilhooly's note. He answered on the second ring.

"This is Celie Lowell. I'm the Volvo woman in the thunderstorm from this morning."

"You're not calling from your cell phone."

"Stolen, long story. I'm using a neighbor's phone across from 431 Washington Street. The owner—I don't know her name, an older woman, with . . ." she hesitated, the irrelevance of physical description hitting her. "She just called the police from here. The kids I'm looking for—"

"APBs on both of them just came over the wire. I don't know who managed that, with less than 24 hours, but we're on the look-out officially now."

"They're here."

"With you, ma'am?"

"No, no. Across the street at 431. At least I think it's them. I can't see them, but they're screaming and there are men inside, loud voices, cursing. The door's locked. I can't get in. I wanted to be sure you were coming. I mean, the police."

"Hold up a second."

She waited.

"The 911 feed shows they're on their way."

"Great, I'll be over there."

"Don't do that. Just sit tight. They could have weapons."

He hung up and Celie shivered where she stood. Weapons were not in her vocabulary. But the children were in trouble and she'd wasted enough time.

"They're coming, aren't they?" The old woman had her hands raised in prayer. "He's always listening."

"Yes, thank you so much. Is there a back door?"

"What's a matter with my front door? Good enough for you to come in."

"Across the street. A back door across the street?"

"Oh." The woman looked confused for the first time. "There oughtta be. All these row houses have the same layout. People used to plant vegetables out back before the war."

Celie understood she meant the second World War and was impressed all over again with how alert she was for someone that old. "Thank you again," she called back from the sidewalk. Who knew what was happening at Antoinette's?

When she leaped up from the sidewalk to the side yard of 431, she tripped on something hard hidden in the long grass, maybe the concrete edge of a low wall for one of the Victory gardens. Brushing off twigs and bits of wet trash, she raced along the pocked stucco side of the row house to the back. Thank goodness the lot next door had been cleared at some point. There were no crumbling foundation walls to slow her down, just the overgrowth. A ragged stretch of chicken wire started at the building's back corner and plunged in and out of the weeds. She picked a low place and eased her legs over one at a time, not eager to fall again in the muck.

More loudly from the back of the house she could hear Meeka yelling and a man's voice, alternately angry and wheedling. A handful of gunk fell on her hair and shoulders. When she looked up, more wood chips sprayed into the air from a small square window next to the back door. A door with six glass panes, cracked and taped. On the inside the whole glass section had been closed over with a bigger piece of plywood. She couldn't see in. The handle wouldn't turn. Of course it would be locked. This was the city after all.

She scrounged in the weeds for something hard, a stick, a bottle. She found an old paint can, but she couldn't get a good grip with the chunky finger bandage. Switching arms, she swung the can as hard as she could on the pane closest to the handle. Slivers of glass fell into the tall grass.

As she drew back the good arm to swing again, she yelled through the door. "Meeka? Rey? It's Ms. Lowell. I'm right outside the door, the one with the taped window panes. Are you in that room, the one with the little window a little bit higher than the door?"

"Are the police with you?" It was Meeka's voice at a much lower level.

"They're on their way. Where's Rey? Is he there with you?"

"No, he's in the other room. With three men."

Her stomach flipped. He was so small. "Tell me about the wall where the window is."

"There's no door in here, just a big piece of some kind of wood nailed to the wall opposite the bathroom door back into the house. That's the only door I see. It's the one I came through. It goes back to where those men are . . . and Rey. I'm trying to dig out the window frame."

Celie saw immediately what had happened. The old door was unreliable. Someone had nailed up plywood to keep people from getting in that way. Two layers to get through, more time wasted.

"Smart girl. Can you yell through the door? The inside door? Tell those men the police are coming to arrest them, they'd better leave now."

The rain of rotten wood stopped. Celie heard a string of unintelligible high-pitched words, and then Meeka's voice, clear and sweet, through the window. "I told them, but I'm not sure they understand. They're so wasted."

Her description conjured up all kinds of horrible images. Celie sucked air into her lungs to swing again. "Let's hope they have enough sense to run. You keep digging. I'm going to try to get through the panel."

The wood shower began in earnest. Celie sent the paint can spinning against the outside door. She reached through the lowest broken pane for the door handle and fumbled for the lock mechanism, but the plywood barrier was jammed against the knob, leaving no room for her fingers to grasp the handle. She'd have to remove the whole section of door where the handle was installed, and then the plywood itself. She swung the paint can again.

They carried both children to the emergency room in an ambulance. Two officers raced off on foot, chasing a shirtless man. The other two were handcuffed along with Antoinette, still mumbling about her party. Separate cruisers drove the prisoners to the station. A fifth person, a woman whose age was impossible to guess from her condition, wouldn't wake up where Meeka had seen her sprawled on the table. She came last in a city ambulance. When Officer Gilhooly reached Jake on the phone, he was already on his way, bringing Ashante and Mary Breeden with him. The Volvo wagon had turned up six blocks over from where it was stolen. Empty wallet and no cell phone, but the rest was intact. Minus the unreliable roof rack.

Gilhooly convinced Celie to get a sandwich in the hospital cafeteria while the social worker talked to Meeka. Rey had been sedated and treated for external bruises, lacerations, and a broken arm. The rest of his ordeal would require a psychologist to sort it out. He hadn't been coherent, but he'd still had his clothes on, so he'd managed to hold them off from the worst.

"You'll have to sign a statement," Officer Gilhooly said to Celie.

"I want those men charged with kidnapping, assault, battery."

"I thought you were a mediator. You sound like a prosecutor."

"I'm done with mediating."

"Two of these guys are repeat offenders. They'll get the maximum on the drug possession charge alone. There'll be more once we can figure out exactly what happened and the lab tests come back."

"Death won't be good enough. And his mother, she ought to be hung."

"Kids survive worse, you know. Your girl says his mother sent him letters, money. Somewhere down deep she cared. It's the drugs. That's your devil. She just couldn't get out of the mess she'd made to get straight."

"He's better off without her."

"Sounds like they've all had a rough time. The girl especially. She did the right thing, didn't jump into the fire, used her brain. She'll get past all this."

"If only I'd offered to go with her when she first mentioned trying to find him herself."

"Listen, you saved her. You saved them both."

"Half an hour earlier and Rey wouldn't have—"

"Ms. Lowell. Stop second-guessing. Most people would have shrugged their shoulders and walked the other way. I'd like to live in Patogansett. They make real good neighbors there."

After the social worker released Meeka to Celie's temporary custody, with Mary's permission over the phone, Celie moved two chairs from the family waiting room to the hallway outside Rey's room so they could wait for the doctor. Meeka insisted they be close by.

"Mama's coming here? She knows?"

"According to my husband she's been talking the whole ride up. Worried you and Rey were running away because she's been so out of it."

"I never meant to make her worry. I thought I was helping."

"You were. You did."

When Meeka didn't argue, Celie thought she was handling the whole mess with amazing aplomb for all that she'd been through.

"I stole those black stones from your house."

Celie tried hard not to let Meeka see her surprise. She'd noticed the stones were back in place, but had never connected their disappearance with Meeka. "It's not important."

"I wanted you to lose something too. It was silly."

Celie thought about her own failure to make Jake understand what she'd lost with the cancer. "Every person reacts differently to grief. When my husband wanted to help, I refused to talk about it. In a way I was punishing him because he didn't understand how I felt."

When Meeka didn't answer, Celie wondered if she should have said more clearly that she forgave her. The truth was she'd never known and wouldn't have blamed the girl even if she had known. The stones, gone and returned, were Meeka's to deal with as she chose. They were the past. Celie was determined to concentrate on the future, Jake's patient voice in her head, someone who loved her despite her mistakes.

"If you know someone is evil, but other people don't see it, how can you make them see?"

"Like Antoinette's friends?"

272

"Yeah, well, other men who are the same way, but can hide it better."

"You can tell an adult you trust. Or the police. You can warn kids who might not realize the danger. Some women learn karate to protect themselves." Celie waited for more details, but Meeka didn't offer anything more. "Does that help?"

She perked up, as if she'd worked it out in her head. "It sounds kind of like what you've been saying about swimming lessons."

"How long do you have to wear the bandages on your hands?" Celie asked.

"Couple three days, maybe a week. They say it's more to keep out germs than anything. Lots of blood, but nothing real deep. Mostly scratches. And they pulled out some really gross splinters." She made an exaggerated grimace. "But the doctor said no nerve damage."

"It looks nice and tight."

"I don't know about that. Aunt Ruthie's a nurse and she's always saying things need to air out to heal."

"That is true about some wounds." Celie thought about scars the doctors couldn't see, but then she remembered Meeka's concern about Maxy and her determination to find Rey. Maybe scars were the shooting stars of a life, indelibly etched, then fading into an echo of that moment in time, already woven into the whole tapestry. They altered your trajectory, but not the bigger points of light, not the planets and constellations that defined where you were headed, who you might become, that marked your place in the universe.

"I miss Henry Lewis." Meeka rested her head on Celie's shoulder.

"You always will. But you have a mother and a sister, cousins, aunts to share him with, and friends. You can talk about him with me whenever you want." She touched Meeka's bandaged hands for just a second. "You know, when I had my cancer surgery, I had a huge bandage, wound around my chest three or four times so it wouldn't slip off. The whole time it was supposed to be healing, it felt like it was leaking. I worried that it wasn't healing, that it was getting infected, I just knew that it was going to be a bloody mess when I took off the bandages." She steeled herself against the old feeling of nausea.

When it didn't come, she took a deep breath and told the story she had kept to herself for so long. "My family wanted to help. They offered to change the dressing for me, but I wouldn't let them. I was so nervous about seeing the part of me they'd cut off and the scar. Just the idea of an open wound scared me. And I was ashamed at being such a sissy. I finally asked a rescue squad volunteer to put the new bandage on for me." She was watching Meeka's face, but the girl didn't look shocked. "I've never told anyone that."

"You can't tell at all that anything's missing."

"Thanks, but having only one breast doesn't bother me. I'm old, and it doesn't matter so much once you've been in love and had your babies. It's not important compared to other things. I guess I was more afraid if people saw the scar, they'd be disgusted. But you know what the rescue squad woman said, before I even explained how I was feeling? She said it was a beautiful scar, neat and straight, that the stitches were tiny and perfect."

"When did you have cancer?"

"I have it now. There's a new tumor. But the first time was last winter. All last year really. The treatments ended two months ago."

"Are you going to die?"

Celie wanted to say no, but she wasn't sure and Meeka had earned the right to the truth. "Everybody dies."

Meeka sniffled a little, started to say something, but didn't finish.

Celie didn't hug her. They'd been through a lot, but they had a long way to go. "When it's their time."

"Is Rey going to die?"

"It's not his time right now. He's going to be fine, thanks to you. You were right when you told me he was tough. And so are you."

"He's way braver than me. He's been talking about how he wants to learn how to swim. Since he threw his chunk of dirt on the casket. He asked if you really would teach him. I couldn't tell you at the funeral because of Mama. And because I was still thinking you just wanted to make us be like you."

"What? Be like me? How?"

"Learn how to swim. Be white."

"I never meant it like that."

"I know that now."

"Friends don't do that. They like each other just the way they are." As soon as Celie said it, she knew it wasn't quite right. "And sometimes they help each other to be the most they can be."

"We can't be friends if you die."

"I don't think I'm going to die just yet. I have to teach some kids I know how to swim."

"And how to use a telescope."

Jake had Mary Breeden's arm in his when they emerged from the elevator. When she saw Meeka, the lines on her forehead eased and she smiled. Meeka ran to her mother.

"Baby, baby," Mary said as they rocked together in the hall. "I'm so proud of you, so proud."

"Where's Ashante?"

"He's coming right up as soon as he lets Ruthie know you and Rey are safe."

Jake stood in the middle of the corridor across from Celie. He fumbled in his pocket with the keys. He looked lost. "You don't know how glad I am to see you."

"Ditto," she said.

Maybe he didn't believe her, but his eyes held hers.

"No note," he said. "This is getting to be bad habit." He worked at a smile. "You are one resourceful woman. Not sure why it's taken me all this time to figure that out."

"Thanks for coming. I could never have driven myself home."

"I don't believe that for a minute." He examined the new bandage on her finger. "Fancy."

"The stitches popped when I was pounding on the door."

"Gilhooly warned me."

"Is that all he told you?"

"Actually he gave me quite a lecture."

"Me, too. Apparently they don't get many visitors who initiate arrests for car theft, assault and battery, kidnapping, sexual assault, and felony possession of a scheduled drug. He told me to come back to Baltimore only if I wanted to see the Orioles play baseball and otherwise stay home."

"He doesn't know you as well as I do, then. Because if you don't want to stay home, there's not a thing the rest of us can do to stop you."

ACKNOWLEDGEMENTS

The story of Meeka and Celie is one of the most challenging pieces I've tackled. It confronts issues from my own childhood, my personal battle with cancer, and a drowning very close to home. While tragedy finds everyone at some point, the particular grief and guilt of a sister contrasted with the guilt and grief of a stranger caught me up in its tangle. This story, imperfect and messy, is the unraveling of that tangle. In my custody and family law cases I worked with rural teenagers who, like Meeka, were exposed early to responsibilities and adult issues that most suburban teens never face.

Thank you to my son Phillip who offered practical insight when I was discouraged and to my book club The Come Heres, steadfast cheerleaders of my river stories. Thanks to my virtual agent Ellen Geiger who gave me invaluable advice along the way, to Gary Kessler for his fine editing suggestions, and to my first and favorite editor Linda Layne, a supporter from the very beginning and a generous friend. Most importantly thank you to Stuart, Elizabeth, Jeremy and Allison, faithful readers all, who, along with Phillip, never fail to email or call at the exact moment I need encouragement. And to Chris, my financial partner for life, who laughs and cries at all the right places.

ABOUT THE AUTHOR

Sarah Collins Honenberger writes about ordinary people in extraordinary situations. Her third novel, *Catcher, Caught* is a Pen/Faulkner Foundation selection for its Writers in Schools program. A fellow of the Virginia Center for the Creative Arts, she has been recognized for her ongoing contributions to the writing field and her support of other writers by the Virginia Writers Club. Her novels and short fiction have won numerous awards including the F. Scott Fitzgerald Literary Fiction Conference runner-up award and first place awards from New Millenium, Antietam Review, and Southern Lit. She regularly appears in the top one hundred authors of literary fiction on Amazon.com. Other books by Honenberger include *Waltzing Cowboys* and *White Lies: A Tale of Babies, Vaccines and Deception.* She lives and writes in Tappahannock, Virginia.

Made in the USA
Charleston, SC
17 May 2014